"WHY DO THEY DO THAT?"

"Blink?" Sam shifted in the grass, pulling himself up on his haunches. "It's a mating thing. The lady fireflies do that to catch a suitor. The guy fireflies find those glowing butts real attractive, then light up their own rear ends to show they're interested." He grinned up at Cassie. "It's the bug world's equivalent to short skirts and high heels."

She tossed the jar at him, causing him to lose his balance and fall back as he caught it. "That's not why I wear what I wear. It's called *fashion*—a word I'm sure you're not familiar with. It just goes to show how similar males are in every species. They only want one thing, and they rely on superficialities to find a mate."

Sam grabbed her elbow, his tight grip making it clear he wasn't letting go. He stood close enough for her to smell him—a faint whiff of cologne and outdoor air. His breath brushed her cheek as he spoke.

"Not all males are alike, Cassie. Some actually make a point of peeling through all that outside stuff to see the real woman underneath. It's hard-won, but what a prize. A man just has to be patient."

Cassie leaned into him, taking the pressure off her ankle. "And are you a patient man, Dr. Parker?"

His eyes glittered from the porch light, reminding her of the fireflies. "Call me Job."

BOOK YOUR PLACE ON OUR WEBSITE AND MAKE THE READING CONNECTION!

We've created a customized website just for our very special readers, where you can get the inside scoop on everything that's going on with Zebra, Pinnacle and Kensington books.

When you come online, you'll have the exciting opportunity to:

- View covers of upcoming books

- Read sample chapters

- Learn about our future publishing schedule (listed by publication month *and author*)

- Find out when your favorite authors will be visiting a city near you

- Search for and order backlist books from our online catalog

- Check out author bios and background information

- Send e-mail to your favorite authors

- Meet the Kensington staff online

- Join us in weekly chats with authors, readers and other guests

- Get writing guidelines

- AND MUCH MORE!

Visit our website at
http://www.kensingtonbooks.com

FALLING HOME

Karen White

ZEBRA BOOKS
KENSINGTON PUBLISHING CORP.

http://www.kensingtonbooks.com

To Chris, for all your encouragement. I miss you.

ACKNOWLEDGMENTS

As always, thanks to Tim, Meghan and Connor for putting up with me and my need to write.

Thanks also to Wendy, Susie, Jenni, Vicky and Karen— for all your great advice, commiseration and hand-holding. And no acknowledgment would be complete without mentioning Donna Michael, whose begging for more chapters kept me writing.

And, of course, thank you ladies of Georgia Romance Writers. Your support has meant so much to me.

Chapter 1

Cassie was dreaming again. It was of her old summers; the summers of bare feet, skinned knees, and homemade peach ice cream that dripped down her chin and made her fingers sticky. Aunt Lucinda rang the supper bell, and Cassie and Harriet raced each other past the gazebo toward the back porch, their sun-kissed legs pumping under white sundresses. The jangling of the dream bell seemed so real, Cassie felt she could touch the cold brass and make it stop.

Her fingers touched Andrew's arm instead, his skin warm under her hand, and she jerked awake, the smells of summer grass and Aunt Lucinda's lavender perfume lingering somewhere in the back of her mind. But the jangling continued, filling Cassie with dread.

She held her breath, looking at the glowing numbers on her clock, and listened for the next ring of the telephone. Only bad news came at three in the morning. Births and engagements were always announced in the bright light of day. But bad news came at night, as if the sun were already in mourning.

Andrew stirred briefly, then rolled over, away from her. Rising from the bed, she stumbled across the darkened bedroom and into the living room so as not to awaken him. She hit her little toe on a chair leg and let out an expletive, her choice of words the only thing about her still reminiscent of her background.

"Dangnabit!" she muttered, reaching for the phone and knocking it off the hook. She grappled with it on the floor before finally placing it to her ear. "Hello?"

There was a brief pause, then, "Hi, Cassie. It's me. Harriet."

Cassie's blood stilled as she gripped the receiver tighter. "Harriet," she said, her voice sounding strained and unsure to her ears. "How are you?"

The words were so inadequately stupid that she wanted to bite them back as soon as they left her mouth. It was three A.M., her estranged sister was calling after more than a decade of silence, and she was asking about how she was in the same kind of voice she would ask a coworker if they liked sugar in their coffee.

"It's Daddy. He's dying."

A siren screamed outside in the dark beyond Cassie's window. She reached across the table and flipped on a lamp. "What happened?" The marquise diamond on her left hand sparkled in the dim light. Andrew came and sat next to her, his forehead creased with a question. Cassie put her hand over the receiver and mouthed, "My sister."

"Hang on a second." Harriet's phone clunked as the sound of a baby's crying trickled through the line. It must be Amanda, Harriet's new baby. Cassie knew each child from pictures her father sent. There were five of them, spread evenly over fifteen years of marriage. Each birth announcement from her father had opened the old wounds, scraping away the scabs, making Cassie bleed again.

Harriet came back. "I'm sorry. The baby's been fussy all day."

Cassie swallowed. "What's wrong with Daddy?"

Harriet sounded as if she'd been crying. "He's had a stroke. We didn't think it was so bad, but he says he's dying. And you know he always means what he says. He's in the hospital now, but he wants us to bring him home tomorrow. It was his idea to call you right now in the middle of the night. He says he won't rest in peace until both of his girls are here. He wants you to come home."

Cassie didn't say anything, but listened to the sounds of the phone being put down again and of the fretting baby fading. She glanced over at Andrew, who had put his head back against the sofa and closed his eyes. Her gaze wandered the living room of her Upper West Side apartment. Nothing in the cool, crisp space, with its black-and-white checkerboard of color and harsh angles, resembled the old house in which she had grown up. The house with porch swings, ancient oaks, and screen doors. Just as the woman she had become no longer resembled the girl of twenty who had left the small town of Walton, Georgia, fifteen years before without a backward glance.

Then a man spoke, his words deep and resonant. "Cassie? It's Joe."

She looked away, trying to focus on the abstract splotch of color on the painting behind her sofa, wanting to block out the memories his voice stirred. The memories of moonlit nights, serenading katydids in the gazebo behind the old house, and Aunt Lucinda's gardenias drooping in the heat, spreading their seductive aroma.

"Cassie? Are you there?"

"Yes." Her voice cracked, so she said it again, more firmly this time. "Yes. I'm here."

Andrew sat up and took her hand, his eyes guarded.

Joe spoke again. "Are you coming home?"

The receiver slipped in her sweaty palm. Every day, she handled difficult clients, the bread and butter of the ad agency, but nothing had ever made her as unsettled as the sound of Joe's voice and the mere thought of returning to the place she swore she would never set foot in again.

"I am home," she said, defiant.

"You know what I mean, Cassie." She could barely hear him, he was speaking so low. "Harriet needs you now. More than either one of you imagines. He's her father, too."

She looked over at Andrew. He wore only boxer shorts, his skin pale in the glare of the lamp. She stared at the contours of the muscles on his chest, every ridge etched in her fingers' memory. Cassie had worked for Andrew Wallace for five years and been his lover for three and his fiancée for one. Like her, he was a transplant to New York, all the way from Newport Beach, California.

Cassie reached for his hand resting on his thigh. He jerked awake, an annoyed expression quickly turning into a smile. She squeezed his fingers, feeling the bond between them, the bond that made her regard them as wild hothouse flowers, uprooted from the tropics and moved to an intricately land-scaped formal garden. They understood each other, sharing a mutual passion for their work and never talking about how very far from home they both were.

Cassie blinked hard. "I'll come. For Daddy."

Joe sighed into the phone. "Whatever it takes to get you here, Cassie. Just come as soon as you can."

Cassie heard whispering on the other end of the phone, then Harriet spoke again. "Let me know which flight you'll be on and I'll pick you up."

"No." She said it too quickly. She wasn't ready for an hour alone in a car with Harriet. "I mean, I think I'll drive. I'll need a car while I'm down there, and . . . I'd like the time to think. If I drive straight through, I can be there by tomorrow night."

"You be careful. The roads aren't safe for a woman driving alone."

"Really, Harriet. I can take care of myself."

Harriet breathed into the receiver. "I know, Cassie. You always have."

Cassie waited a moment, then said, "Tell Daddy . . . tell him I'm coming."

They said good-bye, and Cassie hung up, staring into space for a long moment. Finally, Andrew stirred next to her, and she pulled her hand away. "I've got to go back to Walton. Daddy's sick and wants me there now. He may be dying."

Andrew looked down at his carefully manicured hands and drew in a deep breath. "I'm sorry." He looked up. "I can't come with you, you know."

Cassie regarded him calmly. "I know. That's fine. I think it's better you stayed, anyway. Walton's not your kind of town. You'd be screaming to leave after five minutes."

He set his mouth in a straight line. "It's not that. It's just that one of us needs to stay behind to see to business. You know the BankNorth campaign is scheduled to hit next month, and we've got lots of work to do."

She touched his shoulder. "Really, Andrew. You don't need to explain. I understand."

He nodded, looking down and breaking their gaze.

Cassie rubbed her face as if trying to erase old images. "It's so hard to believe. I just spoke to him on the phone last Sunday. He was telling me yet again that it was time to come home." She smiled at the darkness outside the window. "He said the most peculiar thing."

Andrew flipped off the lamp, then stood, pulling her into his arms. "What did he say this time?"

Cassie nestled into the soft spot below his collarbone, wrinkling her nose at the tang of stale cologne. "He said that Georgia dirt would always stick to the soles of my shoes regardless of how many elocution lessons I took."

Andrew snorted softly. "The old judge never gives up trying to argue his case, does he?"

Cassie shook her head. "No, he doesn't." She closed her eyes, knowing her Italian pumps would never have the patience for the clinging red clay of Georgia.

They stood in their embrace in front of the large plate-glass window. The never-ending traffic below pulsed and vibrated like an electronic serpent, moving with the city's energy. Cassie lifted her chin and stared out at the glittering city skyline, the hulking outlines of the surrounding buildings like the bruises on her memory.

Without being conscious of it, she lifted her hand to the frail gold chain on her neck and placed her fingers around the four small charms that hung from it. The gold was cool to the touch, but it comforted her soul, just as it had many times since her mother had given it to her.

Andrew's voice was muffled. "You're nervous."

Cassie looked up at him. "I am not. Why would you say that?"

His smile lacked mirth. "Because you always play with that silly necklace whenever you're nervous. It's one of your bad habits."

She pulled away. "I'm not nervous. Just . . . thoughtful."

Cassie dropped her hand, and Andrew bent to kiss her neck, his lips warm and lingering on her skin. He lifted his head. "How long do you think you'll be gone?"

She felt a prickle of annoyance. "I don't know, Andrew. My father's sick and may be dying. I'll go for as long as he needs me."

He rubbed his fingers through highlighted hair. "I'm sorry. I don't mean to sound callous. It's just that I've got an office to run, and I need to make plans." He sent her a dim smile. "And don't forget I'm here if you need anything."

Placing her hands on his chest, she fixed him with a steadying gaze. "Actually, there is something. I'm going to drive. And I was wondering if I could borrow your car."

She could see the internal struggle in his eyes from the glow of the lights outside.

He dropped his arms from her shoulders. "My car? You want to drive my car?" He gave an exaggerated groan. "I was afraid you were going to ask me that."

Nobody she knew in the city needed or wanted a car, but Andrew had a house in Connecticut complete with horse barn and garage.

His shoulders slumped slightly. "Couldn't you rent one?"

She took a deep breath, wondering if he would be as protective of her as his wife as he was his car. "I want something safe, reliable—and fast. You know I'll take good care of it." Trying to add some levity, she said, "And it *is* insured, right?"

"Very funny, Cassandra. But what if it breaks down? I don't know if I want a redneck grease monkey under her hood. Those people barely know how to speak English, much less understand the intricacies of a German performance car."

Cassie put her hands on her hips, reminding herself of Aunt Lucinda. She quickly dropped them. "Just because they have accents doesn't mean they're ignorant, Andrew. Most of the boys I grew up with could rebuild your car from a junk pile and it would perform better than it does now." Cassie chewed on her lip, wondering why she had jumped to the defense of Southerners. It wasn't as if she were one anymore. She had rid herself of her accent along with her long hair and penchant for fried foods, although she still couldn't bring herself to wear white shoes after Labor Day or before Easter.

Andrew sighed. "All right. You can borrow my car. But you have to promise me you'll take care of it and have it waxed at least once."

She pulled him closer and kissed him. "Thank you. I promise I'll take care of it."

Several hours later, in the predawn morning, they took the earliest train to Greenwich, Connecticut, and took his car out of long-term parking. Andrew loaded her luggage into the small trunk of the Mercedes and spent twenty minutes going over things she could and couldn't do with his car.

When there was nothing left to be said, he took her in his arms and kissed her deeply, his hands sliding down her back in the practiced way he knew she liked. "I'll miss you," he murmured into her neck. "And I hope things go well for your father. Call me and let me know how things are going."

"Thanks, and I will." She brushed his lips with hers. "I'll miss you, too," she said as she pulled away and sat in the front seat.

She shut the door, put the car in gear, and sent him a

brave smile. She couldn't shake the feeling that this parting was somehow permanent. Swallowing the thick lump in her throat, she shouted, "I'll call you," then pulled away.

Her glance in the rearview mirror revealed Andrew standing in the parking lot, staring after his car until it rounded a corner and he disappeared from sight.

Chapter 2

It was nearly nine o'clock in the morning by the time Cassie started out, the late June sun not yet warm enough to burn the dew off the grass on the immaculate yards she passed. If she drove fast, she'd be in Walton around midnight. She knew the directions by heart. Shortly after moving to New York, when the pull of things familiar was almost more than she could stand, she had stopped at an AAA office and received a Trip Tik. The pages were now worn and crinkled, the holes around the plastic binding torn in places. It lay on the passenger seat, unopened, but there just in case she got lost.

She fed CDs into the stereo, singing aloud to keep her thoughts at bay. She would have to deal with them soon enough. The little red car took her first through New Jersey, then Pennsylvania, then across the Mason-Dixon line and into Virginia. As the sun slipped behind the painted edges of clouds, she swung through North Carolina, the smudge of the Blue Ridge visible on the far horizon. The temperature and humidity rose in steady degrees the farther south she drove, but she was somehow loath to raise the windows and turn on the air-conditioning. Feeling the dampness on her skin and hearing the screeching of the summer insects brought her closer to home faster than the steady roll of road under her tires. She thought of her father but dared not think of anything beyond that; not of seeing her sister again, or Joe. Instead, she studied the endless asphalt stretched out in front of her, the dotted line like a yellow brick road to follow home.

After nightfall, she clipped the northwest corner of South Carolina and entered Georgia. She wasn't sure if it was her imagination, but the air seemed to change. It was as if the red dirt permeated the air, altering it somewhat, distinguishing it from the more ordinary air of other states. She could almost smell the Confederate rose and jasmine that clung to the back porch of her father's house, and a longing to be there, to see her father, consumed her so fiercely that she pushed the gas pedal down farther.

She had just passed the Walton welcoming sign, Where Everybody Is Somebody, when the gas indicator light blinked on the dash, then glowed a solid red. She was sure Andrew had told her how much reserve was in the tank once it hit empty, but she didn't remember. There were no other cars on the road, just hers and the black stretch of highway. A thousand miles from nowhere with an empty gas tank. Cassie shivered.

She spotted a small reflector sign that said: Gas—24 Hours. Cassie followed the arrows off the interstate onto a road that led through the small business district of Walton, Georgia. The road was familiar to her but not the landmarks. Things had changed. She recognized the corner where Virgil's Soda Shop and the drive-in theater had once been and blinked hard. A carpet warehouse and a fast-food restaurant, in squat square buildings, stood there instead.

The streetlights were the only illumination, all of the businesses shrouded in darkness at the late hour. A flickering sign guided her down the street toward the gas station, and she paused in front of it, almost smiling as she read the neon lettering: Bait. Gas. Cappuccino. The cappuccino part was new, but Cassie knew the gas station well. It had been a high school hangout and was owned by the father of a boy she had gone to school with. She couldn't think of the boy's name but remembered how he had hung around the fringe of their group, as if basking in the light of Harriet's glow but afraid to get too close.

Cassie pulled up to a gas pump and jumped out of the car, eager to be done with it and on her way. She was so close now. A handwritten sign was duct-taped to the front of the pump: After Dark, Please Pay Inside First. She opened the car door, yanked out her keys and purse, then locked the door, with a quiet beep from the remote. Squinting to see in the dim yellow glow of outdoor lighting, she spied a large plate-glass window and door, and a man standing inside behind a counter. She walked across the parking lot and through the door.

Cassie crossed the cracked linoleum tiles, passed the racks of MoonPies, breath mints, and chewing tobacco, and handed the man her American Express card. "I'd like to fill my tank with gas, and get a cup of cappuccino for me, please."

Deep blue eyes stared back at her from a face of well-worn leather surrounded by a cottony strip of white hair and beard. The face looked vaguely familiar, but she preferred to remain incognito. She was back in town to see her father, not to stage an embarrassing homecoming. A homecoming that would surely dredge up unwelcome memories.

He smiled, then handed back her card. "Sorry, ma'am. I cain't take American Express."

She frowned. "Oh. Would you take a personal check, then?"

"Sure can. I'll just need to see a driver's license."

A chair skidded behind her, and she whirled to see a tall man unfolding himself from a stool to stand. He wore jeans and cowboy boots, and his button-down shirt had the sleeves rolled up above his wrists, exposing tanned forearms. Cassie's blood swished a little faster in her veins as she looked at him.

"I'll fill your tank for you, ma'am."

Cassie stalled, not sure if Andrew would approve of this

man being near the Mercedes. "That's all right. I can
manage."

Blue eyes regarded her, and she realized they were the
same deep hue as the old man's. The younger man sent a
look toward his father as a smile warmed his mouth. She
had the distinct impression she was being laughed at.

"The pump's a bit stiff, and you need a big grip to hold
it down." He leaned an elbow on the counter. " 'Sides, I
wouldn't feel right makin' a lady pump her own gas while
I sit inside here. Don't worry. You won't need to tip me."

She narrowed her eyes at him, trying to ignore the handsome crease lines around his mouth when he smiled. She
wasn't wild about the idea of standing outside and being
eaten alive by mosquitoes as she filled her tank, anyway. If
he really wanted to, then he was welcome to it. "All right.
I just need to unlock the gas tank first."

He followed her outside, and she fervently wished she
had worn jeans instead of the short skirt she had pulled from
her closet. He moved around the side of the car near the
pump as she unlocked the tank. She turned to go back inside,
then called over her shoulder, "Thank you." The words
seem unfamiliar but somehow necessary. She didn't wait
for him to answer before returning inside.

Facing the older man, she asked, "Could you please tell
me where the cappuccino machine is?"

The old man stood with a grunt and came around from
the back of the counter. "The dang thing's over here.
Haven't had too much business for it, but it was my son's
idea. He goes away to college and comes back with all sorts
of crazy ideas. So, I'm cleaning and filling this here machine
every day." He hitched up his overalls over a considerable
mound at his middle and ambled to the back of the store.
"Don't tell anyone, but now he's got me drinkin' it, too.
Helps me stay awake when the late-shift help don't show
up and I need to fill in. 'Course, I add a drop of JD to
sweeten it a bit." He winked and reached for a stack of
Styrofoam cups.

Cassie looked out the large window at the younger man.

He stood next to the car, waiting for the gas to finish pumping, tossing a coin in the air and catching it. His sandy-colored hair was a bit longer than she was used to, just brushing the back of his collar, but it suited him. He was probably like an Italian sports car: nice to look at but not much under the hood. She wondered what his major in college had been. Probably phys ed.

Their eyes met through the glass. Darn. She'd been staring. She quickly took a sip from her steaming cup of cappuccino, immediately burning her lip and tongue.

"Dangnabit!"

The older man slipped her a glance. "Careful—it's hot."

"Yeah. I noticed." She pulled her checkbook out of her purse. "How much do I owe you?"

He lowered his eyeglasses on his nose and examined a small monitor. "That'll be twenty-four seventy-five."

The bell over the door rang, and she felt the younger man enter but didn't turn around. She placed the cup on the counter and wrote out the check, then slid it over.

The older man examined it closely, then slid it back to her.

"Sorry, ma'am. Cain't take an out-of-state check, and this one says you're from New York."

She held back an exasperated sigh. "Fine. Do you have an ATM machine nearby?"

The man sent her a blank stare, then handed the check to his son. She noticed the young man's hands as he bent over the check; long and tapered, the knuckles bony ripples under the smooth skin. No car grease staining the nail beds, either.

His eyes met hers, lighting with some sort of amusement. "We can take her check, Dad. I know her."

"Oh, really?" Cassie resisted the impulse to put her hands on her hips.

"You're Cassie Madison. We went to high school together, and the first two years of junior college."

She examined him closely, an alarm starting to go off inside her head. Instinctively, her hand flew to the charm necklace around her neck.

"I was with you when you heard the news about Joe running off with Harriet the night of our sophomore fall formal. I held your head over the bushes while you threw up."

Cassie realized the sound of a deflating tire was coming from her own mouth, and she closed it. She should have figured it out as soon as the old man had said the word *son,* but she'd been too preoccupied with getting out of there as quickly as she could. She remembered a young man of twenty with braces and thick glasses that magnified his eyes until they seemed to cover most of his face. Sam Parker: the last person on earth she ever wanted to see again.

"You've . . . changed." Those were the only words she could force out.

His eyes brightened. "So have you."

"I'm surprised you remember."

Half of his mouth turned up. "It's not something a person forgets."

She dug in her purse to find her keys, trying to hide the flush rising on her face. "Well, you have my permission to forget it now."

As she'd tried to do for years. But the recollection of her standing on the front porch of her daddy's house wearing her purple taffeta dress and the engagement ring Joe had given her, waiting for him to pick her up, was written in indelible ink on the creases of her memory. She could still see Sam's face as he walked up the porch steps and handed her the note from Joe and Harriet. The urge to throw up had hit her as soon as she saw both their names scrawled at the bottom of the letter.

Mr. Parker came around the counter. "I guess you're here to see your dad. I'm real sorry to hear the judge is doing so poorly. The sight of you should perk him right up."

His eyes warmed her, his sympathy sincere. For some reason, she wanted to cry and quickly blinked away the tears.

"I have to go now. They're expecting me."

Sam spoke softly. "You can't. You're leaking transmission fluid. Didn't you feel the engine jump a little bit?"

She stared at him blankly. "Not exactly."

"Well, we don't have the right kind, but we can get it for you. Just not tonight. Dad'll take care of it tomorrow. For now, let me drive you home."

She wanted to decline, since every time she looked at him she relived the biggest humiliation of her life. But she relented, realizing her options were limited. "All right."

He didn't move, but seemed to be expecting her to say something else.

"Thank you," she added. "But it's not my home anymore. I'm just here for a visit."

Sam sent her a sidelong glance as he held the door open. "Come on."

He moved her luggage to his double-cab pickup truck and then held the door open for her to climb in. She looked at the big step up and wondered how she would climb up in her short skirt without flashing Sam.

He turned his head away, and she hoisted her skirt up around her hips to step up, then settled it back down as she backed into the seat. The truck appeared to be new, the aroma of leather still strong inside.

Sam closed her door, then approached the driver's side, pausing at the open door as a beeper on his belt sounded. He looked down at the number, his eyebrows tucked into a slight frown. "Looks like I'm heading in your direction, anyway."

Sam slid easily onto the bench seat of the truck. Cassie had half-expected to find a gun rack in the rear window and was almost disappointed to discover the window empty and nothing in the backseat except for a black bag.

He shifted the truck in gear and moved it out onto the road. "You've been gone a long time, Cassie."

She turned away from him, looking out the side window. "I go by Cassandra now, and yes, I have."

He seemed intent on ignoring her body language and filled the empty air with questions.

"Sounds like you've made a pretty big name for yourself in New York City. Your daddy's real proud of you. All he talks about these days are his girls and his grandkids."

Cassie only nodded her head.

He was silent for a moment. "I just never figured you to be the type to run away from things."

She whipped her head around to stare at him, sure she could see the trace of a smile on his lips.

"Now don't you go and be getting all mad at me. I'm just stating a fact. I never thought I'd see the day when Cassie Madison let a situation get the best of her."

Cassie sat up straight in the seat. "I didn't. I always knew that this town wasn't the place for me. The timing just seemed to work out, that's all. I'd always planned to leave."

"And never come back—even for holidays? Did it never occur to you that there were people here who loved you and missed you?"

She turned to look at his strong profile, the passing street lamps casting mottled light on his face. The man had certainly changed since she'd last seen him—and all for the better. She squirmed a bit in her seat. That he'd given her disappearance any thought at all surprised her. She hadn't thought about Sam Parker once in the entire fifteen years she'd been away.

"I met my daddy every year in Atlanta, and we did all our catching up then. That was enough." She looked away, folding her arms across her chest. "Oh, never mind. I don't want to talk about it now."

He leaned forward and turned on the radio to a country station with a man singing a song about his dog, Jake. Cassie gritted her teeth.

"I guess not talking much is another thing you learned up north."

Irritated now, she blurted out, "What do you mean, another thing?"

He shrugged his shoulders, stretching one arm along the back of the bench seat. "Well, I don't remember you being so snooty before. But I do recall how you always got mean when you were scared.''

She glared at him. Then, without speaking, she reached for the volume control on the radio to make it louder so she couldn't hear him. She was already riddled with guilt, and Sam was only making her feel worse.

With the radio blaring, they drove back to the interstate and took the next exit. It was then that she noticed that her teeth were chattering even though the night was warm; balmy, almost. Within ten minutes they were passing Walton First United Methodist on the left, the illuminated sign outside offering up its message: Need a New Look? Have Your Faith Lifted Here. She remembered Reverend Beasley putting up a new sign every week and wondered if he still did.

Sam stopped at a deserted intersection, and a corner of the high school was visible two blocks down. He turned right onto Orchard Street, and she began counting houses: the Ladues, the Pritchards, and old Mrs. Harris. Then another right on Madison Lane, the ancient oak trees creating a veil over the street. The houses were more sparsely set here, growing farther and farther apart until all that was left was the end of the street and a long gravel driveway. Cassie turned her head, staring at two under-contract signs at houses on either side of her father's property. Sam turned off the radio, and the night sounds buzzed all around them.

Slowly, they bumped over the gravel road, the only light that of the moon drifting through the lane of oaks, stealing the colors from the landscape and turning the red truck hood gray. The large white house loomed before them, the sight as comforting to her as her mother's arms, and the old memories hit her again. She felt a gentle touch on her forearm.

"Are you all right?"

She nodded, suddenly not trusting her voice.

He parked the truck in the circular drive, then reached into the backseat and pulled out the black bag. He got out and walked to her side of the truck, and Cassie decided it was time to show him that liberated women existed. But her efforts to let herself out of the truck were hampered by her short skirt, and she would have fallen out the door if it hadn't been for his strong arm guiding her down. His hand held hers for a moment, his palm surprisingly soft and warm.

"It'll be fine, you know," he said softly, his southern accent soothing to her ears.

Cassie removed her hand. "I know. It just takes a little getting used to. I can handle this." She shut her mouth abruptly, cringing at the wavering of her voice. Her hand reached up, her fingers hugging the charms on the necklace tightly.

He watched her hand with a small smile but didn't say anything.

They walked up the porch steps, centered between two of the six fluted columns. Cassie stopped, her confidence sagging. Sam walked ahead of her and put his hand on the doorknob of the screen.

"Shouldn't we knock first?" she suggested, trying to buy time.

He tugged the door open, releasing the poignant aromas of furniture polish and old wood. "I usually don't. Besides, they're expecting me."

She sent him a quizzical look. "What?"

Before he could answer, the patter of running feet on wood floors cascaded toward them, the sound of shouting children reaching them before anyone came into view.

A towheaded boy of about five ran toward Sam, his head bent like a rampaging bull. "Dr. Parker!" he screeched as he was lifted high over Sam's head.

"Doctor . . . ?" Cassie stopped as the sound of more little feet brought her head around. A small girl with red braids ran pell-mell toward her, shrieking, "Aunt Cassie!" at the top of her lungs. Her arms were outstretched, and Cassie had no other choice but to stretch her arms wide, too, and catch the little girl.

Cassie stood there, hugging a child she had never seen before, in the foyer that had lived only in her dreams for fifteen years. She watched the slender figure of a woman appear at the top of the staircase and then gallop down the wooden stairs, another familiar sound that twanged on the strings of her memory.

The woman stopped in front of her and smiled her toothy cheerleader smile, the one that had always reminded Cassie of her mother. She smelled of roses and talcum powder and baby spit-up, and Cassie felt disoriented for a moment, looking at this woman she knew but didn't know. Her sister's smile never wavered.

"Welcome home, Cassie."

Chapter 3

Harriet reached for her sister, her arms tight around Cassie's shoulders. Cassie stiffened in the embrace, unsure of her feelings, the ghost of forgiveness long absent.

Harriet pulled back, her smile fading slightly. "It's good to see you. You look just wonderful." She placed the flat of her hand against the blunt edges of Cassie's chestnut bob, making it bounce. "You look so ... sophisticated." She dropped her arm, her expression suddenly shy. "It suits you."

Cassie stared down at her sister, only fifteen months younger and still a full head shorter. Harriet's petiteness had always brought out the protector in Cassie, even before their mother's death, when Cassie was eight, had forced her into the role permanently. They had been the best of friends ever since Cassie could pick Harriet out of her crib when she cried. She hadn't even minded when their mother held her back a year in school so she and Harriet would start kindergarten together. They had shared everything. Until Joe.

Cassie spoke slowly, taking in her sister's shoulder-length honey blond hair. She still wore it pulled back from her face with a fabric headband. "You look . . . Well, you look the same." A small smile crept to her lips.

The child at Cassie's knees began hopping up and down, her arms reaching up. Harriet swooped down to pick up the little girl. Her words spilled out in a rush, as if to drown out unwanted thoughts. "We let the kids stay up tonight at Pop-pop's house because they were so excited about seeing you. That's Joey, by the way," she said, indicating the boy being jostled up and down on Sam's back. "And this is Knoxie. We named her after Grandma Knox on account of the red hair. We've just been hoping she didn't get Grandma's foul temper, too, although the old woman did have a lot of sweetness in her when she wanted to. . . ."

Cassie resisted the impulse to roll her eyes, missing New Yorkers and their bluntness all of a sudden. "How's Daddy?" she interrupted.

Without skipping a beat, Harriet handed Knoxie to Cassie, then went to pry Joey off Sam. "He was complaining about not being able to sleep, so I paged the doctor. You remember Sam Parker, don't you? Saved me and a bunch of us seniors from failing biology and algebra. He was with us at the junior college, remember? Then, I guess it was after you left, he went away for school, and we're just all so grateful to have him back."

Sam relinquished the squirming boy on his back and headed for the stairs. "I certainly remember Cassie. Didn't recognize her at first, though, until I saw the back of her head."

Cassie caught his grin as he walked past her. With a tight smile, she said, "Funny, I hardly remember Sam at all." She turned to her sister. "Can I see Daddy now?"

Harriet nodded, reaching for the little girl. "He's . . . he's not as you remember him, so try not to be shocked when you see him."

"I can handle it," Cassie said, and followed Sam up the stairs, trying not to notice how nice his backside looked in those jeans as he climbed the steps. They walked down the long upstairs hallway until they reached the dark double

doors at the end. Two girls sat cross-legged on the floor
outside the door, leaning against the hallway wall, their
heads propped against each other, their eyes closed. Cassie
knew the older girl to be Madison, fourteen, and, by process
of elimination, the younger one had to be Sarah Frances,
nine. The younger one had honey-colored hair like Harriet,
but Madison's hair was two shades darker—not dark enough
to be brown but not light enough to be called dirty blond.
It was no-man's brown, as Cassie used to lament over her
own hair. At least before she discovered Jean-Paul and his
salon on the corner of Broadway and West Seventieth.

Sam tapped lightly on the door, then pushed it open. He
stepped back, allowing Cassie to enter first.

She paused on the threshold, her breath tight in her chest.
Sam seemed to sense her hesitation and rested his hand
firmly on her shoulder. The dark hues of the room—the
burgundies, navies, and forest greens—underscored the fact
that there had been no feminine influence on the decor for
over twenty years. An old man, his emaciated frame barely
making the covers rise, rested in the imposing four-poster
bed. It stood high off the floor, a family heirloom in which
generations of her family had slept. Cassie barely recognized
the man as the robust father of her memory, but when he
opened his eyes, almost black against the pasty white of his
face, she knew him. Straightening her shoulders, she walked
toward the bed.

A pale hand, the blue veins visible beneath the paper-thin
surface, reached for her, and she held it, cupping it gently
between hers like a child holding a butterfly.

"Hi, Daddy. I'm home." Her breath caught, and her father
patted her with his other hand.

"It's about time," he said, then closed his eyes. His hand
went slack in hers, and she turned to Sam in a panic.

"Is he all right?"

Sam stepped closer, pulling a stethoscope from his bag.
"I'm sure he's fine. He was just waiting up for you to come
home before he could go to sleep. Sort of like when you
were a teenager."

She stroked her father's cheek before moving back from the bed to allow Sam to examine him. "Not likely. I wasn't the one with a different date every night of the week." She regretted her petulant tone. More softly, she said, "He'll even tell you that most of his gray hairs weren't caused by me."

Sam fixed her with a disbelieving stare before he leaned over the old man with his stethoscope. "That's not how I remember it."

Cassie crossed her arms over her chest. Ignoring his comment, she asked, "Is he okay?"

He straightened, taking the stethoscope from his ears. "He's fine—he's just sleeping." Sam fixed her with a steady gaze. "And when he awakes, we can talk about that unsolved incident our senior year when somebody painted Principal Purdy's front porch hot pink while he slept."

Cassie felt her ears go hot. "Oh, Lord, Sam. You're not going to tell anybody, are you?"

His shoulders shook with laughter as he put the stethoscope back into his bag. "Cassie, that was over fifteen years ago. Do you think anybody still cares?"

Her chin jutted out in the direction of the old man on the bed. "He would." She swallowed thickly. "Is he . . . is he going to be all right?"

Sam took her by the elbow and led her toward the door. He leveled his gaze on her and spoke quietly. "I'm going to be blunt with you because I know you want to hear the truth. No, he won't. His heart is too weak. I'm afraid it's only a matter of time." He lifted his hand as if to touch her cheek, then let it fall. "I'm sorry, Cassie."

She pulled back her shoulders. "Have you considered anything else? What about surgery or a transplant?"

He shook his head. "I've exhausted all options, Cassie. He wouldn't survive surgery, and a transplant is out of the question at his age. I'm sorry, but there's nothing we can do."

Cassie held back the tears stinging her eyes. "If you don't

mind, I'd like to get a second opinion. Not to sound rude, but where did you get your medical degree, anyway?''

He stared down at her, a small flicker of annoyance in his eyes. ''Harvard. Perhaps you've heard of it.''

''Oh.'' Her fighting spirit deserted her. She looked down, feeling the tears start and not wanting Sam to see. ''May I stay with him for a while? I promise I won't wake him.''

Sam paused for a moment. ''Sure. I'll be back in the morning to check on things. You try to get some rest.'' He opened the door, then turned back toward her. ''And I'd bet my best hunting dog that the judge has known about the pink porch all along.'' With a wink, he stepped into the hallway and closed the door behind him.

Cassie turned toward the bed and saw her father's eyes open. She walked closer to him and sat on the bed.

His voice sounded very far away, reminding her of their monthly phone calls. ''You've cut your hair shorter since I last saw you. Makes you look more like your mother.'' He sighed softly. ''Sure wish she was here. Then she could give you a dressing-down, since I don't have the strength right now.''

''Thanks, Daddy. It's good to see you, too.'' She kissed him on his withered cheek, then bent her head, no longer able to contain the tears. Her father patted the mattress next to him, and she collapsed beside him, her head sharing his stack of pillows. She was a terrified child again, faced with losing a parent. She reached for his hand and held on tightly, one of her remaining anchors to her childhood.

''I miss Mama. I wonder . . .'' Cassie sniffled, then snuggled closer to her father, smelling a faint whiff of laundry detergent and cologne. ''I wonder if things would have turned out differently if she had been here.''

The judge spoke with his eyes closed. ''If you mean she might have known about Joe and Harriet and stopped them, I don't think so. Even you can see now that they were meant for each other.''

Cassie turned away, but her hand still clasped her father's, the wrinkled knuckles somehow comforting.

"He was mine." She sounded childish to her own ears, as if they were talking about a favorite doll.

"Yes, Cassie. He was yours. But that was a long time ago. He and Harriet have a wonderful marriage now, and five children." He paused, taking deep, labored breaths. "It pains me to see how in all these years you haven't even tried to make peace with your sister. And you've made no effort at all to get to know your nieces and nephew. They're fine children, Cassie. You'd be proud of them."

Cassie couldn't hide a sob. "I know—and I'm sorry. I've kept all their pictures in my photo album, and I do think about them all the time. But it still hurts, Daddy. It still hurts. Sometimes I don't know if I'll ever get over it."

"What still hurts, Cassie? The fact that you lost Joe or that somebody got the best of you?"

She turned back to him, wondering if those dark eyes held the truth. "I don't know anymore. I honestly don't know. Maybe it's just an old habit that I don't know how to break. Or maybe I just can't get over the fact that you were on her side. You didn't do anything to bring them back."

The old man shifted in his bed. "It wasn't a matter of taking sides. I didn't like the manner in which they let their feelings be known, but I knew deep down that they were meant for each other. And that in time you would forgive them and find somebody who was really yours."

His voice sank to barely a whisper. "It's been fifteen years, Cassie. Not to be blunt, but it's time to get over it. Get on with your life."

Abruptly, she left the bed and went to the window, hiding her hot tears. "You always took her side. I guess that will never change. But I am over it." She had to be; it was fifteen long years ago. She swallowed the knot in her throat. "I'm thirty-five years old, Daddy. I've outgrown all that. I have a new life, and none of that matters anymore. This town, these people—I've left it all way behind me." She sighed, pressing her forehead against the glass. "And the more I've stayed away, the easier it became to not come back."

The judge struggled to sit up on his elbows. Alarmed, Cassie rushed back to his side to hold him steady and prop the pillows behind him.

He sounded strained. "You can go to the moon, Cassandra Lee Madison, but this place, these people, will always run in your blood. You can't get away from it, so you might as well come home."

Cassie helped him lie back against the pillows, the bright spots of pink slowly fading from his face. She'd never been able to back away from a fight with her father, and she was reluctant to start now. He was stubborn, but it was a trait she had inherited from him. Firmly, she said, "This isn't my home anymore."

His long, bony fingers tightened around her forearm, his voice quiet but still just as forceful and fearsome as it was when she was a little girl caught telling a lie. "The hell it's not. And there's nothing you can do that'll change that. If I have any say in the matter at all, you'll never leave again."

Cassie leaned forward to kiss his forehead. Gently, she said, "You don't have any say. I'll stay here until you get better, but then I'm going back to New York."

He didn't answer, and his eyelids fluttered closed. She lay back down beside him, holding his hand, listening to the rhythm of his breathing. She had spent many nights like this as a child, hidden under his bed, listening. Her mother had given up her long fight with cancer in this room, and Cassie, as a little girl, had thought that if she had been there, she would have heard the moment her mother stopped breathing and been able to awaken her. But she had died, and Cassie had vowed to herself that she wouldn't allow the same thing to happen to her father. While Harriet slept peacefully in her own room down the hall, Cassie had kept vigil over their father, dozing off and on, pinching herself awake as the night wore on, until gray dawn eased its way through the dust ruffle. When her father rose to take his shower, Cassie would escape to her room and sleep for two hours before Aunt Lucinda jerked open her curtains. She had done that up through the eighth grade until one morning her father had stuck his head under the bed and told her she was too old to be sleeping there anymore.

Cassie snaked her hand over to her father's chest, feeling the reassuring beat of his heart. To her surprise, his hand covered hers. "I think painting Principal Purdy's porch showed a lot of spunk, you know. I just hope that by now you've learned there are better means to get your point across."

She looked over at her father in surprise. "So you really did know. Why didn't you tell me?"

He shifted under the covers. "Because then I would have had to punish you, and you didn't deserve it."

Cassie stuck out her chin. "You're damned right I didn't. He wanted to cancel prom because of some silly food fight in the cafeteria—and not even everybody was involved. It just wasn't fair."

The judge patted her hand. "It was a damned fine stunt. And you should know that I laughed for about an hour straight after I saw it."

They laughed quietly together for a moment, remembering easier times between them. Finally, Cassie said, "Thanks, Daddy. For not getting me in trouble."

He patted her hand again. "You're welcome." His voice sounded tired. "I'm glad you're home."

Cassie said nothing, but reached over and squeezed his hand. Then she rolled over, turned out the bedside light, and lay in the dark listening to him breathe until he finally fell asleep. Then she grabbed a pillow and lay down by the side of the bed, her feet tucked under the dust ruffle, until she, too, found sleep.

Cassie awoke to hear people talking outside the bedroom door, a triangle of orange sun slapping her in the face as she opened her eyes.

Harriet spoke in a hushed whisper. "Your aunt and grand-father are still sleeping, and you may not disturb them. I'm sure your Aunt Cassie is dying to see you, too, but she's exhausted from her long drive. Just give her time to get up and dress and I bet she'll even tell you stories about New York City."

A young girl's voice came through the door, dripping with sarcasm. "Well, butter my butt and call me a biscuit."

"Madison Cassandra Warner! I'm going to wash your mouth out with soap if I ever hear you use that expression again."

"But it's already ten o'clock! Is she going to sleep forever?"

Cassie felt her lips turn up with a smile at the maternal sound of her sister's voice and wondered again why Harriet had chosen her firstborn to be Cassie's namesake. Still smiling, she listened to the reassuring hum of her father's breathing as she stiffly moved out from under the bed. She walked to the door and pulled it open, finding herself staring into two pairs of matching sea-green eyes. Cassie blinked, looking at her oldest niece. The resemblance to Harriet ended at the eyes. She could have been looking at a mirror image of a younger version of herself. The same no-man's-land brown hair, the pert, straight nose with a spattering of freckles, and the stubborn chin with the small dimple, inherited from Cassie's mother.

"Good morning," Cassie croaked, never a good conversationalist before her morning coffee. She gave her sister a quick peck on the cheek, then turned to her niece. "You must be Madison."

The young girl nodded shyly, her eyes bright.

Managing a smile, Cassie said, "I need a shower and some coffee before I'm fit company, so give me about half an hour and I'll come down, all right?"

Without waiting for an answer, she walked past them to her girlhood room, the pink canopy and rose wallpaper unchanged since she had last seen it. Her luggage had already been brought up, and she grabbed her overnight bag with shampoo, conditioner, and razor and stumbled into the bathroom.

She showered quickly, using a trick she had learned in

graduate school of keeping the water cold. Not only did it cut down on showering time; it also made one alert and ready for the morning. Cassie was pretty sure she'd need every ounce of alertness she could muster this morning. The thought of seeing Joe again made her hand tremble, and she cut her leg with the razor, the trickle of blood pooling like a tear and snaking its way down her leg.

She turned off the water and opened the curtain, realizing there were no towels on the racks. Shivering, she remembered a clean towel someone had put on her bed.

"Damn," she muttered under her breath. She grabbed a wad of tissue and stuck it to her cut knee. Then, with wet hair dripping down her face, she stuck her head out the door. The hallway was blessedly deserted. She clutched her clothes in a ball in front of her and took two quick steps across the wood floor before her wet heel slid out from under her and she landed with a loud thump on her bare backside.

To her horror, she watched the door to her father's bedroom open, and Sam appeared in the doorway. His gaze searched the hallway until it finally rested on her, lingering far too long on her chest area. Cassie held her underwear to cover her breasts, the other hand clutching the rest of her clothes in her lap.

Sam cleared his throat. "Is that a New York thing?"

Her voice was unnaturally high-pitched. "Is what a New York thing?"

"Doing yoga while naked and dripping wet in the middle of a hallway."

She narrowed her eyes. "I slipped."

Sam left the doorway and began walking toward her. "Are you hurt?"

Cassie held her hand with the panties in front of her, then quickly pulled it back. "I'm fine. Please go away."

She could see he was trying to hide a smile. He turned back to the door. "You haven't changed as much as you think you have, you know."

"What's that supposed to mean? Besides, I'm two dress

sizes smaller than I used to be. And I don't wear glasses anymore.''

"That's not what I meant. But don't worry. It's a good thing. You were a pretty neat kid.'' He twisted the knob and opened the door. "Now go put some clothes on before somebody sees you.''

She heard the laughter in his voice, but before she could reply, he had closed the door behind him.

As soon as she heard the latch click, Cassie bolted into her room and got dressed as quickly as she could. She dried her hair, taking care to curl the ends under, and put on her makeup. She'd need all the defenses she had to get through this day.

The smell of frying bacon wafted up to her, causing her stomach to rumble. She stalled in her room, hoping Joe and anybody else would be gone by the time she got downstairs. She certainly couldn't face him on an empty stomach.

She left her room and went to check on her father. She paused on the threshold, seeing Harriet sitting by the side of the bed, holding his hand. Cassie turned to go but was called back by her father.

"Come in, Cassie. I want to see my girls together.''

She walked over to the other side of the bed and sat on the edge, digging her heels into the side rails, as she had as a child. She slid her hand into his and watched his face break out into a broad smile.

"I can die a happy man now.''

His hand squeezed Cassie's hand, the pressure so faint, she cast a worried glance at her sister.

But Harriet was leaning forward, smoothing the hair off her father's forehead. "Don't say such things, Daddy. You're going to be just fine, you'll see.''

Harriet turned away to pour water into a cup from the bedside table, and Cassie's eyes met her father's. She read the love in them, and the fading strength. She also saw the good-bye.

The judge took a sip of the water, Harriet holding up his head. When she put the cup down, he held his hand in hers again. "My girls," he said, his eyes moist. "You've given me such joy all these years. Your mother would have been so proud."

Cassie looked down at a spot on the Oriental rug, blinking rapidly.

"Tell us about this Andrew you're thinking about marrying, Cassie. Is he planning on coming down for a visit? Because if he wants to ask my permission, he'd better hurry."

"Daddy," Cassie started to protest, then stopped when she noticed he had closed his eyes.

"How many kids are you going to have?"

Her hand felt sweaty, trapped in the warm cocoon of her father's big fist. "We, um, we haven't really talked about that yet."

He nodded, his eyes still closed. "They'll need to know their cousins and their aunt and uncle."

"We'll visit." Cassie used her other hand to wipe her eyes. She caught her sister's gaze and gave a weak smile.

Her father's voice had sunk low in his chest, his breathing raspy. "Do you still laugh a lot, Cassie? I've missed that the most." He swallowed deeply, then continued. "It was like that rush of popping bubbles after you pour a Coke. Effervescent. Yes, that's what he called it."

Cassie waited for him to catch his breath before asking, "What who called it?"

When he didn't answer, Harriet's spoke softly. "Sam. He and Sam talk about you a lot."

Cassie flicked her sister a questioning look and was about to ask why Sam would have any interest in her when their father spoke again, his voice so low that Cassie had to lean down to hear.

"So, Cassie—do you still laugh?"

She sagged against the bed. "Sometimes, Daddy. Sometimes."

His eyes flickered open briefly, then closed again as he set his mouth in a stubborn line. "Mm-hmm," he muttered, and Cassie squirmed. That had always been his sign that he was about to mete out punishment following a confession he had forced out of her.

When he didn't say anything else, Cassie relaxed, feeling the stress leave her shoulders.

Harriet smoothed the hair off his forehead again. "You need to rest now, Daddy. I'll stay here in case you need anything."

He nodded, and Cassie leaned over to kiss him again, holding her head near his for a moment longer and feeling his breath on her cheek. "I love you, Daddy." Her voice cracked, and she bent her head close enough for his hair to rub her face.

"I love you, too."

Harriet looked at her sister. "You go get some breakfast. Aunt Lucinda is aching to see you. She's been frying up a storm all morning waiting for you to come down."

Cassie nodded. "Okay. But call me if ... if you need anything." As she turned to go, she thought she saw the trace of a grin on her father's lips, the type he had always worn when he had a surprise for her. She turned back again, but his expression had gone slack, and his breathing held the steady rhythm of sleep.

Slowly, Cassie walked down the stairs, her stomach rumbling at the enticing aroma. As she descended, she paused at each portrait of her long-gone ancestors, naming them in her head, then stopped completely in front of the painting of old Great-great-great-grandfather Madison, who had built the home in 1848 to attract a bride. It must have worked, because the man had had four wives, who gave him a total of nine children. Cassie stared into the dark brown eyes, recalling how she used to scare her sister with stories about how those eyes would watch Harriet as she walked up the stairs. Cassie smiled, remembering how Harriet wouldn't walk up the stairs alone for years.

She reached the kitchen and paused at the familiar sight of Aunt Lucinda's back. Her father's sister had been like a mother to her, moving in when Cassie's mother got too sick to get out of bed. She had been there for all of Cassie's milestones: the birthdays, the recitals, the academic awards, and later, the tears. Aunt Lucinda now stood before the stove, her knobby shoulders more bent than Cassie remembered, wearing her standard uniform of bright red housedress and high heels. Cassie was suddenly taken back fifteen years to the morning she had last seen her aunt standing at the stove, peach oven mitt tucked under her arm as she beat biscuit batter with one hand and fried eggs with the other.

"Aunt Lucinda?"

The older woman turned, her bright red lips parted in an *O*. She walked toward Cassie and squeezed her tight, the familiar smells of Youth Dew bath oil and bacon grease oddly comforting.

"My goodness, Cassie. It feels good to hug you again, but you're all skin and bones. Don't they eat in New York?" Her words couldn't hide the warble of tears.

She kissed Cassie's cheek, but Cassie didn't have the heart to rub off the inevitable red mark. Just as she had as a little girl, she would wait until she was out of Aunt Lucinda's eyesight.

As Lucinda released her, Cassie noticed for the first time the two men sitting at the table. Sam had paused over a heaping plate of grits and sausage, and the man across from him sat with a baby on his lap, feeding it a bottle. Gentle slurpings filled the suddenly silent room as Cassie realized that the dreaded moment had arrived.

Aunt Lucinda squeezed her around the shoulders one more time, then nudged her forward. "You've already seen Sam, and here's Joe." She turned toward the men. "Doesn't she look fine, y'all? Just as pretty as her mother, don't y'all think?"

Cassie blushed to the roots of her hair, suddenly reduced to age twelve and the time she and Harriet had come home from school and interrupted one of Aunt Lucinda's bridge parties. All the ladies had fawned over Harriet, with her gold hair spilling over her sweater. Aunt Lucinda, striking her mother-hen pose, had stood and pushed Cassie forward, telling everyone how smart she was and how she hadn't quite grown into her looks yet. Cassie cringed at the memory.

Sam swallowed a mouthful of food. "You're right, Aunt Lucinda. She sure is. The new hairstyle threw me at first, but I would have recognized her anywhere."

She forced her gaze in Joe's direction, concentrating on the baby in his arms. It was swaddled in pink, the color setting off the baby's rosy cheeks. Slowly, Cassie raised her eyes. Her gaze swept over Joe, looking for the boy she had once loved with all her young heart and waiting for lightning to strike her, leaving nothing but the outline of ash on the ceramic tile floor of the kitchen. But nothing happened. She felt nothing. No spark, no tightening in the chest, no tingling in the belly. Joe Warner no longer made her mouth go dry. He looked like the high school football coach and science teacher he had become, complete with red marker stains on his fingers and a shirt pocket bulging with pens, pencils and the broken cord of a Bunsen burner. He was still drop-dead gorgeous, with laughing brown eyes that narrowed to slits when he smiled, but he'd lost the power to suck the air out of her lungs with just a look. He was her sister's husband, an old friend, and nothing more.

Still, the old ache, hinting of hurt and humiliation, throbbed in the back of her heart. She smiled tentatively, putting her hands in the pockets of her linen walking shorts. "Hello, Joe. It's been a while."

She became aware of Sam watching the exchange, his back rigid in his chair.

Joe stood, awkward for a moment, then smiled back. "Yeah. It sure has. How've you been?"

She took a step forward, close enough to smell the peculiar mixture of baby powder and formula. The baby's blue eyes opened wide, and then she smiled, making milk drip down her chin.

"This is Amanda," Joe said, turning so Cassie could get a better view.

Cassie stuck her finger in the baby's open fist, marveling at the tiny perfect fingers, the almost transparent nails.

Joe spoke to the baby. "This is your Aunt Cassie—the one your mommy is always talking about."

Cassie's head jerked up, her eyes meeting Joe's for the first time. Before she could call the words back, she asked, "Does she really?"

Joe nodded, almost shyly. "Every day, just about. Pictures of you and her are all over our house—even in the kids' rooms. She wanted to make sure they knew who you were." He paused for a moment, then said, "We sent you letters, at first. But . . . but they kept coming back unopened, so we stopped. But that didn't mean we stopped thinking about you or caring for you."

She swallowed, trying to think of what to say. She wanted to tell him that it was okay now, that the anger she had felt each time she marked "return to sender" on the letters no longer mattered. But the memory of her humiliation made the words stick in her throat. It had been there for fifteen years and would not be dislodged so easily.

The baby burped, spitting up over Joe's shirt and creating a needed diversion.

Sam stood, holding a chair out for her, and she sat down heavily. Aunt Lucinda came and put a plate filled with bacon, eggs, grits, and her famous buttermilk biscuits in front of her. She felt Aunt Lucinda kiss the top of her head.

"I want you to eat all of it, you hear? You're much too thin."

Cassie stabbed a slice of bacon, eyeing it speculatively. As she was about to put it into her mouth, Joe said, "You've lost weight, Cassie. A lot of weight."

She dropped the bacon back on her plate and picked up her coffee. She stared at him through the steam. "It's been fifteen years since you last saw me. Plenty of time to change."

He sat down again, putting Amanda over his shoulder, and began to pat her back. "Things change slowly here, Cassie. You won't find anything a whole lot different. Even Mr. Purdy's still the high school principal. He's probably older than dirt by now, too."

Cassie's lips turned up at the mention of Principal Purdy. "It's a good thing I left, then. Because I happen to think that change is good."

Sam scraped his chair back as he stood and picked up his plate. "Not necessarily. Especially when it means picking up strange new customs."

She knew he was referring to the incident in the upstairs hallway, and she scowled at the creases in his cheek as he walked toward the sink with his dishes. Cassie opened her mouth to say something but stopped when she spotted Harriet in the doorway. Her sister wore a peculiar expression, like a person who'd just seen a plane fall out of the sky. Cassie put down her cup quickly, the hot coffee spilling over the sides.

Her fingers grabbed at the gold chain around her neck as the air seemed to still around her, and her gaze roamed the kitchen, searching out objects, people, anything to help her remember things the way they used to be before her life changed once again. Her eyes took in the stack of newspapers in the corner, her father's gardening shoes dumped inside the back door, his glasses on the counter next to the jar of frying grease. She looked down at her feet briefly, willing herself not to cry. There would be time to cry alone later.

"Is Daddy . . . ?"

Harriet's voice was thick, filled with unshed tears. "Oh, Cassie . . ." She looked at her sister, but Cassie broke the connection by looking away, not yet wanting to share her grief with this woman who hadn't shared her life for so long.

Harriet didn't move. "It was . . . peaceful. And quick. I would have called you except that it was over so fast. He just said good-bye and . . . and went to sleep."

Joe stood and went to his wife, putting his free arm around her narrow shoulders, and kissed her on the cheek.

Cassie stood, her knees shaky. Sam watched her closely as she grabbed the back of her chair. "I want to see him."

Harriet looked at Joe and then back at Cassie. "Wait a minute. There's something else."

Cassie swayed, wishing she had somebody to hold her with compassion and understanding, to kiss her cheek. And she couldn't imagine Andrew doing either. "What is it?"

Harriet tilted her head to the side, as if trying to make her news less off-kilter. "He told me . . . he told me . . ." She looked at Joe again, as if for strength, then back at Cassie, still wearing the same odd expression.

Cassie just stared at her sister, her nerves tight. "What?"

Harriet's eyes met Cassie's, and Cassie knew. Her father would do whatever he could to make her stay in Walton. Somebody opened the back door, creating a gust of warm air, bringing in the heavy scent of the boxwoods that lined the back walk. Cassie sucked in her breath, the scent suffocating, intoxicating, painful. She wanted to put her hand over Harriet's mouth, to stop the inevitable words from coming out, but found she couldn't move. The screen door slammed shut.

Softly, Harriet said, "He's left the house to you. And everything in it."

Chapter 4

Cassie stepped outside, carefully closing the screen door behind her so as not to attract attention. She had seen enough deviled eggs, sweet potato pie, and corn casserole to last an entire year, yet people were still arriving at the house with even more food. She wasn't sure if everybody was there to pay their respects to her father or if they were there to gawk at her and see if she had grown horns during the time she had spent away. She looked down at her black suit and saw fingerprints of powdered sugar and grease from the fried drumsticks old Mrs. Crandall had brought. Through the screen door, she spotted the woman in question hovering over the kitchen counter, arranging a tall vase of flowers. Cassie studied the pudgy fingers as they straightened long stems of gladiolas, the same fingers she remembered clutching a stick of chalk and stabbing out long-division problems in fifth grade. All of Mrs. Crandall's contemporaries called her Sweet Pea, but to Cassie's generation, she would always be Mrs. Crandall.

Cassie sighed, tired of being poked, prodded, hugged, and squeezed. Trying to brush off some of the fingerprints, she stepped off the back porch, and her high heel immediately sank into the soft red clay edging the walk. She yanked it back and began hobbling down the cement walkway, trying to dislodge the chunk of red earth clinging to her shoe. Without really knowing where she was going, she headed in the direction of the gazebo, slipping off both shoes before crossing the wide backyard. Too late, she remembered the prickers hiding in the grass and did a combination of hops, hobbles, and leaps before making it to the sanctuary of the gazebo.

She sank down on one of the built-in bench seats and lifted a foot. Dozens of miniature double-pronged hooks clung to the sole, creating small holes in her pantyhose and hurting like hell. How could she have forgotten so easily the stern warnings from her father not to go barefoot in the backyard? Cassie and Harriet had even taken turns giving each other piggyback rides to the gazebo just so only one of them had to don shoes. Shoes didn't exist in the summer world of Walton's children, and Cassie had made sure she'd never go barefoot again once she'd left her father's house for good. Until now.

Staring at the bottom of her foot, stubborn tears filled her eyes. She hadn't cried when Mr. Murphy had come from the funeral home to discuss arrangements. Nor had she cried at the wake as the black-clad citizens of Walton had filed past the coffin like ants at a picnic. And she hadn't cried earlier that morning at the funeral. But now, staring at her ruined hose and the tiny prickers sticking out of her foot, she sobbed. She sobbed for the loss of her father, for his words of wisdom, for his constancy, and for the little girl at his knee she could never be again.

A heel scraped against wood, and Cassie jerked her head up. Sam Parker, wearing yet another pair of cowboy boots— these were black—stood on the top step of the gazebo, looking at her with a curious expression.

She turned away. "I'd like to be left alone right now, if you don't mind."

Ignoring her words, he sat down on the bench next to her. "Those prickers must hurt something awful, with the way you're crying. Didn't your daddy ever tell you not to go barefoot back here?'' He reached for her foot and held it in his lap.

She resisted at first and then relaxed, trying to ignore the warmth of his touch through her stockings. He bent over her foot and began removing the prickers with his fingers one by one.

Cassie gave an unladylike sniff, wishing he'd stop touching her and then worrying that he would. ''What is it about you that you're always there to see me do something humiliating?''

Without looking up, he said, ''Crying's not humiliating. It just lets others know you're human.''

Cassie wiped a drip off the end of her nose with the back of her wrist. ''Do you mean there's been some discussion?''

He put one foot down and reached for the other one. ''Not yet.''

His gaze met hers as he grinned, and she quickly looked away, not sure why blood rushed to her face.

To distract herself, she leaned back on her hands and stared up at the ceiling, painted blue to prevent bees and birds from building their nests in what they assumed to be sky. She remembered Joe telling her that on their first summer. The summer Harriet was away at cheerleading camp and Joe was all hers.

Cassie glanced back at Sam, realizing that he had stopped and was now just resting his hands on her legs in a casual manner, her feet draped on his lap. It felt so normal and comfortable, and definitely disconcerting. Quickly, she sat up and moved her feet to the floor.

He reached into his back pocket, pulled out a neatly pressed linen handkerchief, and handed it to her.

She stared at it for a moment but didn't touch it.

He shook it. ''Your nose is dripping.''

''Thank you,'' she said, sniffing again. She took it, dabbed her eyes, then blew her nose into the clean square of cloth.

Sam spoke softly. ''I'm going to miss him, too. He was a great man.''

Cassie began to sob again, and it seemed the natural thing to do for Sam to put his arm around her and pull her closer. She held the handkerchief to her face, smashing it between her nose and his chest.

Sam patted her shoulder as he spoke. "The whole town will miss him, Cassie. But one thing you should always carry with you is the fact that you and Harriet were his greatest accomplishments. Everything else he did paled in comparison to you two, and he was never ashamed to admit it."

Cassie sniffled into her handkerchief, feeling like a failure for the first time in many years. She had failed as a daughter—for not allowing her own father into her life for over a decade and pretending that monthly phone calls and yearly meetings in Atlanta were enough.

Her voice was muffled against his shirt. "He must have been a very forgiving man, too."

She felt him nod. "That he was. He hired me every summer to do his lawn, even though he could have hired somebody better and cheaper, because he knew I was saving up for college. Even wrote a letter of recommendation. And that was after I accidentally mowed over your mother's rose garden."

Cassie lifted her head for a moment. "I always thought you worked here so you could catch a glimpse of Harriet."

He looked down at her from the corner of his eye. "No. That's not the reason I came over every week to slaughter your father's lawn."

Something in his gaze made her shift and move her head off his shoulder. She slid away, embarrassed suddenly to be sitting so close, and let her gaze drift over to the house and beyond. Bulldozers rumbled in the distance where the old cotton field used to be. Her father had told her he had finally given in to a local developer and sold the land the previous year, and a small neighborhood of executive homes was being raised on the site. Gone, too, was the old stand of trees Cassie and Harriet had once called their enchanted forest, concocting visions of their future princes and the exotic lives they once expected to have.

A dark cloud hovered on the horizon, blocking the sun and dimming the light. The heavy scent of rain filled the air, making the grass smell sweeter. A crisp breeze stirred the linens Aunt Lucinda had forgotten on the back line, making them dance like ghostly apparitions tethered to the earth.

Cassie rested her elbows in her lap, her hands cradling her chin. "I ran away once—when I was thirteen. I only made it as far as the little cluster of trees that used to stand over there. I was chasing a rainbow, and it disappeared from the sky as I walked across the lawn. I sat down on a rock and waited until my father came and got me." She paused for a moment to wipe her nose, then crumpled the handkerchief in her hand. "He said it was okay to be chasing the rainbow's end as long as I always remembered where the rainbow started." She dropped her forehead to her hands. "I guess I'm still trying to understand what he meant."

Sam leaned back on the bench, his elbows resting on the seat back. "I ran away once, too."

Cassie raised an eyebrow, trying to imagine the perpetually relaxed and casual Sam she knew caring enough about anything to make him run away. "You? Whatever for?"

He slid her a narrow glance. "Guilt. And unrequited love."

Cassie sat back. "Guilt, huh? There's certainly plenty of that to go around. What did you do? Break some country girl's heart?"

Sam didn't smile and stared over Cassie's head. "No. Guilty because my brother, Tom, died at the age of twelve trying to save my sorry butt from drowning."

Cassie frowned, remembering the story. She had been about four or five when it happened. Something about being told not to go swimming in the creek by himself and sneaking out to do it, anyway.

Cassie looked down at her feet. "I'm sorry."

Sam picked up a small pebble from the bench and threw

it off the side of the gazebo. "Yeah, me, too. I guess if guilt can drive a man, it had a hold of me with both reins. It's what made me push myself—all through grade school, high school, and college. Then medical school." He sat back again, his forehead creased. "It never made me feel any better, but at least my parents had a child they could be proud of. It was my fault I was an only child, and I was damned determined not to be a disappointment to them."

"Is that why you came back to Walton? You could be doing so much more with your life."

He turned to face her, his eyes dark. "It's one of the reasons."

They sat in silence for a few moments before heavy drops of rain dotted the roof of the gazebo, and Sam and Cassie looked at each other.

Cassie stood. "Do you think we can make it back to the house in time?"

Before the words had left her mouth, they heard a shout from the house. Madison was galloping toward them, a barefoot Knoxie clinging to her back.

"Prickers!" shouted the little girl, her words nearly drowned by the sudden onslaught of rain driving against the gazebo in sheets. Madison raced across the yard and up the steps. Instinctively, Cassie took the dripping Knoxie, and the four of them huddled in the center of the small structure, their backs turned to the spraying rain sneaking in through the arched openings. Sam wrapped his arms over their shoulders, his forehead neatly pressed against Cassie's. The spray of rain chilled her skin but did nothing to alleviate the heat she felt from his touch.

Knoxie dug her head into Cassie's chest, only looking up when the rain finally sputtered to a light drizzle. Her wide green eyes moved from Cassie to Sam. "Dr. Parker, is Aunt Cassie your girlfriend?"

Without ceremony, Cassie plopped Knoxie on the ground and patted her head absently. "Of course not, Knoxie. I'm getting married—to somebody else."

Knoxie's mouth opened a little bit as her gaze continued to jump between Cassie and Sam.

"Maddie says that you and Dr. Parker—"

Madison quickly clamped her hand across her little sister's mouth. With a small smile, she hoisted Knoxie into her arms and made a hasty retreat. "The rain's almost stopped, so we'd best be getting back. People are starting to leave, and Mama wanted us to come and tell you."

She stumbled down the steps and splashed away through the soaked grass and mud. Knoxie called out over her sister's shoulder. "Are you gonna need a flower girl?"

Cassie bit her lip. "I haven't gotten quite that far with the arrangements. But if I decide that I do, you'll be the first person I call, okay?"

Cassie watched them until they reached the house, not wanting to face Sam. "Well, I guess we should go. . . ."

"Have you called your fiancé yet?"

She turned to look into wide eyes, but he couldn't quite pull off the innocent look. "No. Not yet. But I will." Andrew had called three times and left messages with Aunt Lucinda. But Cassie couldn't admit to either Andrew or Sam that the mere thought of mixing her two lives by calling her fiancé made her stomach churn. She had visions of just showing up again in their office and resuming work as usual, without any questions as to what had happened during her absence.

Sam wouldn't let the subject drop. "I imagine you'll need to let him know you'll be here a lot longer than expected. I mean, you own this house now. You can't just leave."

Cassie shrugged, shaking her head. "I can't keep it. I've got no use for it in New York." She picked up her shoes, then stepped down onto the first step. "I need to get back now."

She stared down into the mud, then at her shoes, and hesitated for a moment, simultaneously remembering the prickers and how much she had paid for her shoes on Fifth Avenue.

Behind her, Sam said, "I don't think that's what your father intended, Cassie."

She didn't turn around, fighting the renewed sting of tears in her eyes at the mention of her father. "He's not here anymore. But I know he'd respect my decision." She wasn't so sure that was true, but it made her feel better by saying it out loud.

"But what about the rest of your family?"

Her shoulders drooped. "I'm not as coldhearted as you think. I'll offer it to them first. But if they don't want it, I'll have to sell it."

His voice held his disbelief. "You just can't sell it. It's been in your family for over a hundred and fifty years. It would be like selling your own child."

She continued to stare down into the mud, her words stronger than her voice. "Trust me; it's not my first choice. But unless you're offering to buy it, you really don't have any say in the matter."

"I can't afford it right now." His footsteps approached behind her, and she stiffened, expecting harsh words. But he said nothing for a moment, the rainwater sliding off the gazebo's roof and splattering in the mud the only sound. Finally, he spoke, his voice hard. "Need some help?"

Before she could answer, she felt herself being scooped up into his arms. As he carried her back toward the house, she started to protest, but then fell silent, realizing the alternative. She kept her face turned away from him and limited places where their bodies could touch. When they'd reached the middle of the yard, she tilted her head back and noticed the multihued arc of a rainbow floating over the big white house.

Sam set her down hard on the back-porch steps, then disappeared inside. She stared at his back through the screen door, absently wondering what he had meant by unrequited love. The Sam Parker she remembered had had only close relationships with his textbooks. She had always assumed he'd had a crush on Harriet, like most of the boys at Walton High, but as Joe's best friend, he would have known her to be off-limits. Cassie gave a mental shrug. All the more reason for unrequited love, although she couldn't picture Harriet as Sam's type.

Cassie spent a few moments composing herself, straightening her hair and wiping any mascara that might be smeared under her eyes. Slowly, she pulled open the screen door, her other hand reaching unbidden to her neck, and entered the kitchen. She moved forward through the house and listened to the low buzz of voices, the ebb and flow of the sound like a swarm of bees.

Small groups of people stood around the front parlor, while others hovered over the mahogany pedestal table in the dining room, its surface brimming over with food. The old Sedgewick twins, Thelma and Selma, in their late seventies and still wearing matching outfits, took turns hugging the breath out of Cassie as they left. Their straw hats scratched her cheek, but their eyes were so filled with warmth and sympathy that Cassie easily forgave them their eccentric exuberance.

Selma's brittle hands clutched Cassie's forearm. "Your daddy wanted a clipping of our Red Radiance rosebush for your mother's rose garden. If it's all right with you, I'd like to plant it myself, as a sort of tribute to him."

Cassie stared at the thin line of bright orange lipstick, a garish equals sign at the bottom of Selma's face, and was oddly touched by the emotion and sincerity wrought by a single rose clipping. To Cassie, a rose was something she received by the dozen from the florist on the corner and then stuck in a vase on her desk, where she could watch them slowly wither.

"Thank you, Miss Selma. I'd like that very much." Before she knew what she was doing, Cassie had bent and kissed the old lady's soft cheek, catching a whiff of baby powder.

She spied Mr. Purdy taking his hat off the rack by the front door, and she flushed, reliving the pink-porch incident all over again. He approached her with a smile and outstretched arms and embraced her.

"It's so good to see you again, Cassie. You've been sorely

missed around these parts. I understand your education at Walton High has served you well in the big city.''

"Yes, sir," she said, feeling like a kid again, a shaky grin crossing her face.

"I'm sorry about your father. He will be missed greatly." He paused for a moment, then smiled softly. "Though I must say that the best thing to come of this is that it's brought you home. I hope you're giving some serious thoughts about staying here permanently. I know it was your father's wish."

Cassie's throat constricted, and she had trouble forcing the words out. "I'm sure I'll think about it, but I really don't—"

Mr. Purdy cut her off by patting her hand. "No need to rush to any hasty decisions right now. There's a lot of other things going on in your life that will take your mental energies, so take your time." He put his hat on his head. "Just try to stay out of mischief while you're here."

Cassie's eyes widened, but he only smiled as he turned away and let himself out the front door.

Slowly, the crowd thinned, all of them patting, kissing, or hugging her on their way out. Her tiredness made it hard to suppress the tinge of annoyance that crawled over her at their prying questions and curious stares. When she caught sight of herself in the hallway mirror with her arms crossed tightly in front of her, she looked like a foreboding crow. She purposefully moved her arms to her sides.

Harriet approached Cassie from behind, her pale skin and blond hair an angelic backdrop to the severity of her black dress. Black had never been Harriet's color, but now she looked even more peaked and tired than Cassie remembered. "You know they're not being nosy just for the sake of it. They're curious about you because they care for you." Harriet touched her sister on the arm. "We've all been worried about you these past years. We feel that, well, that it's our duty to check on you—to make sure you're all right. And that you haven't changed too much."

Cassie turned to face her sister. She wanted so much to resume the closeness she and Harriet had once shared, to take Harriet to the gazebo and talk about their father and their childhood and to share their tears. But it was too soon. Harriet was almost a stranger to her and no more comfort at a time like this than Andrew would be.

The thought had come from nowhere, and in her surprise and annoyance at hearing herself think it, Cassie said the first thing that popped into her head. "Well, one thing that's changed is my knowing how to dress. What is it with all these wide lace collars and big hair? Don't they sell *Cosmo* here?"

Harriet regarded her calmly. "You always did turn mean when you were scared. I guess some things never change." She kissed Cassie's cheek quickly, then left to say good-bye to the last of the mourners already congregating in the foyer.

Cassie stared after Harriet's retreating back, feeling terrible about what she'd said and wanting to deny that she was scared of anything. But somehow the words wouldn't come out. She needed to talk to her father and even started toward his study, until she remembered. The familiar sting of tears hit her again, and she ducked her face, heading toward the kitchen and the next best thing to her father.

She flung open the swinging door, quickly stepping inside to the welcome silence of the kitchen, the only noise the soft ticking of the fisherman's clock above the stove. Cassie had given it to her father one year for Father's Day, loving the way the small fish ticked around the face of the clock, marking off the minutes.

Aunt Lucinda stood at the back door, her face pressed against the screen.

Cassie called her name and began to walk toward her, the need for a soft shoulder to cry on moving her forward. But something in the way Aunt Lucinda stood, her shoulders rounded and her hands, for once, empty and still by her sides, made Cassie stop.

"Aunt Lucinda," she said again, and her aunt turned around.

"Oh, Cassie," she cried, and stumbled toward her.

Cassie, unused to being in the role of comforter, snapped open her arms and gathered her aunt to her as sobs shook her shoulders. Her hand seemed to automatically pat the black polyester of Lucinda's dress, softly at first and then firmer. She wasn't ready for this. Where was a soft shoulder for *her?*

"There, there, Aunt Lu. You'll see—things will be all right." She only wished she could convince herself.

Aunt Lucinda lifted her head, blinking her eyes, her smile wobbly. "They will be, won't they? Things always manage to work out in the end, don't they?" She grabbed Cassie's hand. "I've got wonderful friends, and you and Harriet and Joe and the kids. Things will be okay." Her smile faltered. "But I'm going to miss him. I've been taking care of him for so long, I hardly know what to do with myself now."

Cassie put her arm across her shoulders. "There's lots you can do. Don't worry about a thing. I'll make sure you're settled before I go back to New York."

Aunt Lucinda's eyes widened. "Go back? You can't go back! What about the house? And your family? You can't just leave us. We need you."

"You've all managed very well without me for a long time. I think you'll survive again. But I promise I'll visit often, all right? I won't be a stranger anymore."

"But what about the house?"

Cassie shook her head. "I don't want it." She paused for a moment. "Actually, I was thinking of giving it to you. You've lived here for so long, you might as well own it."

Cassie stopped, alarmed by the change in her aunt. Lucinda glared at her with narrowed eyes, mascara trails running across her rouged cheeks. "Your father wanted you to have this house. I will not be the one responsible for thwarting his plans. Besides, what would an old woman like me do with a big old house like this? Just keeping it up all by myself would be the death of me."

Cassie followed her aunt through the swinging doors. "But I could pay for help. You wouldn't have to do anything."

Her aunt turned to her. "Your father wanted you to have the house, Cassie, and that's that." Her high heels tapped across the wood floor of the dining room. "I'm sure he had his reasons, and I learned a long time ago that my brother was usually right." She dabbed at her nose with a crumpled tissue. "Besides, maybe it's time I find my own place. Your daddy left me a nice little nest egg—more than enough to buy a house. A small one, of course, but mine. It's been a long time since I was on my own."

Cassie opened her mouth to argue, then closed it as Sam entered the room and leaned against the dark wood casement, crossing one booted foot over the other. Cassie averted her eyes, catching sight of something sticking out from the top of the wainscoting. She walked over to where Sam stood and plucked it out of the woodwork behind him.

She held the tiny pine needle in her palm, the smell of Christmas suddenly filling her nose and the vision of her mother draping the doorways and chandeliers with pine boughs crowding her mind. Aunt Lucinda had continued the tradition of dressing the house for the season, and each Christmas had been more memorable than the last. Cassie sighed, crushing the pine needle in her hand. Andrew's concession to decorating for the season was a three-foot-tall artificial tree in the corner of their bedroom. But at least they had real snow. And Rockefeller Center.

Sam cleared his throat. "I'm leaving now. But I wanted to make a suggestion before I left. This house will be pretty lonely tonight. Why don't you go sleep at Harriet's?"

She shook her head, wondering why she was so opposed to the idea. "No. I want to stay here. It . . . it reminds me of Daddy."

He nodded, his eyes warm. "Then you might consider asking Harriet and her family to stay with you. It will make you both feel better."

A scream from Sarah Frances made them both start and then step back at the sound of running feet. The young girl flew past them, a loose ribbon dangling in her hair, followed closely by Joey. Lucinda pressed herself against the wall, and Cassie flew back against Sam when she spied what the boy was chasing his sister with: a small garter snake, its skin reflecting the light from the chandelier and its red tongue flicking in and out. Joe followed on their heels, shouting at Joey to stop but not quite succeeding in getting the laughter out of his voice.

Cassie disengaged herself from Sam's hold. "Yeah. Great suggestion, Sam. I'll feel a lot better having them in the house with me tonight. Besides, it's a lot of trouble for all of them to bring their stuff over here."

"Don't be so stubborn. Just ask. I know Harriet will want to stay here, anyway. He was her father, too." He straightened. "You won't even have to tell them it was my idea." Without waiting for a response, he said good-bye to Lucinda and turned to leave.

Cassie called out, not quite hiding her smile, "Don't let the door hit you in the butt on the way out."

His only reply was the front door slamming shut.

Aunt Lucinda regarded her with still eyes. "You must be scared, honey. You're acting mean." She grabbed Cassie's arm. "Come on. Let's go talk to Harriet. I know she'll want to keep you company tonight."

Cassie allowed herself to be led away, wondering why everybody seemed to think there was anything she could possibly be scared of.

Chapter 5

The sound of a crying baby startled Cassie awake. Sitting up, she stared at the dark outline of the pink canopy and wondered how she had gone to sleep so easily. She still wore her black suit, having just flopped on the bed right after dinner, not thinking sleep would find her. She didn't want to admit that Sam was right, but she had felt strangely comforted knowing that the bedrooms around her would be filled with the sleeping members of her family.

The wailing got louder as Cassie heard a door open and footsteps come up the stairs, cross the hall, and head back down the stairs. She slid out of bed and opened her door, not wanting to go back to sleep and needing somebody to talk to.

The front door closed quietly as Cassie descended the stairs, then let herself outside. The full moon shone brightly, illuminating the porch and columns in a milky blue light. She spied Joe on the swing, a small twitching bundle in his arms.

Joe held a finger to his lips before bending his head to look at the baby's face. He motioned for Cassie to join him on the swing. She sat down softly, trying not to jolt it.

They swung in the stillness for a while, listening to the unseen insects in the grass humming their ceaseless night-time lullaby. A bullfrog croaked nearby, its lonely call the only percussion to the crickets' string section. Cassie smiled, thankful that Joey wasn't there to add the unfortunate amphibian to his collection. The baby let out a few more cries, each one softer than the last, until she settled down to the rhythm of the swing.

The baby sighed softly in her sleep; a light breeze carried with it the scent of jasmine and honeysuckle and a host of forgotten memories of many summer evenings spent on the same porch. She pictured her mother sitting on the steps and singing to her and Harriet, the cotton twill of her mother's skirt soft under her cheek, while her father read the paper, the discarded pages fluttering like moths on the wooden planks of the floor.

Joe spoke first. "Aunt Lucinda says you're wanting to sell the house."

Cassie nodded. "I don't need it. What would I do with a big old house in Georgia? I don't live here anymore." She looked over at Joe. "But if at all possible, I'd like to keep it in the family." She stilled the swing by putting her feet flat on the floor. "If you want it, it's yours. I'll give it to you."

Joe absently patted the baby's back, and Cassie tried not to look at his hands, the old hands of her memory. "No, Cassie. We couldn't afford it. Even if you gave it to us, we could never afford the upkeep. I don't make much as a high school teacher, and Harriet's boutique barely provides for a few extras. Your father was very generous to us in his will, but we've got five college educations to consider."

Cassie sat up straighter. "But I could help! I could send—"

"No." Joe's voice was firm, causing the baby to stir. He waited a moment, then continued. He eased way back against the swing again. "That's not what the judge wanted. I vote you hang on to it. You'll never know when you might need it."

She shook her head in the darkness. "This house was so much a part of me a long time ago, but that life is gone forever, and there's no need for me to hang on to it. Clinging to the past isn't the most healthy thing." She looked away for a moment. "Like clinging to old hurts. It hampers the growing process."

Joe looked at her as the baby sighed in her sleep, his eyes glittering in the moonlight. "So, what are you going to do?"

She shrugged, jostling the swing slightly. "I guess I could sell it. I noticed the under-contract signs on the Haneys' and Duffys' yards. Somebody's buying property in Walton."

With a snort, Joe carefully moved the baby to his other shoulder. "Yeah, but it's not somebody you want to sell this house to."

"What do you mean?"

"A developer bought those lots—gave the families a really sweet deal. Not that your daddy ever gave them the time of day. Wants to put a high-end retail mall right here." He scratched his chin furiously. "Ever since they put that exit in off the interstate, we've had Atlanta commuters moving in and all sorts of builders wanting to change Walton. It's been like a damned circus around here."

Cassie let her gaze wander out over the moonlit expanse of lawn, the nighttime quiet like a gentle song to her soul. "Is it the same developer Daddy sold the cotton field to?"

"Nah. And you're never going to believe who bought that." He looked at Cassie expectantly.

She tried to hide her impatience. "Just tell me—who?"

"Ed Farrell."

"Ed Farrell? You're kidding, right?"

The swing squeaked as Joe moved. "Nope. He's got his own realty business now, and he's actively recruiting all those suburbanites to move into this new neighborhood down there below your house. He even had the gall to call it Farrellsford."

Cassie's eyes widened, picturing the tall, gangly Ed from high school and the pants he wore that were always a size too small or too large—just whatever his mom could find at the thrift shop. If he was buying up property and building neighborhoods, he'd come a long way since she'd known him. "Wow" was all she could manage.

Joe sat up straighter. "You wouldn't consider selling this house to a developer, now, would you?"

She stood abruptly, the swing rocking in her wake. "I honestly don't know. If nobody wants it, I'll have to sell it. And that's that."

"Would you do that to punish us? To get back for what happened fifteen years ago?"

She leaned back against the railing that stretched between the columns, nudging aside a paint can, the smell of fresh paint heavy in the humid air. "No. Of course not. I'm . . ." She closed her eyes for a moment. "It's funny, but none of that old stuff seems to matter anymore. It did for so long, when I stayed away, but now that I'm here, I realize how inconsequential it all seems to my life right now. It's funny, but right before Daddy died, I told him that staying away was just a habit I'd gotten used to. I think I was right."

"We didn't do it to hurt you, you know. We loved each other, and we loved you, too. But every time we tried to tell you, you'd change the subject or run away. It was like you knew what we were going to say but didn't want to hear it. I guess you're just the type of person who has to be hit over the head with something before you believe it."

She smiled at him across the darkened porch. "Maybe. Not that any of that matters anymore. I have a new life. I've got to do what I need to so I can get back to New York and resume the life I've worked so hard to build."

Joe's voice was quiet, almost completely obliterated by the squeak of the swing. "Are you happy?"

His words surprised her. "Well, yes. Of course. Of course I am. I have a great job, making a great living. I live in one of the most exciting cities in the world. A highly intelligent man is crazy about me, and we're going to be married. How could I not be happy?"

He nodded in the darkness. "I see. Well, all I can wish

for you is that you find the kind of happiness Harriet and I have had.''

Cassie looked away, out across the front lawn to the lane of oaks. ''I wish you would reconsider about the house. It has all the room you need for the kids. I would really rather not have to sell it.''

He swiped a hand through the air at a flying insect that seemed intent on dive-bombing his sleeping daughter. ''You do what you want, Cassie. It's your house. And when you're finished burning all your bridges, we'll still be here, waiting to help you back across.''

The baby began to whimper as Joe stood and walked toward the front door. Before he shut it behind him, he called over his shoulder, ''And don't lean on the railing. I couldn't get to sleep, so I entertained myself by painting it.'' The door shut softly behind him.

She looked down at her black skirt, a telltale white stripe glowing in the dim light. She moved back to the swing and sat down with a thump, the night around her alive with sounds and movement, slithering in the grass, and twinkling in the sky. Fingering the charms around her neck, she thought of her dead father and his house and the paint on her skirt, and she didn't know whether to laugh or cry. So she sat on the swing and listened as the night sounds gave way to morning and the sun cracked the sky.

Cassie's eyes rebelled against her eyelids with every blink, regardless of how many cold water splashes she gave them from the sink. She stumbled out of the bathroom, tying her dark hair behind her with an elastic ponytail holder she had found on the bathroom counter.

''Good morning, Aunt Cassie.''

Cassie looked down at a cross-legged Madison beaming brightly up at her.

She made her lips turn up to form a smile. ''Morning, Madison. Going for a run. See you later.''

Madison scrambled up, her long legs protruding from baby-doll pajamas. "Can I go with you?"

Cassie stifled a yawn. "Do you run regularly?"

Madison looked down, her big toe stabbing the carpet runner. "Well, kinda. In P.E. we run laps around the football field." She glanced up with wide-eyed enthusiasm. "But it would be fun with you. Would you wait a minute while I change?"

Cassie could think of a thousand reasons why she'd rather run alone but couldn't voice any in the face of Madison's eagerness. "Sure. But hurry, okay? I want to be done before the heat gets any worse. I'm not used to it."

Madison darted into the bathroom as Cassie looked at the small anniversary clock on the hallway table. Six o'clock. Andrew would just be getting to the office. He liked to have it all to himself for the first couple of hours of the day. He had made it clear that even Cassie wasn't welcome that early in the morning, She forgave him, realizing it probably had to do with his circumstances as an only child that made him crave the solitude he so rarely found in his busy life.

Feeling antsy to get going but realizing she had time to kill while she waited, Cassie descended the stairs. She stepped on one tread at a time, like a small child, postponing the inevitable as long as she could. Crossing the foyer, she went into her father's study and sat at his desk. As she dialed Andrew's number, she looked at the twenty or so frames backing the enormous desk. There were several of the grandchildren, one of Harriet and Joe with their entire brood, a few of her mother, and an old black-and-white of her parents next to his old MG. But the majority of them were of her and Harriet as children. She listened to the ringing tone as she stared at the age progression of her pictures, ending abruptly with her high-school-senior photo.

She set the phone back in the cradle and picked up the picture, staring at a girl she hardly recognized. Cassie couldn't decide which was worse: the winged bangs of her hair framing the full face and thick glasses or the prominent braces on her teeth. Even her shirt was an embarrassment.

Taken at the height of the preppy look, the wide-collared blouse had whales swimming all over it. She glanced briefly at Harriet's senior photo, taken in her cheerleading outfit, her beautiful blond hair spilling over her shoulders, and slipped her own photo upside down in the top desk drawer, closing it with a soft thud.

Picking up the phone again, she dialed Andrew's number. This time he answered on the first ring.

"Hi, Andrew. It's me."

"Cassandra? It doesn't sound like you. You've, um, sort of picked up an accent, I think."

She found herself frowning, disappointed that those would be his first words to her. "Don't worry. I'm sure it's temporary."

"So, how are you? How's your dad? I called a couple of times and left a message with somebody called Lucinda. Man! Talk about somebody who needs speech therapy. I could hardly grasp what she was saying. Might as well have been speaking Russian, for all I understood."

The staccato beat of fingers on a computer keyboard shot through the phone line to Cassie's ear. She bit her lower lip before speaking. "That's my father's sister. The one who raised me and Harriet when our mom died and has been a sort of surrogate mother ever since."

There was a short pause, filled with the clacking noise. "Oh. Well, I'm sure she's very nice. Did she give you the message that I called?"

"Yes. I, um, just haven't really had a chance to call you. Daddy . . . my father died. We buried him yesterday."

The key tapping stopped. "I'm sorry, Cassandra. I'm glad you made it in time. You know, to see him before he died."

The tapping resumed, accompanied by the sound of a computer modem buzzing in the background. She blinked rapidly, feeling the familiar sting. "Yeah. Me, too. But there's been some, um, developments, which is why I didn't call you back right away. I wanted to make sure that I had explored all my options first."

"I see. What kind of developments?"

Cassie leaned back in her father's chair, curling the telephone cord around her hand. "Well, it seems I've inherited this house and just about everything in it. Neither Lucinda nor Harriet want it, so I'm kind of stuck for the time being."

"Sell it."

Cassie's gaze strayed through the large doorway and up the stairwell, lingering on the old portraits of her ancestors, wondering if she was only imagining the frown from Great-great-great-grandfather Madison. "Well, sure, I could sell it. Which is what I'll probably have to do. But this house has been owned by my family since the 1840s. It'll be a major decision. Not to mention the fact that I'll need to go through everything in the house—especially the attic, which I don't think has been touched in over fifty years."

A fax machine beeped in Cassie's ear before Andrew spoke again. "Why don't you just call a realtor and then hire one of those companies that goes in and gets rid of clutter for you? Then you can be back here within a week."

Madison, wearing gym shorts and sneakers, clambered down the stairs. Cassie waved, noting that the color of Madison's shorts and shirt matched her own. "Andrew, I don't know. I . . . I don't think I can do that."

Andrew sighed into the phone. "Why not? Our clients need you up here. *I* need you up here. I miss you."

Cassie turned her face away from Madison, who was now sliding her back down the doorframe until her bottom hit the floor. Quietly, Cassie spoke into the receiver. "I know. I miss you, too. Just give me a week and I'll call you back. I'm sure I'll have things sorted out by then."

"I hope so. I don't like it when you're gone. The bed seems too big."

Cassie smiled. "I bet. Maybe you should move to the twin bed in the guest room."

Andrew didn't laugh. "Come back soon."

"I'll try," Cassie whispered into the phone before hanging up. She kept her hand on the phone, wondering for a long moment why neither one of them had mentioned the word love.

She looked up and found herself staring into Madison's wide green eyes. "Was that your boyfriend?"

Cassie stood, untangling the phone cord from her hand. "That was my fiancé. We're engaged."

Madison drew her tanned legs up in front of her, resting her elbows on her knees and cupping her chin in her palms. "Is he handsome?"

As if she hadn't thought about it in a while, Cassie wrinkled her brow. "Well, yes. He is. Very, as a matter of fact."

"Do you spend lots of time walking in Central Park and holding hands?"

Cassie frowned, trying to remember if she and Andrew had ever held hands. Probably not, since the only time they ever walked anywhere together was home from work when their hands were filled with briefcases and takeout bags.

"We're usually very busy at the advertising agency that Andrew owns. We have plans for a romantic getaway once things settle down a bit, but there just doesn't seem to be the time right now."

Madison rocked her chin in the cradle of her hands. "When do we get to meet him?"

Cassie pushed against the edge of the desk and stretched her hamstrings. "Oh. Um. I don't know. He's so busy at the agency—especially with me being gone—that it's just about impossible for him to come down here. . . ."

Madison slid out from the doorway and sat in a *V*. Stretching her fingertips to her toes, she gasped out, "Mama said something about throwing you a wedding shower. Maybe he'll come down for that."

Cassie's eyebrows shot up. "A shower? Oh, I don't think I'll be here long enough for that. . . ."

Madison continued to stretch as if she hadn't heard her aunt speak. "Mama's real excited, but I think it's supposed to be a surprise, so don't go and say anything to her." She stood and began to stretch her hamstrings against the knobbed newel post in the foyer. "So what do you and Mr. Handsome do for fun in New York City?"

"Oh, we, um, well, we went to a play once—*Les Miséra-*

bles. I'm sure we'll do more of that once we can hire some more people at the agency, but right now we're just so overwhelmed, it's kind of hard to find leisure time." Cassie switched legs and began to stretch the other hamstring. "We do go out to eat at nice restaurants quite often, but we're always with clients, so I don't think you'd count that as being fun."

Madison bent to tighten her shoelaces. "Do you think it's fun?" She tilted her head to the side.

Cassie raised her hands over her head and leaned toward one side. "Well, sure. It's fun. I mean, what could be better than mixing great food with business?"

Madison stood still for a moment. "Oh."

Cassie held open the front door and watched as her niece preceded her out onto the porch. With a giant leap, Cassie was off and running down the driveway at a brisk pace. She looked behind her to make sure Madison could keep up. Her niece's long legs easily overtook her, forcing Cassie to push harder. They ran in silence for a while, jumping over the large cracks in the sidewalks, dodging out into the street to avoid the fat fists of crepe myrtles and hydrangea blossoms dangling over the pathway. Madison waved to every car they passed, receiving nods and waving hands in return. She paused at the broken walkway to a large Victorian on the corner, jogging in place as she addressed the diminutive figure in a rocking chair on the porch. Cassie stopped beside her, trying not to let Madison hear her gasping for breath.

It didn't even sound as if Madison had been running. "Good morning, Miss Lena. Read any good books lately?"

The old lady grinned a toothless grin, her bespectacled eyes reflecting the blue sky. She held up a paperback novel with a cover depicting two lovers in a near-naked embrace. "I'm just getting to the juicy part. She just saw his wicked manhood for the first time."

Cassie shot a shocked glance at Madison, but the younger girl merely waved at the old lady and took off again.

Cassie shook her head, trying not to laugh and use more breath than necessary. The humidity had crept up on her slowly, and she was already struggling to keep up with the young teenager. "Holy shit! Miss Lena taught my Sunday school in tenth grade—and her daddy used to be the preacher at the Walton First Baptist. What happened?"

Madison scrunched up her nose. "Her sister in Mobile runs her church library. She sends Miss Lena all the donated books she can't use. She reads the same ones over and over because she doesn't remember them."

"Is she still teaching Sunday school?"

Madison nodded and wiped a drip of sweat off her cheek. "Never misses a Sunday. But she's only an assistant teacher now. She mostly just stands in the front of the class and smiles. Her mind wanders in and out of reality, but she doesn't want to go into a home. We all pretty much take care of her now." Madison paused for a moment, taking deep breaths as their sneakers pounded the sidewalk. "Mama takes turns with the other ladies to bring her dinner and stuff."

They ran down Madison Lane and crossed Orchard; an ancient oak towering over the intersection from the Hardens' front lawn blocked the stop sign. A rope swing hung from a high branch, and a small child stood under it, trying to jump high enough to grab hold. The little girl waved to Madison as they passed, and Madison sent her a grin.

Cassie, struggling to breathe, forced out a question. "Do the Hardens still live there? I remember . . . swinging on the same . . . swing."

Madison shook her head. "Mr. and Mrs. Harden sold their house to their daughter, Mary Jane, and moved to Florida. Did you know her?"

Cassie could only nod, not wanting to squander an ounce of air. She remembered Mary Jane Harden. They had been best friends from kindergarten all the way through their second year of junior college. At least they were until Cassie met Joe and everyone else in her life took a backseat in her affections. And then Cassie had left town, cutting all ties. It now seemed so stupid to have deliberately lost contact with Mary Jane, too. Cassie shook her head, sweat dripping off her forehead and falling on her arms. Maybe she'd look up her old friend while she was in Walton. She doubted they still had anything in common, but it would be nice to see her.

They continued down Madison Lane until they reached Walnut and headed east toward Main Street and the town square. Even Cassie had to admit that the downtown area held a certain charm. The tall brick storefronts, with window boxes, bright awnings, and large picture windows, were timeless in their appeal. Diagonal parking spaces jutted out from the sides of the wide sidewalk like legs on a centipede crawling up Main Street. The courthouse towered over the square at the intersection of Main and Monroe Avenue, the neatly trimmed grass complemented by the requisite Confederate monument and another statue on the opposite end.

Cassie jogged toward the other statue before stopping completely, the heat and humidity having taken their toll. She slumped over, her hands on her slippery knees, and looked up at the odd piece of statuary. "Oh, my God," she panted out.

Madison slowed to a stop beside her and stared up at the scaled-down replica of the Statue of Liberty. "Does it look like the real thing?"

Cassie straightened, adjusting her sweatband on her forehead. "Not . . . quite." She examined the wooden head of the thing, recalling how it had been carved with a chain saw from a stump pulled out of a nearby swamp. The upraised arm looked as if it had been made of Styrofoam, and the hand holding the torch was undoubtedly an oversized electrician lineman's glove. The whole thing had been painted a softly glowing green. She shook her head, remembering the parade, flag-waving, and convertibles carrying veterans through the streets of downtown the day the statue was dedicated by the proud men of the Lions Club. "I somehow don't remember thinking it was so hideous when I was seven."

Madison squinted in the sun. "It's really pretty stupid looking, isn't it?"

Cassie studied her niece, the small furrow deepening between her eyebrows, and felt a sharp arrow of guilt slice through her. Madison looked as if she had just discovered her father instead of a jolly old elf stuffing the Christmas stockings.

Cassie sat down on the small ledge at the base of Miss Liberty and searched for the words she needed to say. "You know what, Madison? What those men who erected this statue lacked in sophistication, they certainly made up for in enthusiasm." Cassie stared out over the town square toward the courthouse, remembering an old army veteran on the steps giving a speech about what this statue represented and how proud they all were to have a small piece of it here in Walton. She gave her niece a rueful grin. "You don't really see much of that anymore."

A familiar truck pulled into a parking space on the square, and Cassie stood. "Hey, at least it's not that statue over in Plains. You know—the world's largest peanut in the shape of Jimmy Carter. Now *that's* embarrassing."

Madison grinned, then shrugged her shoulders. "Yeah. I guess it could be worse."

They both turned their attention to the truck as two people climbed out. Cassie squinted, holding her hand over her forehead to block the sun. She spotted Sam and a woman pulling long garlands of something green out from the bed of the truck. The couple then approached the two runners, their arms wrapped around the greenery.

As they got closer, the woman smiled at Cassie. "Bet you don't remember me."

It was the smile that Cassie recognized. The smile with the dimple in the left cheek—cheeks that were thinner now, set below a head of hair that was shorter and blonder, too.

Cassie smiled back. "Mary Jane Harden—of course I recognize you. We just ran past your parents' house and saw some kids swinging on the tree swing. Are they yours?"

Mary Jane shot a quick glance at Sam and shook her head. "No. Don't have any kids. Not married—yet. Those were my brother's. He and his wife are visiting for a couple of weeks."

"Stinky got married? You're kidding!" Cassie pictured the roly-poly younger brother of her old friend, his nose always stuck in action-hero comic books and trailing a scent of old sweat because of his penchant for avoiding baths.

Mary Jane nodded. "Yep. But we don't call him Stinky anymore. He's changed a lot. Actually takes baths now."

They all laughed as Mary Jane and Sam dropped their burdens.

Mary Jane sobered quickly. "I'm sorry about your father, Cassie. I wanted to come to the funeral, but one of us had to stay at the clinic."

Cassie tilted her head in question, and Mary Jane smiled. "I'm Sam's nurse and general office gofer. We run the clinic together—along with a few rotating doctors and nurses from Providence Hospital in Monroe."

"Oh, I see." She pulled her soaking shirt away from her midriff, suddenly self-conscious about her appearance. "It's great seeing you—and I'd give you a hug if I weren't so sweaty. I hope we'll have time to talk before I leave."

The other woman frowned. "You're not planning on leaving soon, are you?"

Sam shifted, but Cassie didn't look at him. "Not today, anyway. But as soon as I get everything settled."

"Are you staying at your father's house?"

Cassie nodded.

"Good. I'll call you, and we'll go have lunch at the Dixie Diner—just like old times. We'll do some catching up."

Cassie watched as Madison picked up a branch that strongly resembled a kudzu vine. "Great. That'll be fun." Cassie stepped back. "Madison, what is that?"

Sam reached down and picked up an end, his long fingers fiddling with an oversized heart-shaped leaf. "It's kudzu. Surely you haven't forgotten what it looks like?"

She stuck out her chin. "I know what it is, I just wanted to know why it's here."

Mary Jane chipped in. "It's for the Kudzu Festival. It's

coming up, and Sam and I are on the decorating committee.''
She smiled up at Sam and touched his arm. Cassie studied
Mary Jane with a critical eye, noting the plain khaki shorts,
sandals, and button-down cotton shirt—the same dull,
figure-evading clothes they had both worn in high school.

Cassie pointed to a green strand. ''Won't that stuff die
in two weeks?''

Sam snorted. ''If it were only that easy. We'll stick an
end in the dirt, and it will start growing as if it's always
been here. Our only problem will be pulling it down after
the festival before it has time to take over the town.''

Mary Jane laughed out loud, as if what Sam had said was
the funniest thing she'd ever heard. Still smiling and with
her hand on Sam's arm, she looked at Madison. ''Your
mom's supposed to be here in a minute to help. All the
former Kudzu Queens are supposed to help out, and Harriet's
so good with decorating and things that Sam and I just
grabbed her to work on our committee.'' She sent another
sickening look at Sam, making Cassie even more self-
conscious about her bedraggled and sweaty self. ''We felt
bad about your father's funeral being yesterday and everything, and we even told Harriet she didn't have to come,
but she said she wanted to. I guess it helps to keep her mind
off of things.'' Her hazel eyes regarded Cassie casually.
''Sort of what running must do for you.''

Sam looped several long strands around his neck and
rubbed his hands together. ''We'd better get started. I'm
supposed to be at the clinic at one, and we've got lots of
this leafy stuff to drape. Madison, why don't you and your
aunt stay and give us a hand?''

Cassie glanced at her bare arm, realizing she'd forgotten
her watch. ''Sorry—I'd love to, but I can't. I've got an
appointment with a realtor at eleven-thirty. Plus I desperately
need a shower.''

Sam paused with the kudzu around his neck and a small
pucker between his eyebrows. He looked for a moment as
if he were going to question her about her appointment but

then changed his mind. "Yeah, you're right. You could use a good hosing down with soap and water."

Cassie stuck her hands on her hips. "You should try running yourself sometime. It'll keep some of that fried food you eat off of your stomach." Her gaze strayed to his knit shirt smoothed over a flat abdomen and tucked into a pair of jeans. The ever-present cowboy boots were on his feet.

He grinned. "But I do. Five miles a day. I just go at night when it's cooler and I won't be running into anybody who might catch a whiff of me. You should go with me sometime."

Mary Jane hadn't moved during the entire exchange, nor had she been able to look anywhere else but at Sam's face as he spoke to Cassie. Madison had walked across the square to where Harriet had pulled up with the van and was slowly unloading a double stroller.

Cassie smirked. "No, thanks. I prefer to be alone."

Sam picked up more kudzu from the ground and handed it with a smile to Mary Jane. Without looking at Cassie, he said, "That's another bad habit she's learned in New York. We'll have to do our best to break her of them while she's here."

"Don't bother," Cassie said, waving a dismissive hand in the air. "I won't be here long enough for anything to stick."

Mary Jane cleared her throat. "Is your meeting with Ed Farrell?"

Cassie nodded. "I was surprised to hear he had a respectable job. You'd think he'd be scratching out a living on the old dirt farm he grew up on." An evil grin split her face. "Hey, Sam, weren't you Ed's favorite punching bag in high school?" As soon as the words were out of her mouth, she regretted them. She pictured the old Sam, all legs and arms, with thick glasses and a sweet smile. He had never been anything but kind to her and never failed to laugh at one of her pranks. She saw Sam's jaw clench.

Mary Jane saved her by speaking. "And those two are

still at it—but in a more civilized way now. As a matter of fact, they're both running for the vacant town-council seat.''

Cassie reached her hand around her back to squelch a drip of sweat rolling down between her shoulder blades. "Gosh, Sam. Do you ever have time to do any doctoring? With all your other activities, it's a surprise that you have any time left at all.''

A stiff grin crossed his face. "Actually, I do. That's one of the main reasons I left Boston to practice medicine here. Unlike living in the big city, I can have a life and a career at the same time.''

Without thinking, Cassie's hands went to her hips in a defensive posture. "I have a life!''

Sam turned back to his kudzu. "I'm sure you do, Cassie. A very exciting and glamorous one.''

She dropped her hands, feeling very unsettled all of a sudden. Facing Mary Jane, she said, "I'll talk to you later. Tell Stinky I said hello.'' Without looking at Sam, she waved in his direction, then turned to run across the square and join her sister.

Cassie stood next to Harriet, the old, familiar feeling of being overly large next to the smallness of her younger sister as strong as ever.

Harriet wiped a strand of honey blond hair out of her eyes and stared up at her sibling. She seemed pale and tired, but her smile was as bright as Cassie remembered. "I'm so glad I found you. My baby-sitter canceled last minute, and I can't get a thing done here with Knoxie and the baby. At least Joey and Sarah Frances have vacation Bible school this week. Otherwise I might as well just duct-tape myself to the kitchen sink, since I wouldn't be moving from there, anyway.''

Harriet handed Knoxie to Cassie. "Just stick her in the back of the stroller. I learned not to put her in front because Amanda grabs hold of Knoxie's pigtails and it really puts her in a state.''

The little girl smiled at her aunt as Cassie took her, holding her suspended over the double stroller and not sure how to proceed. Cassie spied two feet holes and began lowering the toddler, kicking legs and all. The child ended up with her right leg in the left foot hole and her left foot somehow in the front seat. Knoxie began to whimper.

"Here," said Harriet, handing Amanda to Cassie. Effortlessly, she scooped up Knoxie and had her seated properly in the stroller without breaking a sweat. Calmly, she took the baby and set her in the front seat. "See? It's easy with just a little bit of practice. You won't have any problems."

Cassie's eyes opened with realization. "Wait a minute. I don't know anything about taking care of children. Besides, I have an appointment at eleven-thirty, and I need to shower." The baby gurgled, and Cassie stared at her with apprehension.

Harriet waved her hands dismissively through the air. "Don't be silly. You took care of me when I was little. It's just like riding a bike; you never forget how. And I'll ask Madison to help. She's got a tennis lesson at eleven, but she can help until then." She reached into the van and pulled out an enormous diaper bag and looped the shoulder strap over the handle of the stroller. "Everything you need is in here. And there's a few bottles already made in the refrigerator at your house. She'll probably be hungry in about an hour."

Cassie rested her hand on the handle of the stroller and then yanked it off as if she had been scorched. "But what about my appointment?"

Harriet slid the large, heavy door of the van shut. "I'll try to be back by then, but if I'm not, just bring them with you. Everybody in town knows them, and they'll be glad to keep an eye on the girls while you do your business." She waved and took off at a brisk walk toward Sam and Mary Jane.

"But . . ." Cassie's objections died in her throat as a little hand pulled on her fingers. She looked down at the stroller, and Knoxie grinned up at her, her light green eyes completely without guile. Cassie looked up and saw Madison jogging slowly toward her.

"Mama says you need my help more than they do. I'm kinda glad. I'm pretty tired of hearing all of Mama's stories about her stint as Kudzu Queen."

Cassie tugged on the stroller, but it didn't budge. Madison leaned down, unhooked the lock, and began walking next to her aunt.

"When I get old like you, I'm not going to have any babies, either. Mama had me nine months after she was married, and she's been stuck here ever since." Madison lifted her ponytail off the back of her neck and wiped off the sweat. "I'm going to live in New York, have an exciting career, and be just like you. I don't want to have anything to do with diapers and bottles. I've had enough of that to last me a lifetime."

Cassie decided to ignore the "old" part and concentrate on the baby part instead. "I never said I didn't want babies . . ." She stopped in mid-sentence, aware that she had never told Andrew she wanted any, either. She pictured her apartment, with its clean lines and white carpets, and couldn't picture anywhere in it where the primary colors of baby toys or a lace-covered bassinet wouldn't look wildly out of place.

Knoxie had been singing tunelessly to herself but stopped suddenly. She twisted her head around, her red hair almost gold in the morning sunlight. "I'm not a baby. Do you like me?"

Cassie poked her head around the top of the stroller and stared into the wide eyes of her niece. "Of course I do. You're pretty darned cute."

Without warning and at the top of her lungs, Knoxie shouted, "I need to go potty. Right now!"

Amanda, jerked out of a doze by the commotion, began to cry.

"Uh-oh. When she says now, she means now." Madison picked up the baby and handed her to Cassie, then yanked Knoxie from the stroller. "I'll be right back."

Madison ran with her little sister up to the front door of the nearest house. When a woman answered, Madison disappeared inside with Knoxie.

Amanda's cries had now turned into yelps, and Cassie stood on the sidewalk, helplessly bouncing the baby up and down in her arms. Eventually, she began practicing with different handholds, finally placing the baby over her shoulder and patting her on the back. After a huge and decidedly unladylike burp, Amanda quieted down and cuddled against Cassie's shoulder.

Cassie stared down at the sweet cheek next to her jaw, the soft plumpness of it rising in a delicate swell. Cassie kissed it lightly, smelling that mysterious baby scent that is as intoxicating as any love potion. The baby snuggled more deeply on her shoulder, and Cassie smiled. They stood in a contented stupor until Madison and Knoxie reappeared.

She continued the rest of the walk with the baby perched on her shoulder, not too concerned about the drool sliding onto the bare shoulder outside her tank top. When they reached the house, Madison held the door open for Cassie, and she walked slowly up the stairs with the now-sleeping Amanda. She nudged open her sister's door with her foot and spied the portable crib in the corner. All the sheets had been pulled off the double bed, and Cassie felt an odd pang, realizing her sister and her family would be going back to their own house that night.

Slowly, she lowered the baby into the crib and watched her rumpled bottom wiggle until she settled down again. Cassie stood in the hushed room for a long time, staring at the familiar wallpaper and furniture. Nothing at all had changed, and it was easy to see in her mind's eye herself and Harriet sitting cross-legged on the rosebud-covered bedspread, whispering to each other about crushes, dances, and fights with friends. Cassie had done most of the listening, and she had done so happily, grateful for this connection to the world of the in-crowd and scores of friends. And mostly, what it was like to go through life getting attention by just walking into a room.

The baby sighed in her sleep, jerking Cassie out of her reverie. She looked frantically at her arm, trying to figure out what time it was. She hated being late for appointments, even if this one was with Ed Farrell.

She stared down at the smooth skin of her arm, wondering how she had forgotten to put on her watch. She lived by that timepiece and was as naked without it as if she had just run outside in the altogether. Feeling almost disoriented from not knowing the exact time to the second, she rushed out of the room, closing the door as quickly and softly as possible. She hurried down the hall to her own room and the comfort of a cool metal band on her wrist that regulated her day and helped her get things done.

Chapter 6

The stroller bumped into the curb, then rolled back onto Cassie's foot. She winced at the pain, then winced again as she noticed the scuff mark on the toe of her shoe. She pushed it harder this time, bringing it successfully over the curb, then strolled the children down the sidewalk to where Ed Farrell had told her his office stood. The building had once housed Hal's Heavenly Bakery, and as she stood before the large storefront window, she had a brief memory of herself on her father's shoulders, eating a doughnut on the way home from church. She saw her mother holding Harriet, a wide smile on her face as she reached up to stroke Cassie's cheek.

Cassie stared at the brick three-story building sandwiched between Bitsy's House of Beauty and Walton's Drug Emporium and blinked hard, erasing the memories along with the tingle of nostalgia in the pit of her stomach. Propping the door open with her foot, she maneuvered the double stroller into the office. The strong odor of new carpet and crisp air-conditioning hit her hard.

She paused for a moment inside the door while she took off her sunglasses and tried to stick them into her purse.

Her smart leather bag was now crammed with two pacifiers,
a small squeaky toy, and a container of Cheerios, leaving
little room for anything else. With a sigh, she stuck the
glasses on top of her head. She lifted her gaze and caught
a glimpse of a richly furnished waiting room, with dark,
polished wood floors, Oriental carpets, overstuffed leather
sofas, and real oil paintings on the walls. Nothing remained
of Hal's bakery, not even a lingering aroma of baking bread.
Cassie's first thought was to step outside and make sure she
was in the right place.

A squeal from a corner erupted when a woman pulled
herself to a stand behind an elaborate mahogany desk. A
wide pink headband cut through a near-bouffant hairdo, and
sat upon the whitish-blond hair like a lipsticked smile.

"Cassie Madison! I can hardly believe you're standing
here in front of me." The woman enveloped her in an
embrace of downy arms and bosom, then held her at arm's
length as if to get a good look at her.

Cassie stared at the woman in her soft-pink knit suit, more
cleavage showing than was necessary for a receptionist in
a realtor's office, and tried not to smile as she thought how
much this woman resembled a dish sponge.

The woman spoke again, small white teeth peering
through the brightly hued lips. "You don't remember me,
do you?"

"Um, sure I do. You're . . ." Cassie leaned over the baby
to tuck a blanket around her, racking her brain for the identity
of this stranger.

"I'm Laura-Louise Whittaker." She paused, seemingly
waiting for a glimmer of recognition. "You probably
remember me as Lou-Lou. I was on the cheerleading squad
with Harriet all through high school."

Cassie's eyes widened with recognition. "Of course. I
didn't recognize you with, um, your hair. It's, ah, you're
doing something different with it, aren't you?"

Lou-Lou patted it gently with the palm of her hand. "I'm
a blonde now." She leaned forward with a conspiratorial
air. "And it's true—we really do have more fun." She let

out a shrill giggle—the same giggle that had made Cassie's
skin crawl in high school. Some things never changed.

Lou-Lou straightened and smoothed her skirt. "My.
Where's my professionalism? I'll tell Ed, um, Mr. Farrell,
that you're here. But we'll have to chat later. I'm just dying
to hear all about New York City."

She slid behind her desk and pushed a long pink nail on
an intercom button. She winked at Cassie. "Mr. Farrell.
Your eleven-thirty is here."

Cassie gave Lou-Lou the warmest smile she could find.
"Lou-Lou, I hope you don't mind, but I was wondering if
you could watch my two nieces while I meet with Ed?"

Lou-Lou threw her hands up in a picture of apparent
delight. "Why, I'd love to. Me and Harriet are practically
sisters, and I love her kids—all five of them!—like they
were my own. Just leave that stroller right there and Aunt
Lou-Lou will take care of these little dumplings while you
attend to business."

At that moment, a door at the back of the office opened,
and a man appeared in the doorway. Cassie noticed the
man's height first. His dark slicked-back hair, parted in
the middle, almost skimmed the top of the doorway. She
remembered that Ed Farrell had played on the junior varsity
basketball team his freshman year before quitting for a reason she couldn't quite recall.

He approached her with an outstretched hand, his broad
smile traversing most of his slender face. She looked again
at his hair. She remembered that it had been the same mousy
brown as her own and wondered absently if he dyed it. His
double-breasted suit made a slight swishing noise as he
walked, and the sheen of it under the fluorescent lights
convinced Cassie it wasn't made with natural fibers. She
chided herself silently for being such a snob. Ed Farrell had
apparently done very well for himself, and she should be
admiring him for his success instead of belittling him for
an unfortunate choice of suits.

He shook her hand while cupping the back of it with his
other hand. His skin was rough, a cold reminder of his years

pulling a hoe. As if reading her thoughts, Ed slipped his hands from hers a little too quickly.

"You look wonderful, Cassie. Long time no see, huh?"

His deep voice was that of a smoker's, like hot tar over gravel. She smelled nicotine mixed with mint as he spoke.

"Thank you, Ed. And, yes, it has been a long time. But it wouldn't be gentlemanly of you to make me remember exactly how long it's been." Cassie stopped herself from saying anything else, wondering why she was talking like Scarlett O'Hara all of a sudden.

He winked, then touched her on the elbow. "Let's go back to my office where we can sit down and talk."

Cassie glanced over at Lou-Lou, who seemed to be having a marvelous time shaking a rattle and making funny faces at the girls. She watched as Lou-Lou sent a luminescent gaze toward Ed. "I'll bring you some coffee in just a minute, Mr. Farrell."

He nodded with a wink, then ushered Cassie into his office.

The office decor was even more elaborate than that of the reception area. Built-in bookcases with recessed lighting illuminated small objets d'art. An oversized crystal chandelier dangled from the ceiling, each pendant tipped with gold. A blueprint, almost the size of the huge mahogany desktop, hung in a gilt frame over the fireplace. Cassie was about to sit down on a sofa when the print caught her gaze.

Slowly, she walked over to it, staring closely, and pointed at a small rectangle in the lower right of the paper. "That's my house."

Ed approached her with a small smile. He spread his blunt fingers, a gold signet ring circling his pinkie, over the northwest quadrant of the paper that was covered with about two hundred blue squares.

"Yep. That's my development. That used to be your cotton fields, now quickly becoming Farrellsford swim and tennis community. Bought it from your daddy."

Cassie could only nod. After a moment, she said, "I didn't realize how big it was—and how close to the house."

Ed led her back to the sofa and motioned for her to sit. He joined her on the opposite end of the cushion. "Don't worry about your privacy. We've plans to plant pine trees at the boundary line that will eventually block the view from your house entirely." He smiled, and she noticed how incredibly white his teeth were.

Cassie waited a moment for him to continue, and when he didn't, she said, "Looks like you've done pretty well for yourself, Ed."

He stuck his shoulders back, puffing out his chest. "Yep. Well, there really wasn't anywhere for me to go but up. You know what I mean?"

She looked down at the hands in her lap, unsure how to respond.

He spoke first. "So, you want to sell your house. You've certainly come to the right place."

She smiled up at him, grateful for the change in conversation. "Yes. I'd like to put it on the market as soon as possible. I have some cleanup to do—like the attic and all the closets need to be gone through—but I have a job and a fiancé waiting for me in New York, and I'm really eager to get back."

"A fiancé, hmm? You marryin' a Yankee?" He winked at her but gave the impression that he really wanted to hear an answer.

Cassie flattened her hands on her lap. "He's not from New York originally. He was born and raised in California, but he's been in New York for twenty years. He owns an advertising agency there, and I work for him."

Ed nodded. "Yes. Well, I hope you're both patient people, because it could take a while to unload an old house like yours. People these days wanting to spend that kind of money want something new—like what I'm offering them in Farrellsford. Sure, an old house is nice to look at and all, but it lacks a lot of modern conveniences that today's sophisticated buyers want." He stood, his brows furrowed as if in deep thought.

"If you don't have a jacuzzi in the master bath or Corian

in a super-large kitchen . . ." He paused, pursing his lips together. "Let's just say it'll be a hard sell. Even if you add all those things, you'll still be competing with new homes in the same price range."

Cassie's face fell. "I've never sold a house before, and I just had no idea. How long do you think it could take?"

He lifted his shoulders. "A month. Two months. A year. Who knows?" He smiled warmly. "Now, don't get me wrong. It's a beautiful house, and I'm sure there's a buyer for it out there somewhere. It could just take awhile. Unless you're willing to look at other options."

Cassie sat back on the sofa. "Like what?"

Ed leaned against the edge of his desk, concentrating on a brass globe on its surface. "Well, you could always sell the land. It's a lot more valuable than the house."

Her eyes widened, and dread settled in her stomach area. "But what would happen to the house?"

The suit rustled again as Ed folded his arms across his chest. "It would be up to the land developer. If they put up a golf course, they could use the house as a clubhouse." He gave her a pointed look. "Or a pool."

She sat up. "A pool? But . . ." She stopped, realizing the implication.

With a compassionate smile, he said, "I know. It's not what we want, but I wanted to mention that you had options." His brows furrowed. "And I wanted to thank you for coming to me first instead of Roust Development. They're the ones who've already bought the property on either side of yours. They want to put up a mall—can you believe? Imagine the noise and traffic—and all in our backyards." His tongue clucked. "That's what happens when outsiders move in. They don't care about what was here first." He shook his head solemnly. "So, I'm glad you came to me. I'll make sure that whatever happens to your property, it's for the benefit of both you and the town of Walton."

He walked back over to her and sat down. "I'm here to help you make the right decision for you." He patted her hand in her lap.

Cassie stood, needing to move. "I'd like to start with trying to find a family to buy the house. If that doesn't work, then we can discuss plan B."

He nodded compassionately. "I understand. And I will do my very best to find a nice little family for your house." He stood and moved to the chair on the other side of his desk, looking up as Lou-Lou walked in with a silver tray and coffee service.

Ed grinned again, and his perfect white teeth, definitely a new acquisition since high school, beamed at her. "Let's just fill out some paperwork now and schedule a time for me to come out for an appraisal." He looked up expectantly. "And I'll need a spare key to put in the lockbox on the front door. I'm assuming I won't need to call each time I come to show a client the house. You get more traffic that way."

Cassie agreed, then moved her chair closer to the desk, trying not to stare at the light brown hair roots cropping up under the slicked-back dark hair of her newly hired realtor.

Cassie slumped over her father's desk, the drawers open and their innards stacked all around the floor, like an old teddy bear with its stuffing pulled out. The hall clock struck six times, and she rubbed her eyes. She had accomplished virtually nothing. There had been a steady stream of visitors, friends, and neighbors of her father's calling to give their condolences and bring food. Lucinda had made so many trips out to the huge icebox inside the detached garage that a well-worn path now marked her way. There was enough macaroni mousse ring, lemon parsley chicken casserole, and scalloped eggplant to feed an entire city block, and then some.

Most of the visitors were familiar faces, and all had stayed for an extended social call to catch up on what Cassie had been doing in her long absence. Her throat was parched from telling them the same thing over and over: Yes, she lived and worked in Manhattan, and yes, the taxi drivers

did drive like maniacs, and no, she had not yet seen the
Statue of Liberty, although she had seen a Gay Pride parade,
but only because it marched on the street in front of her
building.

The desk chair squeaked as its occupant sat back and
stretched. She found some comfort sitting in her father's
chair, the wide, well-worn feel of it behind her a gentle
reminder of her father's never-ending love and support—
even when she least deserved it. Especially the last fifteen
years. The familiar sting of tears threatened again, and she
rubbed her eyes harshly with the heels of her hands.

Almost without thinking, Cassie reached out to the plate
carrying old Aunt Millie's famous nut cake. She stared in
horror, realizing she had eaten nearly half of it, pinching
off a bite at a time. Her thighs seemed to stick to the leather
chair as it occurred to her that it had probably been made
with real eggs and butter. She just couldn't imagine Aunt
Millie, with her jowly arms and double chin, thinking egg
or butter substitutes had any business being in her kitchen.
Cassie pinched another small bite off the side of the cake.
She had to admit that nothing tasted better than the real
thing.

With a sigh, Cassie slammed the drawer shut. The drawers
had been a jumbled mess, consisting of old letters, paid bills,
canceled checks, and an assortment of school papers and
report cards from when she and Harriet were in elementary
school. There was no rhyme or reason to their organization.
They had seemingly just been tossed into whatever drawer
had the most room and forgotten. Until now. Now they lay
in separate piles, ready to be distributed as Cassie saw fit.
The largest pile, with her high school graduation photo on
top, had a date with the garbage can.

She stood, grabbing a large fist of cake and shoving it
into her mouth. As she crossed the foyer, the doorbell rang.
Her eyes widened in horror as she realized that Sam Parker
had already spied her through the lead-glass sidelights next
to the door. She tried to swallow the nut cake, but such a
large amount had been stuffed into her mouth that it couldn't

be budged without a tall glass of milk. Resignedly, she pulled open the door, her cheeks puffed out like a chipmunk's. As an afterthought, she swiped the back of her hand across her mouth.

Sam raised his eyebrows. "You missed some."

"Harrumph?" She dared not open her mouth.

"Crumbs. You've got crumbs all over your chin."

She left the door standing open with Sam on the threshold and quickly ran into the powder room off the hall. When she was done, she came out and found, to her irritation, that Sam had let himself in, closed the front door, and was seated comfortably in a chair in the front parlor. He was staring up at the crown molding on the fourteen-foot ceiling but stood when she entered the room. "The woodwork in this house never ceases to amaze me. They just don't make anything like it anymore."

"Is there something you need?" she asked, wondering if she should have checked her teeth for more crumbs.

"Just you."

It was her turn to raise an eyebrow. "Excuse me?"

"Harriet and Joe have requested the honor of your presence at dinner tonight. They know Lucinda's gone to Atlanta to visit her cousin and didn't want you left alone. They think you'll starve if nobody's here to feed you." She could tell he was trying to hide a smile. "As if the fine folks of Walton would let that happen."

Self-consciously, Cassie brought her hand to her mouth to search for crumbs, then dropped it with annoyance.

Sam smiled brightly. "So they've been trying to reach you for most of the day to invite you for dinner, but your phone's been busy."

Cassie shrugged. "I took it off the hook. Everybody and their mother were calling to find out how I was, and I just couldn't get anything done. So I took it off the hook." She didn't know why, but she felt embarrassed to tell him the truth. She wondered if she should have made up a more altruistic story.

He crossed his arms, revealing well-muscled forearms

that protruded from rolled-up sleeves. He wore the ubiquitous jeans and cowboy boots, and Cassie had to admit that he looked good in his choice of clothing—even if it wasn't her style. He stared at her expectantly.

"What?" she asked, wondering if something was still clinging to her chin.

"I'm ready when you are. Unless you've spoiled your dinner with too much nut cake." He pointed his head in the direction of her father's desk and the half-eaten cake. "I peeked."

"Of course not. I didn't have that much. I offered some to the visiting hordes today." She didn't feel guilty because it wasn't a complete lie. She had offered some to her visitors but just hadn't had any takers.

"Then let's go."

Cassie tried to think of an excuse, but she was tired of going through her father's things, and maybe some real food would settle her stomach. She also wanted to talk to Harriet—to reminisce about their father, to bring him to mind and to reassure each other that he still lived in their hearts. After discarding so much of his life in piles lined up against the study wall, she needed reminders of his existence.

"All right—hang on. I need to get my shoes." She ran up the stairs, feeling his gaze on her backside and wishing again that all her skirts weren't so short. Everybody was wearing them in Manhattan, but she'd yet to see anything above the knee since she'd been in Walton.

She flicked on the closet light in her bedroom and eyed the various shoes, finally deciding on the beige pumps. Sliding her feet into them, she closed the closet door and went back to the stairs. She found it hard to resist galloping down the wood steps, as she had as a child, but instead walked sedately down to where Sam stood in the foyer.

His gaze slowly swept down the length of her legs, finally resting on her feet. "Heels?"

She looked down. "What's wrong with heels?"

"Nothing at all. In fact, they look real fine on your feet. But wouldn't you be more comfortable in something else?"

She lifted her chin and swept past him, opening the screen door before he could reach it and open it for her. "No, I wouldn't. I'm used to them. Besides, I don't own anything else."

He followed behind her, his boot heels clumping on the wood floor of the hall, then out onto the porch. Cassie stopped and used her key to dead-bolt the door, then pulled on the knob to make sure it was locked tight.

Sam leaned one arm on one of the tall columns of the porch. "That's not necessary. Nobody's going to take anything while you're gone. Unless you're trying to stop people from bringing more food, of course, then by all means you should lock up."

Ignoring him, she turned and walked down the porch steps, spotting Andrew's Mercedes in the circular driveway. "Finally! I was wondering when I'd see it again."

Sam didn't answer, but instead rapped his bare knuckles against the solid wood column. "This house is amazing. You don't know how lucky you are."

"You think so? Ed Farrell thinks I might have a hell of a time trying to unload it." She dropped her keys into her purse and hoisted it on her shoulder.

He paused for a moment, looking as if he wanted to say something, then continued across the yard in the opposite direction.

Cassie called after him. "Where are you going?"

"I'm getting into my truck."

"I can see that—but we've got my car back."

He turned on the ignition, and a blast of country music danced out of the open window. "*You've* got your car back. I'd rather not be seen in it. People round here might think I've gone New York on them."

Cassie stuck her hands on her hips. "Then how'd you get it over here?"

Sam slammed his door, then leaned over to push open the passenger door. "My dad and Mr. Anderson. Looked like a couple of fools going through their midlife crisis two decades late. Now get in or we'll be late for dinner."

Cassie didn't budge. "This is a very nice car, I'll have you know. I could blow the doors off your truck without even trying."

"Can't haul anything in it, and the third passenger has to lie down horizontally in the back. I think they should halve the price, since they're only giving you half the car. Now climb in."

"Where are my keys? We could waste gas and take two separate vehicles." She shifted her feet, already feeling the sticky perspiration under her arms and not wanting to be in the un-air-conditioned air one second longer. She wondered why she was being so stubborn about something so stupid. Yes, she wasn't particularly fond of trucks and dreaded stepping up into them in a short skirt. But it was more than that. Maybe it was his attitude that anything that smacked of the city was something to be avoided.

He raised an eyebrow and grinned. "In my pocket."

A drip of sweat crept down her back between her shoulder blades. "May I have them, please?"

Grinning more broadly, he said, "You'll have to get them yourself."

She pulled the front of her blouse away from her chest where it had begun to stick. The air-conditioning blew Sam's hair off his forehead, and she could almost feel its chilling breeze. She looked again at the Mercedes sitting in the hot sun, then back at Sam's truck. Without another word, she climbed in and sat down, regardless of whom she flashed.

Sam directed the vents to blow in her direction as Cassie donned her sunglasses.

"I can only hope that nobody recognizes me." That was mean, but he asked for it with his snide comments about Andrew's car. Maybe now he'd call it even.

Sam slid the truck into gear. "There are worse things than to be recognized as a small-town country girl, you know. Like being thought of as a big-city snob."

That did it. Cassie's sunglasses had moved down her nose with sweat, and she pushed them up with a well-manicured index finger. "At least I don't think genitalia is an Italian airline."

Sam snorted as he pulled the truck down the gravel drive to the main road. "I think you've been listening to too many Jeff Foxworthy jokes."

They rode along in silence for a few blocks. Cassie tried to ignore the driver, but her gaze kept straying to his side of the bench seat. Even the way he sat, his left knee drawn up casually, his right elbow resting on the back of the seat, and his light hold on the wheel, screamed confident self-assurance. This man, with his pickup truck, cowboy boots, and drawling accent, seemed more sure of himself than anyone she had ever met. And it irked her no end.

"Did you really go to Harvard?"

He glanced at her briefly. "Yep. But only for med school. Went to Yale for undergrad. I transferred there from the junior college after you left."

She studied him for a moment. "Then why on earth did you come back here?"

He kept his gaze straight ahead, the light from the windshield brightening his eyes. "Because this is home. I figured life had to be about more than just work and making money. I wanted a place to grow roots. Become part of a community. Raise a family in a familiar environment." He stole a glance at Cassie before returning back to the windshield.

"You forgot guilt. Your parents must have pulled on you at every chance. At least I wasn't an only child, so I had the option."

Sam sent her a hard glance. "Guilt over my brother, you mean? That had nothing to do with it. My parents never once asked me to come back. I did it on my own."

Cassie was surprised by his vehemence, wondering whom he was really trying to convince.

"But didn't you like Boston? There's so much excitement there. So much to do."

Sam shrugged. "It's fine—to visit. But I never really fit in."

She gave him a sardonic smile. "Gee, I wonder why? Could it be the way you talk or the way you dress?"

He caught her with a withering glance. "And what's wrong with the way I dress?"

Unobtrusively, Cassie eyed the plaid shirt rolled up on his strong forearms, the jeans hugging his well-muscled thighs, and the cowboy boots. She opened her mouth to say something, then swallowed thickly. "Oh, never mind."

He shrugged. "I found out later from a friend of mine that a lot of people at school thought I was gay. Could never figure that one out."

She laughed out loud. "It's the boots. In Manhattan, that's a dead giveaway."

"Humph." Sam pulled to a stop at a light and rested his wrist on the steering wheel. "I guess I didn't date much, either, which probably fueled the fire. Not much time with all that studying, plus those city girls just seemed too harsh for my taste. I guess I prefer something softer." He reached up and adjusted his rearview mirror. "You know, someone who doesn't reveal all her feminine secrets in the first fifteen minutes."

Cassie stared out the window with studied nonchalance. How dumb were those northern girls, anyway? One didn't have to know Sam Parker to know there wasn't a gay bone in his body. He practically reeked of masculinity, and sitting this close to him in his truck made her squirm. She shifted closer to the door.

Sam spoke without looking at her. "I understand you had a long meeting with Ed Farrell today."

Cassie raised her eyebrows. "News sure travels fast in a small town."

Sam nodded but didn't smile. "That's certainly one thing you can bank on here. That and plenty of contestants for the watermelon-seed spitting at the Kudzu Festival. It just is. And that Lou-Lou Whittaker is the biggest gossip this side of the Mississippi."

He turned onto Harriet's street. "What did he have to say besides that it will take a long time to sell your house?"

"Why do you want to know?"

Sam pulled into the driveway of a neat two-story brick colonial. Bikes, bike helmets, and roller blades decorated the neatly clipped yard. He pulled the truck into PARK and switched off the ignition before turning to her. "There are many people in this town who believe Ed Farrell is in the developers' pockets. The old farm his parents worked was the first thing to be bulldozed. They're building a poultry processing plant on it now. That's all well and good, but now he's focusing on other chunks of land throughout the community."

The front screen door opened, and Sarah Frances and Joey tumbled out and ran down the stairs toward the truck.

Sam continued. "One by one they're selling out, and Ed's pocketing lots of cash brokering these deals. They all know him as one of them, and they trust him. I think that's why the developers are using Ed to work with them. All I know for sure is that if we're not careful, we'll be a commercial wasteland in a few years. Nothing but plants and industrial parks. And big neighborhoods with cookie-cutter houses. No character, no history. Nothing left of what makes this town so great." He yanked the keys out of the ignition. "And don't believe him when he tells you he's one of us and not one of those other developers who want to tear apart our town. If he's not in cahoots with them, he's still cut from the same cloth."

Sarah Frances tapped on the window, and Cassie reached for the door handle. "I think I understand your point, but it's got nothing to do with me. Ed's merely going to help me find somebody to buy my house; he even mentioned a family he already had in mind." She pushed the door open, angry at him for lecturing her on something that was none of his business. "But even if I were to sell it to a developer, that would be my own decision. Ed's opinion wouldn't sway me one way or the other."

Sam held her forearm for a moment, preventing her from leaving the truck. "You're wrong, Cassie. It's not just your decision. Your house is part of Walton's history. There's a lot of people here who would care very much what happens to your house. Including me.''

She yanked her arm out of his grasp and stepped out of the truck. Four small arms encircled her waist. A warm glow started somewhere deep inside, surprising her. Even more surprising was that she hardly gave a second thought to the dirty handprints that were bound to be smudged on her skirt.

Cassie hugged them both and rumpled their hair, then reached for their hands. But they pulled out of her grasp and raced to Sam.

"Dr. Parker!'' they shouted in unison, running and jumping on him. He eagerly caught them, then adjusted them easily on each hip before sauntering toward Cassie.

She turned her back on him and walked up the three brick steps to the front door, where Harriet now stood. As Cassie neared, Harriet's cheerleader smile faded. She stuck out her hand and gingerly touched the necklace around Cassie's neck, letting the charms slip silently through her fingers.

With a shaking voice, Harriet said, "I remember this. Keeper of hearts, right?''

The memory of her mother's voice uttering those same words stilled Cassie's breath. She felt, rather than saw, Sam slipping by with the two children. She reached up to the charms and touched her sister's fingers.

"Keeper of hearts.'' The words barely made it past her lips. Before she realized what she was doing, she hugged her sister, holding on tightly.

"Mama! Sarah Frances won't help me set the table.'' Madison's voice came from back in the house amid shouting and the clatter of small feet on wood floors.

Cassie smiled, then awkwardly pulled away, the silence of fifteen years still heavy between them but the bond of a father's death bringing them together by a degree. Then she followed Harriet back into the kitchen, her hand still clutching the gold charms around her neck.

Chapter 7

They found Sam in the kitchen, leaning over a steaming pot on the stove.

"Something sure smells good. If you're not careful, Harriet, you're going to find me hanging around your doorstep every night around suppertime."

Harriet tapped him gently on his flat abdomen. "That's what I like about you, Sam. You're so easy to please."

Cassie rolled her eyes, then turned toward the table and her niece.

Madison was busy throwing place mats, napkins, and silverware on the table with a heavy scowl on her face. A tall stack of dishes awaited her attack on the corner of the table. When she spotted her mother's sister, she beamed. "Hey, Aunt Cassie."

Cassie smiled back, admiring Madison's new hairstyle. "I like what you're doing with your hair."

Madison slid a spoon and fork across the table's surface, sending them almost careening off the table. "I've pinned it up to see if I like the shorter hair. Then I'm going to have it cut—just like yours." She slapped a place mat down in front of her before dumping silverware on it. "I wanted you to go with me to show Bitsy."

"Sure." Cassie grabbed a stack of plates and began placing them around the table, picking up the disarrayed silverware and placing it neatly next to the plates. "I'd be happy to." She shook her head. "I can't believe Bitsy is still cutting hair. She gave me my first real haircut."

Sam grinned. "It was a hideous David Cassidy shag, if I recall correctly. And you wore a handkerchief over your head for a week."

Cassie paused for a moment with a fork in midair, her expression a mixture of surprise and annoyance. "Yeah, I did. And you have my permission to forget about that, too."

The sliding-glass door opened, letting in Joe and the smell of barbecue. Cassie looked up and froze, unsure, still, of how she felt about him. She was no longer smitten by him, that much she knew. But he had been the source of so much pain for so long, she didn't know how to talk to him or even look at him. The few times she had spoken to him directly, she had found her gaze centered somewhere between the tip of his nose and his left ear.

"Hi, Cassie. Sam." He nodded in their direction.

Sam watched her intently, making her even more self-conscious.

Joe spoke again. "Hey, Sam. Why don't you grab a beer and come outside with me. I want to show you my new gas grill. Does just about everything but pluck the chicken and wash dishes."

Sam whistled. "Now that's an offer a man can't refuse."

Joe pulled two beer cans from the refrigerator. He left the room with Sam, sliding the door shut behind them as Harriet gave an exasperated sigh. "Men and their toys. They never really grow up, do they?" She turned toward the counter and started tearing lettuce into a salad bowl. But there was something in her smile that told Cassie there was nothing Harriet would want to change.

Over her shoulder Harriet said, "Please hurry up with setting the table, Maddie. You're moving slower than a herd of turtles through molasses. I need you to finish this salad so I can see to the rest of dinner.''

Cassie spoke up. "I'm not that handy in a kitchen anymore, but I can help chop stuff for the salad." She stood next to her sister and grabbed a cucumber and sharp knife. Their arms brushed, and they looked at each other as if simultaneously remembering the same image of their helping Lucinda prepare dinner in their father's house.

Harriet grinned. "Remember when Aunt Lucinda went on that health-food kick?''

"Oh, Lord! How could I forget? That's when he almost set the house on fire trying to fry chicken in the middle of the night so he could get a decent meal." Cassie shook her head, smiling at the memory. "He said it was his God-given right as a Southerner to eat fried food." She sliced a few chunks off the cucumber, her voice quieting. "He still had those grease-fire burns on his hand, didn't he? Don't think he minded, though. Man, how he loved fried chicken."

They were silent for a moment as tears sprang to Harriet's eyes.

Cassie spoke, staring at the cucumber. "Don't you dare start or I'll start, too, and not be able to stop. Then dinner will never be ready."

Harriet sniffled, then nodded, tearing another leaf of lettuce into small bits.

They were eventually rejoined by the men, and when Amanda's fretting sounded from the baby monitor, Joe went upstairs to get her. He settled her in the baby swing in the corner of the kitchen, then joined his wife in the dinner preparations. Children ran in and out, the door swinging open and shut in a rapid procession, while all sorts of conversations were shouted across the room and to the backs of departing children.

"Supper's almost ready. Don't go too far, you hear?"

"Don't pick your nose, Joey. Now go wash your hands and get ready to eat."

"Go practice your scales, Sarah Frances, until it's time for supper."

Through all the commotion, Joe and Harriet created their own private space. When they were near enough to each other, they would touch. A brisk sweep of a hand on an arm, a pat on the elbow, a nuzzle on the cheek. And as much as Cassie found herself watching them, she found Sam closely regarding her with the same frequency. She shrugged and went back to slicing tomatoes.

The whole crew, with the exception of baby Amanda, who was busily gnawing on a rattle in her swing, sat elbow to elbow around the large pine table in the kitchen. Cassie was relieved to find herself far enough away from Joe that she wouldn't have to stare right into his face if she needed to talk to him. Unfortunately, Sam was seated to her direct right, and she felt quite certain that every time his arm rubbed against hers, it was intentional. She found herself anticipating the brush of his arm every time he reached for something, so she discreetly moved her chair an inch away.

Harriet said the blessing, forcing everyone to join hands. Cassie reached tentatively toward Sam's fingers, then found her hand swallowed by his. She bowed her head and listened to Harriet's voice, trying to ignore the warm pressure of Sam's fingers against hers. When the blessing was over, she looked up and found Sam watching her closely. Looking away, she reached for the collard greens.

The children were amazingly civilized at the table, with no arguing and lots of "No, ma'ams" and "Yes, sirs" when they were spoken to by their parents and the other adults.

Cassie had just taken a bite out of a tangy piece of barbecue brisket when Sam brought up the subject of Ed Farrell again.

"Did you give Ed the key to your house?"

She washed down her food with a quick swallow of sweet tea. "Yes, I did. How can he show the house if he can't get in?"

He didn't answer her right away. Instead, he got involved in a conversation with Joey about the best time to go fishing in Senator Thompkins's creek, and then Cassie's attention was diverted by a request from Knoxie for another glass of milk. Letting Harriet sit for a change, Cassie went to the refrigerator and retrieved a carton of milk, placing it in the middle of the table after refilling four glasses.

The family continued to eat in relative peace, and Cassie hoped the entire subject of Ed Farrell had been dropped. But during a lull in the conversation, Sam turned to her again.

"I don't think it's a good idea to give Ed access to your house." He began buttering a large piece of corn bread.

Putting down her fork, she stared at him. "Excuse me?"

He placed his knife carefully on the edge of his plate. "I don't think somebody like Ed should have free access to your house."

"Really. And you call *me* a snob. You're certainly no better. Just because the guy was poor as a child, you think he's out to rob us blind. Let me tell you something, Dr. Parker. If his office is any indication of how well he's doing, he doesn't need anything from me or you or anybody."

Sam slid his chair back slightly so he could turn to face her. A throbbing tick had begun on his left cheek. "He wasn't the only one born poor, Cassie, if you'll remember. But he sure as hell"—with a guilty expression, he looked across the table at the youngest of three children staring at him with large eyes—"um, heck, has not reached his current level of affluence by playing by the book. And I'm not just saying this because of the way he used to bully me in school. I'm referring to the way he's convincing all those families to sell out to him so he can bulldoze their homes and put some god-awful-looking poultry processing plant on the land. And now he's running for that town council seat and saying he's got Walton's best interests at heart." He forced air out of his lips. "He doesn't care about anything except lining his own pockets."

Cassie narrowed her eyes. "So what does this have to do with me giving him my house key? He seemed perfectly nice to me, and he sincerely wants to do what's best for me."

Sam dropped the corn bread on his plate. "I'm sorry, but I just don't trust the man. There's always the question that lingers in my mind of how he found the money not only to go to college but to start his own business. There's something there, and I don't like it. He's the last person in the world you should be giving your house key to."

Cassie picked up her fork again. "Well, I like him, and I want him to sell my house as quickly as possible. Whatever he wants me to do to facilitate that, I'll do."

Sam rested his hands on the table for a moment and stared down at his plate. The throbbing in his cheek beat faster. Finally, after wiping his mouth with a napkin, he pushed his chair back.

"Thank you, Harriet, Joe. It was delicious. But if you will excuse me for a bit, I need to go out to my truck and check my messages and make some phone calls."

Without looking at Cassie, he slid his chair out farther and left.

Harriet and Joe switched their gazes from Sam's retreating back to Cassie.

"What crawled into his boots?" she asked, trying to hide her chagrin by taking a heaping forkful of collard greens.

Joe spoke quietly. "I think it's stress about tomorrow's election. He's always hated to lose at anything, but especially this time, since he believes so much is at stake."

Reaching for her glass, Cassie asked, "Election? What election?"

Harriet dabbed at her mouth with a napkin. "Sam and Ed are both running for a town-council seat. Sam's under the impression that Ed will have Walton looking like an industrial park within a matter of years if he wins—no matter how much Ed shouts about being the 'good' developer in town." She sent Cassie a wry smile. "I don't know. I know Sam's heart is in the right place, but I also think a little bit of progress is good. Those old houses Ed had torn down for that poultry plant were eyesores, anyway."

Joe leaned back in his chair, lifting the front legs off the floor. "I dunno. I pretty much agree with Sam. Sure, Ed's raising a ruckus about that mall developer buying those lots, but it would take a miracle to make me believe that Ed wouldn't be doing the same thing if he'd thought of it first.''

Cassie shook her head. "Oh, no, Joe. Ed loves my father's house. He even mentioned that if I couldn't sell it to a family, he would be interested in maybe making the house a clubhouse for a golf club. I mean, it's not ideal, but at least the house wouldn't be torn down.''

Harriet and Joe looked at each other, but Cassie missed their expressions when she bent to retrieve a rattle Amanda threw on the floor.

Harriet cupped her chin in her hands. "I have to say I'm surprised Ed has done so well for himself. Remember how we used to tease him about the dirt under his fingernails?''

Cassie stopped chewing, the shame of the memory constricting her throat. "Oh, God. I'd forgotten about all that. You don't think he still remembers, do you?''

Joe leaned back, patting his ample stomach with one hand. "I don't think Ed Farrell's the kind of man who forgets anything. Like the time his father traipsed across the basketball court in the middle of the game to haul Ed back home. Said he needed help with the plowing and that was that, basketball game or not. I don't think Ed ever came back to school after that.''

"Pass the cornbread, please,'' shouted Joey, his lips, chin, and cheeks covered with the remnants of his first piece.

Madison stretched her arm toward the bread basket.

Harriet nodded. "Remember how he used to cuss? I still don't know what some of those words meant. You'd think he'd grown up in the city or something.''

Madison's fingers gripped the edge of the basket, shifting it in the opposite direction.

Joe sat up. "Now, really, Harriet. People in the city don't cuss any more than they do out here. I don't know where you get all these stereotypical ideas about city people.''

Madison, still reaching for the cornbread, managed to flop her elbow on the table at the precise spot where a glass casserole lid lay. The force propelled it into the air in a perfect somersault before crashing to the floor and splitting in half.

"Holy shit!" she yelled, effectively silencing all and sundry at the table, with the exception of the cooing baby and Knoxie, who had the sudden impulse to imitate her older sister.

"Bowly shit!" she shouted with glee.

Harriet stood quickly. "Madison Cassandra Warner! Get to your room this instant. You've never heard that kind of language in this house, and I certainly don't expect it coming out of your mouth. I've a good mind to wash it out with soap."

Cassie looked down at her plate, feeling the color deepen in her cheeks.

Madison slowly slid out of her chair. "I didn't mean nothing by it. It just sorta slipped out. . . ."

Her mother leaned toward her, her eyes lit with fury. "Where have you heard that word before?"

Madison glanced over at her aunt, and Cassie swallowed, then nodded her head.

"I . . . I must have said it without thinking, Harriet. I'm sorry. I didn't realize—"

Harriet shook her head, cutting her off. "It doesn't matter. Maddie is old enough to know what's inappropriate language for a young girl." She turned back to her daughter. "We'll discuss this later. Up to your room, please. And no peach ice cream for you tonight."

"Mama . . ." Madison's whole demeanor whined, along with her voice.

Joe spoke, his words soft but strong. "Do as your mama tells you, and do it without complaining or there'll be a worse punishment than being sent to your room."

Madison banged her chair up against the table and ran out of the room. Her feet could be heard stomping their way up the stairs, the sound punctuated by the slamming of her bedroom door.

The front door shut quietly, and Sam returned to the

kitchen. "Was that an adolescent girl or a tornado I saw flinging its way up the stairs?"

Joe shook his head, then stood. "Don't go there, Sam. Don't even go there. I can only question God as to why he gave me four hormonal girls and just one levelheaded boy." He reached across the table and started stacking dishes.

Harriet stood, too, the stern expression on her face doing nothing to hide its inherent sweetness. "Watch it, buddy. The couch in the living room isn't all that comfortable."

Joey dropped his fork on his plate with a clatter. "Let's go catch lightning bugs!"

His pronouncement was followed by the sound of three chairs being scraped back from the table.

Harriet waved her hands in the air. "Don't think this excuses any of you from your after-dinner chores. They'll be waiting for you when you get back." She walked to a cabinet and pulled out four empty peanut-butter jars, all with lids that had small holes poked in them and a different initial painted on the front.

Sarah Frances grabbed two, then took Knoxie's hand and followed Joey out the door.

Harriet squatted and reached into the far back of the cabinet and pulled out two more jars. These appeared older, the bright yellow lids pale and faded. She approached the table again, holding the jars out so Cassie could read the "C" and "H" on the sides.

"I can't believe you kept these." Cassie ran her thumbnail against the ridged side of the lid.

"How could I throw them away?"

Without looking at her sister, Cassie examined the jar closely, trying not to think of all the things of her childhood she had discarded in the last fifteen years without a second thought.

Finally, she looked up. "Thanks. Thanks for keeping them." And she meant it.

Madison lingered in the doorway. "Can I come down now?"

Her mother turned toward her. "Are you ready to apologize?"

Madison nodded, then mumbled, "I'm sorry. I won't say it again."

Harriet just stood, looking at her eldest child with a mixture of love and incredulity, as if she couldn't believe she had a daughter old enough to be cussing like a sailor. Then she walked over and handed Madison a jar with an "M" on it.

A small smile tugged at the corner of Madison's mouth. "Thanks, Mama. Can I have peach ice cream, too?"

Her mother frowned. "Don't push it, young lady. Now go outside and keep your sisters out of the mud puddles."

The screen door banged open, and Joey poked his head into the kitchen. "Dr. Parker—c'mon. It's us boys against the girls to see who can catch more."

Sam looked up at Harriet and winked before turning back to the small boy. "Hold on a minute. I'm going to need another jar, and I need your permission to expropriate a female for our team."

Joey wrinkled his nose. "Huh?"

Sam laughed. "Okay. How 'bout your Aunt Cassie joining us on our team? It would make it more even."

A chair slid back from the table as Cassie stood. "Sorry—can't. Not only am I woefully out of practice, but somebody's got to help your mother clean up this mess." Cassie drained the last of her sweet tea, making the ice cubes tinkle against the glass.

Harriet touched her briefly on the shoulder, making Cassie start. "Oh, you go on, Cassie. Joe and I can handle this, and the kids will finish up when they come back in. I insist."

Cassie scanned the faces of the people around her like a caged animal. "But I've got loads of work to do back at the house, and I should really be getting back."

Sam sent her a level gaze. "How are you going to get there?"

"I'll drive, of co—" She stopped. "Oh."

"I promise to drive you home just as soon as we can catch us more fireflies than the girls."

"I'm really not dressed for running around outside." Cassie looked down at her short skirt and heels. "How about if I just stayed inside and rooted for your team?"

Madison plopped down at the table next to her aunt. "We're too old for kid games like that. We'll stay here."

"Now, Maddie . . ." Cassie stopped, wondering why it was so important to her that Madison go outside and have fun instead of staying inside with her. "Look, it's not because I'm too old; it's just that it's hard to run in heels."

"I'll help." Sam leaned over and picked up the bug jar with the big yellow "C" on the outside.

"And anybody who stays behind has to scrub the pots." Harriet smiled brightly.

Madison stood, making the chair wobble in her haste. "Come on, Aunt Cassie. Please?"

Amused by her niece and only halfway reluctant, Cassie followed Sam and Madison out into the humid night.

A chorus of hundreds of tree frogs hummed and burbled in the tall pines on the far side of the property. Bright lights from the houses at Farrellsford could be seen clearly through large gaps in the trees. Cassie stepped tentatively off the path, feeling her heel grip solid ground. So far, so good.

"Over there—look! By the trees." Madison ran, her long hair swinging loose behind her. Joey ran after her, shouting, "Don't get all of them, Maddie. Save some for me!"

A cluster of blinking lights pulsed underneath a giant magnolia, and Cassie ran toward them, her feet crunching on the ground cover of faded magnolia leaves. Quickly, she unscrewed the lid and swiped the jar through the air.

"I got two! I got two!" She put the lid back on, then held the jar up proudly to show Sam. As she began walking toward him, her heel held fast to a hole in the ground, twisting Cassie's ankle and sending her sprawling, facedown, into the bed of leaves. Her bug jar rolled a few feet away, coming to rest on its bottom. The fireflies inside winked at her.

"Dangnabit!" she shouted, struggling to a sitting position.

"Don't try to stand." Sam's voice was filled with concern as he lifted her under her arms and slid her gently to rest against the trunk of the tree.

"I'm fine. Really." Mortified by her clumsiness, she put her foot under her to try to stand but was only rewarded with shooting pain from her right ankle.

"Umph," she groaned.

"I told you not to stand." Sam knelt in the grass in front of her and picked up her foot. With studied concentration, his fingers gently probed her ankle, foot, and calf. The blood under her skin warmed to his touch, and she barely suppressed another moan—but this time not from pain. It was a struggle not to force her other leg, or worse, into his hands, and beg for the same attention.

His hand slid up the back of her calf, and she bit her lip hard enough to make it bleed. Anything to distract herself from the torture of his hands. And it had nothing to do with her ankle. He asked her to rotate her foot as he supported her leg, his fingers brushing her thigh, and she forced herself to think of fireflies and prickers in the grass and the shouting children running around in the dark. She picked up her jar and clutched it tightly, thinking she could feel the thrumming of the energy inside, causing the little bodies to light up with an inner heat.

She needed to talk or go crazy. "This tree reminds me of that large magnolia in the yard back at the house. Did you know my mother planted it as a sapling when I was born? I can't believe it's still there. And it's just huge now."

Sam's movements paused for a moment as he regarded her. "Its roots go pretty deep. It's not going anywhere for a long time."

Heat from his touch seemed to burn her skin, and she looked away, not able to meet his eyes. Prickly grass tickled the heel of her foot, and she realized he had set her foot down.

"It's not broken. Most likely you've got a little sprain. I'll bring you inside and wrap it with ice."

Cassie nodded, knowing an ice-cold shower would be

even more therapeutic for what ailed her. She found she still couldn't look at him and instead stared intently at the jar.

"Why do they do that?"

"Blink?" Sam shifted in the grass, pulling himself up on his haunches. "It's a mating thing. The lady fireflies do that to catch a suitor. The guy fireflies find those glowing butts real attractive, then light up their own rear ends to show they're interested." He grinned up at her. "It's the bug world's equivalent of short skirts and high heels."

She tossed the jar at him, causing him to lose his balance and fall back as he caught it. "That's not why I wear what I wear. It's called *fashion*—a word I'm sure you're not familiar with."

Hoisting herself up using the trunk for support, she resisted his offer of help. "It just goes to show how similar males are in every species. They only want one thing, and they rely on superficialities to find a mate."

Sam grabbed her elbow, his tight grip making it clear he wasn't letting go. He stood close enough for her to smell him—a faint whiff of cologne and outdoor air. His breath brushed her cheek as he spoke.

"Not all males are alike, Cassie. Some actually make a point of peeling through all that outside stuff to see the real woman underneath. It's hard-won, but what a prize. A man just has to be patient."

Cassie leaned into him, taking the pressure off her ankle. "And are you a patient man, Dr. Parker?"

His eyes glittered from the porch light, reminding her of the fireflies. "Call me Job."

Suppressing a grin, she allowed herself to be lifted and carried inside.

The ride home with Sam was silent except for the soft twangings of a Dwight Yokum CD on the stereo. Cassie didn't remember to be nauseated by it until they were almost at her father's house.

Sam came to her side of the truck and lifted her out,

closing the door with the heel of his boot. Effortlessly, he carried her across the drive and up the front steps to the porch. A full moon crept through the trees, dappling the porch and front door with mottled light and illuminating the bandaging around Cassie's ankle. She tried her best to keep her head away from Sam, but the sturdy wall of his chest and the soft cotton shirt was the natural spot to rest her cheek. With seemingly reluctant hands, Sam set her down but didn't release his hold.

He stared at her neck. "I remember that necklace."

Her hand instinctively went to the four small charms.

A brief flash of white appeared on his face as he smiled. "I remember you always clutched at it when you felt nervous. It's a dead giveaway, but I think it's endearing."

Her defensive hackles had been raised with his remark about her habit, recalling Andrew's negative comments about it, but now she warmed toward him, smiling softly.

"My mother gave it to me."

She moved her hand away, and he touched the charms tentatively, his fingers brushing the tender skin under her chin.

"What do they mean?"

An unseen insect hummed, teasing the air between them. Cassie took a deep breath. "The three hearts are for me, my father, and Harriet." She brushed at the air, listening to the humming fade away. "The key is for me—the keeper of the hearts." Swallowing, she continued. "My mother gave this to me right before she died."

He stared at her openly, not blinking. She looked down, not wanting him to see the shame in her eyes. He lifted her chin with his finger, forcing her to meet his gaze.

"Keeper of the hearts."

She blinked rapidly. "Yeah. It's kind of silly. And I would laugh if I hadn't been such a failure at the one thing my mother wanted me to do."

He let go of her chin and stroked her cheek softly before dropping his hand. A humid breeze, filled with the summer smells of grass, jasmine, and wisteria, lifted her hair. "I don't think so. You may have taken a detour, but you're not a failure."

This man, with his cowboy boots and bright eyes, was standing too close. Way too close. She dropped her gaze and began fumbling for her keys. "I've got to call Andrew."

Sam didn't say anything, but continued to regard her evenly.

"My fiancé."

His expression didn't waver. "Give me your key. I don't want you falling over and hurting yourself opening the door." He took the key and turned, stopping abruptly. A lockbox hung from the door handle.

"My, my. Our Ed Farrell does move fast, doesn't he?" He frowned at the heavy metal combination box hiding a house key inside.

She hopped over to him and leaned against the sidelight. "Where I'm from, that's called not wasting time. I'm glad to see he's taken the initiative."

Sam raised an eyebrow but didn't say anything. He stuck the key into the lock and turned it, pushing the door and letting it swing open.

"Would you like me to carry you upstairs to your bedroom?"

His expression was so innocent, she couldn't understand why his suggestion made her heart flutter like the fireflies in her jar.

"No, thanks. I can manage."

He handed her the key. "All right. But page me if you need me. Anytime—day or night. You have the number."

She held up his business card. "Right. I got it. Thanks."

"Well, then. I'd better let you call Andy."

"Andrew."

"Yeah. Whatever. Good night."

"Good night. Thanks for the doctoring. You can bill me if you like."

He waved a hand at her before turning away and walking toward the steps. "It's on the house."

He waved again as she called out good night and shut

the door. The dead bolt slid home with a solid, final sound. She dropped her purse on the hall table but brought the bug jar upstairs with her.

She took off her clothes and left them on the floor, too tired to hang them up. After sliding on a long T-shirt, she collapsed into bed and turned out the light. Andrew would be angry, but he'd have to wait until the morning to talk to her.

The flickering light from the jar on her nightstand illuminated the room briefly before casting it into darkness again. She thought of her father, straining to hear his footsteps walk up the wooden stairs, just as she'd done all those years ago as a child. But the house remained quiet, her father's tread now forever silenced.

Outside, the sounds of the tree frogs and crickets crept into her room, singing to her like a forgotten lullaby. It was as if this place had frozen in time and she was a little girl again, safe in the cocoon of this house and her family's love. She snuggled deeply into her pillow, the pulsing light from the jar growing dimmer and dimmer, and fell asleep.

Chapter 8

Something thumped downstairs, bringing Cassie out of bed in one leap. Sun streamed through the open blinds, illuminating the mantel clock in her bedroom. Ten o'clock. She never slept late. Never. Even on weekends she was in the office by eight.

A thump followed by a scrape emerged again from downstairs. Bleary-eyed, she searched for a weapon. Lucinda was gone all week, and Cassie was supposed to be alone in the house. She grabbed a fireplace poker, then cracked the door open and waited. Her blood pounded in her ears as she stood with the poker poised over her shoulder. The stealthy sound of a key turning in the latch and the front door opening echoed upstairs. Cassie moved quietly to the top of the steps and peered down into the foyer. The two-toned hair, viewed clearly from her vantage point, was unmistakable.

"Ed? What are you doing here?"

He glanced up, his eyes wide. A broad smile quickly replaced his look of surprise. "Cassie, darlin'. I'm so sorry. I knocked, and when no one answered, I thought nobody was home." His gaze swept Cassie's T-shirt, then looked away as if he were embarrassed. "I, uh, was here to do the appraisal."

"But you were supposed to call me this afternoon to let me know when you'd be over."

His gaze bounced from the newel post to the light fixture and back, as if he were studiously avoiding looking at her. Sensing it was her state of undress that was bothering him, she ducked into her room and grabbed her bathrobe. It only came to mid-thigh, but it was better than the almost-sheer T-shirt. She dropped the poker on the floor, feeling foolish.

Her bare feet slapped the wooden risers of the stairs as she jogged down to the foyer. Her ankle, still wrapped, felt stiff but no longer painful. "Why didn't you call first?"

His smile never wavered. "I wanted to get down to business as soon as possible. I know how anxious you are to sell."

Mollified, Cassie relaxed. "I guess since you're here, then, we might as well get started." She yawned. "But I've got to have some coffee first. May I make some for you?"

Ed seemed absorbed in studying his surroundings and made no indication that he had heard.

"Ed?"

He jerked and faced her. "I'm sorry, darlin'. Did you say something?"

"Yes. I asked you if you wanted coffee."

He blinked, as if wondering why she was there. "Ah, yes. Coffee. That would be fine. And if you don't mind, while you're doing that, I want to go ahead and get started."

Cassie turned toward the kitchen, wondering where he had learned his get-up-and-go attitude. From what she could recall of his family and childhood, he certainly hadn't been born with it.

When she returned with two steaming mugs of coffee, she couldn't find him. She called his name twice before he responded. She found him in her father's study, sitting at his desk and staring at the photos of her and Harriet.

"What are you doing?" Her voice still held an early-morning scratchiness.

He seemed to be trying to pull himself together and quickly began gathering his notepad and pen off the top of the desk.

"I was just trying to get a feel for the ambience of this house. Buying a house is rarely based on something you can touch. If I can give them the feeling of the house, I'll have a better chance of selling it, even with all of its problems."

She handed him his mug. "Problems? Like what?"

The question seemed to take him by surprise. "Oh, well, ah . . ." His eyes brightened. "There's no central air-conditioning. That's a big no-no in this market. Especially with these tall ceilings—I bet it's hotter'n a fire ant's rear end in the middle of July." He chuckled at his own joke.

Cassie recalled the days before they had even the window units, the days when her daddy would take her and Harriet for a ride in the car with the windows open just to catch a breeze. But she didn't think of it as a problem. It was one of those recollections that brought back a pleasant feeling in the pit of her stomach, a happy, albeit long-forgotten, memory. Cassie frowned.

"It's not so bad, Ed. Yesterday it was ninety-eight degrees and ninety percent humidity, and I was completely comfortable inside." That wasn't entirely true, but she was quite certain that any stickiness she had felt simply from moving from one room to another was due to the fact that she wasn't acclimated yet. She pushed aside the memory of Aunt Lucinda walking about her household chores with a wet washcloth right out of the freezer around her neck.

"Hmm." Ed walked toward the velvet draperies and touched one reverently. "Are you leaving any of the furnishings?"

She took another sip of her coffee. "I hadn't really thought about it. I don't have room in my apartment, but I'm assuming Harriet and Lucinda would want at least a few pieces. Maybe I could auction off the rest."

He clutched the curtain tightly in his fist, then let it go.

"That's a good idea, Cassie. I'm sure you don't want to be saddled with any of this old stuff."

Her gaze skipped around the room, taking in all the highly polished mahogany and cherry antiques. She felt a proprietary surge creep into her veins.

"It's not just old stuff, Ed. This furniture has been in the family for generations."

He nodded, his eyes filled with a knowing compassion. "Well, family heirlooms to you; just old stuff to other people. Personally, I love it. Just like I love everything about this house. But a prospective buyer might not have the same sense of history that you and I share."

She took another sip of coffee and found herself eyeing his suit—a double-breasted number with a tie that had reached its fashion zenith about five years previously. Feelings of doubt assailed her. Even though he was the only realtor in town, did she have to use him? Sure, they both wanted to keep the house intact, but was he savvy enough to attract a prospective buyer? She looked down at her bare feet on the wood floor. She would give him a try, even if only to redress the childhood cruelties she had undoubtedly inflicted upon him. If it didn't work out, she'd find another realtor in a different town if she had to.

"Do you need me to show you around?"

Ed shook his head. "Nope—I've been here before. You just go on about your business and don't mind me. I'll be fine."

She looked at him with a perplexed frown. "When . . . ?"

"Your father showed me around. When I was here to talk to him about selling that land."

"Ah, yes. Well, I'm going to use the phone in the study. If you need me, just holler." Holler? Why on earth did she use that word? "Um, yell. I'll be in here." Raising her mug to him in a salute, she headed for the desk.

As she sat down, the scent of leather and pipe smoke settled on her, making her feel her father's presence, if only for a minute. She looked behind her, half-expecting to see him standing there, an expression of quiet support and patient understanding crossing his face. She had the strongest urge to call Harriet to see if she felt their father still, too, but instead dialed Andrew's number.

It took a few moments for the receptionist to patch her into Andrew's office. Hitching her feet under her in the desk chair, she waited.

"Andrew Wallace here."

"Hi, Andrew. It's Cassie—Cassandra. Sorry I didn't call you last night—"

He cut her off. "I'm glad you called. I've got Joan Dorfman from BankNorth here in my office right now. We've got a problem."

She closed her eyes, her heart sinking with disappointment. This isn't what she wanted right now. She wanted soft words of warmth and love, not the frigid words of market share and the cost of full-page four-color print ads in *Time* magazine.

Pulling open a desk drawer, she slid out a pad of paper and a pen. "Okay, Andrew. What's the problem?"

Pushing aside the feelings of disappointment, she allowed the comforting, familiar lull of work to fall over her, obliterating all bothersome thoughts of her family, the house, and Sam. The pen scratched over the yellow paper; one page, then two. The back of the third page was covered in price-per-share calculations. Finally, she sat back in the chair and let go with what she did best: the negotiation. Her voice soothed and cajoled the client on the other end of the line. Cassie was so engrossed in what she was doing that she didn't even look up at the brief knocking at the door. She ignored it and swiveled her chair so that her back was to the entranceway.

Cassie continued on the phone. "Joan, I'm sorry you didn't like the sixty-second spot. We had our best people working on it, and we were pleased. We just weren't aware of your negative feelings regarding John Tesh. It will take some juggling to replace him, but it can be done."

She turned the chair around so she could rest her elbows on the desk. As the client talked, Cassie doodled on the pad in front of her, not paying attention to what she was drawing. The Sedgewick twins, in matching sundresses, appeared in front of the desk, making her jump in surprise.

"We brought those Red Radiance clippings for your mother's rose garden and a few clumps of violas for that front bed. We were thinning ours out this morning and thought you could use them."

Cassie stared at them in horror, her finger to her lips to get them to be quiet. The older women managed to look like chastised two-year-olds.

Holding her hand over the receiver, Cassie whispered, "I'm sorry, but I'm on an important phone call."

Selma smiled. "Is that Lucinda? Please tell her that we said hello and that the bridge-club meeting has been moved from Wednesday to Friday."

Thelma broke in. "And please remind her that we need her black-currant-jam recipe. We're going to serve it on Tuesday at the Women's Guild meeting."

Keeping her hand on the receiver, Cassie vigorously shook her head at the two women.

Thelma stepped closer to the desk, reaching for the phone. "Well, I never! It's only a silly jam recipe. Please tell her that I would like to speak with her."

Cassie shook her head again and clutched the receiver closer to her chest. Thelma reached over to take the phone.

"No!"

Joan Dorfman, marketing director for one of the nation's biggest banks, stopped her diatribe. "Excuse me?"

The front door opened again, and Harriet and Sam appeared in the foyer, carrying an assortment of large packing boxes. Sam set his boxes down on the floor, then reached for Harriet's. He nodded toward the two women. "Thelma. Selma. How are y'all doing today?"

Cassie was mortified to find that Selma had tears in her eyes. "Joan, I'm sorry. That wasn't meant for you. I've got to call you back."

Joan kept talking, ignoring Cassie's request.

Ed Farrell came down the stairs and joined the fray in

the study. Sam, with his arm around Selma's shoulders, looked at him oddly. Cassie ducked her head in an effort to hear Joan better, and her gaze rested on her doodlings. Sam's name, in big block letters, danced across the page in thick black ink, while hearts, doodled in all different sizes, covered the rest of the paper.

She jerked her head up to see if anybody else had noticed, and her eyes met Sam's widened ones. She didn't know if he was surprised at what she had drawn or just wondering why she was making Selma Sedgewick cry.

"Yes, Joan. I'm still here. Yes. I'll talk it over with Andrew, but I've really got to go right now. . . ."

Her voice was cut off by the door flinging open, and a large animal—she wasn't sure if it was a dog or a pony— bounded into the house and into the study. It leaped on top of the desk, then onto Cassie's lap, toppling over her and the chair, and yanking the phone cord out of the wall.

"George—sit!"

At Sam's command, the beast trotted away from Cassie and sat down. Cassie struggled to get her T-shirt and robe over her thighs as she stood. Sam reached her side in one long stride.

"Are you all right?"

Furious, the disconnected phone still in her hand, she shouted, "What in the hell was that thing? And why are all you people in here? Doesn't a closed door mean anything to you?"

Selma and Thelma, their chins waggling like a pair of twin turkeys, pulled their shoulders back and left the room. The genteel ladies didn't slam the front door as they left, as if to show Cassie that even if she lacked breeding, they certainly didn't.

Sam scowled at her. "I hope you know you've just insulted two of the finest people I have ever met. Your father would be ashamed."

His words stung. It was one thing to feel ashamed, and that she did in spades. It was another thing to have it pointed out to you. That only made her angrier. She met his gaze head-on.

"You didn't answer my question. What in the hell are you doing here?"

Sam's jaw muscles began throbbing wildly. Harriet stepped between them.

"We came to help with the attic. Remember? We talked about it last night while Sam was patching your ankle. Sam mentioned he had some boxes at the clinic and offered to bring them here for me."

As if in response to Cassie's ungratefulness, the box at the top of the stack slid off and landed with a soft thud on the wood floor. The hairy beast gave one loud, sharp bark, then stumped its fat tail against the rug for an added effect.

Deflated, all Cassie could think to say was "Oh." She placed the telephone receiver on the desktop, but stopped herself in time from sitting down on empty air. Then she caught sight of the hairy mutt.

"What is that thing?"

Sam didn't answer, but seemed intent on staring at her scantily clad body. The scowl reappeared on his face. "And why is Ed Farrell coming down your stairs at ten-thirty in the morning when you're wearing next to nothing?"

Ed's eyes widened, accompanied by a smirk. "Come on, Sam. We aren't in high school anymore. Whatever Cassie chooses to do—whether to herself or her house—is none of your business."

Sam folded his arms across his chest, clenching his hands into fists. His cheek thrummed wildly. "Oh, really. And since when did Cassie give you permission to speak for her?"

"Enough!" Cassie moved to stand between the two men. "Sam Parker. You have some nerve. How dare you question Ed's or anyone's presence in my own house. It's none of your damned business. And besides, he wasn't the one ogling me in my nightshirt and robe." She waved her hand between them to stop him from speaking. "Look, I'm going to go take my shower, then make a phone call to hopefully repair a badly damaged client relationship." She took a deep, cleansing breath. "While I'm gone, Ed, I'd like you to finish up with the appraisal." Turning to Sam, she said, "And I would like you to bring those boxes up to the attic." He frowned at her, prompting her to add, "Please," as an after-thought.

Rubbing her hands over her face, she turned to her sister. "Thanks for your help, Harriet, but I really think I can do all this myself. But if you want to go up to the attic and see if there's anything you want, go ahead. Feel free to take everything. I'm sure there's nothing I'll want. My apartment has absolutely no storage space as it is."

Mustering all the dignity she could, considering she wore next to nothing and hadn't even brushed her teeth yet, she stepped over the hairy beast named George and headed for the stairs. "When y'all leave, please lock the door behind you. And don't forget to take that . . . that . . . him"—she pointed at the animal calmly appraising her from the floor— "with you."

As she climbed the steps, a stunned expression came over her face. Y'all? Had she really said that? Oh, Lord. She'd been in Kansas way too long. She'd better leave soon before it was too late.

The attic door in the middle of the hallway stood open, puddling light onto the floor. Quiet voices slid down the stairs, like ghosts from her past, drawing Cassie toward the attic. The large space with the sloping ceiling and porthole window had been her sanctuary—hers and Harriet's. At first it had been their playroom, and then, as the girls got older and Lucinda had decided she was too old to be climbing so many stairs, it had become their refuge. The attic walls held all the confidences of adolescence and the tears of frustration, disappointment, and loss, as only a young girl could express them. Facing the attic now was like opening the cover on a dusty and cobwebbed scrapbook album. She took a deep breath and began her ascent.

Her high heels clicked on the wooden risers. Her ankle still felt a bit tight from twisting it the night before, but well enough to wear heels—as long as she walked slowly. Which was a good thing, considering she didn't own anything else and going barefoot was not an option.

The voices grew louder as her head reached the attic-floor level. Her view was blocked by the railing slats, and she didn't spot Harriet and Sam until she reached the top step. They were kneeling on the floor in front of a trunk, apparently oblivious to the thick carpet of dust that lay everywhere, and they were laughing at something Sam held in his hand.

Cassie stayed where she was, watching them. It was such an unguarded moment—a sweet slice of time spent in the company of a friend, reliving shared memories over a good laugh. It was almost like a damned Hallmark commercial. She tried to reach for her protective cynicism but only came up with a longing to be a part of that closeness, that sharedness, that belonging.

A cloud of dust drifted across the floor and tickled Cassie's nose. She sneezed, turning both heads in her direction.

"God bless you," they said in unison. Harriet sent a guilty look toward Sam, then stuffed something back inside the trunk.

"What are you looking at?" Cassie tap-tapped her way across the attic floor.

"Oh, nothing. Just some old high school stuff."

Cassie peered into the trunk. "What was so funny?" She looked at where Harriet's hand seemed to be covering something. "What's this?" she asked as she reached under Harriet's fingers and pried something soft and white out of the trunk.

"Oh ... my ..." The bra inserts were still in pretty good condition—still white, fluffy, and perfectly round, like oversized tennis balls. "I can't believe somebody saved these."

Harriet wasn't being completely successful about hiding her laughter. "I think Aunt Lucinda is responsible. She doesn't like to throw away anything."

Sam didn't even try to hide his mirth. With a broad grin, he said, "Harriet and I were just reminiscing about how you went from an A cup to a double-D cup overnight your freshman year. Like nobody would notice."

They both gave up all pretense of hiding their merriment and let out big roars of laughter.

Cassie stood with her arms folded, feeling her anger rise. They were laughing at her, not even trying to hide it. She looked down at the inserts still clutched in her hands, remembering how ridiculous they had looked under her sweater, and felt her lips twitch. Now that she thought about it, it was really pretty damned hysterical. She tossed them back into the trunk, trying to remain stern, but the memory overwhelmed her, and she was soon joining them, laughing until the tears rolled down her face.

When she could breathe, she nudged her sister. "It was all your fault, you know. It was embarrassing having a younger sister with bigger boobs. I was only trying to even the playing field."

Sam looked up at her, his eyes sparkling. "Instead, it looked like you took something off the playing field and stuck it in your shirt."

All three of them buckled with laughter again. Cassie punched Sam on the shoulder as she leaned over the trunk and pulled something out. It ruffled like taffeta, but whatever the fabric, it had been covered with green plastic kudzu leaves all sewn closely together. The only thing that verified it was actually a dress was the neck and armholes.

"My Kudzu Queen gown!" Harriet reached for it, and Cassie dropped it in her waiting arms.

As Cassie rooted around the trunk, she said, "I wouldn't go modeling that to Maddie if I were you. I think she's pretty much kudzu-festivaled out."

Harriet was standing now, holding the dress in front of her. "I know, but it's not all my doing. Lucy Spafford is mostly to blame."

Cassie examined a bundle of Barbie dolls, all roped together with rubber bands at the neck, and dropped them on the floor outside the trunk. "You can have those." She wiped her hands on her skirt. "Who's Lucy Spafford?"

"The bane of Maddie's existence. Since the beginning of junior high, she's made the cheerleading squad, and Maddie hasn't. It wouldn't be so bad if she were a nice girl, but she's real snotty about it to Maddie. Drives her out of her mind to see Lucy in her cheerleading skirt. Maddie swears it's because Lucy's mom—do you remember Doreen Cagle?—is the squad leader." She placed the green dress over her arm and reached for the Barbies. "I don't want to fuel any rumors, but let's just say that I wouldn't be surprised if Lucy being on the squad and not Maddie might have something to do with Lucy's mother. But it's not nice to gossip, so I won't."

Cassie and Sam looked at each other with eyebrows raised. "So what does that have to do with your kudzu dress?"

Harriet kneeled in front of the trunk next to Cassie. "Lucy's the Kudzu Queen this year. I think Maddie's planning on coming down with pneumonia on the day of the festival so she doesn't have to go and see Lucy on her parade float."

Sam stood, brushing dust off his jeans. "I remember the year you were queen, Harriet. That was when somebody dressed the Statue of Liberty in a woman's bra and panties and filled the fountain with bubble bath. I thought I'd bust a gut laughing. But then, when Cassie showed up behind your float, walking a pig dressed in kudzu, I just about died." He shook his head, smiling broadly. "They never did find out who did that to the statue and the fountain."

Both Sam and Harriet looked at Cassie, but she remained silent, pointedly studying the inside lid of the trunk. She kicked off her shoes and tucked her feet under her as she rooted under a pile of stuffed animals. Her hands touched something curved and smooth, and she pulled it out. The old pipe still hinted of the aroma of tobacco, and Cassie closed her eyes, the picture of her father as clear to her at that moment as if he were sitting next to her.

Harriet came and knelt next to her. "It's Daddy's old

pipe. Remember when you hid it in here when you were trying to get him to stop smoking?'' She smiled gently, taking the pipe from Cassie and running her finger slowly down the stem. ''I think he tried to quit, for a week or something, but he ended up just buying a new one.'' She handed it back to Cassie. ''You can keep it if you like.''

Cassie nodded, her words crammed into her throat with unshed tears. She took the pipe and held it closely to her chest. ''Thanks,'' she managed.

''Hey, what's this?'' Sam had walked past the area illuminated by the bare bulbs overhead and pulled out a wooden box from the dark corner of the attic. ''It looks like an antique writing box.''

He walked over to the sisters and placed it on the floor, a billow of dust rising in its wake. It was made of a dark wood, probably cherry or mahogany, with tarnished brass hinges and a nameplate on the front. It was sloped on top with a ledge at the bottom, as if to hold reading material. Sam pointed to a key sticking in the keyhole. ''That's certainly not much of a challenge, is it?''

Cassie moved to get a better look at the nameplate: HRM. ''That certainly narrows it down to about fifty people. There's been a Harrison Robert Madison in our family in every generation—except for ours. Daddy didn't have a son to leave the name.''

Harriet interrupted. ''So I got stuck with it. I always wanted a pretty girl's name like you, Cassie, and instead I got stuck with Harriet. Please give me credit for not inflicting such torture on my own children.''

Absently, Cassie rubbed the nameplate. ''I guess he was waiting for one of us to use it.''

She looked up at Harriet. ''Well, this could be Daddy's, although I don't ever remember seeing it before. Do you want to open it?''

Harriet shook her head. ''No. You're the oldest; you do it.''

Kneeling in front, Cassie gingerly turned the key, half-expecting it not to work. Like Sam, she felt there needed to be more of a mystery to finding a locked writing box in the attic.

With one last glance at Sam and Harriet, she opened the lid. The smell of old wood and stain wafted out of the box as the three of them peered inside. Scattered around the bottom of the box were stamped envelopes, with an elegant handwriting on the front. The capital letters in the words were enormous, with swirled tails and large loops. It could only have been written by a woman. On top of the pictures lay an old black-and-white photograph of a man and a woman standing in front of a small two-door sports car.

Gingerly, Cassie lifted the picture and showed it to Harriet. "Look, it's Daddy and his old car, but I'm pretty sure that's not Mama." She peered closely at the woman, her head swathed in a chiffon scarf knotted under her chin, and pointy cat's-eyes sunglasses blocking her eyes.

Harriet took the picture and stared at it for a moment. "That's definitely not Mama." Her gaze met Cassie's, an unspoken question between them.

Cassie reached inside and sifted some of the envelopes off the top, only to find more of the same underneath. All were addressed to her father, at this house. She checked the postmarks. All she could see were postmarked in Walton except for one that came from Atlanta. The dates on all of them were from 1962 to 1963. She did a mental calculation. Her parents were married in 1965, and she was born in 1966. She looked up excitedly.

"These might be from Mama!"

She picked up the one with the Atlanta postmark, gingerly opening the neatly slit top, and pulled out a letter.

April 10, 1963
My dearest Harry,
    You are a father. Our child was born this morning at two thirty-eight. The baby weighed 8 pounds and 7 ounces, is as long and skinny as a string bean, and looks just like you.

I have decided it would be best if you didn't know if you had a son or daughter. This way your dreams of your child will end in babyhood and you won't see it grow into a young man or woman in your mind. Still, I hope you will always hold this child in your heart, as I will. This is the hardest decision I've ever had to face, but know it is the right one. Your heart belongs to another, and even though your intentions were good in offering to make an honest woman out of me and be a father to our child, I can not stand in your way of happiness. The bitterness would find its way into our home and destroy whatever love there might be. I would rather see it die now, while in its youth and passion, than see it wither and fade. This way, I can live with my beautiful memories and never have to face the loss. Perhaps I am a coward, or maybe I'm too prideful, but this is the way it has to be.

I have been promised that our baby will go to a loving family, and you shall have your true love. And I, well, I will be content knowing that I loved you once, and those days were the happiest of my life. I will treasure them always.

Please do not try to find me or our child. My parents sent me to visit family in Louisiana for two months and then to Europe until after the baby was born. When I return, this will be behind us. You don't even have to acknowledge me when we pass on the street. I'll understand. And the new parents and our baby will be getting to know each other. This is a tender process, and I don't think it should be disturbed. I know it goes against your nature to let things take care of themselves, but please respect their privacy.

I wish you nothing but happiness and joy the rest of your days. I love you. Always.

E.

Cassie stared at the letter, her voice dry. Without a word, she handed it to Harriet. When Harriet finished reading, she looked up at her sister, eyes wide.

"Our mother's name was Catherine Anne. If these aren't from her, then . . . ?" Her gaze strayed to the woman in the picture.

Sam spoke, and both women looked startled, as if they'd forgotten he was still there. "What is it?"

Harriet handed the letter back. "Do you think he should see it? He might . . . know something."

Cassie looked at Sam, noticing the way the murky light in the attic made his eyes glow an intense blue. They were warm and filled with compassion, and Cassie knew right away he was one of those rare doctors who had a remarkable bedside manner.

"Will you keep it confidential?"

"Of course." He took the letter from her and read it.

Regardless of the dust and dirt on the attic floor, Cassie collapsed on it, her back against the large trunk. "Well? What do you think?"

He squatted in front of her and handed her the letter. Feeling as if she had invaded somebody's privacy, she tucked the letter and picture back on top of the stack and closed the lid.

Sam grimaced, displaying a deep dimple made for kissing on his left cheek that she'd never noticed before. Quietly, he said, "Well, beyond the obvious implication that you two might have a sibling out there, I think there's a story worthy of a novel behind the words of this one letter."

Clutching the box tightly, Cassie's face hardened. "She wasn't my mother. I don't think I want to know any more of that story."

Sam smoothed his hand over the letter box, brushing Cassie's fingers. "It was before your parents were married, so it would appear your father was faithful to your mother. If anything, I think this letter is a testament to how much he really loved her. This 'E,' whoever she is, knew that what was between your parents was the real thing and bravely stepped out of the picture.''

Cassie scowled at him. ''My father had a baby with that woman. I can't imagine that she really stepped out of his life forever. I bet the rest of those letters are from her, begging for him to come back.''

Harriet touched Cassie's shoulder. ''There's only one way to find out.'' She looked pointedly at the box.

Looking down, Cassie furrowed her eyebrows. ''Yeah. I guess I should. Maybe it will hold some clues as to what happened to the baby.'' She glanced up at her sister. ''Unless you'd like to do the honors.''

''No. I think you should do it first—and then share them with me. Sort of like how you used to do—always protecting me from something that might hurt.''

With a lopsided grin, Cassie struggled to stand, still clutching the worn box. ''I knew better than to come up to the attic. I really did. This house—it's like quicksand. The more I struggle to extricate myself, the harder it is to get free.''

Sam's voice was even, carefully measured. ''Feeling scared, Cassie?''

Cassie glanced at wide blue eyes before brushing by him, headed toward the stairwell. ''No. But I am upset. How would you like to find out that your father had a lover before he married your mother?'' She shook her head, blowing out a heavy breath. ''I wish I'd never come up here.''

Sam held her back with his hand. ''Maybe this is a chance to get to know your father better. Even now, after he's gone.''

She pulled away. ''This isn't part of him that I want to know about.'' Straightening her shoulders, she faced Harriet. ''Stay up here as long as you like. I've got some business stuff I need to take care of.''

Harriet leaned against a trunk, looking suddenly exhausted. ''I'll probably go through a few more boxes before calling it quits. I know how eager you are to get through with this.'' She waved weakly, and Cassie nodded.

Harriet's face, for a moment, looked so much like that of

the young girl she had once been, her eyes a mirror of the gentle soul that lay within. A slice of guilt wormed its way through Cassie's veins, prodding gently at her heart. She loved this house, this attic, and all its memories. So why was she so eager to move on? Was she scared that if she stayed too long she'd forget who she'd become? Who she *was*?

Tucking the letter box snugly under her arm, she began her descent, her free hand fingering the gold hearts dangling from the frail chain around her neck.

Chapter 9

"Snake in the grass!"

The children of Walton had congregated on Madison Lane and were now standing in two lines on opposite curbs. The snake was a blindfolded Sarah Frances. She stood in the middle of the street as the children tried to cross the space between the lines without being caught.

The shrill calls of the children in the dusky air slowed Cassie's pace. Running at night was certainly cooler, if not less humid, and at least she didn't have to bump into anybody she knew while sweating like a horse. Or "glowing," as Aunt Lucinda referred to it.

She stopped completely to watch the children, a smile tugging at her mouth. It was so much like the summers of her youth, when all she had to worry about was saving enough of her allowance for the Friday-night movie and running faster than the snake in the middle. Cassie breathed deeply, smelling the freshly cut grass and her own sweat. Things didn't change much in Walton, but somehow, at that moment, it didn't seem like such a bad thing.

Heavy footsteps pounded behind her. She turned to see

Sam jogging toward her. He stopped, panting heavily, his hands on his hips.

Her heart seemed to skip a beat, and she turned back to the children. Sarah Frances had taken hold of somebody's pigtail, and the girl was shrieking for her to let go.

"I see you took my advice about running at night. It's a lot better, huh? Not like New York, where you need an armed guard once the sun sets."

Cassie refused to argue with him. She tilted her head into the warm breeze, remembering the same sights and smells that had drifted into her bedroom through the screened window all those years ago. Her breathing slowed, reaching a harmonious rhythm with the cicadas and crickets.

"As your doctor, I don't remember telling you it's all right to run on that ankle so soon. You should give it at least a week."

Reluctantly, she turned her attention toward Sam. "Right. And I'd be as big as a house if I didn't run off some of that food everybody's been shoving at me. The town's conspiring to make me fat, I swear. Either that or they want to send me into cardiac arrest. I've never seen so many fried foods in my life. They seem to know just what to tempt me with." She shifted her feet, watching the children once more. "Besides, the ankle feels fine. Good as new."

Sam watched with her, laughing softly as Joey pinched Sarah Frances on her bottom as he sped by his blindfolded sister. He cleared his throat. "Since you asked, I'll be happy to tell you firsthand that I won today's election. I'm the newest member of the town council."

"Hmm?" Cassie murmured, mesmerized by the padding of bare feet on the asphalt as children scurried back and forth across the lines. Offhandedly, she said, "Oh. Congratulations."

She continued to watch the children, a wistful smile on her face. "Remember playing that when we were younger? I don't think I was ever caught. I must have been too fast for everybody."

Sam looked at her from the corner of his eye. "You think

so, huh? I remember that people were afraid to catch you because when they did, you would hit them. Really hard.''

Cassie turned to face him. "How would you know? I don't remember you ever being there."

His smile faded slightly. When he spoke, his voice was low, almost a drawl. "Oh, I was there. You were just too busy chasing Joe Warner to notice anybody else."

She glared at him in the fading light. "That's ancient history. Everybody else seems to have forgotten it, so why don't you? You seem to remember an awful lot of bad things about me. I hope your memory is as good with important stuff."

He moved closer to her, and wild thoughts of whether or not she used enough deodorant ran rampant in her head. She tried to turn her attention back to the game, but his nearness unnerved her. Bending over, she began stretching her hamstrings, if only for an excuse to move away. Unfortunately, it only brought his strong calves at eye level, making her hot and flustered all over again. She closed her eyes.

"After casting my vote, I went over to Town Hall to see what kind of public records I could access about your father's child. Mr. Harmon said you'd already been there."

Cassie jerked back up. "Did you really?" Somehow the fact that he cared enough to check on her mystery sibling himself surprised her.

"Yes, I did. Really." He gave her a facetious smirk. "Although I knew before going there that the adoption records would be closed to all but the involved parties. Not that I think your father's name would have been used, anyway."

Laughter spilled from the street as a mother called her children in for supper, the sound safe and comforting to Cassie. She turned her head back to Sam. "You're right—there was nothing there to help me. I think my next step will be to go to the library and check old newspapers for birth records for April of 1963. It's a long shot, but I have no idea where else to go. The letter was postmarked Atlanta, so I'll check the Atlanta papers, too. But I have a feeling that whoever this woman was, her priority was keeping her privacy and the baby's identity a secret.''

"That's a good idea. Have you had a chance to look through the rest of the box yet?"

She shook her head, feeling chastised. "No. Not yet. I've been busy. But I'll get to it."

He nodded, watching her closely for a moment. "If you don't find anything between the letters and the library, I'm going to Atlanta at the end of the month for a medical conference. I can check hospital records while I'm there."

Two frown lines formed between Cassie's eyebrows. "Why are you helping me out? What do you want from me?"

Sweat beaded on his forehead and dripped down his face, but he didn't wipe it away. "It's called helping out a friend. Perhaps that's not a familiar term in the big city. And no, I don't expect payment. I enjoy challenges." He sent her a pointed look.

"Good. Because I happen to be engaged." Why did she say that? He had said nothing that might be construed as an interest in a physical relationship, and she had gone and blurted that out. Mercifully, he only raised his eyebrows, giving him that wizened look she had come to admire from afar.

With a final glance at the disbursing children, she started to walk away. "I've got to get back. Harriet wants to talk about plans for a wedding shower. She can't seem to take no for an answer."

Sam began to walk with her. "But you could say thank you. Assuming you remember how."

She halted, putting her hands on her hips. She stopped so suddenly that Sam bumped into her, grabbing her upper arms to stop them both from falling over. He didn't let go.

"Thank you, Sam. For taking the trouble on my account. I do appreciate it." Gently, she pulled away and resumed walking.

Sam fell into step beside her. "It's a great story. I know;

that's easy to say because it's not about my parents. But I'd like to find out what happened to 'E' and her child."

Cassie looked down at her feet, concentrating on not stepping on the sidewalk cracks, recalling the little verse she and Harriet would sing as they walked to school: "Step on a crack and break your daddy's back." Purposefully, she stepped on the space between two squares, silencing the singsong voices in her head. "Well, you and Harriet both. She thinks it's this wonderfully romantic story. This horrible thing has happened to this woman, she's losing both the man she loves and the child they created, yet she wishes him joy and happiness for the rest of his life. And then tells him she'll love him always." Her voice caught, and she coughed to hide it. "I wonder . . . I wonder if she ever found somebody else. Had more children."

She stopped in front of the house and looked up at the sky, the same sky from her childhood, with the fading ribbons of pink and red strewn on the horizon and framed by the graceful limbs of the oak trees. It was as comforting to her as a mother's kiss. "Even the cynic in me wants to believe that she did."

Sam stood close, and she could feel the heat from his body. When he spoke, his breath brushed her hair. "Maybe there's only one love for everyone out there. And if you miss it, that's it. You don't get another chance. You can hang around waiting for them to be free and then hope they'll love you back, but it's all pretty much chance."

Cassie tilted her head to look him in the face. "You don't really believe that, do you? That out of the millions and millions of people out there, there's only one for each of us?"

An air conditioner whirred to life from the bedroom window above them. Sam's face stilled in the near darkness as he spoke. "Angelfish mate for life. When one of them dies, the other one simply floats to the bottom of the ocean and dies, too."

Cassie tried to add levity to her voice but only half-succeeded. "And black widows eat their mates." She tried to laugh but couldn't. "I'm glad I'm not an angelfish, then, or maybe I would have crawled up into a ball and died after Joe." She regretted saying that, but Sam seemed to bring out the confessor in her.

Sam sat on the bottom step, crossing his long legs at the ankles, and Cassie joined him as if it were the most natural thing in the world. "Maybe you did. There's lots of ways to die that don't involve physical death."

She stretched out her legs, leaning over her toes to stretch the hamstrings. "Stick to doctoring, Sam. You're no philosopher. I'm very much alive and kicking."

Sam remained silent, watching her.

She waved her hands in front of his face. "See? I'm here. And I'm just fine."

Finally, he spoke. "I see." His tone was unconvincing. "Maybe Joe wasn't your one and only."

Leaning back, Cassie rested her elbows on the next step. Serious now, she angled her head back and watched the evening stars poke holes in the growing darkness. "I know that now. All anyone has to do is watch Harriet and Joe together to know that there could never be anybody else for either one of them. At least not on that level. But try telling that to a twenty-year-old." A fine sigh escaped her, the sadness of it surprising even Cassie. "Oh, to have the wisdom of thirty-five at the age of twenty."

Sam leaned back, too. "But why all this time? Why did it take you so long to forgive and forget?"

Cassie straightened, facing him. "It's none of your business, Sam. You have a nasty habit of sticking your nose into things that have nothing to do with you."

Sam remained where he was, casually studying her. "It wasn't so much Joe, was it? It was more your loss of pride. And you Madisons have enough pride to fertilize a field."

She leaped off the step and stood in front of Sam, her hands on her hips. "You have a lot of nerve. You don't know anything about me—anything about the kind of life I live now. I'm very happy with the way things have worked out, and it's never even occurred to me to return here."

She began marching up the stairs, but he blocked her way with an arm stretched out to the opposite railing. "The truth hurts, doesn't it? And I know a lot more about you than you think."

"Excuse me, please." Her voice thickened with sarcasm.

He stood slowly but without moving out of her way. Their faces were only inches apart. "One more question—and this is one I asked your father but never got an answer. Why did he never visit you in New York for all those years?"

Surprised by the question, Cassie took a step back. "It's not because I never asked him to, because I did in every letter and every phone call. But he wanted *me* to come home and visit, and I wouldn't. So we just talked on the phone and met once a year in Atlanta. It was a neutral-enough place for both of us, I guess."

"I guess that means you come by your stubborn streak honestly."

She ignored his jibe. "Can I get by now, please?"

As he stepped out of the way, he said, "Oh, just one thing before I leave that I thought you should know. One of my first acts as town councilmember will be to find support for an ordinance to protect over twenty historical buildings in this town. I'm also preparing the groundwork to have large chunks of the town, including your house, placed on the National Registry. It shouldn't affect you at all—unless you decide to do something with this house besides sell it to a nice, well-deserving family."

She stared at him in disbelief. "You've got to be kidding. This is *my* house, and it's nobody else's business what I decide to do with it. Now, please get off my property. Nobody"—she wagged her finger at him—"not you or any of your small-town, small-minded people are going to tell me what I can or cannot do with my own house."

He paused for a minute, chewing on the corner of his mouth. Slowly, he turned around, speaking in a drawl as he walked away. "Good night, Cassie. Was a pleasure as always."

Her only answer was the slamming of the front door.

* * *

Cassie sat under the large circular window of the library, trying to shade the screen of the ancient microfiche machine from the full sun streaming in. Her back ached, and the beginnings of a headache began to throb in her temples from squinting her eyes at the blurry words on the screen. Computers at the Walton Public Library were still a thing of the future, and Cassie cursed under her breath again at the ignominy of having to use something as archaic as microfiche. The damned thing belonged in a museum.

She had checked every birth and adoption announcement for the month of April 1963 in not only the *Walton Sentinel*, but also the *Atlanta Journal-Constitution*. She had jotted down all the pertinent information for mothers whose first names started with the letter "E" but realized she'd need help to follow up on all of them. Not that she expected anything to turn up from these voluntary announcements. Sighing, she slid out the tray holding the film and began winding it back into the cartridge. What a waste of time. She should have just hired a private investigator to begin with. Andrew and her life were waiting in New York. She had no business allowing her feet to get mired in the thick Georgia clay.

Clutching her notebook, Cassie jogged down the library steps and toward the curb where the Mercedes was parked. That was one thing good about this town: One never had to hunt for a parking space. Or pay for it, either.

Sliding into the driver's seat, she stuck the key into the ignition and turned. Instead of the soft hum of the engine, it choked, then did a fine impression of a dry heave. Successive tries yielded the same result, the only addition being Cassie's cussing, which grew exponentially worse with each key turn.

A familiar truck pulled alongside her car. With a wave and a honk, Sam guided his vehicle into the parking space in front of hers. Cassie ignored him, turning the key once more. Grind, cough, splutter, splutter.

Sam came to stand next to the passenger side of her car, speculatively eyeing the thick cloud of smoke billowing out of her exhaust. With a barely concealed grin, he drawled, "Cassie, I'm afraid that dog won't hunt."

Ignoring him, she tried the ignition one more time. A hideous clunk banged under the hood, followed by a thick cloud of smoke from the exhaust pipe.

"I'll call my father to have him tow it into the station and have a look at it." Before she could protest, he had flipped open his cell phone and was speaking to his father's service station. Sam wore an Atlanta Braves baseball hat, the front brim casting his face in shadow as he talked. She had always hated baseball hats on men, wondering what the appeal was. Until now. There was something irresistible about the way Sam Parker looked in a stupid baseball hat.

Cassie swung herself out from the car and slammed the door. "What's wrong with it?" Her voice sounded high and panicked. She had to remember to lower it when she told Andrew about his ailing baby.

Sam closed his phone, then tipped up the brim of his hat. "Dunno. These foreign cars can be mighty temperamental and will throw fits to show you who's boss. Don't know why people buy them." A lopsided grin lit his face. "Hey, I thought you weren't talking to me."

"I'm not. I'll stay here and wait for the tow truck. You may leave."

He looked at her as if he found something vastly amusing. His smile faded as he spotted Ed Farrell approaching them on the sidewalk.

Ed's drawl almost hid the animosity in his voice. "So, it's Walton's own king of antiprogress. Forgive me if I don't congratulate you, Sam. But I can only see your winning as the beginning of Walton's untimely death. Tell me when the funeral is and I'll be sure to come."

Sam's face closed, all signs of humor quickly erased. "I'll do that." Without another word, he turned his back on Ed to face Cassie. "I guess you'll be needing a ride. Where can I take you?"

Ed stepped around the car to stand beside Cassie. "Car trouble, sugar? I've got my nice air-conditioned Cadillac parked right on the corner if you need a ride. It's the least I could do for a client." His smile broadened. "And a beautiful one at that."

She was too old and wise to fall for that kind of flattery, but it couldn't be helped. She smiled up at him. "Thank you, Ed. I'm on the way home if you wouldn't mind." Turning to catch Sam's expression, her satisfied smile faded. He wasn't even watching her. Instead, his attention was focused on Mary Jane Harden walking down the sidewalk, her hands clutching bags from Walton's Drug Emporium.

"Hey, y'all." She beamed at everyone, but her warmest smile was for Sam.

Sam took her packages and stored them in the back of his truck. "I'll give you a lift back to the clinic."

"Thanks, Sam." She faced Cassie. "Do y'all have your tickets yet for the Kudzu Festival? We're selling them quickly, so you'd better hurry. Don't forget—this year we're having a prize for the cutest couple." She indicated Ed and Cassie with her index finger. "Are y'all going together?"

Ed put an arm on Cassie's elbow. "Well, I hadn't quite gotten around to asking, but now's as good as time as any. Would you do me the honor, sugar?"

Flustered, all she could do was stammer, "Um, well, uh, I probably won't be here. When is it again?"

Mary Jane stepped closer. "It's this weekend. Surely you won't be leaving before then?"

"Uh, no—unless Ed sells my house for me by then."

"Now, sugar, you know nothing would make me happier, but it's probably not likely. I'd love for you to do me the honor of being my date."

Cornered, there was nothing she could do but agree. She watched as Mary Jane completed her web.

"Sam, you don't have a date yet, do you? Seeing as how we both have to leave right from work, why don't we just go together?" She reached her hands around Sam's forearm and squeezed.

Sam's face was closed, his thoughts unreadable. He smiled gently. "Sure. That's a great idea."

Cassie reached for Ed's elbow. "Come on, Ed. Let's go. I'll call you, Mary Jane, and we'll do lunch." As an afterthought, she called over her shoulder, "Sam, tell your dad I'll call him about the car."

They walked to the corner where a large white Fleetwood monopolized the space like a hulking polar bear. Ed opened the door for her, and she slid onto dark red leather upholstery. All it needed was a crystal chandelier hanging from the ceiling to complete the look of a bordello.

Ed crawled in behind the steering wheel and pulled out onto the street. "Like it, huh?"

Cassie was busy staring at the large gold pinkie ring on his finger. "Uh, the ring? Yeah. Sure. It's very nice."

He lifted a hairy finger, the gold catching the light. "It sure is nice, but I was talking about the car. Never thought Ed Farrell would be driving one of these, did you?"

His grin was wide enough for Cassie to see the gold fillings on his back teeth. "You've certainly come far, Ed. You're a real tribute to this town." Her sentiments were genuine. He had come far from the dirt farm where he'd grown up. She looked down at her hands in her lap, remembering the boy with soiled clothes and how she and her friends had teased him. Reaching over, she patted him on his arm. "I'm real proud of you."

Under his dark skin, she could have sworn she saw him flush. She assumed it was from pleasure but couldn't tell because he turned his face toward the side window.

After a few moments of silence, he said, "Just ran into Lou-Lou walking past the library. Said you were doing some research."

Cassie sat back against the cushy seat. "Now, that was something I never expected to see: Lou-Lou Whittaker in a library. She told me she was there to check out books for you on American antiques." She stopped before adding what an additional surprise that had been.

Ed shrugged, turning left on Oak Street. "Yeah, well, I'm

trying to educate myself on things they don't teach you in community college. I want to be able to furnish my house the way rich folks do, and I have a feeling going to the furniture section at Sears isn't going to cut it.''

Cassie smiled to herself, wondering yet again where he'd gathered his get-up-and-go.

He turned onto Madison Lane. ''So, what were you researching?''

Her fingers found their way to the necklace around her neck. If her sibling's mother still lived in Walton, she needed to be very careful about protecting her identity. At least for now. ''I'm doing some genealogy research on my family. It's all the rage now, and I thought that while I had time to kill, waiting to unload the house, that I might try to be useful.''

Ed nodded as he pulled the car into the circular driveway in front of her house. Harriet's minivan was parked farther down the drive. He got out of the car and walked around to let her out. ''Just give me a call if you need a lift anywhere. I'd be happy to do it for my prettiest client.''

Obviously, the waves of political correctness had bypassed this neck of the woods. ''Thanks, Ed. Oh, and by the way, just to let you know. You've probably already heard, but Sam told me that he's petitioning the town council for a moratorium on any further development. Not that I think it will affect the sale of my house; it might in the long run if we decide to exercise another option for the property besides keeping it residential. Is there anything we can do now to keep our options open?''

Ed's face turned an unhealthy shade of red. ''That son of a . . . damn! No, I didn't know.'' He reached for the cell phone clipped to his belt. ''I've gotta make some phone calls. I'll get back to you.''

Without a good-bye, he flung open his car door and left in a hasty gust of red dust.

Cassie turned and mounted the porch steps, an odd feeling of sanctuary possessing her as she approached the front door. It had been a long time since she'd felt that old feeling. The familiar pace of work had been a fine substitute. She stepped onto the top step, then stopped. The squeak of the floorboard, or maybe the scent of the boxwoods, brought the memory flash so clear-cut, it made her skin tighten. She could almost hear the snatches of old conversations coming through the screened windows, reminding her of the many nights she had lain in bed listening to the comforting voices of her parents downstairs, and then, later, of her father and Aunt Lucinda. The memory was like food to her soul, and she held her breath, unwilling to let go of it.

The front door opened, and Harriet stood on the threshold, holding a cordless phone. Placing her hand over the receiver, she said, "It's a guy from *Preservation* magazine. He's doing an article on endangered historical structures and wants to know when it would be a good time to come out and take pictures of the house. Says Sam Parker gave him your name and number."

Cassie's eyes widened, all peaceful thoughts deserting her completely. "He what?" She took the phone from her sister, pushing the OFF button without speaking to the person on the other end. Harriet watched as Cassie marched up the stairs. She could almost feel the accusing stares of her ancestors from the portraits on the wall. Her M.B.A. training and years of working in New York had taught her to ignore that twinge of conscience. "That no-good damned redneck sonuvabitch. He's going to regret messing with me." She stomped into her room and began rummaging in her garbage can for the business card he had given her. It was time to show Dr. Parker that she could play dirty, too. She punched the numbers on the phone with a shaking finger, trying to erase the image of Great-great-great-grandfather Madison's accusing glare.

Chapter 10

The older woman's voice on the other end of the phone surprised Cassie. She sat down on the small bench in front of her dressing table.

"Hello? I'm trying to reach Sam . . . uh, Dr. Parker. I might have reached the wrong number."

"Oh, no. This is his mother. He forwards his calls here when he comes to visit, and I'm expecting him soon. Who's calling?"

Cassie caught sight of her reflection in the mirror. Her geometric bob was in dire need of a trim, and her roots were no longer exactly matching the chestnut brown of the rest of her hair. "This is Cassandra Madison. Perhaps I should try at the clinic. . . ."

"Cassie Madison! Why, this is a pleasure. So sorry to hear about your daddy. What a fine man. This town will certainly miss him."

"Thank you, Mrs. Parker." She vaguely remembered Sam's mother. Mrs. Parker had worked in the lunchroom at the high school. She was round with gray hair, even then, fixed tightly in a bun on top of her head, with lines crisscrossing her cheeks from being in the sun too much. But her smile brightened her plain face and warmed the room around her. What Cassie remembered most was the way Mrs. Parker would give her second helpings of dessert without an admonishing stare or a pointed glance at her thighs. She pictured her now wearing a sleeveless apron with lace frills on the edge.

Cassie sat up straighter, pulling her shoulders back. "Thank you so much for the sweet-potato pie. That was so kind of you. I've put it in the freezer for when Aunt Lucinda comes back. I remember it was her favorite. I must get your recipe before I go back home." Recipe? She didn't even think she could remember how to turn on an oven. "I've been meaning to write you a thank-you note, but it's been so busy—"

Mrs. Parker cut her off. "Oh, no need for that. Take all your time to grieve, and don't worry about no thank-yous. Just know you're in our thoughts and prayers."

Tears parked themselves in Cassie's eyes. God—where was that coming from? If all it took to set her off these days were kind words, she needed to get back to New York as soon as possible before she softened too much. She couldn't even imagine Andrew's reaction if she burst into tears every time a client said he didn't like her idea.

"Thank you, Mrs. Parker. I appreciate that. Um, could you have Sam call me when he gets in?"

"He's at the clinic right now. Would you like the number?"

Cassie glanced back down at the business card. "Ah, let's see . . . no. It looks like I have it. I meant to dial it to begin with, but my eyes switched lines on me."

Mrs. Parked laughed. "Happens to all of us as we grow older. I wish my arms would grow longer so I could hold a book at a distance I can read it."

Older? Thirty-five wasn't old. Well, maybe here, where most of the girls from her graduating class were not only married but had several children by now. "I guess so. Well, sorry to have bothered you. . . ."

"No bother at all. And I'm glad you called. I'd like more

of a chance to chat. Why don't you come by for dinner tonight?''

A flood of panic rushed over her. "Ah, tonight? No, I really couldn't impose . . .''

"It's no trouble at all. When I cook fried chicken, I make a whole mess of it, so there will be plenty to go around. Sam will be here, too.'' She made it sound as if Sam would be the icing on the cake.

Cassie stared at her reflection again in the mirror, her eyes looking like those of a condemned woman. "Well, thank you. What time would you like me to be there?''

She finished the conversation, then dialed the clinic while trying to revive her anger. Mary Jane picked up the phone.

"Cassie, hi. Are you calling to make lunch plans?''

"Uh, yes, actually. Are you free tomorrow? Thought we'd do that lunch at the diner we talked about.''

"Great. I normally take lunch at about one o'clock. I'll check with Sam and let you know.''

Cassie swallowed. "Speaking of Sam, is he there? I need to speak with him.''

There was a brief pause. "Actually, no. He just left. Shall I leave a message?''

Another pause as Cassie chewed her lip, wondering how much she should tell Mary Jane. "Um, no, thanks. I'll just see him tonight.''

She didn't realize how insinuating those words were until after she'd already said them. With some perverse pleasure, she didn't elaborate.

"Okay, then. I'll let you know about tomorrow. 'Bye, Cassie.''

As she hung up the phone, her shoulders slumped. She needed to go back and take a refresher course in assertiveness training. If she kept it up, Andrew would never recognize her when she got back. She looked back at her reflection. Her cheeks were softer, rounder, pinker. The perpetual circles under her eyes had faded, making her brown eyes brighter. She leaned forward on her elbows and sighed. Perhaps that would be a good thing.

Her gaze caught sight of the writing box on the dressing table behind her, and she swiveled to stare at it. She hadn't opened it once since it was brought down from the attic, feeling that in reading the letters she was trespassing on her father's secret. If he hadn't told her, he obviously didn't want her to know.

With slow steps, she approached and opened the lid. Her father was dead now, and if she had a sibling somewhere, she wanted to know about it. She thought briefly of her father's will, the house he had left her, and his obvious motivation for doing so and smiled softly to herself. This wouldn't be the first time in her life she'd gone against his wishes. He had been a lovable but bullheaded man, but it was a trait that ran thick in her veins.

Her fingers gently rifled through the small stack of letters, feeling the brittleness of old paper against her skin, and studied the beautiful handwriting of the unknown woman once again.

A glossy corner stuck out of the stack, and Cassie pinched it between her fingernails to pull it out. She looked at the photograph in surprise, recognizing her sixth-grade school picture. There she was, standing next to Mrs. Browning, her knee socks drooping around her ankles and her hair part looking like a fault line. Harriet stood nearby in the front row, looking perfect and wearing a hair bow that matched her outfit. Joe and Sam stood next to each other in the back row, making horns over each other's heads. Sam's eyes were invisible, the sunlight reflecting brightly off the wide frames of his glasses. Cassie squinted, trying to recall knowing Sam in sixth grade, but the memory eluded her.

She was about to slip the photo back into the box when she noticed the tall figure in the back row, standing slightly apart from the other children. Ed Farrell. He had been held back two different years, and sixth was the first time they had been in the same grade. His eyes were downcast, as if to remain invisible to the camera. She could see the top of his stained overalls and remembered with abject embarrassment

how she and the rest of the children had teased him mercilessly for being a bona-fide redneck.

With heavy remorse, she dropped the picture back into
the box as if she'd been burned, wondering why it had been
put there instead of downstairs in her father's desk with the
rest of their school pictures.

Tentatively, her hand floated over the stack of letters like
a curious butterfly before settling down and pulling out the
first yellowed envelope. Bringing it over to the bed, she sat
down and opened it.

September 25, 1962
My dearest Harry,

    *My daddy said he spotted you waiting for me after
church last Sunday. When he asked me why you hadn't
been to hear the sermon, I said it was because you
were Episcopalian. I thought his head would explode,
it turned so red.*

    *I always knew this would be a problem, which is
why I insisted we be quiet about us. But it seems now
we are found out. Daddy says he doesn't want me to
see you anymore. I think things between us are too
far gone for that, don't you? I've never disobeyed
him before, but what I feel for you makes me forget
everything else.*

    *I wear the beautiful necklace you gave me every
day, but I'm careful to keep it under my blouse. I like
feeling it so near my heart, and it keeps you in my
mind until I can see you again.*

                        Love,
                        E.

Cassie sat for a long time with the letter opened on her
lap, her emotions moving rapidly between guilt, disgust, and
a strong dose of romance. Eventually, she got up and put it
back into the writing box, gently closing the lid.

* * *

Cassie found Harriet in the attic again. Her sister was leaning over an antique sewing table, trying to reach a small box on a shelf behind it.

"You're going to hurt yourself, Har. Let me get it. There are advantages to being big and bulky, you know."

Harriet stepped aside to let Cassie grab the box. "You're not big and bulky. I always thought of you as Wonder Woman from TV. You were so tall and strong. I wanted to be like you."

A frown puckered Cassie's brow. If Harriet had ever had one jealous thought in her head regarding Cassie, this was the first she'd ever heard about it. Her gaze slid over to Harriet, who had just sat on an old steamer trunk. "I don't believe that for a minute, Har. All of the boys at Walton High went for the blond petite type—not the Amazon brunet. Considering how tall I am, I was pretty invisible."

Harriet shook her head slowly, her head tilted to the side. A narrow beam of sunlight stretched from the dormer window and touched her hair, spinning it into gold. "You're supposed to be the smart one, but sometimes I'm not so sure." Her mouth held a silly grin. "So, are you still mad at me?"

Reaching into an old appliance box, Cassie looked up. "About what?"

"About my thinking that daddy and his lady friend had a terrific romance."

Cassie shrugged, burying her head in the box again. "No, I'm not angry. Even I have to admit there's something terribly romantic about it all. I read a letter today. I'll show it to you later." She scratched her nose, feeling the dust tickle it. "I didn't see any letters dated after that one we read up here—the one about the baby. I have to admit I'm pretty relieved about that. Maybe the love affair really was over before Daddy married Mama."

Harriet turned to look out the small window. "I hope we

find her. I'd like to know that ... that everything worked
out for her."

Cassie offered a gentle smile. "Things usually do, I think.
I lived, after all." She ducked her head back into the box
and pulled out a past-its-prime naked baby doll. It had been
neatly decapitated at some point. She dug back into the box
to find the errant head.

Harriet spoke softly. "Yes, you sure did, didn't you? They
say that living well is the best revenge."

Cassie held up the doll head, wondering what her sister
had meant by that last remark.

"Baby Betsy!" Harriet reached out her hands for it but
didn't stand. She took the doll from her sister and stuck the
head on top of the neck. "Remember when Cousin Nathan
cut her head off with his daddy's hunting knife?" She
laughed softly. "You went after him with the knife until
Aunt Lucinda caught up with you. Then you glued the head
back on, but it never would stay." She eyed the doll wist-
fully, then gave it a soft hug. "You were always trying to
fix things for me. It made you mad when you couldn't fix
everything."

Cassie stopped her rummaging for a moment and turned
to her sister. Her gaze roamed around the dusty attic, touching on the piles of boxes, clothes, and trunks—all the
reminders of their shared past. She faced her sister again.
"I guess I didn't want you to know what it was like not to
have a mother. It was bad enough that one of us did, but
we both didn't have to."

"Keeper of hearts, right?" A corner of Harriet's mouth
tilted up.

"Yeah. Right." Cassie turned back to the box she'd been
digging into.

"Do you still miss her?"

Cassie didn't need to ask whom Harriet meant. She sat
back on her heels. "Yes, I do. Not every day, like I used
to. Just sometimes. Like when I get a whiff of that perfume
she used to wear." She threw her head back and laughed.
"Or when I walk around my apartment in my slip. I swear

I'm the only woman under sixty in New York who wears a slip. Mama had such beautiful ones—all silk and all sorts of colors. She used to call it her 'secret femininity.' I just remember her running around before church, wearing her slip and jewelry and trying to get us ready. I remember how soft they felt on my cheek when I hugged her."

Harriet dipped her head. "I don't even remember that much. But I've missed her—especially at those times when a girl needs her mother." She tilted her head back, a distant smile on her face. "I missed her on my wedding day. I wanted her to help me pick a dress and put her pearls around my neck." She shook her head slightly. "Not that I ended up having those things, but I couldn't even ever dream about them. But most of all I missed her during all my pregnancies—especially the first. I needed her guidance." She looked directly at Cassie. "And I missed you, too. I wanted you to experience it with me. I will always regret that you weren't here with me when they were born." Her eyes misted, and she dabbed at them with the corner of her dress.

Cassie remained silent, not comfortable talking about these things. Her sister was supposed to be a stranger to her now. It had been too many years, and the hurt and betrayal still ranked up there on the list headed by the word *unforgivable.*

"You know, Har, I can clean up this attic myself. Just give me an idea of the things you want me to save for you and I'll pile them up in a corner."

When she received no response from her sister, she turned around. Harriet still sat on the trunk, but her eyes were closed, her eyebrows knitted together.

"Are you all right?"

Harriet opened her eyes slowly. "Yes. I'm fine. I'm just so . . . fatigued. I don't seem to be snapping back so fast after Amanda's birth like I did with the others." She gave a feeble laugh. "Guess I must be getting older."

Cassie reached deep inside the box. "I'm sure owning your own boutique and raising five children has nothing to

do with it.'' Her brittle smile dimmed as she noticed what
her hand had latched onto. Purple taffeta. After fifteen years
the vibrant hue had hardly faded. She held it up, the small
arc of light bouncing off it and making it sparkle. The place
inside her, where a person keeps her deepest hurts, tightened,
pushing the feeling of pain and humiliation into her blood,
as if it had happened yesterday. She tried to tuck the dress,
unnoticed, back into the trunk, but Harriet's voice called
out.

"Wait, Cassie. What was that? It might be something
Knoxie or Sarah Francis might want to play dress-up with.''

With a resigned sigh, Cassie dredged up the dress again
and held it up for her sister to see. "Here. You can have it.
I certainly have no use for it.''

She turned her face away, not wanting Harriet to see the
shameful tears hovering in her eyes.

Harriet stood and walked over to Cassie, sitting down
with a deep sigh. "I'm sorry, Cassie. I've always wanted
to tell you that. I really am. Not about me and Joe but about
the way you found out. And you leaving. We never meant
that to happen.''

Her voice broke, and Cassie could hear the tears but still
could not look at her sister. She shrugged. "Yeah, well . . .''
There was nothing she could think of to say. It wasn't okay,
nor did she really want to hear an explanation for something
that happened so long ago. She wanted to bury all of the
old ugliness away in the old trunk, along with the dress.
Just looking at it was like touching a bruise—tender to the
touch but easily ignored if one didn't get too close.

Harriet kneeled next to Cassie on the dusty floor. "We've
wanted you to come back ever since you left. It just isn't
the same without you here. We want you to be part of our
lives, part of our children's lives.'' As if to elicit a response
from her sister, Harriet touched Cassie's arm. "We were
hoping this visit would make you forget all the bad feelings
and make you want to come back.''

Turning, Cassie looked at Harriet. In fifteen years she
hadn't changed. The wide green eyes and perfect features.

The blond hair and trim body. The little sister Cassie had once loved and protected as if that were her mission in life. The woman who had run off with and married the love of Cassie's life. Cassie looked down at her fingers, studying the French manicure, sorely in need of a touch-up.

"It doesn't matter anymore, Har. All that old stuff is over now. I have a new life. I'm engaged. Moving back just isn't an option for me." She looked up, meeting Harriet's gaze. "I'd always wanted to get out of this town, and you gave me a reason to leave." With a stilted laugh, she added, "Maybe I should thank you."

Harriet's gaze didn't falter. "Do you still have feelings for Joe?"

Cassie shook her head slowly. "No, definitely not. I can see him as a friend—or a brother-in-law—but he's most definitely not the type I would marry."

Harriet tweaked her lips into a little smile. "Well, then. Maybe you *should* be thanking me."

Cassie threw a velvet hat with three peacock feathers at her sister. "Don't hold your breath for that one, okay?" Sobering, she looked at Harriet with clear eyes, as if seeing a truth for the first time. "Small hurts that are allowed to fester sometimes seem to grow out of all proportion."

"It wasn't a small hurt."

"Yeah, well." Cassie took a pair of moth-eaten woolen long johns out of the trunk, looking at them closely but not seeing them. "But I shouldn't have punished Daddy and Aunt Lucinda, too. I was just so busy trying to prove to me and everybody else that I didn't care."

Harriet stroked the smooth velvet of the hat, her fingers gently moving over the feathers. "No—I think you were too busy trying to prove to everybody that you didn't belong here."

Cassie stood, brushing off her knees. "Well, I don't. It's nice to visit . . ."

Harriet leaned back against a box, her eyes closed.

"Are you all right? You're as white as a ghost."

"I'm fine. I'm fine. Just tired." She waved a pale hand

in front of her. "I think I just need some rest. But I need to get ready for inventory at the boutique. . . ."

Dropping the long underwear into a growing pile of things to be discarded, Cassie crouched in front of Harriet. "Don't be ridiculous. You're obviously unwell. Go lie down and I'll see if I can get ahold of Sam."

"No, really. This has happened before. I just need a quick twenty-minute catnap and I'll be as good as new. I'll just go to my old room and lie down. Just promise me you won't let me sleep longer than twenty minutes."

Cassie looked at her doubtfully. "Are you sure . . . ?"

Visibly struggling, Harriet hauled herself to her feet. "I'm sure." Unsteadily, she walked toward the stairs, then grabbed the banister tightly. "Twenty minutes, okay?"

Still frowning, Cassie nodded. "But only if you let me go to the boutique with you and help you out."

Harriet's voice had visibly faded. "All right. But only if you really want to."

Her footsteps padded away down the hall, followed by a door shutting gently.

Cassie returned to the purple taffeta dress lying in a puddle of fabric like a crushed dream. She started to turn away but stopped, lifting it off the floor instead. Holding it against her, she swayed, feeling the soft fabric brush the bare skin on her legs. She stopped as if something had bit her and dropped the dress back on the floor. Turning abruptly, she headed for the attic stairs to find a phone and call the boutique to tell them that Harriet was taking the rest of the day off.

Cassie stood in front of the pink Grand Am, thinking it even smelled like face powder. Aunt Lucinda had returned from her trip just in time to loan out her car to Cassie, who otherwise would have to walk. She pondered if walking wasn't a better alternative to being seen in the pink car.

She lifted her arms, already feeling the stickiness, and decided that pink or not, it had air-conditioning. With one last look at the license plate, which read LIPSTCK, she climbed in behind the wheel. As she flipped on the radio, she casually wondered how many skin lotions, clarifying masks, and mascaras Aunt Lucinda had to sell to the fine ladies of Walton to win this car. She turned a quick corner and listened to the boxes and bags, filled with beauty potions, shift and titter on the backseat like giddy children.

The small ranch-style house on Orchard remained much as she remembered. She'd never been inside the Parker house before but had passed it every day to and from high school. The most memorable thing about it was its porch, almost as deep as it was wide, with plenty of hiding space behind large wicker rocking chairs. She had learned this firsthand the night she'd painted Principal Purdy's porch across the street.

After locking the car door and flipping the handle to make sure it was locked, she headed down the front walk. She recognized the tall form standing behind the screen door and immediately felt her anger rise.

"I know it sounds unnatural to you, Cassie, but you don't need to lock your car doors here. Especially not in our driveway." He held the door open for her, an insouciant smile crossing his face.

Cassie stopped, looking around nervously. "Is that animal of yours around here?"

"No, ma'am. On account of your skittishness, I left him at my place. He was mighty upset, though. Seems he's taken quite a liking to you."

Ignoring him, she stomped up the porch steps. "You've got some nerve, Sam Parker. How dare you call that maga—" Her foot caught on the door mat, sending her straight into Sam's chest.

Their arms were wrapped around each other when Mrs. Parker emerged from the kitchen. She caught sight of them, and her wide gray eyes beamed with what appeared to be surprise quickly shifting to satisfaction.

Cassie quickly extricated herself from Sam and allowed herself to be enveloped in the soft pillow of Mrs. Parker's hug. The woman hadn't changed one bit. Everything was the same—all the way down to the little apron with frilly lace sleeves.

"You're just as pretty as your mama, aren't you? Just a picture of her." She bent toward Cassie's hair and sniffed loudly. "That's Saucy, ain't it? Just bought some of that perfume from your Aunt Lucinda yesterday. Just drives my Walter wild."

She gave a throaty laugh just as Mr. Parker stomped down the stairs, rolling down sleeves over still-wet forearms on which the wet hairs curled themselves up like small tufts of cotton. "Yep—that's me. A wild man."

He reached his wife and gave her a big kiss on the cheek. His hand did something behind her, making her squeal like a schoolgirl. She slapped his arm. "Walter! Mind your manners, now. We've got company."

The same dark blue eyes she remembered from the gas station peered at her from under bushy gray eyebrows. The ubiquitous overalls covered his rounded abdomen, and he smelled faintly of soap. The thought of this man being wild with a woman made Cassie want to laugh outright.

"So I see. It's good to see you again, Cassie." He bent forward and kissed her loudly on the cheek. "I'll hardly be able to eat my supper tonight. I'll be too busy staring at the two lovely visions sitting at my table."

Mrs. Parker giggled again and slapped him on his arm. "Be careful, Walter. Flattery will get you everywhere."

He winked at his wife, and Cassie had the oddest compulsion to hug them both. There was something so refreshing and authentic about them. She tried to picture herself and Andrew as old marrieds, and the picture just wouldn't focus.

"Come help me in the kitchen, Walter. Sam, why not show Cassie to the parlor and get her something to drink."

Cassie caught the sly wink Mrs. Parker sent her husband and immediately offered her services. "I'll help!"

Mrs. Parker waved a pudgy hand. "Oh, no, darlin'. You just go sit and chat with Sam. Won't have our guest workin' in the kitchen."

The overalled Mr. Parker followed his wife, with a few

lighthearted remarks about women's work, and disappeared into the kitchen.

Cassie faced Sam, her hands hugging her elbows. "Why does your mother think that I would rather talk to you than chop lettuce?"

He led her into a room off the small foyer and motioned her to sit on a green velvet love seat. "Because I'm her son and she thinks I'm the neatest thing since sliced bread and can't imagine everybody else not thinking the same thing."

He took a seat in a well-worn recliner, the remote control perched on the armrest. She rested her head against a home-made quilt on the back of the love seat and gazed at the angel figurines sitting on a lace table mat on the coffee table. Her fury over the magazine shoot lingered beneath the surface, but she was loath to unleash it here, within earshot of his parents. Their opinion of her suddenly mattered, and she didn't want to be interrupted before letting Sam get an earful.

Standing abruptly, Cassie approached the fireplace to examine framed pictures set among old sailing-boat models and bronzed baby shoes on the mantel. The brick fireplace had been swept clean, but the smell of old ash still lingered. Cassie bent forward to look at an old colored photograph of two boys, one about eleven and the other a mere toddler. Both wore cowboy hats and were grinning goofily into the camera. The younger boy also wore cowboy boots and a strategically placed holster—and nothing else.

"Nice outfit," Cassie said, grinning.

"That's me and Tom."

Cassie swirled around, surprised to find Sam standing so close to her. His eyes burned with a gentle blue light, making her temporarily forget her anger at him. She took a step back and looked down at the picture.

"Your brother?"

Sam nodded. "That was taken the year before he died. We'd gone to the State Fair and got those hats. Thought we were two tough customers."

Cassie ran her finger over the glass, wiping away a thin layer of dust. "I'm sorry. You must miss him very much."

He said nothing, but continued to regard her closely. She stepped back, her fingers toying with the charms around her neck. "Is that why you've come back? To make it up to your parents?"

Sam made a narrow hissing noise as he sucked in his breath, and Cassie knew she'd touched a sore spot. But she couldn't back down.

Gingerly, she placed the picture back in its place, staring at the picture so she wouldn't have to see his face.

"Is that why you're trying to make it difficult for me to leave? Because you're jealous that I have a choice and you didn't?"

Long, tanned fingers moved to the mantel within her field of vision, and she turned to find herself blocked in by his arm and his body. His voice was calm. "Maybe it's the other way around. Maybe you're jealous of me because I have a reason to stay."

His words stung, but she would be damned if she'd let him know it. "I have more reasons to return to New York than you could count. As soon as the house sells, I'm leaving."

He raised an eyebrow, then slowly withdrew his arm from the mantel. He turned away, but not before Cassie spied his furiously working jaw.

Mrs. Parker bustled in at that moment, carrying a steaming platter of fried chicken to the adjacent dining room. She was followed closely by Mr. Parker with a bowl filled with mashed potatoes and a gravy boat shaped like a football. It had the University of Georgia bulldog painted on the side.

Cassie plastered a polite smile on her face and sat down at the table. One glance around at the dishes told her there was more cholesterol and fat on that table than her body had been allowed near in over fifteen years. She closed her eyes and sniffed deeply, rationalizing that she could run an extra mile the next day. When Mrs. Parker came around the table with the platter of chicken, Cassie held her plate up with an eager smile.

After everyone was served, Mr. Parker cleared his throat as he tucked his napkin into the bib of his overalls. "Let's say grace." Everyone bowed his head, and Cassie was relieved she didn't have to hold anybody's hand.

Afterward, Mr. Parker turned to Cassie. "I sure hope you don't need your car before the end of the week. Seems that engine part I need to get it running again has to come all the way from Germany. I saved some time ordering it off the Internet, but it will still take awhile to get here."

Cassie's eyes widened, surprised that he knew what the Internet was, much less how to use it. She swallowed a mouthful of potatoes before nodding. "That's fine. I've still got stuff to clean up at the house. I haven't even gone through half the attic yet. I don't think anything's ever been thrown away since the house was built."

Mrs. Parker reached over and patted Cassie's hand. "More stuff to treasure, dear. Enjoy going through all those memories."

Cassie nodded and went to open her mouth in agreement. But she felt Sam's gaze on her and fell back, silent, not wanting to give him the satisfaction.

After dinner, Mrs. Parker all but ordered Cassie and Sam out to the front porch, pushing aside protestations that Cassie wanted to help with the dishes.

"You two young people go out and enjoy that gorgeous night. It's going to be a full moon, and you can watch it rise over the magnolias. The sight will just break your heart." With a pat on Cassie's shoulder, pushing her in the direction of the door, Mrs. Parker turned to take the pitcher of iced tea off the table. "I'll bring y'all some lemonade and apple pie in just a minute."

Cassie walked on ahead of Sam, knowing if anything was going to break this evening, it would be his head. The cool blue light startled her, making her stop and gaze out at the sparkling night. She never noticed the moon anymore. If she ever thought to look for it, it had already drifted behind

a tall building, hiding it from her sight. She stood still for
a moment, bathing in its ethereal light, listening to the night
sounds all around her.

The squeak of a porch swing made her turn. Sam patted
the seat next to him. Turning her back to the moon, she
ignored Sam and found a comfortable spot in a large rocking
chair. She didn't allow herself to rock, but steeled her feet
on the floor.

"I want you to call that stupid magazine and inform them
that if they show up on my doorstep, I'll have them sued
for invasion of privacy. And then I'll sue you for harassment
just for fun."

He didn't even shift in his seat; just the slow, comfortable
squeak of the swing answered her.

Annoyed, she asked, "Did you hear me? I'm serious.
You're interfering with my life, and it's none of your damned
business."

Sam continued the slow swinging motion. "How come
you didn't change the color of your eyes when you got
contacts?"

Her eyes widened, her fingers flying to her face. "What's
wrong with the color of my eyes?"

The blue light made his smile glow. "Nothing. I always
liked them. Sort of reminded me of a fine glass of whiskey
backlit by a fire."

Cassie sat back, her arms folded in front of her. "My,
my. So we're a poet, too."

He shrugged, and the swing groaned. "I guess I'm just
a man of many talents."

Self-conscious now, she asked, "Then why do you think
I should have changed them?"

"Changed what?"

She stamped her foot. "The color of my eyes. Are you
sure your medical license is legit?"

He stood, the swing swaying drunkenly behind him. "You
changed everything else that didn't need changing, and it
just surprised me that you didn't change your eye color,
too."

His words caught her by surprise. Her voice softened a degree. "They're the same color as my mother's, and I thought hers were beautiful."

"So are yours."

Blood rushed to her cheeks, and she was glad for the cover of darkness. Then sane realization hit her. This man was trying to ruin her life. "Don't try to sweet-talk me. I'm furious with you. And if you don't stop this right now, you'll be hearing from my lawyer."

Cassie stood, trying not to notice how the moonlight outlined the hard planes of his chest and lit his eyes with a glowing fire. She focused on a spot above his head. "Please send my apologies to your mother—tell her I couldn't stay. It was a wonderful dinner." Cassie walked purposefully toward the pink car, now resembling a brilliant marshmallow in the moon glow.

"And yes, it's legit," he called after her.

Facing him again, she put her hands on her hips. "What is?"

"My degree. When you come to visit, I'll show it to you. It's hanging on the wall in my living room."

"Don't hold your breath, Sam. On second thought, please do. That'll be one less irritation in my life I'll need to deal with."

She opened the car door.

"Cassie?"

"What?"

"Moonlight becomes you."

She slammed the door shut and started the engine, feeling blood again rush to her cheeks. She caught sight of herself in the rearview mirror and paused with her hand on the steering wheel. Her skin appeared pale and smooth, unmarred by freckles, like a lake in early morning, before the first fishing line is lowered. Her eyes smoldered, and her hand touched her cheek. It had been so long since someone had said something so . . . so frivolous to her. It made her feel . . . like a woman. Not a businesswoman but a woman. Feminine. She put the car in reverse and looked at herself again and saw her mother's eyes, but the look in them was harder, more wary.

Pulling the car out onto the street, Cassie put it into drive and drove home slowly, one hand turning the steering wheel, the other trailing outside the window. Her pale fingers opened wide as if to capture some of the milky night air and some of the wistfulness that seemed to stir up from the dark road and push at her temples.

Chapter 11

Cassie stood behind the counter at Harriet's Skirts 'n Such and cringed. The Sedgewick twins, with bright peacock feathers perched on identical straw hats, were approaching the shop.

It was only ten o'clock in the morning, but already her day was turning from bad to worse. It had started with a wake-up phone call from Andrew at five o'clock. It hadn't gone well. He had asked, no, demanded to know, when she was coming home. Things were apparently getting out of control at the office, and he needed her there now. Not next week but now. Today. Jump in the car and leave—it was as simple as that.

Cassie had even been about to agree until she realized he'd said nothing about missing her—her body, her self, her. Not her negotiating skills or her ability to handle crises in the office but her. Then she thought of baby Amanda and the way she smelled when she fell asleep on her shoulder. And Joey, Knoxie, and Sarah Frances, with their playful antics. And especially Madison, who reminded Cassie so much of herself that it almost frightened her. She wanted to get to know them a bit better. They were her family, after all. She deliberately left out Sam Parker from the equation, not knowing if he'd weigh in on the side of wanting to stay or needing to go.

"No, Andrew. I can't come now. I've got responsibilities here, too. You can't just tell me what to do."

"The hell I can't. I *am* your boss."

That had clinched it. Not *I am your fiancé and I love you and miss you,* but *I'm your boss.*

"As a matter of fact, Andrew, I think I need to ask for a formal leave of absence. I'll still be available to handle client problems long distance and answer questions if you need me. But I'm sure Cynthia Moore would be more than happy to take my place in my absence. She's really good at brown-nosing." Cassie cringed, hating even the sound of that word. "I won't be gone much longer—maybe a month or so—but you're going to need somebody there to fill in."

She had no idea where this was all coming from; these things just seemed to jump to the tip of her tongue without being summoned. But it somehow felt right. Even the thought of that back-stabbing, ladder-climbing Cynthia Moore sitting at Cassie's desk didn't bother her as much as it probably should have.

There was complete silence at the other end of the line. Then: "What about my car? How am I supposed to get that back?"

Cassie had simply replaced the phone on the receiver without answering.

Now, here she was, fulfilling her promise to help out until Harriet felt better, and she was about to be scolded by two old biddies. Like any errant child, she ducked behind the counter, hunched into a tight ball, and listened to the bells above the door chime as the twins entered the store.

Aunt Lucinda, who worked at the boutique three days a week, stepped out of the stockroom and stopped as she spied Cassie cowering beside the shoulder pads and pantyhose boxes. Cassie held her finger to her mouth.

"Did you drop something, dear?"

Startled, Cassie jerked her head around to stare at the

sweet face of Thelma Sedgewick, the peacock feather bobbing up and down as if nodding a greeting.

"Um, yeah. Got it." Cassie grabbed a handful of shoulder pads and stood, knocking over a stack of hangers. She gave the twins a big smile. "What a pleasure to see you two again. How can I help you?"

The two sisters glanced at each other, then back at Cassie. "We've come to apologize. Harriet told us you were here, and we just couldn't start our day without clearing the air, so to speak."

Cassie blinked. "Apologize? To me? But I think I'm the one . . ."

Selma waved her hand. "No, dear. The misunderstanding was all our fault. We simply neglected to recall where you've been living these last fifteen years." She placed a gloved hand on her chest and rolled her eyes heavenward. "Anybody who has lived in New York City was bound to pick up bad habits—through no fault of your own, of course." She patted Cassie's arm. "We're quite sure that your good breeding and upbringing will soon blossom again."

Speechless, Cassie merely blinked her eyes as Selma plopped a plastic lawn bag on the counter. It reeked of moist earth and hot plastic. "So we're asking your forgiveness and bringing this as a token of our sincerity."

Cassie stared at the bag and moved the top back to see better. There, nestled in a ball of dirt, was a plant.

"What is it?"

Two pairs of identical eyes stared back at Cassie, as if amazed she couldn't identify the species of whatever it was that sat on the counter.

"It's a gardenia clipping from our garden. Our great-grandmother planted the first one, and we've been giving clippings ever since we can remember. I would say that most of the gardenias in the county are related to ours."

Cassie lifted the bag gingerly. "What, um, what do I do with it?"

Again, incredulous eyes stared at her. "Why, you plant it, you goose. Here, anyway. Don't think you could take it to New York. That's too far from its natural habitat. It would just shrink up and wither, I'm afraid."

She clucked her tongue as if talking about a distant relative. She reached two gnarled hands up to the bag and knotted it closed. Sliding it over to Cassie, she said, "Just take this home and plant it. If you need help or advice, you know where to find us."

The bell over the door chimed again, and Mary Jane Harden stepped inside. Lucinda was the first to greet her.

"Mary Jane—what a pleasure. What can I help you with this morning?"

Mary Jane looked around the room, taking in the Sedgewick twins, her gaze coming back to rest on Cassie. She sent a tentative smile and a quick greeting.

Mary Jane turned her attention back to Lucinda. "I was looking for something, uh, well, special. Maybe something eye-catching?"

Lucinda pursed her lips. "Eye-catching? That would depend on whose eye you're trying to catch. If it's for Ed Farrell, we don't do T-shirts and jeans. But if it's for that nice manager over at the bank, well, we just might be able to—"

Mary Jane spoke so low it was hard to hear. "No. It's for tonight." She glanced briefly at Cassie, who was pretending to study the fine intricacies of shoulder pads. "I'm going with, um, Sam."

Aunt Lucinda nodded, a smile widening her reddened lips. "I know just the thing."

She walked to a wall of blouses and pulled out a low-cut silk tank top in flamingo red. Cassie watched as Mary Jane's eyes brightened. "I'll take it."

Lucinda fumbled with the hanger, trying to unhitch the shirt. "Don't you want to try it on?"

"I can't. I've got to get back to work. If it doesn't fit, I'll return it."

Cassie stepped away from the cash register to allow Lucinda to ring up the purchase.

As Mary Jane fumbled with the money in her wallet, she

said, "I'm sorry about canceling lunch today. I just got swamped at the clinic. We'll do it another time, okay?"

"Sure." Cassie said good-bye, almost wanting to suggest a purchase of a long-sleeved blouse to wear over the "come hither" shirt. But she had thought better of it. It was none of her business.

The twins left amid busy feather bobbings and bell chimings, and Cassie settled down to work on the inventory list. She wouldn't give anybody the satisfaction of even thinking about what she was wearing that evening until she actually opened her closet door. Hopefully, she'd come down with the plague and wouldn't have to worry about it, anyway.

Ed pulled up in his mobile bordello precisely at five-thirty. He'd called at lunchtime to tell Cassie he wanted to get to the festival early to make sure he got first pickings at the food tables.

He blew the car horn outside, causing Aunt Lucinda to march out to the porch and insist he come to the front door. With grave apologies to Lucinda, his gaze flickered over Cassie's slim black Capri pants and emerald green linen crop top. He held the door open for her, and she could feel his gaze on the low V in the back of her blouse.

"That sure is some outfit, Cassie. You get that in New York?"

"Actually, I did. And thank you."

He opened her car door, then settled himself behind the wheel. "You're always dressed so nice. Like one of them models from those fashion magazines you see at Bitsy's House of Beauty. Maybe I need to go to New York, too, to learn how to dress."

He smiled at her, but she could tell he was waiting for her response, maybe even reassurance. She recalled the tall kid in the back row of her sixth-grade picture, and her heart went out to that friendless boy who still seemed to lurk beneath the surface of Ed Farrell.

"You know, looking at those pictures is a great way to

learn what's new and what works with what. I mean, I'd even be happy to go shopping with you sometime, if you'd like."

His eyes lit, and he seemed to struggle for the right words, his eyebrows jerking up and down in seeming confusion. Finally, he started the engine, his face now a mask of studied concentration.

"Well, thanks. Maybe sometime. But clothes are pretty expensive. I mean, your outfit must have cost you a pretty penny. Bet your daddy sent you lots of money, huh?"

Cassie stared at his profile, wondering if he really expected an answer. He looked at her with raised eyebrows, showing her he did.

"Actually, no. He offered, but I didn't need it. I make a pretty decent living myself." Her hand reached up to touch the gold charm necklace around her throat.

He narrowed his eyes, producing a look that made it seem as if he didn't believe her, then turned his attention back to the road.

Cassie situated herself onto the seat, the leather sticking to her bare legs, and changed the subject. "Guess who called me today? Jim Roust himself, from Roust Development. Wanted to talk to me about my house."

Ed's eyes widened. "And what did you tell him?"

"That you were handling the property for me and that we had no immediate plans for anything other than to keep it residential. He kept pressing for a meeting, but I was pretty firm. I remembered what you told me about them, and I'd really rather have somebody local take care of this deal for me. I told him that, and he seemed pretty mad."

Ed nodded, redirecting an air-conditioning vent that was blowing on his hair. "Well, I certainly appreciate the business. I'm actually surprised it took Jim this long to call you. He or one of his people is usually out on your front porch before the For Sale sign is even in the ground. Did I tell you that your old neighbor is working for Roust now? That Richard Haney fellow—the one with the three hulking teen-aged boys who are always up to something. After Haney sold his property, he decided to stick around and see what other kind of damage he could do to Walton. Like selling his house to Roust and creating those three boys wasn't enough. Unbelievable.''

Cassie shook her head. "I've known the Haneys all my life. I can't believe he's working with Roust. Maybe with the boys heading toward college he needed the money."

Ed shrugged, his eyes focused on the road ahead. They crunched over gravel, stirring up clouds of red dust as Ed maneuvered the car into a spot in the field behind the high school stadium. The sun lay low on the horizon, spilling yellow onto the grass like a giant cracked egg.

Thick, dark clouds mottled the sky off in the distance, hinting at foul weather to come. Cassie lifted the hair off the back of her neck, already sticky from the thick layer of humid air that seemed to congeal on everything and everyone during the late July days of a Walton summer.

A familiar truck pulled past them, kicking up a red dirt cloud. It drifted over their heads for a brief moment before collapsing and adhering to sweat-dampened skin.

Ed crossed his arms over his chest. "Well, well, well, if it ain't Walton's antiprogress police."

Sam stepped out of his truck, gave a brief nod in their direction, then opened the passenger door to help out Mary Jane. The red tank top skimmed over well-rounded breasts and was tucked into a pair of black linen walking shorts. She hadn't looked like that in high school, Cassie recalled, wondering where Mary Jane had stolen a copy of *Cosmo*. Then, standing close together but not touching, they approached Cassie and Ed.

The sky rumbled in the distance.

Sam smiled congenially. "Sure am glad to run into you. I was afraid we'd be the only people here over eighteen and under sixty."

Finding his expression contagious, Cassie smiled back. "There will be at least six of us. Harriet and Joe and their brood are already here. They didn't want to miss the parade.

Even Maddie seemed pretty anxious to see it. Probably wanted to see if Lucy fell off and broke her nose.''

Sam looked at his watch. ''The midpoint of the parade is the town square. My guess is they'll be there in the next ten minutes or so. If we hurry, we'll see it.''

Ignoring Sam, Ed pulled on Cassie's arm, leading her away in the opposite direction. ''I'm gonna get me some of those fried dumplings first. We'll catch up.''

Annoyed, Cassie pulled her arm back. ''Come on, Ed. I don't want to miss the parade. I promise, as soon as it's over, we'll get you something to eat.'' She sent him a smile he couldn't refuse, and he relented.

She wasn't sure why it was so important to her. It had been years since she'd seen a parade. The last time was the summer before her sophomore year in junior college, and she had gone to the Kudzu Festival with Joe. They'd held hands, their palms slick with sweat, and shared a cotton candy. He'd won her an enormous stuffed pink elephant by biting an apple out of a barrelful of water. His shirt had been soaked and plastered to his skin, giving Cassie the first stirrings of teenaged lust.

It had been just one of many shining moments of her girlhood, unmarred by all that had happened since. Their reminders decorated her bedroom in her father's house like a museum—the pennants, dried corsages, faded invitations. Even the pink elephant. Many times since her return, she had gone to her room with an empty garbage bag to clean it out, but she hadn't yet succeeded in removing one frayed streamer. The old Cassie might be gone, but she wasn't ready to be swept up, boxed away, and forgotten.

The four of them raced across the open field, past the stadium and through several backyards before coming up behind Town Hall. Cassie's shirt now clung to her skin with sweat, and she dared not think about what state her hair was in. She looked at Mary Jane and saw that her old friend had fared no better.

They spotted Knoxie's bright red hair right away. She

was perched on her father's shoulders, her head a veritable beacon in the fading sunlight.

Mary Jane waved to catch their attention, and Harriet waved back. They pushed their way through the crowd as they made their way to Joe and Harriet. They had claimed a spot on the curb in front of the square—a perfect vantage point for the parade. Joey and Sarah Frances sat on the curb eating ice-cream cones, most of it dripping down their chins and forearms. Baby Amanda slept peacefully in her stroller, her lips pursed in a perfect bow. Cassie looked over at Madison, expecting her to be wearing a glum expression, but was surprised to see the young girl fairly bouncing with excitement.

Knoxie wore the remnants of her ice-cream cone on the front of her dress and her face, along with something that looked like congealed ketchup and mustard. When she spotted Sam, she stretched toward him. "Hold me, Dr. Parker!"

Heedless of the artistic arrangement of food on the child, he held out his arms, and the little girl fell into them.

His smile slowly dipped as he stared into Knoxie's face. "Are you feeling all right, peanut?"

She shook her head. "My tummy hurts a little bit."

The trill of a cell phone sounded behind them. Everybody in the vicinity turned to stare. Sam pulled his phone off his belt, then shook his head. "Not me."

Ed yanked his out of the pocket of his denim shirt as Cassie noticed the wide lapels for the first time. Either Ed was getting a jump-start on a new fashion trend, or he'd hung on to that shirt for at least a couple of decades.

He put the phone to his ear. "Ed Farrell."

Cassie watched as his color deepened on his cheeks.

"Well, you just tell them that I had it surveyed and that's the damned property line. Show them the papers, for Pete's sakes."

He stayed on the line for a few more moments, shaking his head and muttering expletives. Finally, he ended the call and shoved the phone back into his pocket.

"I gotta go. Those idiots by the old MacLaren farm are

threatening my guys with shotguns, telling them it's private property. I'm goin' to get the sheriff, and then we'll decide who's right.''

He glared at Sam. "And if I find you're responsible for this, I'm hauling you to jail, too."

Sam didn't notice. He was too busy watching Knoxie. Mary Jane had moved to stand next to them and was smoothing the sticky strands of flaming hair off Knoxie's face. A distinct green tinge covered the little girl's pale cheeks.

"I don't feel so good." Without warning, she leaned over Mary Jane and vomited up what food had escaped her face and clothes and actually made it down to her stomach. The glorious red silk tank top now closely resembled an elementary-school art project.

Miraculously, no one else had sustained any damage. Sam sat Knoxie on the ground as the rest of the adults stood in shocked silence and the younger children added the requisite potty-humor remarks. Only Harriet, her skills honed by years of motherhood, flew into action. Delving deep into the diaper bag that hung suspended on Amanda's stroller, she pulled out a box of diaper wipes and a handful of cloth diapers. She handed several wipes to Sam for Knoxie's forehead, then set to work on Mary Jane's blouse.

Sam sent a wry grin to Cassie. "Guess it kinda runs in the family."

Cassie blinked, trying to understand what he meant, then remembered the humiliating scene on her father's porch the night of the fall formal. Patently ignoring him, she turned her attention to Mary Jane, who appeared close to tears as Cassie moved closer to help.

"Don't worry. If you take it to the dry cleaners tomorrow morning, I'm sure they'll be able to get it all out." The stench of throw-up mixed with scented diaper wipes made her throat constrict. She swallowed thickly and closed her eyes.

Mary Jane shook her head. "I need to go home. I reek to high heaven."

Cassie patted her friend on the shoulder. "But you just

got here. Why don't you at least stay and see the parade and then see how you feel.''

''No. I'm . . . I'm not in the mood anymore. I want to go home.''

Sam looked up from a quickly recovered Knoxie, who was asking for more ice cream. ''I'll take you home, if that's what you want. Harriet—I'll take you and Knoxie home, too, but I think she's back to form now. Just needed to empty her stomach.''

Harriet cast a glance at her daughter. ''Yeah—I knew better than to let her eat all that stuff. I'll let her stay if she promises not to eat anything else.''

Knoxie frowned at her mother, but Harriet turned her attention back to Sam. ''But it's silly for you to leave. It looks like Ed has to go, too, so why don't we have him drive Mary Jane back?''

Ed shifted impatiently, then eyed Mary Jane closely, his eyes focused on the middle of her chest. ''Sure, I'll do it. Just hope you don't mind if I drive real fast. I got business to attend to.'' He cleared his throat. ''And by the time I'm done, I'll swing back by your place to bring you back. That will give you plenty of time to get all prettied up again.'' He cast a quick glance at Cassie. ''That all right with you, sugar?''

Cassie nodded, anxiously eyeing Mary Jane, who looked as if she might burst into tears. Mary Jane looked around at the adult faces as if waiting for an objection or another solution, but none seemed forthcoming. Straightening her shoulders, she moved toward Ed. ''Fine, then. Let's go.''

Without saying good-bye to anybody, she followed Ed into the crowd.

Cassie felt a nudging in her ribs and turned to see Harriet winking at her.

''What . . . ?'' Cassie's eyes widened as she realized what Harriet was trying to tell her.

She started to give her sister a piece of her mind when a large roar went up from the crowd lining the main square. The tinny sounds of a marching band could be heard coming down the street. Everyone sitting on the curbs now stood and stepped back onto the grass, pressing the crowd backward. Cassie found herself wedged against Sam Parker but couldn't extricate herself.

A convertible came first, carrying the retired state senator and his wife, who were perched incongruously on the rear of the backseat and waving stiffly. Cassie recognized Senator Billy Thompkins. He lived in an old Victorian on the edge of town and raised chickens in his yard. She remembered being chased by the man as a child when she'd been caught trying to mix dish soap in their feed. She'd wanted to see them cackle up bubbles. Senator Thompkins hadn't been amused. She laughed at the memory and found herself waving back.

Young girls in leotards of red and white stripes, the high school colors, marched by, their skinny legs off-step but their silver batons flashing in unison as they tossed and twirled them over their heads and across their bodies. One fell and rolled to the curb nearby. The girl rushed over to retrieve it and caught Madison's eye. With a wink and a smile, she ran back to her position.

Next came the marching bands, the members sweating under their tall hats and pom-poms, their capes rising limply in the humid air. The perennial disco favorite "Celebration" bounced around the crowd, encouraging not a few people to start singing.

Finally, the float carrying the Kudzu Queen ambled by, pulled by an old bright red pickup, the driver looking to be of the same vintage as the truck. Lucy Spafford stood on a tall platform, waving proudly, her chiffon-and-feather dress floating dreamily around her. Cassie smiled to herself, thinking how much she resembled cotton candy. Kudzu vines and bunches of plastic flowers and balloons clustered around Lucy like clouds, and her celestial expression added to the effect. Out of sight of the float's occupants, cream-colored balloons edged the rear of the float, jiggling up and down with every bump in the road. They seemed stiff and oddly shaped, making Cassie do a double take. She nearly choked when she realized what they were.

She turned to Harriet, who was squinting at the back of the float, where a whole line of the peculiar balloons were strung together like a tail. "What on earth . . . ?"

Cassie caught Sam's gaze over Harriet's head. Together, they turned to focus on Madison, who was now doubled over in a seeming coughing fit.

Harriet gave firm pats to the middle of Madison's back. "You okay, honey? What's the matter?"

Cassie leaned down to her niece and spoke quietly. "Do I take it that you were in charge of the decorations on the float?"

Madison only managed a nod.

Sam's hand gripped Madison's shoulder. "Come on, Maddie. Let's go get you some water." He steered her away from her mother just as Harriet's eyes widened in comprehension.

"Were those . . . ?" She lowered her voice to a mere whisper. "Condoms?"

Cassie patted her sister's arm. "I'm going to go check on Maddie to make sure she's okay. I'll be back." She turned and followed Sam and her niece into the crowd.

She found them standing by the drink stand, Sam holding a cup of water out for Madison. Her face was deep red, tears rolling down her cheeks.

Cassie fought the urge to laugh out loud and congratulate her niece on a prank well done. Sam's stern expression stopped her from patting Madison on the back.

Sam's expression didn't change as he spoke to the young girl. "When Lucy sees those, uh, balloons, she's going to be mighty embarrassed. And I don't think she'll need to look far to figure out who's behind it."

Madison looked up at Sam, her face now a fading pink, and took a deep swallow of water. "No, sir."

"How do you think your mother's going to like getting that call from Lucy's mother?"

For the first time, Madison looked chagrined. "I only

meant to embarrass Lucy. She deserved it. But my mom doesn't need to get involved.''

Sam straightened. ''I think it's a little late for that.''

They all turned to see Joe and Harriet marching toward them, pushing the stroller like a weapon, their faces grim. Joey and Sarah Frances ran behind them as Knoxie clung tight to her daddy's shoulders. They all came to a stop in front of Madison. Sam and Cassie took their cue to leave, but not before Cassie gave her niece's shoulder a reassuring squeeze.

Sam grabbed Cassie's hand and led her into the thick of the crowd.

''Where are we going?''

He didn't answer, but kept his hand firmly gripping Cassie's.

She asked again, ''Where are we going?''

When he didn't answer, she dug in her heels. As he faced her, she realized that he was laughing—hard. His eyes sparkled with merriment. When he caught his breath, he gasped out, ''That was about damned near the funniest thing I've ever seen. Almost as funny as that pig you got for Harriet's float when she was Kudzu Queen.''

Cassie's lips twitched in an effort not to smile. ''You mean you're not really mad at Maddie? I think you had her about ready to cry.''

He swiped his hand over his face as if trying to sober himself up but didn't completely wipe the grin off his face. ''Well, I had to at least pretend to be a grown-up with no sense of humor. I've got a reputation to keep in this town.''

At that, Cassie finally lost the last of her control, and she burst out laughing, not able to stop. She clutched Sam's arms for support and looked up into his face. Breathless, she asked, ''What are you staring at?''

His smile softened, but his eyes never dimmed. ''You. Your laugh. I've always loved the sound of it.''

The smile dipped on her face as she watched something flicker in Sam's eyes. Lou-Lou Whittaker walked by, her bleached hair teased out into perfect roundness, a bright red headband bisecting it and making it look like a beach ball. Her arm was tucked into the crook of the arm of a tall cowboy Cassie didn't recognize, but she practically purred as she passed Cassie and gave her a knowing look.

Cassie swallowed her laughter when she realized there were about another dozen sets of eyes staring at her and Sam and probably coming to the same conclusion Lou-Lou had. She dropped her hand from Sam's arm.

"I need a drink." She headed for a concession stand.

Sam moved in front of her. "Allow me. What would you like?"

She smacked her lips. "I want some of that kudzu punch. I was never allowed to have it when I was a kid, so I think it's about time."

"One kudzu and one water, please."

While waiting for their drinks, Sam turned around and leaned both elbows on the counter. "I'd join you, but I'm on call tonight. You do realize that there's mostly grain alcohol in the punch, right?"

Cassie looked at him with a practiced smirk on her face. "I can handle alcohol. We have that in New York." She took the Styrofoam cup and stared inside at the bright green liquid. "Perhaps not exactly any in this particular hue, but we do have alcohol."

She took a small sip and smiled. "It tastes like lemonade. I doubt there's very much alcohol in it." With that, she took a large gulp, ignoring Sam's protests. She slapped her empty cup on the counter. "May I have another one, please?"

Raising an eyebrow, Sam leaned against the counter while another cup was slid over to Cassie. "Guess you hadn't heard the rumors about this punch, then."

Cassie took a big gulp. "What rumors?"

A broad grin split his face. "That it's what they call an aphrodisiac. More babies are born in Walton nine months after the Kudzu Festival than at any other time. I know never to schedule vacations or conferences in the month of April."

Cassie plopped her half-filled cup on the counter. "April? Oh, Lord—I was born in April!"

Sam straightened and winked. "So was I."

"Ew. I'd rather not think about that." She shook her head, wondering why things appeared to be swimming in front of her. The rumbling and shouts from the roller coaster caught her attention. "Let's go on that."

Sam held her back. "You might want to rethink that. Aren't you feeling a bit woozy right now?"

"I'm perfectly fine." She stumbled over a piece of trash on the ground. "I want to go on the roller coaster. It's just a kiddy ride, anyway."

He studied her for a moment. "All right. I know better than to get in the way of a determined woman. Come on. We should go now before it starts to rain." He grabbed her hand and led her across the field to the roller coaster.

The first tremors of nausea didn't hit her until they had clack-clacked up the rickety track to the first plunge. By the time they had reached the second plunge, Cassie had her face buried in the side of Sam's shoulder. At the third one, she was holding her hand over her mouth and begging to get off.

Sam had to help her out of the car and almost carry her away from the roller coaster and to the open field behind the festival buildings. Without warning, she stopped abruptly and knelt on the grass. Unable to stop herself, she bent over and threw up.

With gentle hands, Sam pulled her hair away from her face and placed his fingers on the back of her neck. When she had finished, she sat back on her legs but kept her face down.

Sam rubbed her neck. "Just like old times, huh?"

She threw out a halfhearted punch that barely brushed his shoulder.

He dug into his back pocket and handed her a handkerchief.

Cassie took it and wiped her face. "Thanks. I'm starting quite a collection of these."

Sam said nothing, but continued to rub her neck and back.

Cassie sighed. "You know, if you weren't such a burr

under my saddle, I'd say you were a pretty nice guy, Sam Parker.''

"Thanks. I think."

A few sprinkles began to fall on them from the darkening sky, the moon all but obliterated by the hulking clouds.

Sam sat back on his heels. "Guess we're not going to make it to the watermelon-seed-spitting contest."

Cassie looked at him sharply. "I don't spit, and I have no intention of being seen anywhere near it." She clutched her forehead, the skin slick and clammy.

"Hmm. I seem to recall you winning it one year in high school—our senior year, right? You should have that trophy somewhere in your room."

She did. The faux brass trophy, an enlarged replica of a watermelon seed, was indeed still displayed proudly on her dresser. Whenever she got around to cleaning out her room, that would be the first thing in the garbage. For a brief moment, she pictured bringing it back to her apartment in New York and placing it on the black lacquer of their bedroom dresser and explaining its significance to Andrew. The thought made her laugh out loud.

Sam quirked an eyebrow. "What's so funny?"

She studied him for a moment before answering. Damn, he was good-looking—better-looking than such an annoying man had any right to be. He was comfortable in his skin, in the way he moved and talked. And in the way he dressed. Not like the carefully orchestrated persona Andrew constantly worked at portraying. Sam was cotton flannel to Andrew's linen, and she couldn't help but think that flannel was a heck of a lot nicer to cuddle up to.

Cassie shook her head. She needed to get away from this man. Now. "I need to brush my teeth. Where're the bathrooms?"

Sam threw his head back and laughed. "Let me guess. You carry a toothbrush and toothpaste in your purse at all times just in case you get caught at a client dinner with spinach between your teeth."

Her mouth fell open. Those had been Andrew's exact

words to her when he'd given her the little travel set of dental hygiene. "Just show me where the bathrooms are."

In one fluid motion Sam stood and helped her up. The ground tilted a bit, then leveled out.

"I'll take you up to the high school. I know the night security guard. He'll let you in."

As they crossed the field, the sky opened up and dumped water on them, drenching them to the skin. She turned her face to the sky, welcoming the cool rain on her face. By the time they reached the high school, their clothes were plastered to their bodies. Sam waited outside the building while she tried to make herself presentable.

She scrubbed her teeth with the toothbrush and paste, gargling twice, then splashed her face with water from the tap. After looking into the mirror, she realized she resembled a drowned rat and improving on the situation would be hopeless. She was more than ready to go home but had no idea how to find Joe and Harriet in the crowd. And she hadn't seen Ed since he'd left with Mary Jane.

She found Sam outside, leaning against the brick building in the shelter of an overhang and chewing on a strand of long grass. She hated asking him for anything, but her options were limited. "Would you mind taking me home? You could still come back for a chance to win the cutest-couple contest with Mary Jane."

He studied her for a moment as if weighing her request, then simply nodded his head and pushed off from the building. "Let's go." The rain had slowed to a light drizzle as they found their way through the soggy grass and muddy parking area.

His truck still smelled like Mary Jane's perfume. Despite the rain, Cassie cracked open her window, then leaned against the seat back. She closed her eyes and promptly fell asleep for the duration of the short ride home.

Cassie awoke to the feel of Sam touching her cheek. She opened her eyes as he helped her slide her soggy bottom off the seat. He closed the door, but Cassie didn't move forward. She remained where she was, groggy and light-headed but feeling that rare feeling that all was right with her world. The wet grass tickled the exposed part of her foot in the high-heeled sandals, but still she remained rooted to the spot.

Flashes of light echoed in the sky as the trees dropped their watery burden onto the already sodden ground. All around them in the hushed night the water dripped, a heady background beat to the resumed chorus of the crickets. Steam rose off the gravel drive, floating like apparitions in the glare of the porch light.

Cassie stared at the way Sam's rain-soaked hair fell over his face. She lifted her hand and pushed it back, her fingers reluctant to leave the smooth skin of his forehead. The backs of her fingers swept over the bristles on his cheek, then slid along his jawbone.

His hand wrapped around her wrist and pulled it away.

Embarrassed, she said, "I'm sorry." Her words stumbled and tossed against each other, making her feel like an awkward teenager. "I'm . . . I'm sorry for getting sick. I should have known better about that kudzu punch. I mean, it's not like I've never been to a fraternity party." She attempted a smile.

He stood so close, she could feel his heat. She almost expected to see the steam rise from his shirt. She should step back.

"We all make mistakes." There was no smile in his voice, and his jaw seemed to tighten with tension.

She should go inside now. "Some mistakes are more permanent than others."

His eyes brightened in the dim light. "Nothing's permanent, Cassie. Things change."

The sky exploded with light, illuminating Sam, the house, the truck, this place. It made things so clear for a moment, as if she were staring at a Polaroid picture. His head bent closer to hers, and she closed her eyes, swaying in his direction. A rippling wave of thunder rent the sky, but he made no move to kiss her. She forced her eyes open and found herself staring into probing blue eyes. She placed both hands behind his neck and pulled him forward, closing the gap between them.

His lips were warm, soft, responsive, making her knees soften like butter in a frying pan. His hand fell to her waist as the fingers of his other hand crept through her hair at the base of her skull, cradling her head. The move was so unexpected, so different, she almost pulled back. It made her feel . . . cherished.

Rain pelted down now with renewed force. Cassie opened her mouth, tasting warm rain and skin. She sucked on his lower lip until he took control and opened his mouth, touching her tongue with his.

Light flashed under her eyelids, but it wasn't the lightning. Burnt ions from the electrified air popped and fizzled between them, creating a storm of its own deep inside her. He moved her against the truck, and she welcomed the solid feel of him against her, his need pressed against her hip.

The rain beat steadily on them, dripping down her neck and beneath her blouse, thudding gently on the hood of the truck. Her hands clutched the back of his shirt, and she pulled on it, releasing the shirttails.

He pulled back, and she found herself gasping for air. He didn't say anything, but stood staring at her, rivulets of water running down his face.

Cassie blinked the rain out of her eyes.

His chest rose and fell as his gaze dropped to the ground. The rain plopped and splashed on the wet gravel between them.

He shook his head before looking back at her. "Do you want me to come inside?"

She swallowed thickly, wondering why her New York cool had suddenly deserted her. In a small voice she said, "Sure."

Sam reached behind him and began tucking in his shirt. "No."

She stared at him, growing humiliation quickly extinguishing the fire in her blood. "No?" She swallowed again.

"You practically toss me over the hood of your truck to ravage me and then you just stop cold?"

She knew she was being unreasonable, but humiliation was never a feeling she could take lying down.

Sam merely raised an eyebrow, then turned to rest his hands against the truck, trapping Cassie neatly between them. "Believe me. It's not because I don't want to." He reached down and adjusted his jeans, as if emphasizing the truth of his words.

Cassie ducked under his arms to escape him, her feet squelching in the mud as she made her way to the porch steps.

"I want more from you than a one-night stand, Cassie. It's all or nothing with me."

She pulled open the door. "Better get used to that nothing part, then, Sam Parker." Stepping inside, she was about to shut the door when she heard him laughing.

"Ravage, huh? I don't think I've ever heard anybody use that word in a sentence before. That's too funny. You haven't changed a bit."

She slammed the door and leaned against it, a small smile forcing itself on her face. She wanted to be mad at him, and she had every right to feel humiliated. But somehow she didn't. He'd acted like, well, like a gentleman. So different from most of the men she knew. So different from Andrew.

Andrew. The keys fell from her hand, falling with a thunk on the wood floor. Oh, Lord—she hadn't even thought about her fiancé since their disagreeable phone call that morning. Out of sight, out of mind, indeed. She wore the man's ring on her finger, yet she'd been pawing at the body of the first available candidate. She was humiliated, all right, alcohol or not. And it was all her doing.

Slipping out of her shoes, she ran up the stairs as fast as she could to call Andrew. He needed to come down to Walton for a visit. As soon as possible.

Chapter 12

Cassie stared at the ceiling in her bedroom, the flashes of lightning creating odd shadows on the plaster. She turned on her side and listened to the steady fall of rain, a sound she usually found sleep-inducing. But not tonight.

Finally, she dragged herself out of bed, threw on her robe, and went downstairs, hoping a midnight snack might help her sleep. She was surprised to see a light under Aunt Lucinda's bedroom door. Without hesitating, she knocked.

"Come in."

Aunt Lucinda sat propped in a chaise longue in the corner of the room, her feet resting on a pink chiffon pillow. Each toe shone with crimson brilliance, the smell of fresh nail polish hovering about the bedroom. A fluffy cotton ball was wadded between each digit like a punctuation mark. Pink bristly curlers covered her head, and Cassie would have laughed if it weren't for the tears glistening on Lucinda's cheek.

Cassie stood on the threshold. "What's wrong, Aunt Lu? Do you want me to leave?"

Lucinda shook her head. "Oh, no, honey. I was just finishing up one of Miss Lena's books. Those happy endings always make me cry.'' She moved her feet and patted the chaise. ''Come sit, sweetie, and tell me what's wrong.''

Cassie did as she was told. ''Nothing's wrong. I just couldn't sleep.''

Lucinda bent over and started removing the cotton balls. ''Who were you talking to on the phone?''

''Sorry—didn't know I was talking so loud. That was Andrew. I had to convince him that he needed to come down here.''

Her aunt clapped her hands together. ''Why, that's wonderful. I'll tell Harriet, and we can get those bridal-shower invitations out. We'll make it one of those couples showers—maybe an outdoor barbecue. Let him meet the whole town.''

''Like a sort of 'Donald Trump Meets the Clampets.' Yeah, sounds like fun.'' She had meant it to be a flippant comment but realized too late how it must have sounded to her aunt.

Lucinda used one of those looks Cassie remembered from childhood, the one reserved for times when she was due a spanking but managed to elude her aunt's grasp.

''There's no need to be scared, Cassie. We'll behave ourselves.''

Cassie's eyes widened. ''Scared? Why would I be scared?''

''Well, you're acting mean, and that's always meant just one thing. But, sugar, if this is the man you're going to marry, you've got to let him meet us sometime. You can't go hidin' us forever.''

''I wasn't trying to hide you.'' Cassie looked down in her lap, wondering whom she was trying to hide from whom. She stood. ''He says he'll be here a week from Friday. He doesn't know what flight he'll be on, so he'll call from the airport to let us know when to pick him up. That's probably not enough time for Harriet to organize a shower.''

Lucinda adjusted one of the curlers that had drooped precariously over her forehead. ''Nonsense. She's already got it half-planned already. Even has the invitations addressed. Just didn't know the date or time. I guess we do now!''

Cassie leaned against the dressing table, her arms folded over her chest. ''Wonderful.''

Lucinda sent Cassie that look again but didn't say anything. She took out a file and began filing her fingernails. ''I think we should both help her out. Harriet just hasn't been herself lately. She's so tired all the time. And did you notice how pale she looks?''

''I just figured that's what a mother of five should look like. She's probably exhausted. Sure, I'll help. Maybe I can work on damage control. You know, warn everybody on the invitations about making 'damn Yankee' remarks.''

''Cassie, honey, what are you so afraid of? That he'll be so appalled by all of us that he won't want to marry you? Because if that's the type of person he is, maybe you shouldn't be marrying him, anyway.''

Cassie sent her aunt a sharp look, but Lucinda was studiously filing her thumbnail. ''It's not that. It's just that Andrew is so . . . different from everybody here. I'm afraid he'll feel out of place.''

Lucinda smiled. ''Honey, we all have something in common; we love you. And if he loves you like we do, then he'll fit right in.''

Cassie pushed away from the dresser. ''Yeah, well. I guess I should turn in. You've always told me to make sure I got my beauty sleep.'' She paused for a minute. ''Aunt Lu?''

The older woman looked up, her thin eyebrows raised expectantly. ''Yes, pumpkin?''

''Do you remember any of daddy's old girlfriends—girls he met before Mama?''

Lucinda thought for a moment, then shook her head. ''I really don't. But remember, I was living in Mobile back then, so I really wouldn't know.'' She smiled softly. ''The first woman I ever remember him mentioning in a letter was your mama, though. That's when I knew he was really in love.'' She bent back to her filing. ''Why are you asking?''

Cassie pursed her lips thoughtfully for a moment before deciding that trespassing into her father's life had gone far enough without sharing the letters with his sister. "No reason. Just curious, I guess."

Lucinda sniffed, the file stilling against her thumbnail. "I miss him so much. I wasn't . . . ready . . . for him to go yet. It's hard losing a sibling. It's like losing a part of my past."

Blinking back her own tears, Cassie gave her aunt a hug. "I know. I miss him, too." Kissing her on the cheek, she said softly, "Good night, Aunt Lu."

The older woman didn't look up. "Good night, honey." When Cassie reached the door, Lucinda sniffed loudly, then said, "Was that Sam Parker's truck bringin' you home tonight?"

Cassie's face colored, wondering how much her aunt had seen. She tried to sound nonchalant. "Um, yes. It was. We couldn't find Ed to bring me home. . . ."

"He's a real nice boy. And so good-lookin'."

Cassie tried to look nonchalant. "You mean Ed?"

Aunt Lu lowered her head, raising her eyebrows and piercing Cassie with a look that said she wasn't fooled. "No. That's not who I meant. I was talkin' about that delectable Dr. Parker."

Cassie sent her a sidelong glance, but Lucinda had returned to her nails. "Really? I hadn't noticed."

"Uh-huh. Sugar, would you mind bringing over my Brunswick stew to Miss Lena tomorrow? It's my turn to bring her supper and visit for a spell, but Harriet's so tired, I thought I might just spend the day with her and help her out with the kids and the party plannin'." She handed her the book she had just put down. "Would you please bring this back to her, too? Be careful, though. She might want to discuss it with you. And you, being a single lady, wouldn't have any idea about some of the stuff that goes on in those books."

Cassie colored again, realizing she had probably blushed more in the last few days than she had in fifteen years.

"Sure, I'll do it first thing." She took the book, said good night again, and left the room.

The storm continued through the night and into the morning. Cassie stood on the front porch, balancing the stew pot with one arm while she wrestled the umbrella with her other hand. A car door shut, and she glanced up just in time to see Sam's dog, George, bounding toward her. Sam caught the pot just in time as Cassie moved the umbrella between her and the large animal.

"Afraid he's going to ravage you?"

Cassie heard the smile in his voice, but she refused to smile back. "Could you call off your dog, please?"

The animal lay down on top of Cassie's feet, exposing his underbelly.

"He likes you. He wants you to scratch him."

Cassie was about to step over the animal, but something soft and sweet in the dog's expression made her pause. It reminded her of her father's faithful companion, Hunter. Her earliest memories included the mixed-breed bloodhound: memories of her pulling on his tail and putting Harriet on his back to carry like a horse. Hunter had died after she left home, and looking at George's face, she suddenly missed him terribly.

She bent down and rubbed the sable hair on George's belly, the fur soft and damp from the rain. The dog went limp in an attitude of supreme satisfaction, making Cassie grin.

"Why are you darkening my doorstep, Dr. Parker? Anybody sick that I should know about?"

"Lucinda called me last night and asked me to drive you to Miss Lena's, seeing as how I needed to visit her today, anyway."

Cassie raised an eyebrow, wondering what Lucinda had really been thinking, especially to call the doctor so late at night. She wished for Lucinda's pink car. Anything would have been preferable to being in close proximity to Sam

Parker. But Lucinda and her car had already left for Harriet's. It was either Sam and his truck or a walk in the pelting rain with a stew pot and an umbrella balanced precariously in her arms.

"I'm only going to say yes because I don't want to dump Brunswick stew all over Madison Lane. And because I need to get out of the house. Ed's bringing a couple by today to look at it, and I'd rather not be here."

"Let's go, then." As George raced to the back of the truck and leaped in, Sam took the umbrella from Cassie and held it over their heads. Sending her a warm look, he said, "Unless you're afraid that I'm going to try and ravage you again."

She wished she had her hands free to throttle him. "Look. About last night . . ." She paused, hoping Sam would wave a dismissive hand in the air and relieve her of the need to continue. Instead, he looked at her expectantly.

She found she couldn't look directly into his eyes. "I . . . I must have had too much of that kudzu punch. I wasn't in my right mind, and I apologize for acting like that."

"Like what?" Sam opened her door and took the stew pot from her while she settled herself inside.

Cassie studied the dash in front of her. "Like a sex-starved maniac. I'm not like that at all."

Sam leaned in close enough for her to feel his breath on her cheek. "I never thought you were. Besides, I'm not complaining." The door closed with a solid thunk.

When Sam drove his truck to the end of the drive in front of the property, Cassie noticed that the For Sale sign in front of the house was lying prone on the ground, conspicuous tire tracks marring the red-and-white logo of Farrell Realty.

"Stop!" she yelled.

She dumped the stew pot in Sam's lap and clambered out of the truck and into the teeming rain. She ignored the squelching sound of the clinging mud that sucked at her shoes as she stomped over to the sign and righted it.

After hoisting herself into the truck again, she glared at Sam as she took back the pot. "That was pretty juvenile.

How about next time you just hang a bucket of water over the front door?''

Sam put the truck into gear. "Or maybe I'll just attach inflated condoms to the sign."

Cassie coughed to stifle her laughter, then turned her head toward the window so he couldn't see her broad grin.

Leaning an elbow on the doorjamb, Sam glanced over at Cassie. "Have you made any headway yet on finding your missing sibling?"

"Nope. But I put a classified ad in the *Sentinel*'s Sunday edition. It's pretty discreet, not mentioning any names or anything—just asking anybody who was born and adopted around April 1963 to give me a call. Didn't mention my name, either, and I used my cell-phone number just in case anybody got too nosy." She sighed, slapping her hands on her thighs. "Well, it's a start, anyway. I'd like to think I can do this on my own. I mean, if whoever it is is hiding so well, then he or she doesn't want to be found. I might just have to leave it at that."

Sam glanced at her for a hard moment. "You mean you'd walk away with that secret because you respected their privacy? Or because it would be one more thing to tie you down in the quicksand?"

She stuck her chin out but didn't respond. Instead, she rode the rest of the way watching the town of Walton flash by outside the car window, aimlessly fingering the gold charms around her neck.

Despite the weather, Miss Lena sat on her front porch, stockings rolled down around her swollen ankles, the ever-present romance novel clutched in her hands. She waved wildly, her smile showing perfect white dentures.

Her smiled softened as Cassie walked up the porch steps. "Catherine Anne," she said, reaching for Cassie's hand. Cassie put the pot down on the floor and placed her hand inside the old woman's.

Sam's voice was gentle. "No, Miss Lena, this is Cassandra. Catherine Anne's oldest."

The woman gripped Cassie's hand tighter. "She was such

a pretty young thing—no one knew why she wanted to marry the judge. She could have had any of the young men in the county, but instead she chose a man old enough to be her father.'' She studied Cassie's face closely. ''Nobody would have ever thought he'd outlive her.'' She stroked Cassie's cheek with her other hand. ''You're the spittin' image of her, too.'' She glanced up at Sam. ''Is she just as sweet?''

''Sweet as vinegar.'' He reached for Miss Lena's elbow. ''Come on; let me help you inside.'' The old lady giggled as Sam gently pulled her from the chair.

Cassie was left to bring in the pot, and she resisted the impulse to dump the contents on Sam's sandy-brown head. She walked inside the small but immaculate house, making her way to the back kitchen. The wood floors gleamed with polish, and the stainless sink shone. As Cassie opened the refrigerator door to deposit the stew, she noticed a large color-coded chart on the door. Curious, she looked at it closely.

Days of the week and familiar names filled out the chart's heads. On closer inspection, she realized it was a food-and-cleaning schedule. Apparently, most of the women in the town contributed to Miss Lena's daily upkeep. Every day somebody was scheduled to come by and clean and keep her company, while somebody else brought breakfast, lunch, and dinner.

As Cassie made room for the stew pot in the tidy and clean refrigerator, she thought briefly of the old homeless woman who appeared frequently on the corner of the street in New York where Cassie worked. She was dirty, her hair unkempt, her clothes tattered. The crowd on the sidewalk swayed in unison, like a great big roiling wave, to avoid her. It was doubtful anybody had ever brought her a covered casserole.

She shut the refrigerator door with a thoughtful thud and returned to the living room, where Miss Lena sat comfortably in a worn recliner as Sam took her blood pressure.

The older woman smiled. ''Come over here so I can see

you better. I don't think I've seen you in a very long time. Where have you been, child?''

Cassie sat on a stuffed vinyl ottoman next to the chair. ''I live in New York now.''

A frown shadowed Miss Lena's face. ''You poor, poor child. I'm so sorry. Will they let you come home soon?''

Cassie bit her lip as she looked up at the older woman. ''I'm quite happy there, actually. I'll be going back soon.'' She reached up and placed Lena's soft and gnarled hand in her own and patted it gently.

A confused frown covered Lena's face for a moment, then she smiled. ''Do you read, sugar? I've just finished the best book, and I'd love for you to borrow it.''

Sam took the blood-pressure cuff off her arm, and she leaned to a nearby table. ''Here—take it, and when you're done, we'll discuss it.''

She handed Cassie the same book that Lucinda had given her to return. The book that was still in her purse waiting to be given back to Miss Lena.

Cassie stared at the cover of the half-naked people. ''Thank you, Miss Lena. I'll look forward to it.''

As Cassie opened her purse to put it next to the other book, Miss Lena sat up and leaned forward so Sam could place his stethoscope on her back.

''I know you'll love it, too. It has the best love scenes. His swollen manhood is supposed to be just absolutely enormous and is quite adept at pleasuring his women.'' She chortled gleefully. ''My favorite scene is when they're riding bareback—naked. Oh, my—it just about gives me heart palpitations every time I read it.''

Cassie swallowed, then smiled, nodding agreeably. ''I see. Why, aren't they lucky!''

She could see Sam valiantly trying not to laugh as he spoke to his patient. ''Miss Lena, I need you to lean back now and unbutton the top button of your dress so I can hear your heartbeat.''

Miss Lena's eyes clouded, and she looked up at Sam as

if she'd never seen him before. "Young man, I hope you're not taking liberties with me. I might have to tell your mama."

Sam calmly took a step back. "No, ma'am, I wouldn't think of it. I just need to put this on your chest to hear your heart beat—like I do every week. It will just take a second."

The older woman pressed her lips tightly together. "No, sir. I'm an unmarried woman."

Cassie looked at Sam. His expression remained calm, his arms relaxed against his sides. He seemed to be weighing different tactics to get Miss Lena to cooperate.

The patient sat indignantly in her chair, bright spots of color suffusing her cheeks. Her eyes remained cloudy, momentarily confused with what was happening around her.

Cassie leaned forward and placed the woman's hands in her own. "Miss Lena, I'm here. How about if I stay next to you and hold your hands while Dr. Parker listens to your heart? I'll make sure that he treats you with the utmost respect."

Miss Lena blinked, as if trying to focus. "Doctor?"

Cassie nodded. "Yes, this is Dr. Parker, and he needs to listen to your heartbeat. Will you let him?"

The older woman gripped Cassie's hands tightly, then nodded her head.

Gently, Sam undid her top button, then slid his stethoscope to her chest. The room was in complete silence, the only sound that of the clock ticking away life's moments on the mantel.

As Sam put the stethoscope back into his black bag, Cassie buttoned up the collar. When she moved her hand away, Miss Lena held it. "Thank you, dear." Her gray eyes were suddenly clear and moist with unshed tears. The look of gratitude in them made Cassie's heart feel as if it had swelled just a bit.

She leaned forward and kissed the older woman's cheek, surprised at the softness of it. "You're very welcome," she said, and meant it.

When they were ready to leave, Sam leaned over Miss Lena with a smile. "You're still healthy as an ox. We'll see you next week, all right?'' He, too, planted a kiss on her cheek.

She beamed up at him, her early reticence apparently forgotten. ''I'll look forward to it.'' She pushed herself up to whisper in a conspiratorial tone, ''And don't forget to bring Catherine Anne's daughter. Although I'm sure I won't need to ask you twice.'' She elbowed Sam in the ribs, making him grunt.

''I'll try, ma'am. But that woman is like a pig in grease to pin down.''

They each winked at each other, looking like accessories in a great plot and making Cassie want to laugh out loud.

The clouds had scattered along with the rain, leaving no obstacles in the sun's direct rays. George barked in greeting from the truck as Sam and Cassie walked down the porch steps toward him. ''If I'm not mistaken, Sam Parker, you just called me a greased pig.''

''Not exactly . . .''

Cassie stopped, holding up her hand. ''That's all right. I'll forgive you because you were so sweet to Miss Lena. And I guess I don't need to ask if you ever bill her.''

Sam opened the truck door and threw his bag in the backseat. ''It's one of the perks of being old. You get a lot of things for free. Which reminds me, I gotta ask Ed if he can trade mowing days with me at the end of the month. I hate even talking to the man, but we're the only two on the schedule, and I've got to switch. I'm going down to Atlanta for a conference. I thought I'd check through the hospital birth records while I'm there, if you like.''

Cassie looked up into those infernal blue eyes, trying to read them. ''Why are you being so nice to me? It's not like I've gone out of my way to ever be nice to you.''

Sam studied her for a moment, his eyes unreadable. ''Because . . .'' He looked away for a moment. ''Because you used to make me laugh. After Tom died, I didn't find much to laugh about. And then, in sixth grade, we were put in the same homeroom together, and you put that giant cockroach in Susan Benedict's lunch box because she'd said something mean about Harriet. I laughed till I almost wet my pants. I was hooked after that; you changed my life. You showed me that there's nothing in life that can't be laughed about." His eyes turned somber. "I guess you could say I'm still a fan."

His mouth was so close to hers, reminding her of how delicious his lips had tasted the night before. She stepped back, her hand flying to the necklace around her neck.

"And I appreciate what you did for me in there with Miss Lena. I don't know what I would have done without you."

Cassie shrugged and scrambled into the truck. "Glad I could help," she said, staring out the windshield as Sam shut the door.

After Sam climbed in, Cassie turned to him. "Do you have any plans right now?"

Something flickered in his eyes, but his expression remained neutral. "I don't have office hours until one o'clock, and I have my beeper in case anybody needs me sooner. Why?"

"Could you drive to Harriet's? She's been complaining of being fatigued and out of sorts lately, and she is looking a little peaked. I asked her if she had been to see you, but she said she hadn't seen you for an appointment since her postpartum checkup after Amanda was born. I thought that since she wouldn't go to you, I could bring you to her. Maybe you can prescribe her some vitamins or something."

Sam cranked the engine but didn't answer right away. He looked oddly distracted.

"Sam?"

"Um, yeah. Sure." With a slight grin, he said, "Still taking care of your little sister, huh?"

Cassie stuck out her chin. "Old habits die hard, I guess."

He pulled out onto the street. "Careful, Cassie. People might start thinking that you care."

Cassie didn't answer and remained silent for the short ride to her sister's.

Screaming and laughter led Sam, George, and Cassie to the backyard of Harriet's house. Aunt Lucinda stood in her red heels, leaning over the patio table and cranking an old-fashioned ice-cream machine. Madison stood next to her, trying to hold the table steady so it wouldn't rock in response to Lucinda's exertions.

Sarah Frances, Joey, and Knoxie were running around with what looked like the majority of the neighborhood kids, telltale signs of peach ice cream dripping down their chins. Another bin of homemade ice cream, the frost on the outside quickly dissipating in the heat, stood open, a puddle of peach-colored liquid swimming in the bottom.

A card table stood nearby with large wedges of watermelon decorating a red-and-white-checked tablecloth. Two boys stood next to it, globs of the pink fruit staining their faces and shirts, large chunks of watermelon gripped in grimy hands as they spat out the seeds to see who could spit the farthest.

Lucinda greeted Sam and Cassie with a wide smile, and she momentarily lifted her hand from the crank to wave. "Hi, y'all. Come join the party. I should have known that the sound of this here machine would bring people out of the woodwork."

Homemade peach ice cream. The name alone brought back memories of long summer days spent in the gazebo with Harriet. The cones would drip down their forearms in the ever-losing battle of trying to lick the drips before they fell. They'd spend hours out there during summer vacation talking about everything, especially boys. And the summer when Harriet was away at camp, Cassie had sat in the gazebo eating her ice cream alone, watching Joe slap coats of blue paint on the ceiling and falling in love in the process.

Cassie searched the crowd of little people for her sister. "Where's Harriet?"

Lucinda straightened, putting a hand on her hip. "That girl was just about give-out. I had to force her to go inside and take a rest. She said she'd only go in for a minute, but last I checked on her, she was sound asleep."

Sam stowed his bag underneath the table. "In that case, we'll let her rest a while longer. That'll give me a chance to dig into this ice cream.'' At Lucinda's direction, he went inside to the large freezer and brought out another bin.

Cassie held out two cones as Sam dropped generous portions on top. When Cassie bent her head to get a bite, her nose bumped into the large mound of ice cream, leaving a dollop of the peach stuff on the tip.

"That's cute, Cassie," Sam said after taking a small bite from the side of his.

"Here, then." With her index finger, she scooped up some ice cream from her own cone and gently placed it on the tip of Sam's nose.

Knoxie, who had come to stand by her aunt, giggled uproariously and stuck her nose in her own cone.

Sam looked at the little girl. "You think that's funny, sweetheart? Watch this." He stuck three fingers into his cone and deposited a sticky cold chunk onto Cassie's cheek.

With that, Cassie squeezed her hand over her cone, making sure her fist was full of the sweet stuff, and carefully wiped it through his hair.

Most of the children had now stopped to stare at the two adults making spectacles of themselves.

Lucinda stopped cranking and came and stood between them. "All right, you two, that's enough. It's going to take forever to get all that sugar out of his hair. . . ."

"Excuse me, Lucinda." Gently, Sam guided Cassie's aunt to the side. Then he calmly plopped his cone upside down on Cassie's head.

Cassie decided that she really should be more angry, but laughing made it difficult. God, it felt good. When was the last time she had laughed so hard?

"Cassandra?"

The voice brought her back to reality, and she immediately quieted, turning on her heel toward the sound of the voice.

Andrew stood at the corner of the property by the swing set. His double-breasted suit jacket hung open, the front of his shirt saturated with sweat. His blond hair appeared streaked with brown, and perspiration dripped down his forehead. He clutched his suitcase with his left hand, his rumpled Burberry raincoat tossed over the other.

Cassie stared at him for a moment, feeling the ice-cream cone on her head slip to the side and then fall with a gentle plop on the ground beside her. Then she said the first thing that came to mind. "Well, butter my butt and call me a biscuit."

Chapter 13

Cassie grabbed a couple of napkins off the red-and-white-checked tablecloth and handed one to Sam. She wiped the other one over her face, pieces of paper sticking to her nose and cheek. Forcing a smile, she approached her fiancé, trying to ignore his look of shock. "Andrew. This is a . . . surprise. We weren't expecting you for another week."

He dropped his suitcase on the ground and loosened his tie. "After our last phone conversation, I decided I'd better come earlier. What the hell's going on, and who's that guy?"

Before she could answer, Sam swaggered forward. She blinked, wondering why he was walking as if he spent most of his days straddling a horse. He stuck out his hand toward Andrew. "Hey! Now ain't this a pleasure. You must be Cassie's beau. I'm Sam Parker."

Cassie didn't know whether to laugh, cry, or just run away screaming. The ice cream in Sam's hair had started to melt and drip down the side of his face, while pieces of yellow napkin stuck to his beard stubble and fluttered as he moved. He looked utterly ridiculous but amazingly, completely, appealing.

Andrew looked down at the outstretched hand for a

moment before shaking it. "Nice to meet you. Andrew Wallace." When he let go, he rubbed his hands together.

"Nice to meet you, Andy. Our Cassie's just been talkin' up a storm about you, and finally gettin' to meet you is just about gooder'n grits."

It was Andrew's turn to blink. "Um, it's *Andrew.*"

Not able to stand looking at the yellow scrap of napkin stuck on Sam's nose, Cassie reached over and pulled it off, Andrew scrutinizing her movements. He stepped toward her, grabbed her arm, and pulled her close in an intimate embrace. When she looked up to protest, he kissed her, sliding his tongue against her lips. She stiffened, but he didn't let go of her. He smiled as he lifted his head. "I've missed you."

She put her hands on his chest and tried gently to push away. "I've missed you, too." When he bent his head toward her again, she raised her hand between them to wipe sweat off her forehead. "Gosh, it's so hot. Let's get you home so you can change into something more comfortable."

He dropped his arms from around her, his lips smiling but his eyes cool.

Cassie looked at the large suitcase in the grass. "I'm assuming you had a taxi drop you off at Daddy's house and nobody was there. Why didn't you leave your suitcase on the porch?"

Andrew sent Cassie a curious glance. "That's expensive luggage. I wasn't about to just leave it on a porch." He glanced around at the children running around the backyard. "Some old guy wearing overalls in a pickup truck even offered me a lift. Hard to believe. But he at least told me where I could find you."

Sam leaned down and scooped up the suitcase. "Heck, Andy, people here in Walton are so honest, they'd put stuff *in* your suitcase." He gave them both a wink. "Now, seein' as how you're without transportation, let's all just pile into my truck and I'll take you home."

Andrew's face blanched. "You mean my car's not here? Is there anything wrong?"

Cassie smiled brightly. "Nothing that can't be fixed. I'll fill you in later."

Sam waved to Lucinda and led the way to the front of the house. Cassie briefly introduced Andrew and Lucinda, then rushed to follow Sam. George gave them all a welcoming bark, making Andrew take a step back, but he withheld any complaints he might have had as he saw his suitcase lifted into the bed of the truck with the dog.

Sam pulled open the driver's side door. "We'll all have to squeeze into the front seat. Got all my huntin' gear back there, and there's just no room."

Narrowing her eyes, Cassie regarded him closely. She knew the backseat was filled with presentation materials and handouts for the following week's medical conference in Atlanta. Before she could protest, he threw an old flannel blanket from the truck bed onto the pile.

Cassie slid into the middle, then tried not to laugh as she watched Andrew negotiate his way into the truck. Sam flipped on the air-conditioning full force and turned to them with a silly grin. "Man. It's hotter'n a goat's butt in a pepper patch."

Cassie elbowed him in the ribs, then focused her attention on the dashboard as she tried to ignore Andrew's proprietary hand on her thigh. As soon as Sam put the truck in drive, his hand snaked its way over the back of the seat, coming to rest on her right shoulder. The ride home was the longest five minutes of her entire life.

The truck stopped in front of the old house, and they climbed out. Cassie stared up at the familiar façade, with its stately columns, and felt an odd surge of pride. Turning to Andrew, she waited for his reaction.

"So, this is the old pile of lumber." He put his hands on his hips and walked back behind the truck as if to get a better view. He turned in a circle, surveying the property. "I didn't get a good chance to look at it before. But now I see why you're having such a problem selling it. It's so old."

Sam slammed the truck door a little louder than necessary.

Cassie tugged on Andrew's arm. "How can you say that? You haven't even seen the inside."

He turned toward the house again, squinting into the sun. "It's old. Not my style. But really, the land it's sitting on could be a real gold mine."

Cassie bit down hard on her lip, wanting to defend her house and the place she had called home throughout the many happy years of her childhood. But she kept quiet instead, catching sight of Sam watching her closely.

Sam hoisted the suitcase out of the truck bed and slung it solidly onto the ground and right in the middle of a small puddle.

"Sorry 'bout that, Andy. Didn't see the puddle."

Andrew yanked on the handle and lifted it up. Cassie recognized the belligerent jut of his chin and knew she had to separate the two men before things came to blows.

She pulled on his coat sleeve. "Andrew, let's go inside and get you cleaned up. Thanks for the ride, Sam." She tugged on Andrew's elbow and led him toward the steps. Andrew moved ahead and stopped at the front door. Cassie hung back, turning toward Sam. "Sam? Please don't forget. . . ."

"I won't forget." The foolish grin disappeared as he spoke, the country hayseed gone.

A small grin crept across her face. "How did you know what I was going to say?"

He didn't return her smile. "I've known you for a long time." He turned and opened the door to his truck. "Don't worry. I'll go check on Harriet now. But you're probably going to have to be a real pain in the butt to get her to make an appointment for a complete office checkup." He climbed behind the steering wheel, slammed the door shut, then leaned one muscular forearm out the window. "I know you can be real good at that." He started the engine and pulled away before she could think of a response.

When she approached the waiting Andrew, his scowl turned into a practiced smile. "Alone at last." She allowed herself to be pulled into his embrace, her face plastered against his custom-made Egyptian cotton shirt. She sniffed, smelling the familiar expensive cologne, the starch of his shirt, and tried to nestle into his arms until she found a comfortable spot. She sniffed again, wondering what was missing.

Jerking her head up, her gaze met his.

"What's wrong?" His voice deepened as he pressed her closer to him.

She closed her eyes for a moment, trying to figure it out. Her eyes widened with realization. There wasn't anything wrong. There was just something missing. The smell of outdoors, Dial soap, and the rough feel of denim. *Sam.*

"Nothing. It's just so hot, that's all." She broke away and opened the door. "See? It was unlocked. You could have just put your stuff inside."

He followed her into the foyer, plopping down his dirty suitcase on the Oriental rug and gazing about the room. "It's like a museum in here. Who are all those goofy-looking people in the portraits?"

Cassie crossed her arms in front of her. "Your future in-laws. So be nice."

"Oops. Sorry." He faced her, not looking at all repentant. "Are we alone?"

Her fingers strayed to the charms around her neck. "Ah, yes. But Aunt Lucinda should be back soon. . . ."

He dropped his raincoat on top of the suitcase and approached her with a purposeful look. "Where's our bedroom?"

Something akin to panic rippled through her. What had gotten in to her? This was the man she was supposed to marry. "Our bedroom? Oh, you mean mine?" She tried to picture Andrew in the pink canopied bed, making room for the giant stuffed elephant that had been keeping her company of late. "It's upstairs, but—"

"Come on, then." He pulled on her hand, dragging her toward the steps. There was no mistaking the look in his eyes. It occurred to her to wonder why she felt nothing at his touch.

Before she could think of an excuse, she heard a car door slam outside. She pulled away. "That's Aunt Lucinda." She almost skipped to the front door and flung it open.

"Hey, Aunt Lu." Even to her own ears her voice sounded as country as collard greens. She didn't bother to turn around to catch Andrew's expression.

Lucinda fairly ran up the stairs and into the house, breathing heavily as she teetered in her four-inch heels. She wore freshly applied Bingo Night Red lipstick and smelled of baby powder. Cassie spied lines of the white stuff in the elbow crease of her aunt's arm.

The older woman tottered toward Andrew and smothered him in an embrace, leaving powder smudges on his jacket and a look of alarm on his face.

Lucinda smiled brightly. "I didn't get the chance before over at Harriet's house, but I just had to give you a hug and welcome you to the family, Andy. It's so good to finally meet you."

A small smile plastered itself on Andrew's face. "That would be Andrew. And, yes, it's nice to meet you, too. You're exactly how I pictured you."

The wattage on Lucinda's smile didn't dim. "Why, thank you. And you're exactly what I pictured, too." She looked down at the muddy suitcase. "Here, why don't I take that and let you get settled in your room. I'm putting you down here in my room. It just wouldn't be fittin' to leave you and Cassie alone upstairs. I'll sleep in the guest room instead."

With a wink at Cassie, Lucinda hoisted the suitcase and sashayed out of the foyer and to the back of the house.

Cassie ignored the stunned expression on Andrew's face and silently thanked her aunt. She wasn't sure why she should be so relieved to be rescued by Lucinda; after all, she was no stranger to Andrew's bed. But there was something about seeing Andrew here, in this town, in her house, that illuminated him in a strange new light—a light that wasn't entirely flattering. He stuck out like snow in July, and as she stared at him with new eyes, she realized for the first time in their relationship how very different they were.

She couldn't remember ever thinking that before, but maybe he had changed in the short time they'd been apart.

Cassie gave him a quick peck on the cheek before escaping past him and up the first couple of stairs. "I've got to shower and get this sticky ice cream off me before I start attracting ants. When I'm done, I'll show you the house."

"Oh, boy," he said, looking entirely unenthusiastic. "Can't wait."

As Cassie turned to run up the rest of the stairs, she could have sworn the eyes of Great-great-great-grandfather Madison sent her a scolding look.

Cassie sat on the porch swing, her bare feet skimming the surface of the floorboards, her eyes closed and head tilted back to catch the breeze from the ceiling fan. The door shut with a bang, and she jerked up.

Andrew's hair was still damp from his shower. With the high humidity in the air, it wasn't going to dry by itself anytime soon. Splotches of perspiration already marred his pale green silk shirt, and wet streaks snaked down under the waistband of a pair of mocha-colored linen trousers.

"Damn it's hot! How can they stand it?"

She eyed his outfit with amusement. "Well, for one thing, they dress appropriately."

His gaze traveled from her bare feet up to the denim shorts and cotton tank top with spaghetti straps she had bought on the spur of the moment during a trip to the local Wal-Mart. "I have my standards."

She moved over to make room for him on the swing. "Then stop complaining about being hot."

He eyed the swing speculatively, awkwardly maneuvering himself next to her. He slid back on the seat, then rested his arm around her shoulders, his fingers caressing her collarbone. They swung in silence for a moment before Andrew spoke.

"So, Cassandra. What's going on here?"

She looked down at her hands, noticing her peeling fingernails. She hadn't bothered to get a manicure since she'd been in Walton. "What do you mean?"

"Well, for starters, who's that guy? Sam something or other."

Cassie swallowed in an effort to make her voice sound nonchalant. "Sam Parker. He's the town doctor. An old family friend."

Andrew shook his head. "Oh, great. I guess everybody here spends a lot of time praying they won't get sick. What a bozo."

Cassie pulled away. "You don't even know him. You can't always tell who a person is by the way they look." Cassie pushed at the floorboard with a dig of her heel, sending the swing into an odd rocking pattern.

Andrew snorted. "Well, what about the way he talks? He reminds me of that Goober guy on *The Andy Griffith Show*. Hell, he's so perfect, we might be able to use him in one of our commercials as a redneck gas-station attendant. He'd be a natural."

She almost mentioned Sam's Harvard degree but kept silent, figuring it would be a lot more amusing to have Andrew find out for himself.

They turned their heads in unison at the sound of tires on gravel. Ed Farrell's Cadillac, its white walls sparkling, pulled into the drive and parked. Slowly, Ed slid out of the car and sauntered toward them, his pinstriped suit reflecting the sunlight.

Cassie stopped the swing and stood. "Hey, Ed." There was that word again. When had the word *hello* fallen from her vocabulary?

"Hey, Cassie." He approached Andrew with an outstretched hand and a smile. "And you must be Cassie's fiancé. It's a real pleasure to meet you."

Andrew stood and shook hands. "Andrew Wallace. Nice to meet you." He studied Ed's face closely. "Have we met before? You look vaguely familiar."

"Nope. Don't think so. Can't imagine there being somebody looking just like me, though. Pretty scary, huh?"

He chuckled as Andrew simply nodded. Cassie noted Andrew's smirk as his gaze took in Ed's suit, and she had the oddest desire to go stand in front of Ed as a protective shield from ridicule.

Seemingly oblivious to Andrew's expression, Ed hitched up his pants. "So. What do you think of the property? Cassie's got a nice thing here. Have you had a chance to check out my new neighborhood, Farrellsford?"

Andrew's eyebrows rose with interest. "You're a builder?"

Ed's gaze shifted to Cassie for a moment. "Not exactly. I'm a realtor who just dabbles in land development and improving the town of Walton. It's been pretty lucrative these last few years."

"Really?" Andrew's attention had been aroused. "How lucrative?"

"Follow me." Ed led Cassie and Andrew off the porch and around the side of the house where the backs and chimneys of some of the houses in Farrellsford could be seen. Ed pointed. "I bought that piece of property for a song not three years ago. Now I've got close to a hundred and fifty houses on it, each going for around two hundred thousand." He grinned widely at Andrew. "Now that's what I call lucrative."

Cassie narrowed her eyes at the slate gray hip roofs of the houses in Farrellsford. "But Ed also believes in keeping the integrity of Walton. Which is why he's not pressuring me to do anything with the house besides sell it to another family for residential use. Right, Ed?"

"Well, yes, Cassie. As long as that solution remains feasible." He hitched up his pants again, looking uncomfortable in the stifling sun. "But I told you it would be hard, since everybody wants new construction these days. I've shown it to four families so far, and every single one of them has decided on one of the newer homes. That's why I came over today. To start talking about our plan B."

Cassie looked beyond his shoulder to the white house behind him. Every brick, every shingle, every floorboard, was as familiar to her as her own skin. The squeaks and sounds of the old house had been her nightly lullaby ever since she could remember. Her gaze strayed to the front lawn as a small breeze blew toward them, carrying on it the scent of her mother's roses. Beyond the house, towering over the driveway, the magnolia her mother had planted as a sapling when Cassie was born twittered its leaves in the breeze.

Ed continued. "And the good news is, I think I've got part of the town council on my side about that moratorium to halt further development. The police chief and Judge Moore have sworn to oppose, and I'm working on the others. Sam can't pass it without a majority, and I don't think he's going to get it." He smiled gently at her. "I'm not talking about bulldozing the house, Cassie. You know I'd hate that as much as you would. I'm just talking about finding some other uses for the existing structure with just some minimal changes."

Cassie's gaze fell to the backyard. There she saw the ghosts of her childhood friends playing hide-and-seek in the twilight of a long-gone day. She smelled her mother's roses again and turned back to the men. "I don't know if there is going to be a plan B, Ed. I know that's not what we originally talked about, but the more I think about it, the more I'm pretty sure I'd never be able to see this property used for anything else except for a family who wants to live in the house." She stared at the two men evenly. "I can wait. For however long it takes."

Andrew gave her a contentious look. "I beg to differ, Cassandra. First, you have a job in dire need of your attention back in New York. Second, there's an awful lot of money to be gained here."

Cassie stared at her fiancé, waiting for him to say something about how much he needed her and loved her. Then she realized what she wanted most was for him to turn around and look at the house, to see it through her eyes and to know that the brick, mortar, and wood were worth far more to her than money. He did neither. Instead, he frowned as he tilted his head back. "This old place looks like a fire hazard."

Cassie looked at Andrew in disbelief, then turned at the sound of her aunt's voice.

Lucinda stood on the edge of the porch, waving at them. "Hey, y'all, I brought out some sweet tea. Thought you could sure use it on such a hot day."

Without waiting for the men, Cassie charged forward toward the steps. Her hand shook as she poured herself a glass. She paused for a moment, looking intently at the fuschia aluminum cup. She held the frosty metal up to her cheek and closed her eyes, remembering going to the Green Stamp store with her mother to buy them. With her mother's help, Cassie had licked and pasted all those stamps into their little book until they had enough to get those silly aluminum cups. They were as much a part of her childhood as church picnics and swimming in the creek behind Senator Thompkins's house.

The two men walked up the steps, deep in conversation. Cassie handed Andrew a fluorescent blue cup and watched with amusement as he raised an eyebrow before placing his lips on the curved edge to drink.

Ed chose a bright yellow cup and took a sip before addressing Andrew again. "If you like, I'd be happy to show you around Farrellsford and some other projects I've got going on around town. I'm always looking for investors." He winked.

To Cassie's surprise, Andrew nodded. "I'd like that."

"Aunt Cassie!"

They all turned to see Madison walking up the drive, Knoxie on her hip and Joey and Sarah Frances following close behind.

"Dr. Parker said Mama needed to rest, so he sent us over here."

The children clattered up onto the porch and stopped, staring at Andrew. Cassie made the introductions and was proud of the children as they each held out a small hand to him.

Knoxie slid down from Madison's arms and wailed, "I need to go potty."

Madison grabbed her hand and led her into the house. Quickly, the screen door popped open again, and Madison stuck her head out. "Before I forget—are batteries made of metal? Like, would they set off a metal detector?"

Cassie puckered her eyebrows as she regarded her niece. "Yes, I believe they are. Why do you need to know?"

Knoxie wailed again from inside the house. "*Now,* Maddie. I don't wanna wet my pants."

Madison smiled. "Oh, no reason." She let the screen door slam behind her as she disappeared inside.

Andrew stared at Joey and Sarah Frances who were now sprawled on the porch swing. "Oh, my god! You mean your sister has four children?"

Cassie put her cup down and poured more tea. "Actually, five. Baby Amanda must be home with Harriet."

Sarah Frances's small voice piped up. "Mama says we shouldn't use the Lord's name in vain, Mr. Wallace."

Andrew's eyes widened before he turned to Ed. "You know, I'm not doing anything right now. If you've got a few minutes, I'd love to take that tour."

Ed put his cup down on a railing. "Nope. Got nothin' planned at all. It would be my pleasure."

Andrew turned back to Cassie. "Assuming that's all right with you."

Cassie waved her hand in dismissal. "It's fine with me. I'll stay here and play with the children."

Andrew kissed her quickly on the cheek, then left to get into Ed's Cadillac. Ed faced her for a moment with a sympathetic smile. "We'll talk later, all right? And if you just want to wait it out until we find the right family for your house, then that's fine with me."

He winked and began walking toward the Cadillac with the same lanky gait he hadn't seemed to have outgrown. Cassie paused for a moment, recalling the memory of going with her mother to deliver a bucket of apples and old clothes to Ed's mother. Ed had walked away from them without a word as soon as they reached the bottom broken step of the front porch. His bare feet had stirred up clouds of red dust as he strode across the parched and bare yard in front of the dilapidated house, as if the embarrassment of facing charity was more than he could stand.

Cassie turned and opened the screen door. "Maddie. When you come out, grab some apples and meet us under the magnolia out front."

She reached for the hands of the two children, and the three went running across the lawn, the freshly cut grass tickling her bare toes. They sat under the welcoming branches of the old tree, leaning against the trunk, their legs stretched out in front of them. They were soon joined by Maddie and Knoxie, and the air was filled with the juicy crunchings of apples.

Maddie sat cross-legged on the grass in front of her aunt. "Is that the guy you're gonna marry?"

Cassie nodded, her mouth filled with apple.

The younger children squealed and giggled, and Joey blurted out, "Ew, they're gonna kiss!"

Madison gave her brother a stern look, and he quieted. "Why does he dress so funny?"

Cassie nearly choked. "It's not 'funny.' Just different from what you're used to. That's how many of the men dress in New York. It's more fashionable."

Madison munched thoughtfully, then said, "It doesn't look very comfortable, but I suppose I could get used to it."

Cassie raised both eyebrows in amusement as she took another bite. Leaning her head back against the trunk, she startled at seeing a large bug close to her head. Turning her face to examine it more closely, she realized it was the shell of a cicada embedded in the tree trunk, the occupant long since gone. She plucked it from its prison, holding it gently between two fingers, and brought it close to her face to stare at it intently.

The shell appeared nearly transparent, the wings, long gone, now fragile paddles of stray breezes in a new life. It was as if the body of the insect had taken flight, leaving its soul in the place it called home, under the gentle fanning of the magnolia leaves. Digging her bare toes into the cool summer grass, Cassie placed it into her palm and blew hard, letting the delicate shell drift slowly to the ground.

Behind Madison's shoulder, she spotted Sam's truck pulling up the drive. Madison turned around and watched as Sam got out and walked toward them.

She faced her aunt again with a grin. "Dr. Parker's much cuter than Mr. Wallace, don't you think?"

Watching Sam approach, wearing those thigh-hugging jeans, boots, and a knit golf shirt, Cassie wanted to agree. He had obviously just taken a shower, for his hair was still wet and she smelled the soap as soon as he stood in front of them.

He greeted each of the children, giving Joey a high five. Then he turned to Cassie and reached for her hand. "We need to talk."

Something in his eyes made her drop her apple core and grab hold without question. He didn't let go of her hand as they walked toward the house, finally stopping in front of the porch.

Grim lines etched the corners of his mouth, but his eyes were soft as he regarded her. "I need you to do me a favor."

She tilted her head, curious. "Depends. What do you need?"

He lowered his head for a moment, then looked back at her, his eyes darkening. "I've scheduled an office appointment for Harriet next Wednesday morning at eight o'clock. I need to make sure she doesn't forget or postpone it. Can you make sure she gets there?"

"Yes. Of course. Why?"

He didn't say anything right away, but continued to stare hard into her eyes.

Unbidden, her hand flew to the chain around her neck, her fingers clutching at the small gold hearts, then sliding to the key that hung lower than the other charms. "Is she . . . is she sick?"

He didn't look away. "It's too soon to say anything. Her fatigue has me worried, but I'm not here to jump to conclusions. We'll know more after her appointment."

Cassie's gaze slid over to the four children sitting under the giant magnolia, their high voices traveling over the green expanse of lawn. She looked up at Sam again. "Our mother ... she ... had breast cancer, you know." Her hand began to shake, and his fingers closed over hers to still them.

"I know. But don't you start worrying. There's lots of reasons for fatigue, and four of them are sitting right over there under that tree."

Cassie's smile warbled as she nodded. He rubbed his knuckles gently over her jaw, their hands clasping the necklace together. "It will be all right, Cassie. I'll be right here with you, okay? You can count on it."

She squeezed his hands tightly, sure of that one truth, and looked at him with grateful eyes. They turned in unison at the sound of Ed's car coming toward them. Dropping their hands, they moved apart, but Cassie felt his comforting presence just as surely as if his arms were around her, holding her tight.

Chapter 14

Cassie sat on the swing in the cool shade of the porch, the writing box settled next to her. The breeze from the fan above rustled the pages of the yellowed letter in her hand, whispering its secrets.

October 1, 1962
Dear Harry,

I was nearly caught last night. The window jamb slammed shut after I had crawled inside, and I think it woke Daddy. I threw myself under the covers just in time. It was so hard to make myself breathe slowly, but I think I had him fooled. I don't like this sneaking around. I'd like to shout our love from the town square, on top of that soldier's horse, but until Daddy's heart is feeling stronger, it's just something we need to keep to ourselves.

I have a little favor to ask of you. There's a new girl in town, Catherine Anne Abbott. I know you've heard me talk about her, because she's my best friend in the whole world. She's moving here from Columbus and will be living with her aunt, old Miss Shrewster.

Catherine Anne's parents died recently in a horrible car wreck, and her aunt is the only living soul in her family. I know her because our parents were friends and we've been spending summers together ever since I can remember. She's quite a few years younger than me, but just as sweet as can be. But she's come here to live now, with that old, shrunken, prune-faced aunt of hers, and I'm afraid she'll become just like Miss Shrewster if she isn't brought out at all. If you do happen to run into her in town, introduce yourself. Don't mention you know me—I don't want to force her to keep our secret—but do say hello and make her feel comfortable. And please tell all your single friends about her. Maybe, when we're free of our secrets, we can double-date or something.

Daddy has just come home, so I'll close this letter. I don't know if I can stand waiting a whole week to see you again. Think of me kissing the locket and thinking of you.

Love,
E.

A car door slammed in the driveway, making Cassie look up. Harriet approached, a crisp yellow linen sundress hanging loosely on her small frame. "I thought you might like a ride over to Bitsy's." She held up something in her hand. "And I brought you one of the shower invitations—for your scrapbook. I'm having napkins printed, too, and I'll save you one from the party."

Cassie nodded, feeling a little shell-shocked. She moved the writing box to her lap and allowed Harriet to sit next to her. "How are you feeling?"

Harriet sighed. "Oh, the same, I guess. I suppose I'll find out what kinds of vitamins I need to be taking when I see Sam on Wednesday." She indicated the letter with a nod of her head. "Anything interesting?"

"I'd say so." Cassie handed her the letter.

The moving air from the ceiling fan played with the fine

blond hairs that had strayed out of Harriet's headband as she bent over to read. She finished and handed the letter back, her blue eyes wide. "So. That's how it happened. Sort of like it was meant to be."

Cassie stuck the letter back in the box, slamming the lid a little too hard. "Meant to be? She practically threw Mama at Daddy. Imagine how she must have felt." Cassie turned away and stuck out her chin. "No, never mind. You couldn't. But trust me, it feels awful."

With a wry grin, Harriet ducked her face. "I guess I deserved that. But we're not talking about you and me and Joe. We're talking about Mama and Daddy. I know they were the loves of each other's lives, and nothing will ever change that. Unfortunately, Daddy was also the love of Miss E's life."

Cassie stood abruptly, clutching the box to her chest. "How can you say that? She left him. She abandoned him and took their child and gave it up for adoption. If she really loved Daddy, I'd hate to see what she'd do to somebody she hated."

Harriet twisted the gold wedding band around on her finger, her gaze focused far beyond the front porch and green grass. "She loved him so much that she sacrificed everything she loved so he could be happy." Her eyes met her sister's, her expression somber.

Cassie shook her head. "Love isn't about sacrifice. It's about meeting each other's needs. It's about companionship. Not to mention the fact that Miss E's sacrifice makes Daddy sound incredibly selfish."

"I don't think Daddy was being selfish, because that's not like him at all. I don't think he was given a choice. I read that letter up in the attic, too. It seemed that Miss E was doing everything she could to make sure Daddy didn't find their baby—and for good reason." She pushed hair out of her eyes, her gold band catching the sunlight. "And I think you're wrong about the sacrifice part. Love is all about sacrifices—big and small ones. It's only when you know how much you could give up for somebody that you know what true love really is."

The whirring fan spun above them, the only sound on the silent porch, the unspoken words of what lay behind their fifteen-year estrangement lying scattered about them like fallen leaves. Yes, Cassie knew all about being sacrificed in the name of love, and it didn't seem right that so much pain could walk so easily with love.

Finally, Cassie hoisted the box under one arm. "We're going to be late if we don't get a move on. Let me go put this inside and I'll be right out."

Without waiting for a response, she disappeared inside the house, the screen door banging shut behind her.

The ladies sat under domed dryers at Bitsy's House of Beauty, their hair wrapped in bits of foil and brightly colored curlers. Cassie frowned, feeling as though she could pick up the local radio station with the contraptions on her head.

She shifted her attention, warily eyeing the comb and scissors in Bitsy's hand. "I just want a sleek bob—nothing fancy. Just what I have now, but trimmed up a bit." She chewed on her lip, trying to think of other ways to make her point. She was afraid that if she wasn't very explicit, she'd wind up looking like Lou-Lou, her hair teased within an inch of her life. "I don't want big hair—no need to tease it at all, okay?"

Bitsy patted her shoulder, a patient expression on her face. "Don't worry about a thing, sugar. I'll have you fixed up, sleek and pretty, in no time."

Chewing on her lip, Cassie glanced toward the chair next to her. Harriet sat holding a small stack of tiny tissues, handing them one by one to Ovella, Bitsy's sister and co-owner of the salon. Harriet's skin appeared dull and flat in the glare of the fluorescent lighting, the circles under her eyes dark and unforgiving.

Ovella's words were muffled by the bobby pins in her

mouth. "You look wore out, Harriett. Why don't you leave those little ones with me for a bit so you can get some rest?"

Harriet smiled and patted Ovella's arm. "I'm just a bit tired, that's all. But you watch out. I just might take you up on your offer." Harriet's gaze slid to Cassie's reflection in the mirror. "Miss Lena stopped by this morning. She wants to give you a copy of *Sweet Wicked Love* for a shower present. Before she earmarked all the juicy parts to use on your honeymoon, she wanted to make sure you hadn't read it yet."

Cassie noted Harriet's obvious attempt to change the subject. They would have plenty of opportunity on Wednesday to talk about Harriet's health. She waited for Bitsy to raise her chair before responding. "For an unmarried older woman, one would wonder about her fascination with sex. Do you think she's ever done 'it'?"

Harriet turned to Bitsy. "Do you ever remember Miss Lena having a boyfriend?"

Bitsy's forehead creased. "She's a good bit older than me, you know. She used to baby-sit for me and Ovella and our five brothers. We were monsters, really. She used to tell me she only did it for the money, because we were truly terrible. Climbing out windows after she put us to bed and that sort of thing." Long red nails combed through Cassie's wet hair, preceded by the snip of the shiny metal scissors. "She was working as the church secretary back then, right before her parents decided to send her to Europe to get 'cultured,' whatever that means. I'm pretty sure she had a boyfriend, though. Sometimes she'd be dropped off at our house in one of those cute British convertibles and be all dreamy and googly-eyed. Don't know who it was, though. Too young to care, I guess."

Her fingers straightened Cassie's jaw, then clipped off more hair with the scissors. "Couldn't have been very serious. Once she got back from Europe, she started back to work at the church again, and that was it. Never got married, which was a shame. She was so good with us kids and would have been a wonderful mother. She was always volunteering at the church's nursery, and those kids just loved her." She sighed heavily. "Even me and Ovella and our brothers. Oh, well. I guess not everybody can find their true love, like me and my Henry. 'Course, I had to go to another county to find him, but I think it was destiny. We would have found each other no matter what."

Cassie glanced over at her sister, whose own eyes had gone soft and wistful. Cassie looked down at her hands, focusing on her diamond engagement ring. She tried to think of Andrew and get all warm and mushy but couldn't. Maybe they were right. There was only one mate out there for everybody. You could spend your whole life searching and come up empty-handed. Or you could settle for "good enough." She sighed and looked back at her sister's reflection and was once again shocked at the pallor and sheer exhaustion etched on her face.

They regarded each other in the mirror. Before Cassie could comment on her sister's appearance, Harriet crossed her eyes and stuck out her tongue. Looking away, she handed another tissue to Ovella.

Madison walked in from the back of the shop, her gait stiff as she hobbled on her heels, her toes separated by cotton balls, the nails painted a bright fluorescent green.

Harriet only half-succeeded in looking shocked. "Are your toes radioactive, Maddie? I don't want them changing the taste of my cheese straws at the shower."

"Very funny, Mama. This color is very fashionable. I just saw it in *Seventeen*. All the girls are wearing it."

"Not in Walton, they're not." Even Harriet's voice sounded tired, and when Cassie looked back to her, her eyes were closed.

Wanting to defuse any mother-daughter tensions, Cassie suggested, "Why don't we go for the works, too, Har? We can have a manicure and pedicure—maybe even a facial. My treat."

Without opening her eyes, Harriet smiled. "I'd like that. Maybe Aunt Lucinda can do our makeup, too. I don't think I have the energy to even put on mascara."

Madison stood by her mother. "And why don't you borrow something out of my closet with a waist to wear tonight. I'm tired of seeing you in those muumuus. It's all you seem to wear anymore."

Before Harriet could respond, the bells over the door jangled, and Cassie looked through the strands of wet hair combed over her forehead. The two women that walked into the salon could have been a matching pair of bookends, but one generation apart. They both were pale blondes with slender builds and creamy skin and were wearing matching pink sweaters with pearls.

For a moment, Cassie was back in high school, rounding her shoulders and trying to disappear. Of all times to run into Doreen Cagle again; with her wet hair, in her Wal-Mart shorts and flip-flops, and wearing an unattractive orange vinyl cape, Cassie looked like something the cat dragged in. In her younger days, Doreen had eclipsed even the beautiful Harriet, and her daughter was her spitting image. Cassie watched as Madison eyed her nemesis.

"Hey, Lucy."

The girl appeared to be about Maddie's age but was much shorter and fine-boned, giving her a delicate look. She eyed Madison's toenail polish with a raised blond brow and without comment before answering. "Hello, Maddie. What are you doing here?"

The question sounded innocent enough, but Cassie could see Madison pulling her shoulders back. "What does it look like I'm doing?"

Lucy sniffed. "Well, it's just that I've never seen you here before." She regarded Madison casually with clear gray eyes. "I mean, you're on the girl's basketball team. They'd probably have you kicked off if they found out you were here."

Cassie held up her hand, making Bitsy step away. Flinging her hair out of her eyes, she approached the two women with a smile. "Doreen, it's so nice to see you again. What's it been—fifteen years? Gosh—is that the same hairstyle you wore in high school? I haven't seen that look in New York, but it suits you. How have you been?''

Without giving the other woman a chance to speak, Cassie gushed on, ''And those cute matching sweaters—how sweet! I just don't think those designers on Fifth Avenue know what they're doing when they ignore the homey styles that so many small-town girls cling to. It's just so, well, quaint. And I for one miss it terribly.''

Doreen and Lucy gave her identical plastered smiles. Cassie grabbed Madison's arm and brought her closer. ''Now just look at this gorgeous girl. I can hardly believe that she's my own flesh and blood. She's got that height and that dark 'look' that all those New York modeling agencies are going for these days. I can't believe y'all have been keeping her hidden here in Walton all this time.'' She reached her hand around her niece and squeezed.

All six women wore stunned expressions.

Doreen put her arm around her daughter. ''Yes, well. It's good to see you again, Cassie. It has been a while.'' She smiled, adjusting her purse on her shoulder. ''And you're right. Most of Walton hasn't changed a bit. Did I tell you that Lucy was Kudzu Queen this year? Guess we're lucky that the petite blonde is still in style here in Walton.''

Suddenly struck dumb, it was Cassie's turn to give them a plastic smile.

Doreen, leading her daughter away, said, '' 'Bye, y'all. Lucy's got a big date tonight with Kevin O'Neal, so we'd better let Bitsy get started working her magic. See y'all later.''

Madison looked as if she'd been struck. Harriet stood and walked over to them, clutching Cassie's arm and leaning on her heavily. She spoke softly into her sister's ear. ''You can't fix everything for everyone all the time, you know.''

Cassie shrugged, feeling the gold charms move against the skin on her neck. ''I suppose. But I can at least try.''

Harriet looked up at Cassie and spoke loud enough for Madison to hear. ''Come on, let's get finished here so we can go get our toenails painted neon green.''

Cassie grinned, wondering how she'd lived so long apart from this woman she called sister.

As they left Bitsy's, Cassie heard her name being called and squinted into the sun toward the sound of the voice.

"Wooeee! Be still my heart. I must be in heaven with all this beauty."

She couldn't stop the grin that spread across her face as Sam slid his truck into a parking space and joined them on the sidewalk.

He studied Madison and Harriet closely. "My. A vision of loveliness. It's a good thing I don't have a weak heart." He turned to Cassie and eyed her hair judiciously. "Hmm. Not as big as I usually like a lady's hair but simply stunning just the same."

Sam dodged Cassie's hand as she reached to slap his arm. "I'm heading to the Dixie Diner for lunch. It would do me proud to have you beautiful ladies join me."

Harriet squeezed his arm playfully. "You're such a flirt, Sam. Don't ever stop."

Cassie noticed how the sun played on her sister's hair, illuminating the bright gold strands. For the first time, she saw several gray hairs mixed in. The sun took no prisoners as it highlighted Harriet's face, accentuating every fine line and dark circle and stealing the color from her skin. Maybe we're just getting older, Cassie thought as she slid a glance at Sam. Almost two years older than Harriet, he radiated good health and youthful energy. The contrast between them was hard to miss. Sam's gaze met hers, and she knew he was noticing, too.

Harriet pushed Cassie toward Sam. "You two go on. Me and Maddie need to head toward home and get ready for the shower. I hope you're planning on attending, Sam. Joe's doing his famous barbecue." She winked. "And lots of beer, too. That should guarantee your presence."

Sam squeezed her arm. "Sure, Harriet. I'll be there. Wouldn't want to miss Senator Thompkins's clogging routine. He likes to save that for special occasions, so I don't get to see it as often as I like."

Harriet started to move off, Madison in her wake. "Yeah, I bet. You're terrible." She stepped off the curb, wobbling a bit until her daughter took her elbow. She faced Sam and Cassie with a wide smile. "We'll see you two at six, then."

Cassie stepped toward her. "I can help, Har. It's really silly for you to do all that work."

With a dismissive wave, Harriet stepped away. "I've got Lucinda and Maddie and a ton of other helpers. You're the guest of honor, and I wouldn't dream of putting you to work. I'll just see you later."

Cassie watched as Harriet and Madison walked toward the van parked on the town square.

"She doesn't look good, Sam. I'm worried about her."

She felt him grab her hand and turn her around. "Hey, no need for you to eat all that worry alone, okay? I'll be happy to split it with you."

Her face puckered as she regarded him. "Every time I see you, I either want to slap you or give you a hug. Why is that?"

She allowed him to lead her toward the diner. "It's because you've never tried any of the in-between stuff. You just give me a time and place and we can get started."

Facing him to give him a retort, the words died on her tongue.

"Where have you been, Cassandra? I've been waiting for over half an hour."

Andrew stood outside the door of the diner wearing olive linen pants and a dark yellow silk shirt with sweat stains showing under the arms. His annoyed gaze flickered over Sam before turning his full attention back to Cassie.

She'd completely forgotten she was supposed to meet Andrew at the diner for lunch. "Oh, Andrew. Sorry. Took a little longer at Bitsy's than I thought."

He bent to kiss her lips, but she tilted her head so that his lips merely slid across her cheek. Cassie smiled at him

as a sickening picture of her squeezed between Sam and
Andrew on one side of a booth flickered in her mind.

The bell over the door tinkled as they pushed it open and
went inside. Andrew put his arm around Cassie. "Does this
place have sushi? I could really go for some sugata rolls."

A pager beeped, and both Sam and Andrew patted their
pockets. It was for Sam. "It's the clinic. Sorry I won't be
able to join y'all for lunch. Guess I'll see you tonight." He
pushed open the glass door. With a slack grin and an accent
as thick as lard, he said, "And, Andy, only place you'll get
sushi around here is at the bait shop." With a wink, he let
the door close behind him.

Cassie stood in the doorway of Andrew's room, watching
him in the mirror as he knotted his tie. She recognized it as
the Hermes she had given him for his last birthday and
wondered if he had ulterior motives for wearing it.

Lunch together had not gone well. He had insisted on
sitting on the same side of the booth as she and then rubbing
her thigh throughout the meal. She was sure the other customers noticed, and it embarrassed her. These people had
known her parents and knew that she had been raised better
than that.

Things had further deteriorated when even Brunelle
Thompkins, the senator's wife and longtime waitress at the
diner, had her perpetually chipper demeanor darkened by
Andrew's carping at fat grams and ingredients as he scruti-
nized the menu. At first, she had simply stood by the side
of their booth, pad and pencil poised, as she suggested the
chicken fried steak with cheese fries. After ascertaining that
the cook didn't use low-fat vegetable oil for frying, he'd
eliminated half the items from the menu. Eventually, Cassie
took over and ordered them both house salads, minus the
fried chicken and bacon bits.

The final straw had come after they'd left the diner and
were walking across the town square. Andrew had spied
Miss Liberty glowing particularly green in the direct light

of the midday sun, her Styrofoam arm and lineman's glove proudly holding the torch aloft.

"Good Lord, what is that?"

Cassie drew herself up tall. "It's a replica of the Statue of Liberty. We're very proud of it."

Andrew's only response was to laugh until the tears sprang to his eyes. When he could finally speak, he gasped out, "That's the stupidest thing I have ever seen in my life. Are you sure it's not a joke?"

Cassie's lower lip quivered. She felt as if her family pride, her honor, her whatever, had been gravely insulted. She wanted to do something with that torch that would make it so Andrew would never think a bad thought about it again.

Instead, she said, "No, Andrew. You're the only joke around here. I'm going home." She turned on her heel, walking quickly in the opposite direction.

He had to jog to catch up with her, placing his hand on her arm to make her stop. "Damn it, Cassandra. It's not like it means anything to you. It's just a stupid statue."

She took a deep breath, wondering where her deep-felt indignation was coming from. "No, it's not. It's much more than that. But even if I explained it to you, you still wouldn't understand, so I'm just not going to waste my breath. You're warped, Andrew. If you can't see and recognize the gentle things in life, then living in New York has hardened you." She could tell from his blank expression that nothing she said was sinking in. "Never mind. I need to go home and change for the bridal shower. Just try not to embarrass me in front of my friends and family tonight, all right?"

He snorted. "Right. Like you have to worry about that. Isn't it the other way around?"

She shook her head at him. "You're so stuck-up you'd drown in a rainstorm. Maybe you should try harder to fit in; then we wouldn't have to worry about anybody embarrassing anybody else."

Before he could make her any angrier, she pulled away and walked all the way home, Andrew following doggedly at her heels.

That had been two hours earlier, and she still felt the sting of anger. Pushing it aside, she took a moment longer to scrutinize him without his being aware she was there. His long, tapered fingers—artist's fingers, that's what she'd always called them—jutted in and out of the silk tie as he adjusted it to perfection. Leaning her head against the doorframe, she studied those fingers, wondering if they knew her body better than he knew her mind and soul. And how well did she know him? She knew he had been born and raised in Southern California, the only child of a dentist and a salesclerk at Neiman-Marcus. She had never met them, and Andrew had only been to see them once in the years she had known him.

Andrew loved the ad agency and his work there, and their relationship had evolved around the rise of the agency's success, feeding off it like parasites. They lived the agency; breathed it morning, noon, and night. There was never any time for anything else. But his affection and admiration, coupled with their success, had seemed to be enough. But what had any of that to do with marriage? She realized with a start that she didn't know his favorite color or his life's secret dream or what his grandparents were like. She didn't know the color of the house he had grown up in or the name of his first-grade teacher or his first serious crush. She blinked hard, moving away from the threshold before he could see her.

She had reached the first step before his voice called out, "Cassandra? Are you ready for the big hoedown?"

He stuck his head out of the room, and Cassie looked at him and his carefully groomed hair. "Better stay away from the barbecue pit. That stuff on your hair looks flammable." She gritted her teeth. *Oh, Lord. I must be scared, because I'm sure as hell acting mean.*

He looked hurt, and Cassie felt a stab of remorse. With great effort, she smiled and offered her hand. "Come on. Lucinda's driving." She grinned, anticipating his reaction to Aunt Lucinda's pink car.

If the Free Book Certificate is missing, call 1-800-770-1963 to place your order. Be sure to visit our website at www.kensingtonbooks.com.

To start your membership, simply complete and return the Free Book Certificate. You'll receive your Introductory Shipment of FREE Zebra Contemporary Romances. Then, each month as long as your account is in good standing, you will receive the 3 newest Zebra Contemporary Romances. Each shipment will be yours to examine for 10 days. If you decide to keep the books, you'll pay the preferred book club member price of $15.95 – a savings of over 20% off the cover price! (plus $1.50 to offset the cost of shipping and handling.) If you want us to stop sending books, just say the word… it's that simple.

BOOK CERTIFICATE

Yes! Please send me FREE Zebra Contemporary romance novels. I understand I am under no obligation to purchase any books, as explained on this card.

Name _____

Address _____ Apt. _____

City _____ State _____ Zip _____

Telephone (___) _____

Signature _____

(If under 18, parent or guardian must sign)

Offer limited to one per household and not valid to current subscribers.
All orders subject to approval. Terms, offer, and price subject to change. Offer valid only in the U.S.

Thank You!

CN062A

Zebra Contemporary Romance Book Club
Zebra Home Subscription Service, Inc.
P.O. Box 5214
Clifton , NJ 07015-5214

PLACE
STAMP
HERE

"I hope my car's fixed soon and that Mr. Overalls knows what he's doing. I'd hate to make him pay for any damages."

Cassie's grin faded as she led him to the door.

Cars lined both sides of the street approaching her sister's house. Lucinda pulled into the one open spot in the driveway, claiming it was reserved for the guests of honor. Her gaze met Cassie's in the rearview mirror, and she winked. "Well, y'all. This is it." She didn't drop her gaze, and Cassie couldn't help but wonder if there was double meaning to her words.

They stepped out of the car and headed toward the squeal of children and the hum of adult voices from the backyard.

"I hope to God this thing is inside, because if I have to spend another minute in this heat, I'll melt."

"Have you ever been to an indoor barbecue, Andrew?" She grabbed his hand, feeling it already perspiring, and led him to the gate in the fence surrounding the backyard. Her first stop would be at the drinks table. Hopefully, there would be kudzu punch. She had a feeling she was going to need it.

Lucinda walked past them and into the milieu of people, but Andrew and Cassie stopped. Small children, dressed in their Sunday best, ran around chasing each other, playing a wild game of tag. Cassie recognized the shrieks of one child and turned to see Sarah Frances, a ribbon hanging precariously onto the end of a long braid, chasing a boy her age.

Old Mr. Crandall, the husband of Cassie's fifth-grade math teacher, sat on a stool, a large vat of lemonade in front of him, stirring the lemon-dotted liquid with a broken oar. He tipped the brim of his straw hat as he spotted the couple.

The spicy aroma of barbecue in an open pit teased Cassie's taste buds as she spotted Joe, beer in hand, basting the chicken parts with his secret sauce. Nearby, Joey and several of his friends were spitting watermelon seeds at each other while little girls hung behind them, squealing as each small dart hit its target.

Thelma and Selma Sedgewick, in matching Hawaiian print sundresses and large straw hats, spied Cassie and Andrew and headed toward them, brims nodding, like a couple of parakeets on a mission. It appeared that the whole town was there, standing or sitting around the deck, patio, and backyard. Old people sat in lawn chairs with grand-children, or even great-grandchildren perched on creaky knees or cradled in wrinkled arms. Miss Lena, the tops of her knee-high stockings peeking out under the hem of her polka-dot dress, sat next to the senator's wife, and Cassie watched in amusement as she took a paperback novel out of her large purse and handed it to the baffled Mrs. Thompkins.

Cassie smiled. It was like looking at an old movie from her childhood. She had been to many such parties as a child. Nothing had changed, not really. Perhaps some of the older folks were no longer here, and some of the town's matrons had progressed to the lawn chairs, the altering faces changing the individual threads of the fabric that made up her home-town. Today Harriet played hostess instead of their mother, and the young boys Cassie and her sister used to chase now had receding hairlines, thicker waists, and families of their own. Yes, the threads were different, but the richly woven fabric remained strong. These were her people. No matter how far she would ever roam, that fact would never change.

Sam leaned against a tree and said something that made Joe laugh. Cassie's gaze caught Sam's long enough for him to dip his head in greeting and raise his beer bottle. His blue eyes seemed to sparkle in the sun, and she found herself winking at him. She turned her head to see Reverend Beasley do his inside-out eyelid trick in front of an enraptured crowd of children. They were probably the third generation of Walton children lucky enough to be privy to such an experi-ence. Cassie breathed in deeply, feeling for the first time in a long while that perhaps lack of change might not be such a bad thing.

She glanced over at Andrew, her smile fading. A bemused

frown sat on his face, as if he couldn't quite make out what he was seeing. He shook his head as he looked back at her. "How long do you think we have to stay?"

It was as if a large spotlight had suddenly turned on above, illuminating just the two of them. Her first instinct was to flee in the face of the harsh reality, to run away from this huge problem looming on her doorstep. She'd done that once before, after all. Looking away for a moment, her gaze wandered back to the yard's edge. Sam's parents and Harriet, with baby Amanda on her hip, had joined him and Joe. Mr. Parker said something with a laugh, making his gray-haired wife nuzzle into his shoulder like a young girl. Cassie watched as Mrs. Parker's hand snaked behind her husband and pinched him through his overalls.

She caught Sam watching her with a questioning look and realized with surprise that she wore a silly grin. He winked at her, and she wanted nothing more at that moment than to go over to that group and be enveloped in the gentle comfort of people who really knew her and loved her, anyway.

Instead, with a deep breath, she faced Andrew again.

"Come on, Andy. We need to talk."

She yanked on his arm and pulled him back through the gate, letting it slam hard behind them.

Chapter 15

Cassie didn't stop walking until she had reached the cool respite of her own porch. Perspiration poured down her face and body from the short walk, making the silk of her dress stick to her skin. Ignoring Andrew, she kicked off her shoes, then reached under her dress and pulled off her pantyhose, throwing them to the ground. She plopped down in the porch swing, breathing heavily. She hadn't said a word, and Andrew hadn't asked any questions. But it was plain on his face that he was annoyed—and very, very hot.

She frowned at him. "You know, you'd be a lot cooler if you wore something that doesn't stick to your skin. Like a nice cotton knit. Or a T-shirt."

He gave her a disdainful look, then wiped the sweat from his forehead. "Cut the bull, Cassandra. What's going on here?"

She tugged at the fourth finger of her left hand, pulling off her ring and grasping it tightly for one last moment. Slowly, she opened her palm, watching as the light played on the large diamond in her hand. "I can't marry you, Andrew."

He blinked. "Why not?"

"We don't belong together. We work well together, but that's not enough to base a marriage on." She looked down at the ring, at its flawless perfection, but saw only a piece of jewelry. It meant nothing to her, and the thought surprised her. She looked up again and met his gaze. "I don't love you, Andrew. At least not enough to marry you."

He took a step toward her, his eyes narrowed. "What? You're walking out on me now? In the middle of the Bank-North campaign?"

She stared at him, incredulous. "I'm not talking about work here, Andrew. I'm talking about you and me and how a marriage between us would never work. Our backgrounds are miles apart. I don't even think I realized that until today. Did you know that we have never even talked about having children? Or where we want to live when we retire? Gosh, Andrew, we never take a vacation because we never find the time to discuss whether we want to go to the beach or go skiing." Her voice shook. This was probably the most honest conversation she had ever had with him, and she wanted to make sure she got her point across. "There's more to life than work, Andrew. And that's all we've got between us."

She stood, the swing swaying drunkenly behind her. Her voice quieted. "I've never even met your parents. And that's probably the saddest testament as to why I can't marry you."

She stopped talking, her breath coming hard and deep. Wide-eyed, she waited for his response, half-hoping he'd defend himself and call to mind why she had agreed to marry him in the first place.

He leaned closer. "It's that Sam guy, isn't it? Are you sleeping with him?"

Cassie blinked once. Then, without a word, she pulled her arm back and threw the ring at him, hitting him right between the eyes. It landed on the floorboards, bounced once, then came to rest near the welcome mat.

Andrew stared down at it but didn't make a move to pick it up. His voice was harsh when he spoke. "You won't even try to deny it, will you? What happened? You get lonely? Or did he make the moves on you first?''

Her anger bubbled up into her head to a point where she thought smoke might emerge from her ears. ''You think this has to do with Sam? After everything I've just said, you think I'm breaking our engagement because I'm sleeping with another man?'' She shook her head. ''You're cracked, Andrew. You're just completely clueless. Seek help—but I won't be there to hold your hand during therapy. Maybe Cynthia Moore would be happy to do it instead.''

He looked at her as if she had just sprouted horns. Almost under his breath, he said, ''I knew better than to let you come down here. These people have changed you. You need to come back to New York and see how real people live.''

She felt the reassuring pressure of the swing against the back of her legs. *''These* people are real, Andrew. It's taken me fifteen years to realize it, but they're *my* people, and I love them. If I've had to change to see that, then so be it.'' She reached up with her right hand to grasp the gold charms on her necklace.

''Does that mean you're going to stay down here?''

''No!'' The response was automatic, emitted without thought. ''Of course not. I love my career. I'm good at it, I enjoy my success, and I've worked too hard to leave it all behind. And I hope . . . that we can still work together. That's one thing that I know we do well.''

He wiped his hands over his face. ''Don't do this, Cassandra. We had something great going between us. We just need to get away from this nightmare of a town and get back to New York. You'll see things differently then.''

With a violent jerk of the swing, Cassie stepped toward him. ''You just don't get it, do you? I *am* seeing things differently, for the first time in years.'' Her fingers gripped the railing as she stared out at her mother's magnolia. ''Did you ever play tag as a kid—you know, where there was one place called base where nobody could tag you? Well, you were my base. I clung to you to keep all that hurt and humiliation away from me, knowing that as long as I had you and my career, they could never touch me.''

She faced him, feeling the warmth of the dying sun on her cheeks. "I don't need a base anymore. I'm okay with my past. I even feel like I want to visit here often. But I don't want to marry you.''

He stood before her, his balled fists on his hips. "Is that it, then? You don't want to marry me?''

She nodded, her voice too tangled with conflicting emotions.

His lips formed a thin line. "Fine. Then I'd better get packing.'' He turned away from her and yanked open the screen door. "Cynthia Moore needs me at the office.''

The screen door slammed, leaving Cassie staring after him. She called out at his retreating back, "You forgot the ring!''

She waited a few seconds before the door swung open again and Andrew reappeared. He got down on his hands and knees and looked for the ring until he found it, nestled between two floorboards. Prying it out, he tucked it inside his shirt pocket and stood.

"You'll regret this decision, Cassandra. All that fried food has turned your brain to mush. But maybe when you're back in New York and you need somebody intelligent to talk to and straighten you out, call me. I just might still be available to knock some sense into you.''

He left her on the porch, his footsteps disappearing inside the house.

Weakly, she shouted at him through the door, "And don't call me Cassandra. My name's Cassie!''

She sat back down on the swing and waited for the big, crushing blow of disappointment and sorrow to swallow her. But it never came. A small breeze teased the hair at her temples, and a little smile played on her lips. Kicking her shoes out of the way, she jumped down the porch steps and began running, feeling the soft grass under her feet and a freedom she hadn't felt in years. Hiking up her dress, she turned a cartwheel, landing solidly on her backside. Lying in the grass, she looked up at the brilliant blue sky, a hint of stars glowing dully behind the sun's glare, and grinned to herself.

Cassie scraped the remains of the potato salad into a large Tupperware bowl and sealed the lid over it. She remained motionless in Harriet's kitchen for a moment, her eyes squeezed shut, recalling the moment she had reappeared at the shower to tell everybody about the broken engagement.

Instead of the shocked looks of disappointment, she had been surprised to recognize looks of relief on the faces of the partygoers. Even Harriet, appearing completely wiped out from the effort of organizing the shower, had a bright smile on her face. She had squeezed Cassie's hand, then looked pointedly at Sam before turning her attention back to Miss Lena's detailed summary of her current novel.

Sticking her finger in the remaining salad still left on the plate, Cassie licked it off with childish enthusiasm.

"I saw that."

Startled, she swung around and found Sam standing in the kitchen doorway.

Guiltily, she lowered her hand. "I missed so much of the party, but I refuse to miss any of Mrs. Crandall's potato salad. It might pack one thousand calories per spoonful, but it's worth every one."

He leaned against the counter and casually crossed his legs at the ankles. "Where's Andy?"

Cassie let the dirty bowl slide under the warm soapy water in the sink, keeping her back to Sam. "He's packing."

"Leaving so soon?"

She shrugged, squeezing another dollop of dishwashing liquid into the sink. "No reason for him to stay, I guess." She began scrubbing the soggy salad out of the bowl.

"I'm sorry."

She scratched her chin on her shoulder. "No you're not. You think he's a jerk."

"Yeah, that's true. But I'm sorry if you're hurting."

Cassie lifted the bowl and rinsed it under the tap, finally turning around to face him as she stuck it in the dish drain on top of the pile of clean dishes. "Actually, I'm feeling pretty good. It was almost a relief."

"Good. And I know what you mean about relief. I don't know how long I could continue coming up with southernisms without going to the library for fresh material."

A reluctant smile appeared on her face. "You were going a little overboard with that stuff. If Andrew wasn't going to deck you one, I certainly was."

He smiled back, blue eyes meaningful. "Hey. It worked. I'd say you owe me one."

Her smile faded as she looked down at her empty ring finger. "Yeah, I guess so."

He lifted her chin. "I'm sorry your marriage plans didn't work out. But I think you'll find that it wasn't meant to be. You two weren't meant for each other, that's all. You'll find somebody. I know it."

The touch of his fingers burned. Stepping back, she picked up the dishtowel. "I guess you're going to tell me the angelfish story again."

He shook his head, his eyes bright, his body close enough to hers that she could feel his heat. "No. But I'd like to tell you another story."

The sliding door opened, interrupting him, and Mr. Parker stepped into the room. Cassie turned back to the sink, expecting Sam to step away. But he remained where he was, and every pore on her skin was vitally aware of his nearness. She felt hot and flustered and knew it had nothing to do with the weather.

To her surprise, Mr. Parker came to her and put an arm around her shoulders. "I hope your heart's not broken over this, Cassie."

Her heart was far from broken, but his sympathy nearly brought tears to her eyes. She sent him a bright smile. "No, I'm fine. Really. As everyone keeps telling me, it's better that it happened now rather than later." Impulsively, she put her arm around Mr. Parker's thick waist and squeezed.

"I was hoping you'd let me keep your shower present, though. I could use a homemade ice-cream maker."

He winked at his son. "Sure, dear. You go on and keep it. Save me the trouble of getting you something else when you do decide to get married."

Sam coughed. "So, Dad, did you get the car running?"

Mr. Parker pulled out a handkerchief and wiped his forehead. His nail beds were stained dark with fresh grease. "Yep. Just finished. Parked it in front of Cassie's house so he'll have no trouble finding it."

Cassie stared at him. "You fixed Andrew's car? Tonight?"

The older man looked sheepish. "I hope you don't take this the wrong way, but after I saw you with your fiancé earlier this evening, I went back to the service station to put in that part I had ordered. I didn't want to be the one responsible for keeping him here one minute longer than needed."

Cassie's eyes widened as she stared at the two men, their only similarity their bright blue eyes—both pairs now sparkling with hidden mirth. Unable to contain herself, she laughed out loud and was soon joined by Sam and his father.

Wiping tears from her eyes, she hugged Mr. Parker. "Thanks. You're a lifesaver. I hadn't quite yet figured out how I could face him for the long drive to the airport tomorrow."

He grinned. "Glad I could help." He shoved his handkerchief back into his pocket. "Better go find the missus now before she tans my hide for skipping out on her when the music started. She'll forgive me, though, when I tell her why." With a wink, he left through the sliding door, latching it behind him.

"There goes a very smart man." Sam lifted a stack of dirty paper plates and shoved them deep into the garbage can.

Cassie leaned back, her arms propped on the counter, a teasing grin on her face. "Too bad you're not more like him."

Sam quirked an eyebrow. "You think I should start wearing overalls?"

"Anything but linen pants and silk shirts." She hadn't meant to say that. It seemed so disloyal. Almost as if she were speaking ill of the dead.

Sam stepped closer to the counter, picked up a clean fork, and stabbed it into Brunelle Thompkins's chocolate bourbon pecan pie. "Did you get to try any of this?"

Glad for the change of subject, Cassie's eyebrows lifted. "Is that what I think it is?"

With a seductive grin, Sam approached with the full fork held aloft. "Ten-time State Fair champion in the pie division and none other. Would you like some?"

She nodded eagerly.

Instead of handing her the fork, he held it in front of her mouth. "Take a bite."

Her gaze never leaving his, she opened her mouth and felt the rich chocolate melt on her tongue. Belatedly thinking of the calories, she bit it in half, leaving the rest still on the fork. As she chewed slowly, she watched as Sam put the rest in his mouth, leaving a small crumb on his lower lip.

Her finger and his tongue reached the crumb at the same time and collided, sending a flash of heat through her hand, up her arm, and coming to a rest somewhere below her lower rib and belly button.

His voice rumbled in his throat. "Want some more?"

The moisture left her mouth with a rush. She could only nod.

He made no move toward the pie, but just looked at her with an innocent grin.

The door opened again, and Lucinda, her fuschia jumpsuit looking a little crumpled, entered the kitchen. She smiled with relief when she spotted Cassie and Sam. "Just the two people I needed to talk to." She leaned against the glass for a moment as if waiting for the scent of her Saucy perfume to reach them. "Harriet's just beat. I'm going to spend the night here so she can rest in the morning while I get up with

the children. Sam, would you mind driving Cassie home?''
She smiled expectantly.

"If the lady doesn't mind riding in my truck, I'd be happy
to.''

Cassie swallowed. "Really, Aunt Lu. I can walk. It's only
a few blocks. . . .''

Lucinda shook her head. "It's hotter than Hades out there,
and you've got all those leftovers to cart back. Just let Sam
take you.'' She winked. "I'll see you in the morning.'' The
door slid closed behind her.

Avoiding Sam's eyes, Cassie said, "Well, that settles that,
I guess. All the dishes are done, so let me go say good-bye
and get my purse.''

When they found Harriet to say good-bye, Cassie was
surprised when Sam leaned over to kiss Harriet's cheek,
then whispered something in her ear. He hugged her, then
turned back to Cassie, his eyes brooding. Curious, she
wanted to ask him about it but held back, knowing it was
none of her business. She was eager not to break the spell
that had somehow enveloped her and Sam.

Ten minutes later, all the food containers stored neatly in
the backseat of the truck, Cassie slid into her seat and waited
for Sam to walk around to his side.

She blinked hard at the dash. Staring at her, propped
upright on its cardboard backing, was her old high school
picture. The same one that had been in the garbage pile in
her father's study. She yanked it off the dash and threw it
at Sam as he opened his door.

"What in the hell is that doing there? Are you sadistic
or something?''

He leaned down and carefully picked the picture off the
driveway. "What are you talking about? There's not a thing
wrong with this picture. I saw you were planning on throwing
it away and figured you wouldn't mind me taking it.''

His smile almost made Cassie forget her anger. Almost.

"Why would you want that? To put it in your attic to
scare the mice away?''

He slid in easily on the leather seat and closed the door.

"No. I wanted to show it to Andy. I figured if that didn't make him run, nothing would."

She punched him on the shoulder, trying not to laugh.

He rubbed his shoulder, pretending that it hurt. "Actually, I wanted you to sign it. You promised me our senior year that I could have one of your pictures, and I guess you forgot. Now's my chance. I figured for my patience I could at least get it autographed."

She folded her arms over her chest, trying to remember promising him a picture, but she couldn't. She couldn't even remember having had a conversation with him prior to the night of the ill-fated fall formal.

"I'm not signing that thing. It belongs in the garbage." Her chin jutted out.

Sam leaned back in his seat and started the engine. "Fine. I'll just sit it up here on my dashboard to keep me company."

Leaning back, she stared out the open window, up toward the inky sky, with its spattering of stars. "Funny, I don't remember asking you for *your* picture." She cringed at the petulant sound of her voice, wondering why she was being so mean.

"You didn't." He glanced over at her. "What's the matter? Feeling scared?"

She noticed she was clutching her necklace and quickly dropped her hand. "Of course not."

But that wasn't true at all. Being near him jangled all the nerves in her body, heating each one like eggs sizzling in a frying pan. The sound of his voice alone sent her pulse skipping and humming in her veins. And that's what scared her. He was as much a part of Walton and her past life as the old house. He lived and breathed the place in which he had been born and where he planned to be buried. But she had long since cut her tethers and moved on to new pastures, now leading a life she had worked very hard to obtain. The thought of returning to this place was as foreign to her as putting "y'all" back into her vocabulary and going barefoot. No, she wasn't scared. She was petrified.

Sam pulled into the drive and stopped the engine but didn't move to get out. She faced him in the bright moonlight.

"Andrew's car is gone."

Sam's voice was quiet. "Yeah, I noticed."

He continued to look at her, his breath soft and rhythmic. A firefly, caught inside the cab of the truck, blinked between them.

Cassie smiled crookedly. "Horny bug. Hope he finds himself a date."

Sam's lips turned up. "Is my butt glowing, too?"

She gave a quiet laugh. "Not yet."

When his mouth touched hers, she sighed and allowed herself to be pressed against the back of the seat. He nibbled at her mouth, making her squirm in her want for more. Impatient, she pushed her fingers through his thick hair and brought him closer to her. Their tongues touched tentatively, then Cassie opened wider, allowing him to invade her mouth more thoroughly.

She sighed again, tasting him, wondering at the rush of heat that flooded into her core. She slid lower in her seat, bringing him down with her. His warmth engulfed her like a hot fire on a winter afternoon. His breath on her neck, as he nibbled along her collarbone, sent shock waves to her limbs, making them tremble. She grabbed his shoulders, holding on for dear life.

What are you doing, Cassie? She opened her eyes, wondering if she'd said the thought aloud. She pushed away, sliding herself up against the door. "Stop. Please. What were we thinking?"

His eyes glittered from the faint porch light, his voice a low drawl. "I know what I was thinking, and if I were a betting man, I'd say you were thinking the same thing."

She pushed herself harder against the door, the handle digging into her back. "I . . . we can't."

He leaned closer, his lips brushing hers. "Why not? Are you and Andy still engaged?"

Breathless, she only shook her head.

He nibbled on her lower lip. "Do you still have feelings for the man?"

She barely managed two shakes of her head.

"I didn't think so." He pressed his mouth against hers, his tongue prying her lips open, and she moaned in spite of herself. He lifted himself slightly so she could slide her arms around him and grab his shoulders. She could have been in the middle of a hurricane but wouldn't have heard a thing for the roaring in her ears. Why was she letting this man affect her so?

She struggled to think clearly. "But I was engaged to the man when I woke up this morning. I don't think I . . ."

Sam raised his head, his breathing hard and heavy. "Now's not the time to be thinking with your head. Feel with your heart for a change."

She eyed him warily. This wasn't fooling around. This was playing with fire. But her body thrummed at a high pitch just from being this close to him fully dressed. If she didn't have him now, she'd never get him out of her system, and she'd always wonder what it would have been like. Something was thinking for her, but she didn't think it was her heart.

He must have read something in her eyes, because he leaned down closer and touched his lips to hers for a brief, tantalizing moment before unlatching her car door. With lightning speed, he jumped out of the truck and was helping her out. She had barely made it to a standing position when she found herself pushed against the side of the truck. His mouth devoured hers as her hands, as if of their own accord, unbuttoned his shirt. His hands stroked her sides, sliding the thin silk of her dress and slip over her bare skin, making her think of bedsheets. She moaned and pushed away from the truck.

They stared at each other for a full minute, breathing heavily, the heat from their bodies rising like steam in the sultry night air. She recognized the need in his eyes, and something else there, too. Blinking slowly, she wondered if the same look was mirrored in her own eyes and prayed that it wasn't. She started to back away from the intensity of his gaze but stumbled, catching his outstretched arm for balance. God help her, she couldn't walk away. Not now. Without a word, his hands cupped her buttocks and pulled her closer, then lifted her until she straddled him.

The thin silk of her underwear, the only thing separating her from his jeans, left nothing to the imagination as he walked up the porch stairs and into the foyer. His pants were stretched tight under her, rubbing her mercilessly with each step. He kicked the door shut behind him with a booted heel, then headed for the stairway.

She stopped him at the foot of the stairs, pulling her mouth away from his and sliding down to stand on the bottom step. "Wait a minute. Where are you going?"

He arched an eyebrow. "To your bedroom." He lifted her and took another step before she slid down again.

"We can't . . . you . . . gosh, Sam, not in my bedroom. That's like . . . like running naked in church or something."

While she spoke, his hand had moved to her back and slowly slid down the zipper of her dress. "Do you have a better suggestion?" Gentle fingers pushed the dress off her shoulders and helped the delicate fabric slide to the ground. He regarded her red silk slip. "A slip?"

She grinned shakily as his fingers relieved her shoulders of the thin scarlet straps and the slip joined her dress around her ankles. "Old habits die hard."

His mouth found a nipple, and she threw her head back with a moan, forgetting for a moment what they had been discussing.

While his tongue wreaked havoc on her breast, she undid his belt buckle and unzipped his jeans. Pulling away from him, she sat down on the step and turned her attention to relieving him of his pants. She grinned impishly up at him. "Well, I guess while we're here . . ." He muttered something under his breath as she cupped him in her hands and then brought him into her mouth.

She took him in deeply, breathing his scent and her own arousal. Her hands wandered up to his taut abdomen, then stroked the back of his legs. Even without his touching her, she felt the restrained strength of his body and its incredible hold over hers.

His voice was strained. "If you don't stop that now, it'll be over before it starts."

With a parting kiss on his inner thigh, she leaned back, resting her elbows on the step behind her. "What else did you have in mind?" Her voice cracked, belying her flippant attitude.

With a growl he lifted her buttocks off the steps and slid her underwear off, throwing it in the hall somewhere behind him. He leaned over her, his hands propping him up. "Lord, you're beautiful." He took a deep breath. "Do you have any idea how long I've waited to see Cassie Madison naked?"

She squirmed under him, pressing her nakedness against him. "Uh-uh."

"If you can't guess, I'm not going to tell you, because it's too embarrassing." He lowered himself, pausing at her threshold, surely feeling her wetness. "Say, 'Y'all.' "

"What?" She looked at him, incredulous.

"I'm not going any further until I hear you say it." His breath was strained.

She pushed herself against him again, crazy with her need for him. "You're nuts."

He didn't move. "Say it."

"Y'all." She could barely speak.

He slid against her. "Now say, 'fried chicken and sweet tea.' "

"Oh, God, Sam, please don't make me wait."

He bent his head and sucked on a nipple, filling her with a ripeness she was sure would burst. "Say it."

"Fried chicken and sweet tea."

He pushed into her with a long sigh. "That's my good ol' southern girl. I just had to make sure."

She slapped him on his bare buttock before grabbing them hard and pulling him into her as far as he could go. She wanted him inside her, filling her, and the void that had resided within for so long. This man, this stubborn, know-it-all, good-ol' boy, too-good-looking-for-his-own-good man completed her in a way she had never felt before. Falling into his arms was like falling home, a return to a place held precious and dear.

No longer feeling the press of the stair digging into her back, she opened herself fully to his thrusts, feeling the heat building within her. He whispered her name into her ear, the very sound an intimate caress, and something inside her chest moved with joy.

The flames that licked at her groin grew stronger as he moved inside her, his rhythm matching hers. Her world seemed to fall off its axis, and only the solid feel of him under her hands held her in place.

Their skin stuck together where their bodies joined, slick with the sweat of their lovemaking. She let her head fall back, and she gazed up into his eyes and saw how easy it would be to never want another thing except this man.

His wanting of her filled his eyes, the most potent aphrodisiac she'd ever encountered, and it shredded the last of her restraint. She shouted his name, and he gasped with relief, filling her with his desire as her world spun out of control, and then brought her spiraling back down to earth like a wind-blown leaf.

She lay back, dazed and wondering what had just happened to her, to her soul. Pulling Sam down with her, she gazed out into the foyer. The moonlight spilled inside from the fanlight over the door, painting all with a blue-white light. She looked up at the shadows of the portraits on the wall, the pictures of all the Madisons who had walked up these very stairs for over a century. With a grimace, she buried her face into Sam's hard chest, hoping that Great-great-great-grandfather Madison wasn't watching.

Chapter 16

The hall clock struck loudly, chiming three times and waking her from a sound doze. She and Sam had moved up to the landing, where they now lay, their limbs entwined. She turned her head, seeking out his gaze, and was startled to find him propped on his elbow, staring down at her. He removed his hand from her hip and smoothed back her hair from her forehead.

"You're beautiful when you sleep."

"But not when I'm awake?"

He didn't pause. "No. Then you're just ornery."

She nipped at his shoulder, tasting his sweat. "This is my house, and if you're going to be mean to me, you'll have to leave."

He made a move to stand, but she pulled him back. "Don't you dare."

He kissed her hard, heating her blood. His lips hovered over hers as he spoke. "Do you think we should go somewhere else, or do you want to stay here and be Lucinda's greeting party?"

That jerked her to a sitting position. "Oh." She rubbed her neck. "I'm so stiff."

"Me, too." She looked past his mischievous smile in the moon-drenched foyer and saw that he was right.

Blushing like a young girl, she looked around at their scattered clothes. "Come on. I don't want to be lectured by Aunt Lucinda." She helped him up, and they collected the stray clothing.

Sam pulled on his pants, using the banister for balance. "I'm going to go move my truck to the back. Don't want to give you a fast reputation."

She leaned against the wall, clutching her clothing in front of her, feeling suddenly self-conscious. "Does this mean you're staying the night?"

He tipped an imaginary hat brim. "Yes, ma'am. A gentleman always stays the night." He kissed her, then trotted down the stairs, whistling quietly. She couldn't help but admire the backside of his retreating form and felt her insides melt to mush again.

When he returned, she was already in bed, the sheets pulled up under her arms. He stood on the threshold. "Can I come in? I don't want to be accused of running naked in church."

She snuggled down into the cool cotton. "I'm over it. Take those pants off and come on in before I jump you."

"Be still my heart." He shucked his jeans and took a flying leap onto the bed. She could feel his heat through the thin top sheet, but he made no move to join her underneath it.

The moonlight spilled through the open curtains, bathing them in its gentle light and making his eyes appear colorless. But the words written in them were as clear as if he spoke them aloud, and it frightened her to her core.

Shutting her eyes to block out the sight, she felt his lips on her neck, moving southward. He found her breast, and he teased the nipple through the soft cotton until it hardened, making her moan.

"Get under here. Now."

"I aim to please." With one flick of his arm, he pulled the sheet off the bed and threw it on the floor.

"I'm cold," she said, wondering if the goose bumps really were from the cool night air.

"Then let me warm you," he whispered over her open lips, covering her with his heat and obliterating all feelings except those produced by his expert hands on her body and by his endearments whispered in her ear.

Cassie awoke slowly in the early-morning light, tired from lack of sleep but her mind more at peace than it had been in years. The curtains puffed gently into the room, and she gave a languid stretch, feeling the warmth of Sam's body pressed against her back. She thought about all the mornings she had awakened with Andrew. She would be cold and lonely on her side of the bed, and he would be curled up on his, facing away from her.

She turned toward Sam and wasn't surprised this time to see dark blue eyes studying her intently. Her voice was thick. "Don't you ever sleep?"

He cocked an eyebrow. "Only when I'm not otherwise occupied."

She placed the flat of her palm on his stubbled cheek, and he held it there. "I've never—" She stopped, unsure of what she wanted to say, of what she could say.

"I know," he whispered back. "I feel the same."

He kissed her softly, his lips warm and inviting.

The front door slammed, and the tapping of Lucinda's high heels floated up the stairs. Cassie jerked upright, feeling the heat of a blush envelop her body from head to toe. "Oh, my gosh. She can't find you here!"

Sam sat up, casually leaning back on his elbows. "And why not? Last time I checked, you were an adult."

She slugged him with her pillow. "Put your clothes on. I'm going to try to sneak you out the back door."

He responded by grabbing her around the waist and wrestling her back down to the mattress. The desire to get him out of her bed evaporated. "What are you doing?" she whispered, her breath catching in her throat as he nuzzled a breast.

"I'm trying to make love to you, but you keep talking and distracting me."

Clinging to what little reasoning she still possessed, she arched her back as his mouth traveled lower. "But . . . Aunt . . . Lucinda . . ."

Somebody knocked on the bedroom door, and they both froze. "Cassie? Are you awake? I was about to start breakfast and was wondering if you'd like something."

Cassie jumped out of bed, hitting Sam on the head with her knee.

"I'm in here, Aunt Lu. I just need to get dressed and I'll be down in a minute."

"All right. I'll be in the kitchen." Lucinda's heels tapped their way down the hall.

Cassie let out a sigh of relief and was about to collapse back on the bed when she heard Lucinda call back, "Tell Sam he'll have a plate waiting with the eggs over easy, the way he likes them." After a short pause, she continued, "And please don't leave your underwear on the coatrack in the foyer, Cassie. It doesn't look nice." The heel tapping continued in the hallway and then down the steps.

Cassie fell back on the bed and folded her arms over her eyes. "I will never be able to look her in the face again."

Sam rolled over her, his body pressing hers into the mattress. "Did you ever stop to think that maybe we were set up? Why do you think Lucinda had me drive you home last night to an empty house?"

Her eyes widened. "It's a conspiracy. I can't win."

He moved against her, and she felt his desire for her. She should get up and leave now, before she decided to stay indefinitely in his arms. Still, she remained where she was.

She touched his earlobe, remembering how it tasted. "Last night you asked me how long I thought you'd been thinking about seeing me naked. How long has it really been, Sam?"

His eyes darkened and narrowed, his gaze boring into

hers as if trying to read her thoughts. "I don't know if I should tell you."

"Why . . . not?" She shifted under him, her need for him making her ache. And it was more than a physical ache. It grew inside her, threatened to take over, and she resisted it. "Sam—" Her words were cut short by a sharp rap on the front door, and then, with a jangling of keys, somebody pushed open the door and walked into the foyer downstairs with heavy footsteps.

"Hello? Anybody home?"

Cassie recognized Ed Farrell's voice and then Lucinda calling for her to answer the door. She pictured her aunt in the kitchen up to her elbows in pancake batter. "I'd better go see what he wants." She put her feet on the floor, but Sam's hand held her back.

"Don't go." His voice was serious, and she knew he wasn't talking about staying in bed.

With a gentle shake of her head, she pulled away, somewhat relieved to have an excuse to leave Sam's touch. His hands on her seemed to scramble her brain, and she needed her wits about her.

"I'm not going to lie to you, Sam. You knew before we even came into this house last night that whatever happened between us was only temporary. We're two different people. We want very different things in life."

Sam slid from the bed, and Cassie tried to keep her eyes off his naked torso and muscled limbs as he bent to retrieve his pants and pull them on. He looked at her, his face a mask of restraint. "We're not so different. You're just so busy denying it that you can't see the truth. I thought that last night, with Andrew out of the picture . . ." He slid his shirt over his head.

Her hands shook as she pulled on her underclothes, shorts, and a shirt. "You don't know me at all. How dare you make assumptions as to who I am." She straightened. "And as for last night . . ." She bit her lip, unable to go on. She had wanted to say it was because she was lonely, but they would both know she was lying.

He approached and stopped directly in front of her. She felt his heat as he spoke. "I have loved you ever since sixth grade, when you put that roach in Susan Benedict's lunch box. There has not been a day since that I have not studied you, thought about you, or loved you. I spent hours with your father talking about you in the fifteen years, three months, and eleven days since you left. It's a sickness, I know. But I can't seem to cure myself." Shaking his head, he walked toward the door. "Last night was a mistake. I told you before, it's all or nothing with me. I won't be your warm body for lonely nights."

He pulled open the door, not looking back. "And don't worry. I'll take the back stairs."

She wanted to say something, but the threat of tears made her mute. Why was she so miserable? She had everything she wanted, didn't she? She'd even had the chance to sleep with him to get him out of her system. So why did she want to throw herself on the bed and cry for hours?

He shut the door gently behind him. She waited a moment, then left to go downstairs.

"Hey, Ed. I'm here. Sorry to make you wait."

Ed looked up, a flush of embarrassment flooding his face. "Gosh, Cassie—I wouldn't have just barged in like that if I thought you were here. I didn't see anybody's car out front, and nobody answered the door, so I let myself in." He held out a stack of papers. "I wanted to drop this facts sheet off to leave on the kitchen counter. Lists all the amenities and things that a prospective buyer might be interested in." A stray blob of white shaving cream clung to his upper lip as he smiled.

Cassie's gaze strayed to the writing box sitting on the hall settee. Scooping it up before Lucinda had a chance to be curious about it, she faced Ed, holding out her hand. "Thanks. I'll put them in the kitchen."

He handed them to her, his gaze catching sight of the box. "That's a beautiful antique writing box, Cassie. Where did you find it?"

"In my attic. It was my daddy's."

Ed nodded, rubbing his jaw. "Was there anything in it?"

She adjusted the bulky box in her arms. "A few letters. Nothing of any value."

"Well, I'm starting a little collection of American antiques, and I'd love to have that. Let me know if you're going to get rid of it, because I'd like to call first dibs."

"Sure. I'll let you know."

He turned to go, but faced her again, his brows puckered. "Have you had any more calls from the Roust people?"

"Well, just one besides the original call I told you about. It was their marketing department. Wanted to find out how long it had been on the market and how long I might wait until changing my mind about keeping it residential. I hung up on them."

He grinned, the blob of shaving cream dangling precariously. "Good for you. I guess they're saving their hassling for me."

Cassie grabbed for the knob and held the door open for him. "What do you mean?"

He sighed heavily. "Well, one of my sites was vandalized last night. You know that condo development off of Route One where the drive-in movie theater used to be? Somebody came and stole all the bathroom fixtures last night. Just plain ripped them out of the walls. It's gonna set me back at least a month to get them replaced and reinstalled."

"I'm sorry, Ed. And you really think Roust had something to do with it?"

"Not that I'll ever be able to prove it, of course, but who else would want to do that? Well, maybe that Sam Parker. He's as bad as Jim Roust. One wants to destroy the town, and the other wants to make sure it remains the armpit of the state." He stepped out onto the porch. "I don't blame you one bit for wanting to leave this two-horse town in your dust. Not one bit."

She leaned back on the doorframe. "I wouldn't exactly call Walton an armpit, Ed. Certainly it's no Manhattan, but it does have its charms."

Frowning, he faced her again. "Are you sure you're not changing your mind about staying here for good?"

The ghost of Sam's touch claimed her, making her skin tingle and her heart thud. Just as quickly, fear gripped her; fear of losing herself, of losing control and everything she had worked so hard for. She would never go back to that vulnerable country girl she had once been. "Never. I'm not staying—I just couldn't. I mean, there's just not a whole lot here to keep me—well, except for Harriet and her kids. I'm sure I'll visit, but I'll never live in Walton again."

A congenial smile settled on his face. "Fine. I respect your decision. I just need to get back to work to find you a nice little family to move in here. Anything but having those Roust people in here trying to turn this into a shopping mall." He snorted, stepping heavily down the porch steps. "And if you see Dr. Parker, tell him that I've got two more councilmembers on my side regarding that moratorium. Tell him to just give it up and stick to doctoring like he's supposed to."

Cassie flushed, wondering if Ed had seen Sam's truck in the backyard. "I'll mention it to him."

He sent her a brief nod. "All right, then. I'll be seeing you later. Think I've got another family interested in a showing. I'll bring them by this afternoon."

"I probably won't be here, but you know how to get in." He flushed, bringing back Cassie's memory of the skinny boy with the hungry look in his eyes. She stepped toward him and wiped the shaving cream off his chin. Showing it to him, she said, "I didn't think you'd want that there."

Something in his eyes flashed, a mixture of gratitude and something else. "Thanks, Cassie. I appreciate that."

Saying good-bye, she closed the door.

When she went back inside and entered the kitchen, she was just in time to hear the back door slam and then the engine of Sam's truck start up. His barely touched plate sat on the table next to a half-empty cup of coffee. Lucinda stood by the stove, spatula in hand and with a worried look on her face. "He said he wasn't that hungry, after all. Said he had business in town he needed to see to."

Realizing he must have heard the entire conversation, she went running to the screen door, flinging it open. "Sam," she shouted, scrambling down the steps toward him.

He lifted a hand to wave but didn't stop as he drove past her, the dust from his wheels floating up over her, settling on her like a cloak of shame.

Cassie's alarm clock rang, shrill and urgent, at six-thirty on Wednesday morning. She hadn't slept much, her thoughts ricocheting between her feelings for Sam and her concern for Harriet. She had counted enough sheep to fill the house and yard, but still, sleep had evaded her.

She had finally resorted to pulling the writing box from under her bed and reading until her eyes blurred. Most of the letters were simply written, the words of a young girl in love. Whatever had been between her father and this woman had been love, even if not the same as what her parents had shared. But a love, nevertheless, which had created a child. Feeling weary but not yet ready to sleep, she pulled the last unread letter from the box.

January 14, 1963
My dearest Harrison,

I know your dear, sweet heart is breaking with mine, and I supposed it's just a part of growing up. I hope this is the last time for both of us, but as Daddy says in his preaching, we never know what the good Lord has in store for us.

I'm not angry with you or with Catherine Anne for what has happened between you. I love you both dearly, and I can easily see why you both feel the way you do. And I had no intention of making my predicament stand between you two. You asked me to marry you, and it would be the greatest honor of my life to be your wife. But it is not to be. I will not be the one responsible for making your life one of "what ifs." You love another, and I am setting you free.

I'm telling Daddy and Mama tonight, but I won't mention your name. They might guess, but I will never give up our secret. Your future children will be grateful for this.

I'm sure I will be sent away, but I'm all right with this. And please don't call me a saint, because you know well and true that I am not. I've prayed a lot about this, and no matter how painful it is, I know I'm making the right decision for all of us.

Love,
E.

P.S. I'm returning the beautiful locket. Keep it safe, for it holds all my love for you inside.

Cassie's eyes stung as she picked up the envelope and turned it over. A thin gold chain with a small heart locket emptied into her hand, puddling in her palm like fallen tears. She turned the locket over to examine it more closely and spotted two sets of initials: HM and EL.

With a rush of excitement, Cassie slid from the bed and put the locket on her dresser. She'd discreetly ask around to find out who the initials belonged to. And then, maybe, find her missing sibling. She crawled back under the covers, shivering. Sam was right. It was like quicksand. If she wasn't careful, just a few more steps and she would be swallowed completely.

With a deep yawn, she turned her head into the pillow, jerking back suddenly as she recognized Sam's scent. No one was looking, so she buried her nose in it, taking a deep breath.

The last time she'd seen him had been at church the previous Sunday, and it had been a lesson in torture. Just about every member of the congregation at First United Methodist had taken turns patting her arm and offering condolences over her broken engagement. That would have

been fine if their sentiments hadn't been followed by broad
hinting about Sam.

The man in question had done everything he could to
remain aloof. He had been a portrait of politeness, but no
teasing, no twinkling eyes or winks in her direction. She
almost wanted him to make some comment on her behavior
or appearance, even if it was mean and nasty, just to know
that he was thinking about her. Not that it mattered. Things
were best this way—and far less complicated.

She had sighed with relief when he walked past their pew
with just a wave in her direction. The empty seat next to
her had gone unnoticed, thank goodness. Until the tenacity
of the Sedgewick twins made its presence known. With
matching wide-brimmed straw hats and white gloves, they
had each taken one of Sam's arms and led him to sit next
to Cassie, chatting the whole time as if to keep him from
noticing what they were doing.

Beyond a polite "good morning," the only time she heard
his voice was during the hymns, when he broke forth with
a surprisingly strong tenor. When they sat down, their legs
had accidentally touched, and he unobtrusively placed a
hymnal on the pew between them.

Cassie had caught Harriet's gaze, and her sister's tired
blue eyes were filled with concern. The fleeting memory of
Harriet's face staring up at Joe during a picnic following
high school graduation fluttered through her mind. As Harriet
had shifted her gaze and seen Cassie standing at the dessert
table with a lemon bar halfway to her face, she had worn
the same expression. Whether it was concern or pity, Cassie
didn't know. Lowering her eyes, she had spent the entire
service staring at the notes and words inside the hymnal,
not seeing them but acutely aware of Sam's presence next
to her.

The man would not leave her alone. Thoughts of him had
chased her into sleep, then accompanied her dreams, so that
once again she felt as if they had spent the night together.
With a heavy sigh, she struggled out of the pillow's depth
and climbed out of bed.

Before her feet had even touched the ground, her cell phone rang. She remembered turning it on the night before to drain the battery but couldn't understand why it would be ringing. As she bent to pick it up, she recalled the ad she and Harriet had put in the paper. Her heart lurched as her hand stilled over the small black phone. On the third ring, she picked it up, her palm sweaty.

"Hello?"

She heard breathing on the other end of the phone but nothing else.

"Hello?" she asked again. "Who is this?"

A distinctive click on the other line answered her.

Lowering the phone, she looked at the incoming number on the little screen. It was a local number, but not one she recognized. Jotting it down, she put the phone on the night table, leaving it on in case whoever it was called back.

She looked at the paper in her hand, then folded it in half. She should get on the Internet and do a reverse search to find out who the number belonged to, but that could wait for later. The image of quicksand came to mind, making her drop the folded paper on the table.

Cassie sighed. Harriet's appointment was at eight, and she needed a run first to clear her head. Hugging the large pink elephant, she pulled the curtain at her window aside and peered out. Her mother's roses drooped in the heavy humidity, the sky thick with gray clouds and the scent of rain. A perfect day to fit her mood. She had every intention of finishing up the attic today, with no time allotment for old memories. She had to move on. Her hard-earned career lay in shambles, her relationship with her boss iffy at best. Yes, her stay in Walton had been long enough, and it was time to start making plans for a return to New York.

The smell of Saucy perfume hung heavily inside Lucinda's car. Cassie blasted the air-conditioning full force and then cranked all the windows down to air it out. It was bad enough driving a pink car, but to smell like it was adding insult to injury. Grimacing at her thoughts, she noticed her hand fingering the charms around her neck. *What are you scared of, Cassie? It's only a checkup. Everything will be fine.*

Harriet opened the front door of her house before Cassie could ring the bell. Her blond hair was worn straight and tucked behind her ears like that of a teenager. Her gingham cotton sundress flapped like a shapeless tent over Harriet's body, but Cassie noticed a roundness to her arms and figure that she hadn't noticed before. Cassie had to remember that her sister had gone through five pregnancies, and a softening of the figure was inevitable.

Harriet raised her fingers to her lips. "Shhh. The children are still sleeping. School starts soon, and I want them to sleep in as much as possible."

Cassie nodded and led the way to the car and slid into the driver's seat. She waited for Harriet to open her door. After watching her sister struggle with it, Cassie reached across the seat and pushed it open from the inside.

"You need to start pumping some iron, Har. You're not getting any younger."

The fatigue in her sister's smile made Cassie want to call back her words. Silently, she put the car in reverse and backed out of the driveway.

"Joe wanted to take off from work today so he could come with me, but I told him no. It's just a checkup. It would just be silly for him to take a vacation day for that." She worried her bottom lip.

Cassie frowned as she pulled onto the road but kept silent. They drove past Miss Lena's house, and they both waved as they spotted the old woman on her porch. She wore a bright pink sweater over her housedress in spite of the heat, and the ubiquitous romance novel lay open on her lap. She waved and smiled as they passed, then bent her head back to reading. Ed Farrell, shirtless but wearing a red bandanna around his forehead and dark socks with his sneakers, pushed a lawn mower around Miss Lena's front lawn but didn't look up.

Harriet leaned back in her seat. "Do you think that'll be us when we're old and gray? Sitting out on the porch, wearing sensible shoes and our stockings rolled down to our ankles, and reading sex scenes to each other all day?"

Cassie laughed. "Oh, Lord—I hope so. It seems to me that Miss Lena's got a pretty good deal going." Her smile faded slowly as she drove, thinking of their mother and her own mortality and what a blessing it was to be allowed to grow old. She pulled into a parking spot but stopped halfway with a start. The idea of sitting on a large porch with her stockings around her ankles and waving at passersby suddenly sounded amazingly appealing and something to aspire to. Certainly more so than working herself into a heart attack and dropping dead at her desk at an early age. She shook herself mentally and finished parking the car.

Cassie helped her sister out and pushed open the glass door of the clinic. The waiting room was empty except for a large black woman sitting against the wall and knitting. Cinnamon potpourri saturated the air, giving the space a warm, inviting air, as did the cozy gingham curtains and matching upholstery. An empty reception desk filled one corner of the room, a box of lollipops propped on a corner.

The woman put aside her knitting and stood slowly, a wide grin splitting her face. "Cassie Madison—I heard you were in town."

Cassie allowed herself to be enveloped in a bear hug and then held out for scrutiny.

"My, my—you're as pretty as a picture. You look just like your precious mama, God rest her soul." Her dark eyes warmed. "You don't remember me, do you?"

Cassie smiled. "Of course I do, Mrs. Perkins." She held her hair back from her forehead. "My scar's almost gone, but I still remember you bundling me into your car and driving me to the hospital."

Mrs. Perkins's smile widened, allowing a gold tooth to shine through. "I'd never heard such caterwauling in all my days. You learned your lesson, though, didn't you? You played pranks after that, but you never tried to climb on the courthouse roof again, thank goodness.''

Cassie smiled, feeling the warmth that emanated from this gentle spirit. Camellia Perkins had worked for her mother as a housekeeper, but she'd always been treated as more of a friend of the family. She had stayed on, taking care of the girls, after their mother had died, until Aunt Lucinda had moved in with them. Her soft bosom had absorbed many a tear from the Madison sisters.

Harriet gave the older woman a hug. ''Good to see you again, Mrs. Perkins. I missed your birthday last month, and I've been meaning to mail a present to you. If I'd known you'd be back in town visiting, I would have brought it over. How long are you here for?''

The black woman put her hand on Harriet's cheek. ''You are always so sweet. You don't need to bring me anything. Just stop by for a visit and that will be a treat enough. I'll be here for another week. I'm watching my grandbabies while their parents take a second honeymoon. Lord knows they need it!'' As if to show a camaraderie between mothers, she winked at Harriet.

Harriet smiled. ''Now, why are you here? You aren't sick, are you?''

Mrs. Perkins gave a deep, rich laugh, a sound like hot melted tar on summer asphalt. ''No, I'm as healthy as a horse. I'm here with Patricia, my oldest granddaughter. She's getting her stitches out. What about you, dear? You look tired.''

Harriet looked away, greeting Mary Jane as she walked into the waiting room. Mary Jane said hello to Cassie, then turned back to Harriet. ''Sam's ready for you. Come on back with me.''

Cassie touched her sister's arm. ''Do you want me to come with you?''

''No, you can stay here and get reacquainted with Mrs. Perkins. I won't be long.'' She flashed a bright smile, then disappeared behind the door with Mary Jane.

She sat down next to Mrs. Perkins, feeling restless.

The older lady turned to her. "Is she sick?"

Cassie plucked at her skirt. "She's just tired. Sam's going to do some tests and I guess prescribe her some vitamins to perk her up."

Mrs. Perkins nodded, satisfied. "I just can't get over how much you look like your mama. I'd think you were her if I hadn't seen that sweet woman in her coffin with my very own eyes."

Cassie looked down at her hands.

Mrs. Perkins leaned closer. "Your mama was such a sweet lady to work for. So kind and gentle. Always had a nice word to say to everybody. I was with her when you came into this world, you know."

Cassie looked up, surprised. "I didn't know that." Lucinda had told her about the circumstances of her birth, but this was new.

The large woman leaned back, resting her knitting on her ample lap. "You've always been impatient—I remember you as a little child. But it started when you were born. I was helping your mama clean her silver and her water broke just like that—no warning or nothing. Thank goodness your Aunt Lucinda was there. I left her with your mama, and I ran as fast as I could to old Dr. Williams." She gave Cassie a gold-toothed grin. "I wasn't so big then, and I could run fast."

A faraway look drifted across her face. "You were born right there on the dining-room floor in the middle of your mama's wedding silver. We'd barely got you wrapped up and your mama on the parlor couch when your daddy came in for lunch. We'd been so busy getting you born that we'd forgotten all about him." She chuckled, then frowned. "My memory's getting fuzzy now, but I'll never forget what the judge said the first time he held you. It was just so peculiar."

Cassie straightened, her attention captured. "What did he say?"

Mrs. Perkins took a deep breath. "Well, he marveled over

how pretty you were, of course. And then he said something like how he couldn't spoil your brother but he'd be darned if he wasn't allowed to spoil you."

Cassie felt the air leave her lungs. "My brother?"

Mrs. Perkins slapped her hands on her knees. "As sure as I'm sitting here, that's what he said. All of us there just sort of passed it off as new father's shock. We honestly didn't think he was in his right mind." A soft look came over her face as she regarded Cassie. "But, oh, how he loved you. I never seen a man make such a fuss over a baby before. You'd think you were the first baby ever born."

The door opened, and Mrs. Perkins's granddaughter walked into the waiting room. After a quick introduction, Mrs. Perkins hugged Cassie again and then left.

Cassie tried flipping through the magazines on the table but couldn't concentrate. The word *brother* kept echoing in her mind, as did the image of her and Harriet as old ladies wearing fluffy pink sweaters in the summertime.

The hands of the clock pushed across its face with each lethargic tick as Cassie paced the room. Her anxiety over Harriet mixed with her eagerness to share her news about the locket's initials and a possible brother. Thunder rolled lazily in the distance, the room darkening by a degree.

The door handle rattled, and Cassie spun around, her words drying in her mouth. Harriet's face was serene, more beautiful than Cassie had ever seen it. A quiet peace, an acceptance, radiated from Harriet, and it chilled Cassie to the bone.

Cassie stepped toward her. "How did it . . . ?"

Harriet held her finger to her lips. "I need to be alone. I need time to think before I see Joe."

Cassie opened her mouth to say something but stopped as Sam followed Harriet into the waiting room.

Harriet continued. "I've asked Sam to talk to you now. He has my permission to tell you . . . everything. I . . ." Her voice trailed away.

"Har, it's going to rain. Let me drive you home. We can talk in the car."

Harriet shook her head and pushed open the door leading to the outside. Cassie walked toward her, but Sam pulled her back. "Let her go," he said, his voice dry.

Cassie pushed away, intent on following her sister out the door. The first drops of rain began to fall as she reached the parking lot and watched Harriet run down the sidewalk as if her life depended on reaching her destination.

She felt Sam's presence behind her and waited for his touch. When it didn't come, she turned around to face him.

"Are you going to tell me?"

Her breath caught when she looked up into his eyes. She felt as if she were looking into his soul—seeing the hurt, the love, the pity. She stepped away, not wanting or needing any of it. "What's wrong with my sister?"

"She's pregnant." The words fell flat, his voice carrying more meaning than the simple words.

"That's good, right?"

He shook his head. "In this case, not necessarily."

She touched his arm, then let it drop. "Tell me straight, Sam. Harriet said she wanted you to tell me everything, and I can take it. Don't give me any wishy-washy drivel. I can take the cold, hard facts." She stuck out her chin and forced it to stop trembling.

He regarded her closely. "All right, then." His eyes softened. "Harriet also has breast cancer. I know because I've just reviewed the results of the biopsy with her."

Cassie blinked. "Biopsy? What biopsy?"

The rain fell in a steady drizzle now, but neither of them moved. "Last week, when Harriet went to Atlanta to get a few things for the party and refused company, she actually went to an appointment to have a biopsy done. I drove her myself. We'll need more tests to see if . . . if the cancer's spread." He wiped his rain-dampened hair off his forehead. "I'm sorry."

Her first impulse was to turn around and run as far away as she could. She even managed to take a step away from him before she jerked around to face him again. "Biopsy? Last week? And you didn't tell me? My sister is horribly sick and you didn't think I should be told?"

Sam slowly shook his head as the rain plastered his white coat to his shirt. "You know I couldn't. My professional relationship with Harriet is strictly confidential. I'm sorry."

She slapped both palms against his chest, the sound sharp against the pattering of the rain. "My sister has cancer and you're sorry? You should have told me. You know you should have told me." She started to cry and was glad for the raindrops gliding down her face.

He placed his own hands firmly over hers, keeping her close to him. "I am sorry, Cassie. It was Harriet's choice not to tell anybody until she knew for sure. She ... she wanted to decide for herself about the baby."

Jerking away from him, Cassie stumbled on the wet pavement. "The baby? Oh, God." She looked up at him, blinking at the raindrops, seeing things as if through a microscope. "She's going to try and save the baby first, isn't she?"

Sam hesitated for a moment, then nodded.

Cassie shivered, feeling cold all of a sudden. "How far along is the pregnancy?"

"Four months—almost five."

Cassie stared at her feet, at her pink-painted toenails, and let her peripheral vision fade. "The baby will make treatment for her more difficult, won't it?"

He didn't pause. "Yes, it will."

Cassie looked at him square in the face, all of the fight in her gone. "Is Harriet going to die, Sam?"

He reached out to touch her but stopped midway. He slid his hand into a back pocket instead. "I don't know. Cases exist where both mother and child have survived. When I'm in Atlanta, I'll be making appointments for her with the best people in the field. If there are treatments for her that won't harm the baby, we'll find them. But I won't lie to you. Chemotherapy and radiation are her best chances. And she won't consider them—at least not until the baby is born."

The wind picked up, whipping her hair across her face. "Harriet's always a mother first, isn't she?"

Sam nodded, his eyes dark. "She had a good example."

Cassie bit down hard, stilling her chattering teeth. "She hardly knew our mother."

"That's not who I was referring to. Despite your best efforts, your nurturing side still shows." He sent her a crooked smile.

Cassie took a deep breath and turned away. The rain had stopped, but the sky draped low and dark clouds over the summer-scorched earth.

"I'm not going to tell you to be strong, Cassie. You're strong enough for all of us. But I do want to tell you that it's okay to cry—that it's okay to ask for help or a shoulder to lean on. There're plenty of people in town who would be happy to have the honor."

She stuck out her chin and grabbed hold of the charms around her neck. Thunder growled in the distance, vibrating the ground.

He shoved his fingers deep into his lab-coat pockets. "And I'm sorry if you think that relying on me or anybody else will make you unwillingly form attachments to us. But I'm here if you need me. As a friend, and nothing more, if that's what you want."

She searched her purse for her car keys. "I need to get going. A storm's coming."

Sam stood in front of her and gently lifted her chin. "It is. Just remember to take shelter when it starts to pour."

Pulling away, she headed toward Lucinda's car. The tall oaks swayed with the wind, shaking loose their acorns. Fat hydrangea blossoms edging the walkway bent over double, their large, showy heads dipped in sorrow.

"You know where to find me." The wind carried Sam's voice to her, and she stopped. She wanted to rush to him, to have him hold her. She wanted to feel his heartbeat against her ear, to know his understanding. She faced him again and watched as the wind pelted his white coat and blew his hair into small tufts. But she could not take what she was not able to give.

Forcibly, she turned toward the car again. Thunder rumbled overhead as a large gust pushed at her, drying her eyes and bringing with it the promise of rain.

Chapter 17

Cassie sped down the street, not seeing anything but the blurry pink of the car's hood. She blinked, clearing her eyes temporarily. The windshield wipers beat a rhythm: *Harriet is sick, Harriet is sick, Harriet is sick.* Desperate for a distraction, she flipped on the radio to Garth Brooks singing about friends in low places. She sang along for a few bars before switching it off in irritation. *Since when do I know all the lyrics from a Garth Brooks song? It's certainly not poetry and definitely not worth the effort of learning them.*

She swerved the car into her sister's driveway. *You're being mean, Cassie. You must be scared.* Cassie caught her reflection in the rearview mirror and said aloud, "You're damned straight I'm scared. I'm scared shitless."

Not wanting to wait while she searched for an umbrella under the seat, she opened the door and ran to the porch. She pushed on the doorbell again and again until she heard footsteps approach.

Joe opened the door and greeted her with a smile that quickly changed to a worried expression. "Where's Harriet? I thought she was with you." Amanda cried inconsolably in the background.

Cassie forced herself to remain calm and pasted a smile on her face. "You mean she's not here?"

He shook his head, opening the door wider for her to come inside. "No, I haven't seen her since she left with you this morning." He shut the door, his hand lingering on the doorknob. "Did y'all . . . have a fight?"

"Oh, no. Nothing like that." Amanda cried louder in the background. "She, uh, wanted to get some exercise and decided to walk home from the clinic. I needed to talk to her." Cassie looked past his shoulder into the hallway. "Do you need to see about the baby?"

He swiped a hand through his hair. "Um, yeah. I was just feeding her when the doorbell rang. Come on back."

Cassie followed him into the kitchen. Amanda sat in the highchair, an upended bowl on the tray and baby cereal covering most of her hair and the floor beside her.

Joe surveyed the mess with a sad shake of his head. "I sure wish I knew where Harriet was. She's a lot better at this stuff than me."

The television blared from the family room, and Cassie peeked inside. The three youngest Warner children lounged around the room, still wearing their pajamas. Cereal boxes, bowls with milk and spoons stuck in them, and various toys were strewn from one end of the room to the other. She turned back to Joe and forced a smile. "Hey, why don't you take the kids upstairs to get dressed and straighten the family room. I'll finish feeding Amanda and get her cleaned up." She glanced over at the baby, who was now making a face rub out of the cereal. "Wherever Harriet is, she'll be back soon."

Stricken, Joe's eyes went wide. "Oh, Lord, she'll have my hide. I'd better hustle, then. Thanks, Cassie. You're a peach." He hurried into the family room as Cassie surveyed the kitchen for the best plan of attack.

Thirty minutes later, trying to hide her impatience, she handed the fed and cleaned baby to her father. She knew where her sister had gone but wasn't yet willing to share the information with Joe. Harriet had been her sister first, after all. And looking at Joe's affable and once-beloved face, she wanted to postpone the inevitable as long as she could.

Cassie stepped out onto the small porch, letting Joe catch the door before it swung shut. "If I see Harriet, I'll tell her to call you. I'm sure she just decided to do some shopping. I'll see you later." Not knowing why she did it, she squeezed his arm, then returned to Lucinda's car and started the engine, the tires squealing as she peeled out onto the road.

She didn't have to think about where she was going. The comforting and familiar scent of mothballs and old cedar of the attic in the big house called to her. It had once been a place of sanctuary and refuge, and Cassie figured that if Harriet ever needed such a place, it was now.

The rain slowed to a steady drizzle as she urged the car under the drooping oaks leading to the house. She spotted Aunt Lucinda immediately, hands clutching a fuschia umbrella with ruffles, staring up at one of the trees. Lucinda wore a bright yellow jogging suit and matching athletic shoes, making Cassie smile. Trying to keep her girlish figure, Lucinda had taken up power walking. She still did her hair and wore full makeup before venturing outside, but it met with Cassie's full approval. Slowing the car, Cassie rolled down the window.

"What's wrong with the tree?"

Lucinda faced her, a frown puckering her penciled eyebrows, her mascara smudged under her eyes from the rain. "Somebody's been stripping the bark off these old trees. Look." She indicated the bottom twelve inches of the bark where somebody had neatly shaved off the bark. Thick tree sap wept over the naked wood.

"Are they all like that?"

Lucinda nodded. "As far as I can tell." She stuck her head in the window, peering closely at Cassie. "You here to talk to Harriet? She's up at the house, waiting for you. Wouldn't tell me a thing until she'd talked to you." Straightening, she slapped the side of the car, her metal rings making a pinging noise. "You go on and see about your sister. I'll see what sort of damage has been done to these oaks."

Cassie waved, then rolled up the window and drove to the front of the house. She ran up the stairs, taking them two at a time, until she reached the attic.

Harriet stood in front of a cracked cheval mirror, a white satin and lace gown held in front of her. She caught Cassie's gaze in the shattered reflection and smiled.

"It's Mama's wedding gown, remember? I always thought I'd wear it when I got married." She sighed, lowering the dress from her chest. "At least you'll be able to."

Cassie tried to smile but failed miserably. "Don't hold your breath on that one. I think I've screwed up things royally on all sides. Guess I'll just be an old maid like Miss Lena. Maybe she'll even let me move in with her."

Harriet smoothed the satin against her legs. "Promise me that you'll remind Maddie that this dress is here and hers to wear. She's so stubborn sometimes, but I think she'll listen to you. She looks up to you, you know."

Cassie swallowed thickly. "Why don't you just tell her yourself?"

With a sigh, Harriet gently laid the wedding dress back into the open trunk. Kneeling slowly, she began tucking yellowed tissue paper around the white gown. Cassie joined her, focusing on placing the paper between the delicate folds of satin, each tuck and flip of the fabric like a gentle reassurance from her mother.

Harriet sat back on her heels, staring out toward the small window where a new wave of rain was now forcing itself against the glass in sheets. The sound of a car door shutting drifted toward them. "Poor Joe, he doesn't even know where I keep the Christmas decorations. I don't know how he's going to manage."

"Stop talking like that, Har. You're scaring me."

Rolling over to a sitting position, Harriet leaned against the chest and breathed deeply. "Sorry. I know you're not easily scared. You were always the one sticking your head under the bed to prove to me there weren't any bogeymen lying in wait." She closed her eyes, her hands resting on her abdomen. "I remember after Mama died and you'd let me crawl into your bed because I was too scared to sleep alone. You told me there was nothing to be afraid of because Mama sent angels to watch over us.'' Harriet opened her eyes to look at her sister, a small smile crossing her lips. ''You said you knew it was true because of my dimple. You told me that before I was born an angel kissed my cheek and left its mark, so you knew they were real. And now Mama was up in heaven to help watch over us when the angels had to go to sleep.'' Harriet sighed deeply. ''I was never scared after that.''

Cassie looked away, hiding her eyes, her voice quiet. ''The only reason I wasn't scared was because I believed it, too.''

Her sister reached for her hand and held it. ''You were a good big sister. You didn't deserve all the pain and hurt you suffered because of me. If it makes you feel any better, I was so jealous of you when you moved to New York.''

Cassie wiped her eyes with her free hand and regarded her sister. ''You jealous of me. Now there's a concept. You had everything you wanted right here. What could there possibly have been in New York for you to envy?''

''Snow.'' Harriet's face radiated with an inner peace, glowing in the dim light from the small attic window. ''I've always wanted to see snow. I guess I'll probably die before ever getting to see the white stuff.''

Dropping Harriet's hand, Cassie scrambled to stand. ''Don't say that. It's bad karma and all that.'' She walked toward the window, staring out sightlessly. ''You're pregnant, and they've found a few cancer cells. That's all we know right now, and that's all I'm considering.'' She turned around. ''And what could you have been thinking, getting pregnant so soon after Amanda? Haven't you ever heard of birth control?''

Harriet regarded her sister from beneath lowered brows. ''Honey, being a single woman, I'm sure you don't know much about the baby-making business, but believe me, thinking has very little to do with it.''

Despite her heavy heart, Cassie laughed out loud. ''Please

stop. I'm getting mental images, and I just don't want to go there.''

Harriet laughed, and Cassie quieted, humbled by the sound that suddenly seemed as familiar to her as her own laugh. She wanted to freeze this moment in time; stop its progression. The musty smell of the attic, the discarded remnants of her childhood strewn about in boxes and trunks, and laughter and confidences shared with her sister. They all combined to form a savory stew of memories, like the recollection of a long-ago Christmas. She wanted to hold this moment inside her forever like a cherished doll, to be brought out for comfort when life seemed to get the best of her.

Cassie picked up a tiny wooden cradle from the ancient dollhouse, long forgotten in its dark corner of the attic. Its windows appeared as sightless eyes, watching the big people play at real life. She didn't lift her eyes from the small toy when she spoke. ''I know you haven't told Joe about the baby. It's not ... it's not too late. . . .''

Harriet interrupted her with the slamming of the trunk lid. ''Don't, Cassie. Don't even say it. I've made up my mind, and terminating this pregnancy is not an option. But I don't guess you'd understand.''

Cassie dropped the tiny cradle, letting it hit the roof of the dollhouse. Her voice rose with the frustration of not being in control of what was happening. ''Not understand? No, you're wrong. You're the one who can't understand. You were too little to remember what it was like watching Mama die and then being left to take care of a younger sister. How dare you say I wouldn't understand.''

With visible effort, Harriet stood. ''I'm sorry, Cassie. I never knew how much of a burden I was for you. But I could never deliberately sacrifice one of my children, and no, you wouldn't understand that because you've never been a mother. You've never heard the heartbeat of a child growing inside you, right under your heart. I could no more kill this baby than I could kill one of my older children.'' Her chest rose and fell with exertion as she leaned heavily against a stack of boxes.

Cassie took a deep breath, trying unsuccessfully to calm down and lower her voice. "I don't believe in terminating pregnancies any more than you do, and I've never even been pregnant. But give me a little credit here, Har. I don't have an M.B.A. from Wharton for nothing. You have to look at the pros and cons. Your existing five children need you, especially Maddie. Look at her. My God, she reminds me so much of me at that age that it hurts. She needs a mother bad. It might not seem like it, but she looks to you for guidance." Tears fell down her cheeks freely now, and she angrily wiped them away. "And what about Amanda? Do you want her to only remember you from wrinkled photos Joe pulls out of his wallet?" She threw her hands in the air. "I don't understand you. You're making this decision with the same 'shoot from the hip' decision-making process you used when you eloped with Joe. You never seem to think about what's going to happen to those you leave behind."

Harriet crumpled onto the top of the closed trunk, her voice defeated. "That's not fair. I was just a teenager then, and it wasn't a life-or-death situation, either."

Cassie kicked a Raggedy Ann doll on the floor, sending it flying into the wall with a slight thud. "No, I guess it wouldn't have been life or death for you then. I was the only one who wanted to die after you married Joe."

Tears glistened on Harriet's cheeks, and Cassie wanted to hide from the shame she felt inside. She hadn't meant what she'd said, but old hurts die slow and hard, and the fear she felt for her sister pulled out ugly thoughts from the darkest place inside.

Harriet swallowed. "If I haven't said it enough, I'm sorry. I really, really am. But I'm not sorry for marrying Joe. I make all my decisions from the heart, and I can't say I regret a single one. But I am truly sorry for hurting you and for being at least partly responsible for the mess your life is in right now. But you're a big girl now, Cassie. And I think it's time somebody filled you in on a few things you've been missing." With a shuddering breath, she fixed her sister with a steady gaze. "Since Mama and Daddy aren't here to do it, I guess it's my job, so here goes. You've got this wonderful thing happening between you and Sam staring you in the face, but you refuse to acknowledge it because you've got it in your head that you're not sticking around here long enough to get involved with anything or anybody.''

Harriet held up her hand, fending off her sister's objections. ''Whether you know it or not, you're too stubborn to admit that maybe you've been wrong these past fifteen years and that Walton really is where you belong—with the people who love you, even when you're being ornery. And you need these people, even if you're blind to it. If you're too stupid to see that, then you're not half as smart as I've always thought you were.'' As if to signal that she was done, Harriet rested her head in her hands and took a deep breath.

Feeling as if her legs couldn't hold her anymore, Cassie sank down on a dusty box and began crying. ''I'm sorry, Har. I didn't mean those things. I really didn't.'' She bent and rested her elbows on her knees, the heels of her hands closing her eyes. ''I'm just so damned scared. And I'm angry—angry that this has happened to you and there doesn't seem to be anything I can do to make it better. For the first time in my life, I don't know what to do.'' She sniffed loudly, sitting up and wiping her eyes with the backs of her hands.

Harriet lifted her head and held her gaze steadily on her sister. ''What are you afraid of, Cassie? I hope it's not for me. Don't waste your energies, because I've got enough fear and uncertainty for all of us. Are you afraid of your feelings for Sam? Or maybe it's just admitting that you're wrong about how you feel about this town and what it means to you? Try it. You'll find that it's a lot better once you get it out of your system. And I promise you nobody will think less of you. Just stop being so stubborn and listen to your heart for a change.''

Cassie jumped up off the box, her voice rising. ''Why does everybody think that staying here will solve all my problems? I can't do anything for you, so I'm useless here.

And it's going to take a hell of a lot more than the best sex I've ever had to keep me here in Walton.''

A throat clearing had both women turning their heads toward the attic stairwell. Sam Parker stood on the top step, his lips drawn together in a tight smile, his jaw working furiously. His gaze sought Cassie's. ''Thank you for clearing that up, Cassie. And you shouted it so loud that I also thank you for the citizens of this town who needed clarification of what you were doing Friday night.''

Cassie kicked a trunk with her sandaled foot, bending back her big toe. ''Dangnabit!'' She clutched her foot while hopping on the other. Sam approached, but she held out her hand to stop him. ''Don't you touch me. Haven't you ever heard that eavesdropping is rude?''

''Hey, I've been standing here for a good ten minutes waiting for you to come up for air. I'm glad I finally got your attention, because I was afraid your head was about to explode.''

Her mouth opened to reply, but she quickly shut it, making her think of a bass out of water. Ignoring him, she turned to Harriet. Feeling very small, she said, ''I think I just broke my toe. I'm going to go find a real doctor to look at it. I'll find you later when I've calmed down so we can talk rationally about you and what our next step is going to be. I also have a feeling I'm going to need to do some apologizing.'' Turning her back on Sam, she hobbled down the stairs.

She leaned against the hallway wall, breathing heavily, her heart pounding. Her first urge was to call Andrew and discuss work. She needed to throw herself into a project, be lulled by columns of figures, negotiate and placate a recalcitrant client. When working, she was competent, in control and respected. There was no fear, no need to shout, and no feelings of inadequacy. She was halfway to the phone when she realized Andrew might not be the right person to soothe her worried mind.

With a heavy sigh, she limped through the house and out the back door and headed toward the gazebo. The sun shone in sporadic fits through scattering clouds as the wet grass soaked her feet through the sandals. With damp blades cling-ing to her bare toes, she collapsed on one of the seats and rested her forehead on her drawn-up knees. She wanted to cry or scream but couldn't decide which. She longed for her orderly world in New York, but when she focused on the black-and-white sterility of her apartment or the stark white walls of her office, it left her cold.

Cracking open an eye, she stared at her throbbing big toe. She wasn't stubborn; she simply knew what she wanted. And sure—she was scared. Scared that her sister might be dying. But certainly not scared of admitting she was wrong. Wrong about what? That she didn't belong in Walton? Hadn't her phenomenal success in the advertising world of New York proven that?

Lord, she needed someone to talk to. But the first person that came to mind was the last person in the world she ever wanted to see again.

As if conjured up, Sam came out the back door, striding toward her across the pricker-filled grass in those damned form-fitting jeans and cowboy boots. He stopped at the bot-tom of the gazebo, one water-splattered, booted foot planted firmly on the bottom step. His eyes were guarded as he spoke.

"So, do you want me to look at your toe? It's either me or Dr. Clemens, the veterinarian. Then again, maybe a vet should be your first choice. You were shouting like a wounded animal back there. And at Harriet, no less. You should be ashamed of yourself."

To her complete surprise and humiliation, she began to cry. Not just tears, but fat tears spilling over her cheeks and accompanied by loud gulping sobs.

Without a word, Sam sat down next to her and pulled her into his arms, resting her head on his chest. She didn't resist, but allowed herself to be held while she soaked his shirt.

"It's . . . my . . . toe," she blurted out between sobs. "It . . . hurts."

Sam held her closer and patted her back. "Yeah, I know."

They remained like that until she had no more tears left.

Slowly, she pulled herself up and took the offered handkerchief. She sent him a quivering smile. "You're not going to have any left if you keep giving them away."

His teeth shone white as he smiled. "Well, you're not supposed to keep them. You're supposed to wash them and then return them."

"Oh." She wiped her tears and mascara off her cheek, then blew her nose loudly into the white linen square.

"Let me see your toe."

She stuck out her leg for him and watched as his gentle fingers removed her sandal and placed it on the bench. She grimaced as he manipulated the digit but kept quiet. With a little smile, she said, "This is getting to be a bad habit—me with a hurt foot and both of us here in the gazebo while you try to make it better."

He didn't smile back as he let his hands rest on her bare leg. "Yeah, some habits are hard to break."

The heat from his hand on her calf burned into the skin, and she hastily removed her leg from his lap. "So, what's the prognosis, Doctor?"

"It's not broken—just bruised. Try wearing open-toed shoes or going barefoot until it's better. No high heels."

She nodded, and silence fell between them, the space filled only with the smell of cut grass and fabric softener blowing at them from the dryer vent at the back of the house.

"I'm . . . I'm sorry, Sam." She wanted to add, "For the things I've said and the way I've treated you," but her behavior appalled her, and she couldn't stand to be reminded of it just yet.

He stretched his arms out on top of the bench and crossed his long legs. "Don't think twice about it. Besides, I'm going to bill you for the consultation."

Cassie looked down, embarrassed, realizing he was trying to save her the humiliation of an apology for her dreadful behavior. She felt like a child who is spared from a much-deserved spanking.

He looked toward the tops of the houses in Farrellsford as he spoke. "I'm heading out to Atlanta now. I've got

Harriet's biopsy results with me, and I'm going to schedule a few appointments for her.'' He uncrossed his legs and stood. ''Oh, and by the way, since the conference doesn't start until Thursday, I'll have a bit of time. If you're still interested in finding your missing sibling, I thought I'd go check out birth records while I'm there.''

She raised her head. ''Thank you. All that sort of slipped my mind.'' She reached into her jeans' pocket. ''I found this in the writing box. Look at the initials.'' She let the locket and chain drop into his outstretched palm.

''HM and EL. Well, HM is most likely your father. But EL . . .'' His forehead creased. ''Nobody comes to mind right off. But I'll think about it and ask around. I'll let you know if I learn anything.''

He handed her back the locket, and she slid it into her pocket, next to the crumpled piece of paper with the phone number she'd taken from her cell phone.

Cassie pushed the hair out of her face. ''When I saw Mrs. Perkins in your waiting room, she told me she remembered my father saying something about a brother when I was born.''

''Really? Well, that should help. I'll let you know if I find anything.''

Silence fell again, and Cassie looked away, completely discomfited. She wondered if Sam also saw her naked whenever he looked at her.

''I guess I'd better go. It's a long drive.''

Cassie stood, too. ''Thanks again, Sam. For everything.''

He raised an eyebrow in reply.

She put her hands on her hips. ''For what you're doing for Harriet. And for searching the birth records. And my toe. I know I don't deserve any of your kindness, but I want you to know that I appreciate it.'' She felt the blood rush to her cheeks.

''You're welcome,'' he said, a slow grin spreading on his lips. His boots clumped down the steps of the gazebo. ''Good-bye, Cassie. I'll talk to you later.''

''Sure. Talk to you later. Drive carefully.''

He walked several yards before turning around to face her again. ''Best sex you ever had, huh?''

She picked up her sandal and threw it at his retreating back, narrowly missing him. She watched as he hiked up his pants and walked toward the back door with a deliberate and exaggerated swagger. Burying her face again on her drawn-up knees, she let herself laugh.

Chapter 18

The rain was dripping off the blue-and-white sheriff's car parked in the drive when Cassie came around to the front of the house. The make and model of the vehicle was most likely a lot more recent than that of Sheriff Hank Adams, whom Cassie remembered from childhood. He'd once played football for the University of Georgia before a career-ending injury had moved him back home to Walton, pinned a badge on him, and slid him into a government-issue Crown Victoria. From her brief run-ins with Sheriff Adams during her youth, she knew his heart was as big as his bulldog chest. Still, the sight of his car gave her a start, and she ran up the steps, wondering what had happened.

She found her aunt pouring iced tea for the lawman in the front parlor. He rose and gave her a wide grin.

"How ya doin', Cassie? Still up to tricks?" He winked, and she blushed, recalling the time he'd caught her hauling Principal Purdy's boxers atop the high school flagpole. He'd promised to keep quiet if she'd return the article of clothing to the clothesline where she'd found it.

"I'm doing fine—thanks for asking." She wrinkled her

nose. "And I'm not a teenager anymore, so you can stop your night patrolling. I stay in bed at night now."

He winked again. "That's what I've heard." He turned to Aunt Lucinda and guffawed loudly. "Mrs. Crandall seems to recall Dr. Parker returning to his house in the wee hours of Saturday morning wearing the same clothes he had on the night before." He sent Cassie a wink as Lucinda looked down into her tea, and Cassie choked.

Finding her voice again, she asked, "Is this a social call, or is something wrong?"

"Well, I hate to say it, but this is official. Your aunt called me about them trees. Seems like somebody's deliberately vandalized them."

"Are you sure? What kind of a person vandalizes trees?"

The large man shrugged. "Same kind of person who hunts an endangered animal—pure meanness, is all. I suspect it's some of those kids from that new neighborhood behind your property. Ain't got nothin' better to do until school starts."

Cassie crossed her arms. "Are there any other houses with damaged trees? I'm finding this a little difficult to believe."

"Yep—yours and two others; the Ladues' and the Pritchards'. Seems they skipped right over the Haneys'. Guess because they don't have any big trees ever since the hurricane two summers ago wiped them all out. But whoever it was stripped the bark clean off the bottom of all twelve of your live oaks. I've told your aunt here to have them tarred just as soon as she can before all the sap runs out of them and they bleed to death." He beat his hat against his knee. "Those trees are over a hundred years old. It would be a real shame to lose them all."

Deflated from the day's events, Cassie sagged into an armchair. "This is unbelievable."

The sheriff rose to leave. "Yep. Sure is. I'll send a patrol car to keep an eye on your place at night, so don't be alarmed if you hear a car. But I doubt you'll have any more problems."

He stood to go, but Cassie called him back. "Sheriff,

would you mind looking at this number and telling me if you're familiar with it?'' She slid the paper from her pocket.

Sheriff Adams took one look at it and smiled broadly. ''Yep. Know this one real well. It's the number of the pay phone outside the Dixie Diner. Used to use it all the time before I got my cell phone.'' He handed the paper back to her. ''Why did you want to know?''

Cassie shrugged, crumpling the paper in her hand. ''No reason, really. I had a phone call come in on my cell phone from that number and just wanted to know where they were calling from.''

The sheriff nodded, drained his glass of iced tea, then tipped his hat and said, ''Ladies,'' and left.

Lucinda picked up the tray with the tea and glasses and headed toward the kitchen just as the phone rang. Cassie grabbed the phone in the foyer before the second ring.

''Hello, Cassandra? It's Andrew.''

She paused for a long moment before answering. ''Andrew? How are you?'' She wanted to smack herself on the forehead. She really wasn't good at these surprise phone calls.

''I'm fine. I've been thinking about you.''

''Really.'' She wasn't going to lie and tell him she'd given him more than a passing thought since he'd left.

''Yeah, really. As a matter of fact, I was just talking to the VisEx people about you today.''

''Oh.'' She tried to calm the excitement in her voice. She had been working on acquiring the VisEx account for over two years. It would have been a real coup to get them to jump ship from their current agency and sign with Andrew's. ''And what did they say?''

''That they were ready to sign with me. On one condition.''

A lump lodged in Cassie's throat. She had a sick feeling she knew what he was about to say.

''They'll only sign if you manage the account.''

She held the phone tightly, her gaze straying outside to the porch and then beyond to the magnolia, its glossy leaves winking in the wind. "I don't know what to say, Andrew. This sounds really exciting, and it would be an excellent opportunity for me. But I meant it when I said we were finished, and I just can't imagine working for you again."

There was a long pause filled with empty air. "I know, and I can understand what you're saying. And even though I still don't understand your reasoning about us, I can promise you I'll back off for now. Because I want you to seriously think of the opportunity this would be for both of us. It would be the biggest account we've got, and you'd be calling the shots."

Just a month before, she would have been beyond elated with this news. But now she could barely find even a drop of enthusiasm. She couldn't say that it was just Harriet's illness, although that was a large part. There was something else there; something she couldn't quite put her finger on. "I don't know, Andrew. This is all pretty sudden."

"Cassandra." His voice was stern, as a parent would speak to a recalcitrant child. "You worked too hard for this to give it up. And think about what it would do for the agency."

Her gaze wandered up the stairs and toward the portrait of Great-great-great-grandfather Madison. His eyes seemed to narrow slightly as she studied it. "I ... I really don't know. And I can't give you an answer right now. When do you need to know?"

"They're in their current contract until next February. But they won't sign without knowing you'll be there. Come on, Cassandra. Do you want me to lose the account?"

Andrew's crowning glory was his ability to elicit guilt. It almost worked now. "I told you, I can't give you an answer right now. I need time."

She could hear his chair slamming against the wall behind his desk, something he did frequently when upset. "How much time?"

"I don't know. A month. Maybe more. I just don't know."

"Cassandra . . ." She pictured him doing his deep-breathing technique. "Okay, fine. If time is what you need, then time is what you've got. I'll talk to Mike at VisEx and get back to you."

"Okay, fine. You do that. I'll talk to you later."

"Yeah. Good-bye."

The dial tone droned in her ear. Slowly hanging up the phone, she walked over to the screen door and looked out toward the row of oaks, her mind deep in thought. Her gaze traveled across the lawn past the live oaks and toward her magnolia, and her eyes widened with a start. Jerking open the door, she ran out of the house toward the tree. Running her hands over the beloved trunk, she checked for fresh scars and was relieved out of all proportion that the tree was unscathed. She sank down onto the damp leaves beneath it and watched as Aunt Lucinda picked her way across the yard in her high heels.

"There you are, precious. I figured this was where you'd run off to."

Cassie peered at this sweet woman who had done so much for her. She knew Lucinda loved Harriet and herself as if they were her own daughters. And what she was about to tell her would hurt deeply. "Sit down, Aunt Lu. I have something to tell you."

Without hesitation, Lucinda sat down next to Cassie on the damp leaves. "It's about Harriet, isn't it?"

Cassie nodded, not surprised at her aunt's intuition. She'd always been like that. The woman had unseen radar that could detect a broken heart or hurt feelings from over a mile away. She'd been the source of comfort for all the bumps and bruises of childhood and then, later, for the biggest broken heart of all.

Before she could speak, the older woman reached out and took Cassie's hand. "It's bad, isn't it? I've had one of my feelings for over a month now, and I just can't seem to shake it."

Cassie squeezed her hand, seeking comfort. "Aunt Lu, they've ... they've found cancer in both breasts. Sam's scheduling appointments for her with some specialists in Atlanta." A lump lodged itself in her throat, and she swallowed. "But she's pregnant, and she won't seek the best treatments because it could harm the baby."

She looked at her aunt, ready to lean her head on the familiar shoulder and wait for the comforting pats that had always made everything seem better. Instead, she watched her aunt's face crumple and tears erupt on the finely wrinkled face. When Lucinda rested her head on Cassie's shoulder, Cassie instinctively placed her arm around her and held tightly. She gave her gentle pats, remembering their powerful healing benefits, and waited for Lucinda's sobs to subside.

A leftover gust from the storm shook the magnolia, making the glossy green leaves weep heavy raindrops down on them.

"Let's go inside." Cassie stood and offered her hand to her aunt. They walked back to the house together, Aunt Lucinda leaning heavily on her, and Cassie wondered exactly when it had happened that she had finally grown up.

The bell over the door at the Dixie Diner chimed brightly as Cassie pushed it open. At six-thirty A.M. there was a surprising hubbub in the small restaurant. The sheriff, Senator Thompkins, Ed Farrell, and Hal Newcomb, the editor in chief of the *Walton Sentinel,* sat at a corner booth. They raised coffee cups in her direction. Cassie thought she caught a glance of sympathy from Sheriff Adams and quickly looked away. Already, Harriet's house was filling up with casseroles, pies, and hams. It reminded Cassie of a funeral, and she wanted to shout at the top of her lungs from the town hall that Harriet was only sick and that Cassie had no intention of letting her die.

She spotted her old friend Mary Jane at the counter, a copy of the morning edition and a steaming cup of coffee in front of her. With a guarded smile, she waved Cassie to the place next to her.

Cassie smiled back, unsure of how things stood between them. Mary Jane had been her best friend for so many years while growing up, but things had changed, and Sam Parker wasn't a small part of that change. She air-kissed her old friend on the cheek, as she had learned to do in New York, wondering why as she did it. "Thanks for meeting me for breakfast. I know I promised you lunch, but I have a feeling I'm not going to have a lot of free time for the foreseeable future."

Mary Jane took a short sip from her mug. "I heard. I think it's a brave thing you're doing, watching all those kids while Harriet and Joe are in Atlanta." She grinned. "Whatever possessed you? Of all the people I can think of who would qualify—"

Cassie held up her hand. "I know, but I owe Harriet. I owe her big time." She didn't say any more, but had a clear picture in her head of the scene in the attic. "Plus, I love her kids. A bit rambunctious, sure, but they're great. Nothing I can't handle."

Mary Jane didn't comment, but raised an eyebrow. The waitress came to take their order, and Cassie placed hers. With just a fleeting thought of fat grams and calories, she ordered the blue-plate special of fried eggs, bacon, hash browns, and grits.

As Mary Jane ordered, Cassie's gaze wandered over the restaurant toward the diner's window. The reverse letters of the restaurant's name arched over the glass, transferring the yellow morning glow that shone through them to pink fingers of light reaching across the laminated tables. She recalled when she and Harriet were small and their father used to bring them to the diner for lunch. They would sit in the same corner booth, and Harriet would always read the letters on the window backward, thinking it was a hoot. She hadn't understood they were just the backs of the letters. Cassie would call her stupid because Harriet couldn't figure it out.

The waitress said something to her, bringing her back to the present. Cassie handed her the menu, then turned toward Mary Jane. "Have you ever wanted to recall words you've said to your brother in the past?"

Mary Jane leaned close. "We all do, Cassie. Especially to our siblings. I think we learn what buttons to push while still in the womb. It just is. And remember, you're sitting next to the person solely responsible for her brother's lifelong nickname of Stinky. Now that's something to be proud of.''

The waitress filled Cassie's mug with coffee as the bell by the front door jangled again. Two men in heavy work boots, stained T-shirts, and overgrown beard stubble stomped into the diner and took seats at the other end of the counter. Cassie and Mary Jane eyed the group of men in the corner warily.

Mary Jane leaned over. ''Those are Roust's men. They're working on the old Olsen property. Remember that big house? They're getting ready to level it and build a new Wal-Mart on the lot.'' She wrinkled her nose as if the men sitting ten feet away already reeked of sweat and hard Georgia clay.

Cassie slid a look at the workmen. ''What's wrong with the old Wal-Mart?''

Mary Jane nodded. ''Exactly. That's what Sam's trying to knock into the council's thick skulls.'' She thanked the waitress as her plate was put in front of her. ''Sam's missing an important town council meeting this evening. They're taking votes on that moratorium; it'll save the Olsen home if it passes. At least for now.'' Taking a bite out of her toast, she daintily wiped her mouth with a paper napkin. ''Sam's asked me to go and speak for him, but I don't have his powerful way of talking. He can be very persuasive when he wants to be.''

''That's for sure.'' She felt herself coloring and took a bite of hash browns to hide it.

Mary Jane sent her an arch look. ''And I guess you would know.''

Cassie stopped chewing for a moment. ''What's that supposed to mean?''

''Never mind.'' Mary Jane took another bite of toast, and they continued eating, chatting about old friends and new clothes, waving to the stream of townspeople that flowed in and out of the front door. The bell chimed again and again, as if to remind the two women of the one subject looming between them that needed to be avoided.

When Ed Farrell got up to leave, he approached Mary Jane and Cassie at the counter. With a nod in Cassie's direction, he addressed Mary Jane. "I guess I'll be seeing you at the meeting tonight. I'm sorry Sam won't be here, but it will be a shorter meeting without him."

Mary Jane swiveled on her stool. "Don't be so sure of that, Ed. Sam has given me a ten-page speech of what he wants covered. I wouldn't schedule any early-morning appointments if I was you."

He looked agitated. "Yeah, well. I gotta go. I'm supposed to trim Miss Lena's hedges, but first I've got an appointment to show your house, Cassie." He leaned closer to her. "Aunt Lucinda told me about the call from New York. You do know that I'd be willing to help you out by buying the house myself and then selling it to a nice family." He held up his hand. "Don't give me an answer now; just think about it. It could be the answer to your problems. You'd be able to return to New York scot-free, and your beautiful house will be left in capable hands."

Cassie nodded. "Thanks, Ed. I'll definitely think about it."

He patted her on the back, then left. Mary Jane looked at her as if she'd lost her mind. "You've got to be kidding, right? I wouldn't sell that man my house if he paid me a million bucks. Don't you remember how mean he was in high school? How he used to pick on Sam?"

Cassie took a brief sip of her coffee. "That was ages ago. He's changed. What you don't seem to recall is how we used to pick on him. I find it nothing short of a miracle that he wants to even do business with me."

Jane shook her head. "There's something up with him; I just haven't figured out what it is yet."

Senator Thompkins left the other table and approached, turning to Cassie with a grim look. "I wish you'd talk Sam out of this foolishness. He's just wasting his energy fighting progress. And I'm sure you've got ways to distract him."

Cassie felt the heat flame her cheeks again as the grill sizzled behind the counter with another order of hash browns. She took a gulp of scalding coffee, burning her tongue but glad for the excuse not to answer. Choking down iced water, she waved the senator out the door.

"I can't believe he said that. I mean, does the whole town know?"

Mary Jane put down her fork. "Know what? That you slept with him last Friday night? Yeah, I'd say so." She smoothed the paper napkin on her lap. "But what I'd like to know is what does it mean? Was it a one-night stand, or are you after a bit more?" Her voice held a note of forced lightness. "I wish you'd just go ahead and stake your claim or leave town, because the suspense is killing me. I'd like to know if I should start nursing my broken heart or give it another chance."

Cassie set her mug down with a quiet thud. "I . . . I don't know. . . ."

Mary Jane leaned closer. "Sam Parker is the most stubborn, pigheaded man I know. I also know he's the most sincere, kindhearted man I've ever met—and a damned fine doctor. It doesn't hurt that he looks pretty devastating in a pair of Levi's, either. And I'd give my left arm for him to look at me just once the way that he looks at you." She wiped the back of her hand roughly over her eyes and turned her head. "I don't know why I'm selling his virtues to you. I should be selling you a one-way ticket out of town. But I just can't stand to see him suffer so. He doesn't deserve it."

"I never meant to hurt anybody—especially not Sam. He knows how things stand between us. And Mary Jane, you of all people should understand. You were with me all through my growing up. I never belonged here; I never intended to stay. Sam belongs here, and I belong in New York—end of story. I have no claims on him." She bit her lip, wondering if what she said was true.

Mary Jane picked up the check from the aqua Formica. She bent over toward Cassie. "You just pretended you didn't belong to separate yourself from Harriet. It made you stand out—like your outrageous pranks. But you're an adult now. It's time you started acting like one." She slid off her stool and stood. "I love him, and everything was fine between us until you came into town. So grow up and make your decision, because watching the two of you is killing me." She pushed in her stool. "Thanks for having breakfast with me, but I've got to get to the clinic."

Cassie watched as her old friend paid her check and left through the door, the bell announcing her exit. She took another sip of coffee, trying to swallow the bitter taste in her throat.

She stayed in the diner for another cup of coffee, waving to people as they came through the door and enjoying the last peace and quiet she would probably see in quite a while.

As she was going through her purse to pay her check, her cell phone rang. Flipping it open, she answered the call.

"Hello?"

Again, there was no response, just light breathing at the other end and then a quick click as the caller hung up. Cassie looked at the number registered on the screen, recognizing it as the same one used earlier. The pay phone outside the diner. Her head jerked toward the front of the building with the two huge windows, realizing that they did not afford a view of the corner where the phone was located.

Leaping from her stool, she ran to the door, almost running into the Sedgewick twins, who were entering the building. Doing her best to squeeze by them, she plunged outside on the sidewalk, only to find the phone abandoned, the receiver dangling by its cord.

Cassie glanced around, looking for anybody running, appearing out of place, or watching her intently. All she saw were people going about their business in the slow, small-town pace she had come to recognize. With a sigh, she turned around and went back into the diner to pay her bill. Fortified now with both adrenaline and caffeine to get her through any difficulty, she drove Lucinda's pink car to Harriet's house.

Joe met her at the front door and handed her Amanda

with a very heavy and pungent diaper. "Thanks, Cassie. Would you mind changing her? And I've got a bottle in the refrigerator if she gets hungry. I'll be upstairs helping Harriet pack if you need anything." He closed the door behind Cassie, then ran ahead of her up the steps.

She held the baby away from her, the little girl's plump legs dangling. Amanda gave her aunt a goofy smile, and Cassie had to laugh in spite of the odor rising from the sodden diaper. Still holding the baby in front of her like a sack of dirty laundry, she carried her up the stairs. "Come on, sweetie. Between the two of us, I'm sure we can figure this out."

As Cassie lay the baby on the changing table, Amanda gurgled with a soft smile, making something in her aunt's chest tighten. The door behind them swung open with force, hitting the wall and bouncing against the doorstop. With a start, Cassie turned around and saw Madison leaning against the doorway, wearing a disgruntled frown. Cassie gave her the warmest smile she could muster, knowing that Madison was the only child who had been told about her mother's condition. The younger ones remained blissfully unaware.

"Have a seat, Maddie, and we'll chat while I'm changing Amanda's diaper."

"I'm not in the mood to chat." She shut the door harder than necessary, then stalked to the rocking chair before slumping into it.

Cassie untaped the dirty diaper and folded it down. Trying to hide her grimace at the diaper's contents, she turned back to her older niece. "How are you doing?"

Madison folded her hands over her chest. "Life sucks."

With one hand, Cassie reached into the diaper-wipe box, grabbing hold of a handful. She shook the wad hard, trying to separate one from the bunch. "Yeah, sometimes it does, Maddie." She searched her mind for the perfect words to say, remembering her irrational anger when her own mother had been ill.

The right words remained as elusive as an unbroken conch shell on the beach, so she spoke with the only words she could find. "That's why it's nice to have family and friends who care for you. You know we'll be here to help you through the rough spots." A clump of wipes fell to the floor, one of them sticking to Cassie's bare leg.

"Yeah, right. My mother's dying, my father's clueless, and you're leaving. Why can't this be happening to Lucy Spafford? Her mother is a witch, and she's only got the one child. It's . . . it's just not fair."

Cassie heard the catch in Maddie's voice but didn't turn to look. She was concentrating on getting the front of the diaper in the front of the baby. "No, Maddie. Life is rarely fair. But you can't start thinking so negatively now. Your mother is going to need your support. Remember, she didn't choose to get sick."

"But she's choosing that baby over us. It's like she doesn't even love us—or why would she take such a risk?"

With one hand pinned on the baby's squirming stomach and the other one trying to pry the adhesive off the clean diaper, Cassie tried to keep her voice calm. "There is one thing that you should never forget. Your mother loves you deeply, as only a mother can. She's only making the best decision she knows how. She could no more sacrifice that baby than she could sacrifice one of y'all. It's a mother thing. You'll understand it one day." The baby stilled for a moment, and Cassie recalled her words. When had she gained such wisdom? The same question that had burned in her mind somehow seemed easily answered and understandable when explained to Maddie.

As if sensing Cassie's peace, the baby smiled her sweet smile again, and it brought a sting to Cassie's eyes. Keeping her gaze on the baby, she said, "I lost my mother when I was younger than you. I can pretty much relate to what you're going through. And I certainly share your anger. But this was your mother's decision, and it's up to us to support her." The baby gurgled and began to kick her pudgy legs like a frog, making it difficult for Cassie to close the diaper. Cassie stopped struggling for a moment and said very softly,

"Be kind to your mother, Maddie. She needs your love and understanding right now as much as you need hers."

She resumed the diaper battle and was near to conceding defeat when Maddie stood. "Let me do that. You've got the thing on backwards." With a small smile breaking through her scowl, Maddie expertly diapered her baby sister and snapped up the playsuit with deft fingers. When she lifted the baby off the changing table, Amanda snuggled into Maddie's shoulder, rubbing her eyes with her little hands. "That means she's tired. I'll put her down for her nap. I don't figure you know how to do that, either."

Cassie sent her a grateful smile. "No, I don't. Thanks." She backed out of the room quietly and closed the door behind her.

Sarah Frances met her at the bottom of the stairs with a mournful look in her eyes. "I'm hungry."

"Have you had breakfast?"

The little girl nodded solemnly. "Yes, ma'am. But we're still hungry. We need a snack."

Cassie looked at her watch. Nine o'clock. Sounded like a good time for a snack. She took hold of Sarah Frances's hand and led her into the kitchen. Knoxie and Joey were already seated at the table. "Okay. What do y'all have around here for a snack?"

With a precise voice, Sarah Frances said, "MoonPies."

Knoxie and Joey looked at each other, their eyes wide.

Cassie walked to the pantry. "All right, then. MoonPies it is." She found the box and pulled out four. "What would you like to drink with this?"

All three children looked at each other, then Sarah Frances said, "Co-Cola. Please."

"All right. Three Cokes coming right up."

They were enjoying their snack when Joe and Harriet entered the kitchen. Cassie waved as she took a sip of her Coke, while the children smiled with angelic expressions, mouths filled with MoonPie.

"Aunt Cassie let us have a snack." Crumbs flew from Sarah Frances's mouth as she spoke.

"Don't speak with your mouth full, honey." Harriet placed her hand on her daughter's head and kissed her cheek. "I guess you didn't tell Aunt Cassie about the fruit bowl we use for snacks, huh?"

The little girl answered with a sweet smile.

Cassie stood. "Sorry, Har. I think I was shanghaied."

Smiling ruefully, Harriet said, "It's all right. A special treat isn't a bad thing. Besides, you're the one who's going to have to deal with their sugar high in about an hour." She turned to the children. "All right, everybody. Come and give me a kiss and a squeeze."

Chairs scraping the floor and little feet running filled the kitchen as hugs and kisses were handed all around. Straightening, Harriet asked, "Where's Maddie? I looked for her upstairs but couldn't find her."

"I left her in Amanda's room to put the baby down for her nap. Was she not in there?"

Harriet shook her head, a pained expression on her face. "I'll look for her outside, but if I don't find her, would you give her a kiss and hug from me? And tell her I love her."

Cassie nodded. "Sure." She reached over and gave her sister a tight hug. "Hey, don't worry about Maddie. I think it's normal to feel a bit of anger. I know I did the same with Mama. I knew I was being irrational, but rational thinking and adolescence don't always fit well together."

Harriet nodded. "I know. But I did want to kiss her good-bye." She faced her sister. "Thanks for letting the kids come to your house to stay. I've got all their bags packed and waiting by the door."

Cassie struggled with a smile. "I feel so stupid, wanting to be home to watch over my trees. I hope the kids will be okay away from home."

Harriet touched her cheek. "They're only a few blocks away. And I think it will be such an adventure for them that they won't think about missing me."

Cassie looked up at the ceiling, trying to stop any tears from falling down her face. "Oh, I've got lots of things planned for them. Painting porches, inflating condoms, dressing statues—all sorts of things. You just concentrate on getting well. I'll take care of everything else.''

''That's what I'm afraid of.'' Harriet reached and took hold of Cassie's necklace. ''I guess I should be buying you some more hearts to put on this chain.''

With a shake of her head, Cassie closed her hand over her sister's. ''Oh, no, Har. You just need to start your own necklace.''

Harriet hugged her sister again. ''Really—thanks. And I mean it. This is a big thing you're doing for us, and we really appreciate it.''

Cassie blinked hard. ''Hey, it's the least I could do. Especially after what I said—''

Harriet put a finger to her lip. ''Don't. We all get scared and angry and say things we don't mean. And you don't owe me an apology—ever. What you're doing for us speaks louder than any words ever could.'' With soft hands, she wiped the tears and smudged mascara out from under Cassie's eyes.

Joe returned from putting the suitcases in the trunk, perspiration already beading his forehead and upper lip. He gave bear hugs and loud kisses to the children, then turned toward Cassie and wrapped his arms around her. Cassie froze for a moment, thinking how this was the first time they had touched each other since she had come home. But the warmth and sincerity of his arms around her made her relax as she received their comfort.

His voice had a forced cheeriness to it. ''You have my cell-phone number. If you have any questions, just call.'' He leaned close to her ear. ''And have Maddie call her mother when you find her. Harriet's sick with worry.''

''I will.''

He turned to his wife. ''We have to go if we're going to make your first appointment.'' Hoisting an overnight bag over his shoulder, he led the group out to the driveway, then helped his wife into the minivan. Harriet's face looked small and pale through the van's window as she waved good-bye. Joe backed out onto the street with a crunch of gravel, then drove away slowly, with Cassie watching the hand waving in the window as long as she could.

She felt a tugging on the leg of her shorts. "Aunt Cassie, I need to go potty."

With a smile, she herded the children back into the house, trying to ignore the last glimpse she'd had of her sister, of the thin white face and the eyes filled with love, pain, and abject fear. She knew if she were to look in the mirror, she'd see the same face.

Chapter 19

"There's a possum in the house again!"

The shriek jerked Cassie from the window seat in the front parlor, where she had been perched, watching for stealthy shadows on the front lawn. Her only reward had been the twin circles of headlights making a slow dance across the yard as a car turned around in the drive. The porch lights had illuminated a police car, and Cassie had sat back with relief.

With her adrenaline pumping again, she raced toward the family room, where the children, with the exception of Madison, were engrossed in a Disney movie. Making its slow, lumbering way across the Berber carpet, a small rodent twitched its nose in Cassie's direction.

"How in God's name did that get in here?" The animal stopped for a moment, as if preparing to answer, then continued its stroll across the family-room floor.

Joey, without taking his gaze off the television screen, said, "Got through the cat door in the kitchen."

With hopefulness in her voice, Cassie asked, "You've got a cat?"

Joey shook his head. "No, ma'am. It was Pop-pop's cat,

and she died last year. Daddy's not gotten around to fixin'
that door yet, and Pop-pop didn't know how. The possum
just sticks her snout around the screen door, pushes it open,
and then crawls in through the little door. Aunt Lucinda
doesn't like it, neither.''

Baby Amanda, swinging contentedly in the baby swing,
squealed and threw a rattle, barely missing the small animal.
In response, it curled into a little fur ball and played dead.

''This happens a lot?'' Cassie moved to stand between
the possum and the baby.

Knoxie nodded. ''Yes, ma'am. Are you going to cook it?
Aunt Lucinda keeps saying she's going to make a pie out
of it if it comes inside again, but she hasn't done it yet. Do
you know how to make possum pie?''

Without turning her back on the animal, Cassie released
the baby from the swing and propped her on her hip. ''No,
I don't. And I don't think a potentially rabid animal should
be walking freely in the house, either. Since Aunt Lucinda
doesn't cook it, I have to guess that you have another way
to get it out of the house?''

Knoxie stuck her thumb in her mouth and twirled her red
hair. Sarah Frances lifted her head from the sofa, where she
was lying. ''When Pop-pop wasn't home, my daddy'd come
over with a big shoebox and just scoop it up and put it
outside again.''

Cassie eyed the still animal, wondering where she could
find a big enough shoebox. In the five days since she'd been
watching the children, she thought she'd dealt with it all.
She had learned that peanut butter does not take bubblegum
out of hair, that a small metal object can travel through the
digestive tracts of small babies with little or no effect, and
that plastic glow-in-the-dark yo-yos should never be put on
top of burning lightbulbs to make them brighter. The process
of removing a wild animal from the house had not even
been considered.

Madison, who'd been upstairs doing her homework,
appeared in the doorway. Cassie looked at her with a start.
Her long brown hair had been cut short, with a few remnants

still clinging to her yellow T-shirt. Except for the color, the shape and style were identical to Cassie's.

"You cut your hair."

Maddie gave her a tentative smile. "Do you like it?"

Cassie nodded. "It looks good on you." She tilted her head to the side. "Actually, it looks great on you." She smiled brightly. "If you like, I'll made an appointment with Bitsy and have her clean up the ends a bit."

"Thanks." Maddie eyed the visitor on the floor. "I see the possum got in again. I guess you'll need to call Dr. Parker." She smiled innocently at her aunt.

"Whatever for? I'm perfectly capable of dealing with this. I did live in Georgia for almost twenty-three years, you know." Cassie looked at her watch. Through her frequent phone calls during the week with Harriet and Joe, she had learned Sam would be returning today. "Besides, he's probably just getting in, and it would be silly to bother him for something like this."

The animal stirred on the floor, its rear end twitching. Cassie glanced at her niece. "Here, take the baby and keep an eye on the possum while I go find a laundry basket."

She returned with one from the laundry room and successfully tossed it over the frightened animal. Kicking it slightly, she began to nudge the basket and its prisoner across the floor inch by inch, hampered only by the animal's claws digging into the carpet. Maddie disappeared into another room before Cassie had even made it to the edge of the rug.

Half an hour later, when she had finally reached the kitchen table with the animal and laundry basket intact, the doorbell rang. When she opened the door and saw Sam, she tried to ignore the flip-flopping of her heart as she greeted him.

He tipped an imaginary hat. "Ma'am," he said in greeting, "I understand you have a varmint that you need rescuing from."

"My hero." Cassie rolled her eyes as she shut the door behind him but was unable to suppress a grin. "I guess Maddie called you. I'm handling it just fine, thank you very much. But since you're here, be my guest.'' She motioned for him to follow. ''Come on—the varmint's back here.'' She led the way to the kitchen.

''Where's Lucinda?'' He took a high five from Joey and patted the little girls on their heads. Baby Amanda got a peck on her cheek, and Madison got a wink, but all Cassie got was a smile.

Cassie took the baby from Maddie and juggled her on her hip. ''Miss Lena's been having nightmares again, so Lucinda volunteered to stay with her tonight.''

He nodded as his gaze fell to the upside-down laundry basket and its prisoner still curled up inside. ''Um, um, um. Now there's some good eatin'.''

She wrinkled her nose. ''That's disgusting, Sam.''

''I guess you've never had possum stew, then.''

''No, I can't say I make a habit out of eating road kill.''

Sam snorted. ''You just don't know what you're missing.'' He knelt in front of the basket. ''And I guess you think eating raw fish isn't disgusting.''

She fisted her free hand on her hip. ''That's different.''

He looked at her and raised an eyebrow. ''Is it?''

''Aunt Cassie, Sarah Frances is breathing on me.'' Cassie stepped into the family room in time to see Joey throw a pillow at the sofa, neatly clipping the back of his sister's head.

Cassie flipped off the television. ''Okay, everybody, movie's over. It's time for bed. Everybody upstairs to put on your jammies. I'll be there in a minute to tuck you in.''

''And say our prayers.'' Knoxie's wet thumb hung poised outside her mouth.

''And say your prayers,'' echoed Cassie.

The little girl plopped her thumb back in her mouth and ran after her brother and sister, her feet padding lightly on the wood floors.

Amanda whimpered, so Cassie blew a raspberry on her neck, making the baby giggle. She turned to Sam. ''I'm going to give the baby a bottle and get her ready for bed while you get rid of that varmint.'' She paused for a moment, trying to find her nonchalant voice. "There's beer in the fridge. Help yourself." Putting the baby on her shoulder, she went upstairs, feeling Sam's gaze on her back every step of the way.

After putting the baby in her crib and turning on the monitor, Cassie made her rounds of the children's makeshift bedrooms. Suitcases and clothes still lay strewn over the floor, but Cassie had yet to find the time to help the children unpack and put everything away.

As she approached Knoxie's room, Cassie paused and watched as the little girl stood on the rug in front of the bed and made a huge leap to land on top of her covers.

"What are you doing, sweetheart?"

Wide green eyes stared up at her. "I don't want the bogeyman under the bed to grab my feet, so I jump." Knoxie crawled under her covers.

"Oh, honey, there aren't any bogeymen under your bed." She got down on her hands and knees and peered into the dark space. "Yep—all empty."

"My mommy uses bogeyman spray to keep them away."

"She sprays under the bed?"

Knoxie nodded, her red curls jostling.

Cassie crooked her index finger, got down on her hands and knees again, and made a hissing noise with her mouth.

Knoxie giggled. "No, Aunt Cassie. She uses a real bogeyman spray."

Cassie peeked up over the edge of the bed. "A real spray?"

"Yes, ma'am. And it really works."

Pulling herself up again, Cassie went across the hall to the bathroom and retrieved a Lysol spray can. Returning to the little girl's bedroom, she held it aloft. "This is my own kind of bogeyman spray." She hunched down and spritzed the area under the bed thoroughly, lifting the bedspread at the foot of the bed to get an extra squirt. "Okay, sweet pea. That's guaranteed to keep away any and all nasty bogeymen."

Sitting on the edge of the bed, Cassie held her niece's

hand, and with bowed heads, they said their good-night prayers. Cassie hid her smile at the stridency in the little girl's voice as she called for God's blessing on every person, beast, and insect Knoxie had ever met. Just as Cassie began to nod off to sleep, Knoxie's words caught her attention.

"God bless Daddy and Mama, and please take care of them on their trip. I miss them and want them to come back soon. And God bless Aunt Cassie for taking care of us, and please let her know that we love her even when she shouts at us for putting our tennis shoes in the oven to dry. Amen."

Cassie stood, not sure she could trust her voice. Leaning over, she kissed the little freckled nose and tucked the sheets tightly around the small girl and assorted stuffed animals. "Good night, sweet pea. I love you, too. And I'm sorry I shouted."

She flicked on the nightlight and let herself out of the room, careful to leave the door cracked open. Leaning against the doorframe, she closed her eyes, wishing for a moment that she could believe that the bogeyman could be held back with a household spray instead of knowing with all certainty that the bogeyman was for real. His name started with a capital C, and no amount of spray would ever make him go away.

When she opened her eyes, she spied Sam waiting for her at the top of the stairs, leaning against the banister.

"You handled that well."

"Thanks." She rubbed the back of her neck, the exhaustion of taking care of five children all day finally catching up to her. She studiously avoided his eyes. "I'm pooped. I think I'll go straight to bed. Hang on a second and I'll walk you out."

She disappeared into her room and reappeared carrying her blanket and pillow, the cordless receiver of the baby monitor clutched in her hand. She headed down the stairs and felt him follow behind her.

"Where are you going with that stuff?"

She threw the blanket over her shoulder. "I'm going out to that old magnolia tree my mother planted. With all that stuff going on around here, I'd hate to have something happen to it. I mean, it's pretty old and all, so somebody should watch over it. I've already told Maddie where I'll be, so she knows where to find me if anybody needs me." She held up the baby monitor. "Plus, I'll be able to hear Amanda if she wakes."

He opened the front door, then followed her outside. She stood awkwardly, her pillow deliberately held in front of her as if to keep her and Sam physically separated. "Good night, then. And thanks for taking care of Mr. Possum for us."

"You're welcome. My pleasure, as always." He tipped his imaginary hat, then slowly sauntered down the porch steps.

As he walked toward his truck, Cassie paused for a moment to admire his backside, then headed across the lawn to her mother's magnolia. Its leaves dully reflected the moonlight, making it almost glow. She propped the monitor against the trunk, then spread out her blanket and pillow. As she lay down, she spotted Sam walking across the lawn toward her, a blanket tucked under his arm.

She sat up. "What are you doing?"

"I thought you might could use some company. Plus, I've been carrying around this blanket in my truck for over a year, and I figure it's time to put it to use."

Her stomach did a belly flop. Struggling to control her voice, she said, "Well, I hadn't really thought I needed any company. But if you haven't got anything else to do, then be my guest."

He spread his blanket on the ground by her feet, allowing him to peer out at the sky.

The wind rustled the tree above them, making the leaves whisper like schoolchildren sharing secrets. The summer scents of mowed grass and jasmine drifted on the humid air, cloaking them like a blanket. Sam crossed his arms behind his head and stared upward.

"By the way, I did have a chance to check birth records while I was in Atlanta. Even with the initials from the locket,

I didn't find anything that might even be a remote possibility. Of course, I'm not really surprised. I have a feeling this was all so hush-hush back then that Miss E's parents probably covered up the paper trail pretty well. The birth certificate might even show the adoptive parents as being the biological parents, and there might not be any adoption papers at all." He crooked up a leg. "It's been known to happen."

Cassie braced herself on her elbow. "Remember that ad Harriet and I took out in the paper—the one that listed my cell-phone number but not my name? I got two calls—I'm pretty sure it was the same caller—but they never said anything. Just waited for me to speak and then hung up." She sat up completely. "I know that the phone used was the one outside the Dixie Diner, and the second call came when I was sitting inside. It was almost as if the person knew I was in there and was watching me answer the phone. By the time I got outside, whoever it was had gone."

"Sounds like whoever it was wanted to check out who you were without returning the favor."

Cassie breathed deeply, smelling the sweet summer grass. "Yeah, that's pretty much what I thought, too." She rubbed her bare feet in the grass, the blades cool and damp on her soles. "I wish my father had trusted me with this before he died. I'm just amazed that he was willing to let this kind of secret die with him. Harriet thinks it's because Miss E is still living and he wanted to protect her still." She shrugged. "I don't really know what to do next. If he or she doesn't want to be found, then maybe I should just let it be. I have enough to worry about now, especially with Harriet . . ." She let her voice fall away and turned her head.

They were quiet for a while, watching the passing lights of a jetliner high above them. Eventually, Sam turned to face her. "Has Ed Farrell been by recently?"

Cassie nodded and turned toward him, admiring the clean cut of his profile in the moonlight. "He's brought several couples through here in the last week. But they'd heard at school about the vandalism and Maddie's bike being stolen last Monday night right off the front porch. I could tell the parents were a bit leery, and nothing I could say would make a bit of difference. One of the women actually said something about the neighborhood going downhill. Can you imagine? I wanted to open a can of whoop-ass on her.''

He turned his head, a smile in his voice. ''A can of whoop-ass?''

She clamped her hand over her mouth. ''Oh, Lord—it's contagious.''

''Sounds like you've been hanging around Ed Farrell too much.'' He snorted softly. ''That Ed—he's like a booger you just can't thump off.''

She tossed her pillow at him, hitting him in the chest. ''You are such a redneck.''

''Right. And saying you're going to open up a can of whoop-ass on somebody is so much more refined.''

''That just slipped out. Besides, yours was disgusting.''

He propped himself up on his elbows, a smirk visible on his face. ''Then why are you laughing?''

She slumped back down on top of her blankets next to him, trying to ignore the heat that seemed to radiate from where he lay. ''You can be so annoying, Sam Parker.''

She sensed his grin in the dark as he spoke. ''So that's what you call it. I always thought 'annoying' was a negative term.''

A laugh crept up her throat and bubbled over into the night air. She had the most outrageous notion to move closer and kiss him. Just once.

Cassie rolled over on her stomach, propping her chin in her hands. ''Give Ed a break, Sam. He's not the same bully you knew in school. He's changed—a lot. I actually kind of like him. I mean, he's still a little rough in spots, but he's seriously trying to smooth them out. I respect that in him.''

Sam's eyes glittered in the moonlight as he sat up to face her. ''I'd respect him a lot more if I knew where all his money came from. How did he go to college and start his business? Those are expensive ventures, and he came from nothing. There's something that's just not right there. And then there's the matter of what he's trying to do to this town—make it into one of those damned planned communities.'' He lay back down, his face toward the sky. "I don't for one moment believe he has anyone's best interests at heart except for his own.''

Cassie opened her mouth to tell him about Ed's offer to buy her house, but Sam interrupted. His voice carried a note of urgency. "Cassie—look up.''

On hands and knees she quickly crawled out from under the shelter of the leaves and looked up into the black sky. The tail end of a falling star skimmed past Orion's belt, glowed like spun gold for a brief moment, then faded into nothingness. Cassie stared up at the dwindling light, realizing how long it had been since she'd last seen a falling star and wondering where all those empty nights had gone.

"Make a wish,'' she whispered, remembering long-ago summer evenings spent with Harriet and their father watching the sun set, the waxing moon rise, and the stars erupt with light. "Wishing on a falling star makes it come true.''

He stood next to her, his eyes glowing brightly, the moon making them shine silver. "Sometimes. I've been wishing on falling stars for a long time, and I'm still waiting.''

Heat flooded her veins. "Be careful what you wish for.'' His warm breath stroked her cheek, an intimate caress. Looking down, she noticed his feet were bare. "I'm going to wish that Harriet gets better and everybody lives happily ever after.''

He didn't say anything, so Cassie raised her head. He was studying her carefully with a slight upturn of his lips. "You're such an idealist. It's one of the things I've always loved about you.''

She tucked a strand of hair behind her ear, feeling self-conscious. "Andrew called me a daydreamer. I think he said it was his job in life to break me of that bad habit.''

"Then he failed. I'm glad.''

Looking up at the sky again, she felt small and insignificant under its vastness, like a grain of sand on the beach of life. She took a deep breath, the great boundless sky somehow making her say the unspeakable, as if the atmosphere could swallow the words and take them away forever. "What if Harriet dies, Sam? How will any of us move on?"

Sam moved to stand behind her and put his hands on her shoulders. She resisted the urge to rest her head on his strong fingers.

"Well, you get out of bed, you eat your grits, say hey to your neighbor, you give extra love to her children, and you live your life. The sun is a pretty stubborn guy, and he'll rise each day just to spite you. But life does go on." He squeezed her shoulders. "You survived when your mother died. I suspect you still grieve for her. I know I do for Tom. But I think you've lived your life the way your mother would have wanted you to, and you should be proud of that."

Her fingers idly tinkered with the gold charms around her neck. "No, I think she's crying with shame up in heaven. Maddie's almost fifteen, and this summer is the first time I've ever laid eyes on her. I've never sent a birthday card or baby gift in all these years." She swallowed thickly. "At least I'm here now—to help Harriet out. It's the least I can do. I don't want to think of Mama crying anymore."

He turned her around to face him, his expression earnest. "She's not crying; she's just waiting. The book isn't closed on this chapter, Cassie. Now, I'm only going to say this because I know you've already thought about it." He stepped closer, his eyes searching hers. "If those children are left motherless, what will you do? Visit them twice a year and send presents from New York every birthday and Christmas?"

She tried to pull away, but he held on to her. "I will not be blackmailed into staying here. And I'm not going to think about any of that now, but I do know that whatever decision I make, it will be made of my own free will. Not anybody else's, including yours, Sam Parker."

His hands clutched her tightly. When he spoke, his words were flippant, but his eyes were deadly serious. "I understand I have strong methods of persuasion."

They stood facing each other for a long moment, their

breaths melding in the small space between them. The tree frogs thumped their rhythm into the night, echoing the loud beating of her heart. She could almost taste his lips, and all it would take would be an imperceptible sway in his direction. . . .

Their lips met, and she was unsure who had moved. She opened her mouth to welcome him in, and he touched her tongue with his, making her insides dissolve like flour lumps in hot gravy. Her fingers threaded through his hair, bringing him even closer, as her hips pushed against his.

His hands moved down to the back of her short skirt and slid underneath to cup her bottom. "No slip?" he asked against her mouth.

"Too hot," she breathed.

"I'll say."

She saw his raised eyebrow before he bent forward to devour her mouth again. He lifted her and laid her gently on his blanket under the tree and slowly undid each button of her blouse with painstaking care. Not willing to wait for him, she reached behind and unclasped her bra.

He bent forward and, with slow deliberation, used the tip of his tongue to trace each nipple, waiting for the small buds to harden. She bucked her hips under him, showing her impatience. The smell of damp leaves, humid earth, and her own musk filled her senses, making her lush and ripe, part of the earth and the tree and this man. Using frantic fingers, she unbuttoned his shirt, losing patience with the last button when it snagged on a thread. It popped off as she pulled the shirt open to slide it off his shoulders.

His warm hands moved up her thighs and tugged at the waistband of her panties, easing them down her legs with calculated precision. She moaned, and his lips claimed hers again and heated her blood until she thought she should see steam rising from her skin. Slow fingers moved between her legs and parted the folds of flesh, rubbing with insistent pressure. She cried out with pleasure as he slipped a finger inside, nearly undoing her.

"Sam . . . please . . ." His belt buckle slipped in her

fingers at her frenzied attempt to undo it and get his pants off. She thought she would drown in the desire for him that seemed to consume her, and it occurred to her that it wouldn't be such a bad way to go.

He pulled his hand away from between her legs and rose above her, his chest hairs tickling her bared breasts. His eyes flashed, and her heart seemed to skip a beat as he regarded her carefully.

"Good night, Cassie."

She let her arms fall to her side, feeling suddenly boneless. "Good night?"

He rolled to her side, his breath coming in quick gasps. "I've already told you—it's all or nothing with me. I won't make love to you without a commitment. We should never have let it get this far." He sat up and reached for his shirt.

She sat up with a jerk. "You're kidding, right?"

He slipped his shirt over his head. "I'm afraid not. But believe me, it's hurting me as much as it's hurting you."

Grabbing a handful of dirt and dead leaves, she threw them at him. "Now's a damned fine time to start acting like a southern gentleman!"

He reached over and held on to her wrist, immobilizing her. "I want you, Cassie. God knows how much. But I told you before—I won't be used. I want to be more to you than a nice roll in the hay." He released her, then sat back and raised an eyebrow. "Even if it is the best sex you've ever had."

"I was just making that up." Scrambling for her shirt and underpants, she said, "Besides, you started it."

"I did not."

She pulled on her clothes and faced him. "Did, too."

"Did not."

She threw her pillow at him. "I can't believe you—you're such a child. I'm leaving." She gathered up her blanket and turned to go, mindless of the clinging leaves and twigs. Pausing for a moment, she faced him, a concerned expression on her face. "Are you going to stay and watch my tree?"

He leaned on an elbow, looking up at her and grinning ear to ear. "Yeah, I'll watch your tree for you."

"Thank you." She turned around and stomped across the lawn. On the bottom front porch step she called back, "I'll bring you your breakfast in the morning."

Quietly, she let herself into the house and crept up the stairs, dumping the blanket and pillow in the upstairs hallway. Then she checked on all the sleeping children, taking comfort in the soft rhythm of their breathing. Amanda had kicked off her blanket, so Cassie gently tucked it around her small body. As she left the room, she caught sight of the baby monitor on the dresser. Realizing she'd left the receiving end still under the magnolia tree, she tiptoed over to it, leaned into the speaker, and whispered loudly, "Did, too."

Smiling with satisfaction, she let herself out of the room, closing the door quietly behind her.

Chapter 20

Cassie struggled with the covered casserole dish and umbrella, the enticing aroma of fried okra making her stomach rumble. Joey, wearing a yellow rain slicker and matching boots, sloshed behind her. He held Mrs. Crandall's cake plate with Cassie's first pineapple upside-down cake perched on top and covered with plastic wrap.

A car horn honked, and they both stopped and watched as Sam pulled up alongside the curb. "Lucinda called and said y'all might need a ride."

"We're fine." Cassie continued walking, lowering the umbrella to keep the wind from blowing the rain in her eyes.

"Aunt Cassie!" wailed Joey. "This cake's heavy, and it's getting wet! Can't we have Dr. Parker drive us?"

Cassie stopped for a moment and eyed her waterlogged nephew, his brown freckles stark against the whiteness of his skin. "I'm sure Dr. Parker has other things to do, Joey. We're almost there, anyway."

Sam hopped out of his truck and took the cake plate from Joey. "Get in the truck, big guy, and I'll put this on your lap."

Cassie resisted when he tried to take the fried okra out

of her hands. "Don't you have better things to do? Like rescue a house or lance a boil?"

He wrested the casserole dish away from her. "Nothing so glamorous, I'm afraid. It was slow at the clinic, and I had to pick up supplies for the office, anyway." He held the door open for Cassie. "And what's this about Lucinda's car?"

She waited until he had seated himself inside the truck before answering. "Somebody slashed her tires last night, and it was parked right in front of the house. I heard Johnny Ladue's motorcycle suffered the same fate. I hate to admit it, but all this vandalism is starting to get to me. And with the way everybody's talking about it, I'll never sell the house."

Sam reached over and lowered the volume on the radio. "Who do you think's responsible?"

"Sheriff Adams asked me the same thing. Besides you, the most likely culprit would be the Roust people."

Sam raised an eyebrow. "Besides me?"

Cassie shrugged. "Well, yeah. You have some archaic idea of leaving my house untouched forever, which is pretty amazing, since you don't even own the property."

"Uh-huh." He didn't say anything else, but kept his eyes focused straight ahead.

"But I figured with all your boil lancing, baby birthing, town counciling, and tree baby-sitting, you wouldn't have had the time to do some vandalizing, too." Cassie paused for a moment, waiting for a response. When she received none, she continued. "Anyway, the sheriff at first thought it was kids pulling pranks—like Mr. Haney's boys. They've always been wild, and now Haney works for Roust, so that would make sense. But he found footprints in the mud around the house, so we have our first clue to go on. He's working on it now and should be able to show whether or not the boys were involved."

She shifted in her seat, readjusting the fried okra in her lap. "And Jim Roust keeps calling me. At least that guy from *Preservation* magazine is polite when he calls. I actually tell him no, thanks before I hang up on him. When Roust calls and I recognize his voice, I hang up right away. I guess that wouldn't really put me in his good graces, but it would be hard to believe that a man of his standing in the business community would resort to guerrilla tactics. Especially with what he did to Ed Farrell's construction site."

A dog ran in front of the truck, causing Sam to slam on the brakes. The fried okra nearly slid from Cassie's lap, and a quick check of the backseat reassured her that the cake hadn't suffered the same fate.

Joey looked up at her with wide eyes. "I got it, Aunt Cassie. I was holding it real tight. It did slide a little bit, but I think it made it a bit straighter."

Sam chuckled, and Cassie elbowed him.

Clearing his throat, Sam asked, "What happened at Farrell's site? I hadn't heard anything."

"He said that all the bathroom fixtures had been taken out of the condo in the middle of the night. He was pretty sure it was Roust."

His brows furrowed. "Funny. I hadn't heard anything about that. And Ed told you about it?"

Cassie nodded.

Sam started to say something when he caught sight of Joey in the rearview mirror. "What kind of cake is that?"

The little boy wrinkled his nose. "Pineapple upside-down cake. Aunt Cassie made it all by herself."

With an interested nod, Sam said, "I can see that. I don't ever think I've seen one with such an, um, interesting shape to it, though. Who's it for?"

Cassie fixed him with an evil look. "The fried okra's for Miss Lena, but the cake is for Mrs. Crandall. My mama always taught me that you shouldn't return a dish without something on it."

Sam tried unsuccessfully to hide a laugh. "Do you think I need to stick around for a while to make sure she's okay after she eats it?"

She slapped him on the shoulder with her wet umbrella, spraying water droplets all around the front cab of the truck.

Still, she couldn't resist a smile, even though the news via phone from Atlanta had not been good. Despite the upbeat tone from both Harriet and Joe and the ever-hopeful words of "more tests," Cassie knew she was not being told the whole story. She was almost glad. The truth would come sooner or later, and she'd have to deal with it. But for now she was enjoying being with her nieces and nephew, allowing them their last days of carefree bliss before their lives would be irrevocably changed forever. She glanced at Sam, noticing the crease lines in his face from grinning and the bright blue of his eyes. Yes, it felt good to smile again.

Mrs. Crandall opened her front door, and Cassie watched the older lady's frown as she examined the cake.

"It's a pineapple upside-down cake," explained Cassie.

Mrs. Crandall brightened, "Oh, yes. I see. And my favorite, too. Thanks very much, dear."

A small black poodle appeared from behind the door, nipping at her ankles. Cassie almost suggested feeding the cake to the dog first, just to be sure. "You're welcome." With a small wave, she walked back down the sidewalk and hoisted herself into Sam's truck.

As she buckled her seat belt, she said under her breath, "You'd think some people had never seen a pineapple upside-down cake before."

"Well, Mrs. Crandall certainly has. She's a major contender in the Kudzu Festival Bake-Off each year with her own rendition. Maybe she'll be calling you later to find out how you did that interesting shape."

Cassie slid lower into her seat with a groan. "Well, at least I didn't make the fried okra. I'd hate to be accused of trying to kill Miss Lena, too."

Joey laughed from the backseat, then joined in with Sam to sing along at the top of his lungs with the man on the radio waxing poetic about a woman named Carlene.

Despite the rain, Miss Lena sat out on her porch, her ubiquitous pink cardigan over her shoulders and stockings rolled down around her ankles. A new romance novel was clutched between aging hands, making Cassie grin.

Miss Lena looked up with a bright smile as Sam approached, Cassie and Joey following close behind with the fried okra. "Good afternoon, Miss Lena." Sam leaned down and gave the old lady a peck on the cheek.

"Well, good morning. What a nice surprise. Did I have an appointment today?" Her smile dimmed somewhat as confusion seemed to settle over her.

Gently, Sam said, "No, Miss Lena. This is just a social call. You remember Cassie, Harrison and Catherine Anne's oldest. And this big guy . . ." He pushed Joey to stand in front of the old lady. "This is Joey. Harriet and Joe Warner's boy."

Miss Lena's eyes sharpened. "Joey?" She shook her head. "No, that isn't right. That's not what they called him." She looked down at her lap, her lips moving. "It was Frank or Fred. . . ." Her sparse brows furrowed, her fingers plucking at her pink sweater in agitation. "I . . . I can't remember. . . ." Her voice faded, her gray eyes staring intently at Joey.

"My name is Joey." The little boy stuck out his lower lip, then hid his face in Cassie's blouse.

Cassie patted Joey on the shoulder. "We've brought you some fried okra for dinner. Aunt Lucinda made it. She said it's your favorite."

Miss Lena didn't seem to be listening. Her eyes seemed to focus somewhere behind Cassie's shoulder as she spoke. "I only got to see him that once, and then they took him away. . . ."

Sam took the casserole from Cassie. "I'll bring Joey more often, if you like. I've just always thought that little boys might be a little rambunctious for you."

A small smile wandered over her lips. "Oh, no. Little boys are wonderful."

Cassie helped the old lady up from her chair, then led her into the house behind Sam and Joey.

As Sam deposited the casserole in the kitchen, Cassie situated Miss Lena in her favorite armchair and made her comfortable. Joey sat as far away as he could on the faded chintz sofa and kept a wary eye on the old woman.

Miss Lena settled back in her chair and opened her book again. "This book is just wonderful. It's one of those Viking stories. I had no idea how lustful they were back then."

Cassie sent a quick glance at Joey and noticed him listening intently. As Miss Lena began to read from the book, Cassie quickly placed her hands over Joey's ears.

"Sorry to interrupt you, Miss Lena, but I noticed a few weeds in your front garden, and I just want to take Joey outside to take care of that for you. I'll be right back." Firmly grabbing his arm, she led Joey out of the house.

When she returned, the older woman had fallen asleep in her chair, the book having fallen on the floor at her side; and a gentle snore rumbled in her chest. Quietly, Cassie picked up the book and put it on a table within easy reach.

She sat on the ottoman and regarded Miss Lena closely. "What are you doing?"

She jerked around at the sound of Sam's voice.

Shrugging, she stood. "Just looking at her. And wondering. Wondering what her story is. She has no family except for her sister in Mobile, but lots of friends, and she's never been married. I wonder why."

Sam leaned against the console TV and crossed his arms over his chest. "From what I understand, it wasn't from lack of interest by Walton's young bucks. Miss Lena was a rare beauty by all accounts. Look at this."

He crossed the room in two long strides to a cherry curio cabinet. Opening it, he pulled out a framed picture and handed it to Cassie.

The woman in the black-and-white colorized picture wore a 1940s dress with large shoulders, big buttons, and a tiny waist. Her hair gleamed in dark curls that framed an oval face with delicate features and large, almond-shaped eyes. Her seductive smile spoke of a secret yet to be revealed.

Cassie gently stroked the glass, wiping off dust. "Oh, my gosh. She's beautiful." She looked back at the sleeping woman. "I can certainly tell there's a story there somewhere.

I mean, look at this expression. She's definitely been up to something.''

Sam grinned. ''Yeah, I've always thought the same thing. I've tried to get her to tell me things, to write them down, but her mind doesn't stay on any one topic for very long. I really hate to think her stories might die with her.''

An unexplainable, deep sadness rushed through Cassie like a wave at high tide, burying all under its force. She stared at the gnarled hands on the armrests and wondered if they had ever caressed a lover's cheek, held another's hand at a movie, or clutched at a shoulder in passion. Had Miss Lena denied herself all these years, not willing to settle for ''good enough,'' or had she simply grown old waiting for the love of her life to show up?

Cassie looked at the portrait again, raising a finger to wipe off a smudge on the glass, then froze. The room seemed to fade from her peripheral vision as she lowered her head to examine the picture more closely. Her breath stilled, her hands shaking, as she studied the necklace the woman wore—a small gold locket.

''Sam.''

He turned quickly, as if recognizing the urgency in her voice. Without a word, she handed him the portrait, pointing at the locket.

He stared at it for a long time, his forehead creased, until he finally looked back at Cassie. ''I can't believe I missed it. Her full name is Eulene. Eulene Larsen. It's written on her medical charts in my office, and it never even occurred to me.'' Quietly, he replaced the portrait where he'd found it.

Cassie moved as if awakened from a stupor and pulled an afghan off the back of the sofa. Settling it gently on Miss Lena's lap, she tucked it around the sleeping woman's bare legs. Afraid to speak, she motioned to Sam to follow her and left.

The ride back to Cassie's house was quiet except for Joey, in the backseat, singing along with the radio. A brief respite from the summer heat had blown in with the storm, and the windows were open to enjoy the coolness of the rain-sweetened air.

Finally, Sam spoke. "So, what are you going to do?"

Cassie continued looking out the window. "I don't really know. I think Daddy kept the secret to protect Miss Lena and her reputation. I'm not sure it would be the right thing to do to let her know that we know."

Sam's voice was quiet. "Not that she'll remember, anyway. There's a good chance that she's blocked out all of that completely."

She rubbed her eyes with the heels of her hands. "Maybe it doesn't matter. My sibling doesn't want to be found, so maybe I should just leave it at that."

Reluctantly, she met Sam's gaze. His eyes were hard and serious. "You do what you think is right, Cassie. Though I don't think a little bit of quicksand ever hurt anybody."

Sam stuck his head out the window and sniffed. "I smell something burning—like leaves. But it's too early for that."

Cassie sniffed, too, and was about to comment when she spotted the fire truck coming out of her driveway, passing them on Madison Lane. Unlatching her seat belt, she clutched the door handle. "Hurry, Sam."

He had barely stopped before Cassie opened her door, jumped out of the truck, and started to run. Without stopping, she called out over her shoulder, "Sam—stay with Joey."

Aunt Lucinda and a small group of people hovered around the old magnolia in the front yard. She recognized a few of the neighbors, too, and they were all shaking their heads.

"What happened?" Her breath came in heavy pants.

Lucinda touched her arm. "It's okay now—thank God. But somebody set fire to the dry leaves under the magnolia. Thank goodness so many of them were damp from the rain or this whole part of the yard would have just gone up like tinder."

Cassie stared at the blackened leaves at the base of her tree, smelling the acrid stench of wet leaves and something like gasoline. Her throat tightened. "Is the tree . . . damaged?"

Mr. Haney, their nearest neighbor, stepped forward. "I don't think so. It just appears to be singed a bit. I'd have a tree surgeon look at it just in case, though. Hate for you to lose such a fine tree." He shook his head sadly.

Mrs. Haney peeked out from behind her husband's shoulder. "I just don't know what's happening to our neighborhood. It used to be so peaceful. I suppose it's because of all them new folks." She cast a disparaging glance in the direction of Farrellsford. "And to think I slept last night with my doors unlocked. Don't think I'll be doing that again."

Cassie eyed the Haneys carefully, wondering why they were there. "How did this happen?"

Aunt Lucinda wiped her hair off her forehead, watching Sam approach with Joey. "I was in the study, going through your father's things, just like you asked, when I smelled smoke. I looked out the window and stared out at the lawn until I saw smoke rising up from this tree. I didn't even think. I called 911 and got all the children out of the house. Madison had just come home from school, and she went and got a hose, but the fire truck came before she even had a chance to get it all the way out here. The fire chief says it's definitely arson. Said something about detecting an accelerant, whatever that is." A small sheen of perspiration shone through Lucinda's flawless makeup.

Cassie stared at the singed base of the tree, a small furrow between her eyebrows. "Why would anybody want to hurt my tree?"

The small crowd began to disperse, giving Cassie small pats and smiles of sympathy as they left. Mrs. Haney mentioned something about a neighborhood-watch group and said she'd call.

Cassie faced the Haneys, fists on her hips. "You do that. And you can also tell Mr. Roust that no matter what he does, I'm not selling him my land. And the guys that are doing this for him are bound to be caught sooner or later, so you might want to pass along that message to your boys."

The Haneys both looked at her with stunned expressions.

Richard Haney stepped forward, his face grim. "You think our boys had something to do with this? Well, you're just plain crazy. Sure, they're wild and all, but they'd never do something like this. And as for Roust being behind all this, believe me—he's got much bigger fish to fry than you. If he wanted this land, he'd have had it long ago." Grabbing his wife's elbow, they stalked away in the direction of their property line.

Sam crouched in front of the magnolia. "Your tree will be fine, Cassie—don't worry. I would like to suggest rigging a spotlight from the house to illuminate this part of the yard. Unless you want to camp out again tonight." He sent her a wicked grin, and she felt herself blushing up to her hairline.

Sarah Frances came racing out the front door. "Aunt Cassie—telephone. It's Principal Purdy." She looked at her older sister with an impish grin and began to chant, "Maddie's in trouble, Maddie's in trouble."

"Hush, child." Lucinda grabbed the young girl by the shoulders, hugging her, her face pressed against her side to muffle the girl's voice.

Cassie sighed. She wondered if it could have something to do with Maddie not making the cheerleading squad again. High school had been in session for a week, and the disappointment hadn't even seemed to phase Maddie. She even seemed almost cheerful.

"Let me go take that phone call. Would you mind coming with me, Sam? I've got a check for your dad to pay for Andrew's car. I keep forgetting to bring it by."

As they walked across the lawn, Cassie noticed Madison disappearing around the corner of the house. She seemed to be in a hurry.

She took the phone in her father's office after first hunting for it amid the piles of papers and boxes. Sam lifted a golf club off brackets on the wall and started practicing his swing.

Cassie held the receiver to her ear and said hello. The principal's voice seemed strained as it came through the phone. "Hello, Cassie. I'm afraid this isn't a social call. I understand you're in charge while Joe and Harriet are in Atlanta.''

"Ah, yes. That's right. What can I do for you?"

"Well." There was a long pause. "This is about Maddie. There's been a sort of . . . incident, and I need to sit down and talk with you about it."

"What kind of incident?"

"It involves Lucy Spafford. And, um, I'd rather not discuss it over the phone, but would like you to come down to my office? Would you be available in an hour, say about five o'clock?"

"Yes, sir. I'll be there." She frowned into the receiver, wondering why a thirty-five-year-old professional was still afraid of her old high school principal.

After hanging up the phone, she went to the desk drawer and handed Sam the check for the car repair. He took it, staring at her with a curious expression. "What's wrong?"

She crossed her arms over her chest. "I'm not sure. But it involves Maddie and Lucy Spafford. Principal Purdy wants me to come to his office to discuss it. I was wondering . . ."

She stopped, and Sam tilted his head, eyes narrowed. "What?"

"Well, if you could come with me. I'm not good at this parenting thing, and I think I'll be needing moral support."

Sam hung the golf club back on the wall. "It's not you who's in trouble, you know. But if you think it will help, I'll be glad to go with you. I am Maddie's godfather, after all. Just let me call the clinic and let Mary Jane know where I am."

She touched his arm. "Just don't tell her why, okay?"

He raised an eyebrow but didn't say anything.

Maddie was conspicuously absent as she and Sam got into the truck. Cassie had a nagging feeling that she'd soon find out why.

Principal Purdy was cordial enough as Cassie and Sam entered the familiar office. Except for the desktop computer and fax machine, not much had changed since the days she had been a frequent visitor. Mr. Purdy accepted Sam's presence and ushered them both inside before motioning for them to sit in two chairs facing his desk.

After he sat, the principal steepled his fingers and was quiet for a few long moments, as if hunting about for the correct words. His hair, now completely white, had thinned considerably, with only thin strands spread over his balding pate like a spider's web.

Finally, he spoke. "I think the best way to get through this is to just start, so let me begin." He cleared his throat. "As you are probably aware, Mrs. Anderson's sophomore civics class took a field trip to the state Capitol last Thursday. Your niece"—he indicated Cassie with a dip of his head—"was on that trip along with Lucy Spafford."

He stood and took a paper cup from a table next to a water dispenser. "Water, anyone?" Cassie and Sam declined and waited for the principal to fill his cup and return to his chair.

"Anyway. At the entrance to the Capitol building there's a metal detector where all visitors to the building must pass through." He took a long drink of water, draining the cup. "When Lucy Spafford put her purse through the detector, it beeped. The security personnel, as is their job, then had to manually examine the purse to find the cause of the beeping." He stopped speaking, then lowered his head, looking up at Cassie through heavy eyebrows.

"What was it?" Cassie's voice cracked, and she swallowed. All of a sudden she had the clear image in her head of Principal Purdy's red-and-white-striped boxer shorts flying high atop the flagpole. She bit down on her lip, hard.

He cleared his throat again. "It was a . . . um . . . a sexual device. I believe the term is a vibrator. A battery-operated model."

Sam coughed, but Cassie continued looking at the principal with a straight face. "And what has this got to do with Maddie?"

"Well, Lucy's best friend, Lauren North, said she's seen a, ahem, *Adam & Eve* catalog in Maddie's locker. Seems anyone can just call their 800 number and request a catalog." Sam and Cassie waited while the principal helped himself to another cup of water. He sat down again and continued. "When I questioned Maddie, she admitted to putting the, uh, device into Lucy's purse. She didn't even try to deny it. I think she enjoys the attention." He looked pointedly at Cassie, who tried to keep a bland expression on her face.

Cassie crossed, then recrossed, her legs. "This happened last Thursday? Why wasn't I notified about this earlier?"

"I, well . . ." He coughed again into his rounded fist. "I was waiting for Harriet and Joe to return, but I understand they're expected to be gone for some time." With a short pause, he continued, "And Lucy and her parents are eager to move beyond this . . . this incident."

Cassie nodded, her grown-up expression plastered seamlessly on her face. "I will discuss this with Maddie and come up with a suitable punishment."

Principal Purdy nodded, his expression one of relief, then slid back his chair in a clear signal that the meeting was over. "I don't think this calls for a suspension—not this time, anyway. I'm sure a lot of this has to do with Harriet's illness, and it's natural for a girl such as Maddie to act out. And your niece is a very spirited girl, Cassie. A good student, too. Reminds me of another student we used to have." He winked in Cassie's direction. "She just needs to rein in that energy—focus it in some other, more worthy, direction."

"Yes, sir. I understand. I'll be sure to bring this up with Harriet and Joe when they return." Rising, she leaned forward and shook the principal's hand, then Sam followed suit.

They left the office quietly, only the soft tapping of their heels following them down the deserted after-hours school halls and out the door. They remained stoic and poised until Sam's truck had turned out of the school's parking lot. Barely past the intersection, they both burst out laughing.

Sam pulled the truck onto the side of the road, howling with laughter. Cassie leaned her head against the seat back, trying to catch her breath. "Oh, my gosh—I have such a mental image here. Can you just see Lucy Spafford looking at what they pulled from her purse? Oh, Lord, it's just so damned funny.''

Sam leaned his forehead against the steering wheel. ''Man, I'm just picturing all those kids staring at that thing and wondering what in the hell it was.'' He shook his head and looked at Cassie. ''That's the funniest damned prank I have ever heard of. I think you're going to have to retire your crown; she's got you beat.''

''I'll gladly relinquish it. She's a worthy successor.'' They were silent for a moment before Cassie suddenly turned toward Sam. ''Oh, my gosh! I just remembered her asking me if batteries were metal. That was over a month ago. To think she's been conniving all this time!''

Sam elbowed her gently, still laughing. ''She comes by it honestly.''

Cassie grinned. ''Yeah. She does. Just a chip off the ol' block.''

''Are you going to tell her parents?''

Cassie shook her head. ''No, I don't think so. I think they have enough on their plate right now. Besides, I don't want to be the one to have to explain to Harriet what a vibrator is.''

He grinned, allowing a flash of white to show. ''Are you going to at least punish Maddie?''

Cassie watched a convertible filled with teenagers whiz by them on the road. ''You bet. Besides an apology to Lucy, I'd say the whole first floor of my house needs waxing, wouldn't you?''

Sam started the engine. ''I seem to remember you with wax under your fingernails a few times.''

Nodding, Cassie buckled her seat belt. ''And I'm a damned fine floor waxer, too, I'll have you know.'' She flipped down the overhead visor and fixed her hair. ''But if she's anything like me, this won't make her sorry in the slightest. It'll just make her try harder next time so she doesn't get caught.''

Sam chuckled. ''I can't believe she's Harriet's child. She's you made over, through and through. Poor Har.'' He shook his head, a wide grin on his face. "I just keep thinking about Maddie explaining to her mother what a vibrator is. If it ever comes to that, I want to get it on film."

That made Cassie start laughing all over again, barely able to contain herself. She laughed until she started to cry, thinking of the marvelous girl who was her niece and of the girl's mother who might not be there to see her daughter grow into womanhood.

As if sensing the change, Sam slid his arm over her and let her nestle in his shoulder. No more words were spoken, but his warmth and understanding were enough. She buried her face in his denim shirt and cried for her own motherless childhood, for Harriet, and mostly, for Maddie.

Chapter 21

Cassie hopped on one foot as she struggled to put on her swimsuit as quickly as she could. Sarah Frances and Joey were already downstairs in the foyer, suited up and with sunscreen-coated faces and bodies, waiting impatiently for her to come down and take them to the creek.

As she fastened the tie on her back, she spotted a deep gash in the wood of her bed's footboard. It was a fresh wound, the wood pale and supple, and it was apparent that something large and heavy had fallen and hit it, taking out a chunk of cherry wood. Leaning to press her fingers on the mark, she noticed three envelopes half-hidden under the dust ruffle of the bed. Kneeling, she picked them up.

One by one, she slid out the letters and examined them. The first two she recognized as having read before from the stack inside the writing box. But the third envelope was smaller than the others and completely blank on the front; no handwriting, postmark, or stamp. She was sure she hadn't seen it before and wondered if it had remained hidden among the larger envelopes in the box and been easily overlooked. Turning it over, she pulled out a letter and unfolded it. Her heart squeezed when she recognized her father's handwriting, with the heavy brush strokes and large capital letters.

August 18, 1981
Dear Son,

   I'm sorry not to be addressing this to your name, but despite my best efforts, I've never been able to find out what they have named you.

   In the possibility that I might die before ever seeing you, I am writing this letter so that you might understand why we have never met. It is likely that you will never read this and that I'm merely writing it to ease my own mind. It is small comfort, but it is the only one I can seem to find.

   Your mother, with your best interests at heart, gave you up for adoption against my wishes. She left the country after giving birth to you and has told me that you were adopted overseas. I have reason to believe that is not the true story, but I have found no evidence to either substantiate it or to refute it. I've wanted to find you—not to take you away from a family who has no doubt grown to love you and accept you as their own, but to make sure that you were happy. But the only news I could ever find out about you from your mother was that I had a son.

   I have pictured you over the years growing up, and I have an idea in my mind of what you must look like. I can only hope that one day I will be able to see you face-to-face and tell you that you have your mother's eyes or my nose or my father's hands.

   Know that I love you—as much as I love your two sisters—and since the day you were born I have prayed daily that one day you might walk into my life. I will keep that hope alive until I am blessed enough to see your face or until I go to meet my Maker and will have to atone for my wrongs against your mother. Please forgive me for not giving you a name. I would

*give up my very home just to be able to hold you in
my arms but once.*

Harrison R. Madison III

Cassie held the letter for a long moment, relief flooding
through her. Relief that her father had not deliberately abandoned or forgotten her brother and that he had looked for
him over the years. Her gaze caught sight again of the gash
in the footboard, and she stood so suddenly that her head
swam. *The writing box. The writing box is gone.*

She had left it on the bed and could still see the indentation
on the bedspread. Dropping to her knees, she peered under
the bed but found it empty except for her slippers.

She slipped the letters into her purse, then, her gaze scanning the room one last time to make sure the writing box
wasn't there, ran downstairs shouting Lucinda's name.

Her aunt stuck her head out from the kitchen, flour from
her homemade biscuits smeared on her nose. "What's
wrong, sweet pea?"

Cassie struggled to calm her voice. "Have you seen a
large wooden writing box? I left it in my room, and it's
gone."

Lucinda's penciled brows furrowed. "No, I haven't seen
it. And you know I wouldn't take anything out of your room
without your permission. Are you sure you didn't misplace
it?"

Cassie shook her head. "No. I know I didn't."

"Aunt Cassie, can we go now?" Joey's voice from the
foyer carried each consonant in a drawn-out whine.

"I'll be there in just a minute." She turned back to
Lucinda. "It was Daddy's writing box. It has his initials on
the top." She thought for a moment. "Did anybody come
look at the house this morning while I was out?"

Lucinda shook her head. "Nope. Not that I know of,
anyway. I was in the back, weeding my vegetable garden."

Cassie frowned, deep in thought. "Well, if you do come
across it, could you please put it back in my room?"

Lucinda nodded, and Cassie slowly left the kitchen, wondering what had happened to the writing box. Maybe because she was so preoccupied she had put it elsewhere and just forgotten where. She turned the corner into the foyer and spied her niece and nephew sitting on the bottom step, already wearing their masks and snorkels, and she couldn't resist a smile. She'd think about the writing box later. It hadn't walked off by itself and would surely show up later.

Cassie stood perched on a rock by the creek, her bare toes gripping its slippery surface, her hair slicked back off her face and dripping water down her back. The temperature had been hovering in the high nineties all week, and the coolness of the water felt heaven-sent.

"Shark attack!" she shouted as she made a shallow dive into the water. When she emerged, eyes tightly shut, the delighted screams of the children in the creek alerted her as to where her victims were hiding.

"Shark!" she shouted again, diving for a nearby squealer that sounded suspiciously like Sarah Frances. Grabbing a small, wet body, Cassie tickled the girl mercilessly until the child shouted, "Shark bait!" Cassie hugged her, then let her go. "Your turn to be the shark."

As the dripping Sarah Frances climbed up onto the rock, Cassie skimmed under the water again, delighting in the cool sluicing of the water over her body. She opened her eyes and stared up at the mottled sky, the surreal sun casting an uneven light under the surface. It was quiet and peaceful under there; no worries, no sickness, nobody clamoring for her attention. And no Sam to mess with her mind. She blew bubbles from her mouth, round little bubbles that rose to the surface and exploded into light and air. A shout from the bank brought her crashing up to reality.

Blinking the water out of her eyes, she spotted Ed Farrell approaching.

"Hey, Ed," she said, waving with an arc of water.

"Hey, Cassie." He smiled broadly and waved back. "I

saw Lucinda walking with Knoxie and Amanda, and she told me where to find you. Thought I'd go for a swim, too." He stopped near the edge of the water, his hair sticking to his forehead in sweaty streaks. His wore a T-shirt and faded blue flip-flops and carried an Atlanta Braves towel.

Dropping the towel, he pulled off his oversized shirt, revealing a powder blue Speedo swimsuit. He thumped his pale chest. "Yep, gotta get my daily workout, and swimming is as good as any exercise." He stepped slowly into the water, adjusting himself to the temperature. "As a matter of fact, I'm planning a fitness facility in downtown Walton, and I can guarantee we'll have an Olympic-sized swimming pool in it. Easier to do laps and all that stuff than in a creek."

Cassie nodded, averting her eyes from the skimpy strip of blue nylon that seemed to bounce on the surface of the water.

"Hey, Ed. Remember my father's writing box? I was holding it one day when you stopped by, and you admired it."

Ed nodded. "Sure do. Beautiful antique. Why? Have you changed your mind about selling it?"

"No. I just can't find it. I don't think I misplaced it, but can't figure why it isn't where I put it. If somebody you brought to the house took it, you'd notice, right?"

Ed splashed water on his face. "Absolutely. It would be kinda hard sneaking something like that into my car without me noticing, you know?"

Cassie breaststroked away from him, enjoying the cool sluice of water on her arms and chest. "Yeah, I guess so. I just can't understand what happened to it."

Joey let out an ear-splitting scream before landing in the water with a perfect cannonball and successfully drenching everybody.

Ed sucked in his breath as the cool water hit his skin. "Hey, kid—watch who you're splashing."

Cassie sent the boy an admonishing glare that wasn't quite successful. Joey stifled a smile, issued a perfunctory "Sorry, Mr. Farrell," then swam over to his sister.

Cassie rolled her eyes, counting again the days until school started. Even though Maddie had been in school almost two weeks, Joey and Sarah Frances attended a small private elementary school, and they started later, much to Cassie's chagrin. Her days were filled with entertaining three boisterous children and a baby, refereeing fights, and feeding them endlessly. At three-thirty, when Maddie returned home from school, the homework battle began. It had taken Cassie three whole days to realize that her oldest niece could be bribed with stories about her life in New York or the promise of trying on some of her clothes. Cassie looked past Ed and toward Joey and Sarah Frances, who were arguing over the use of an orange foam noodle. With a crooked smile, she shook her head. No matter the exasperation and dog-dead tiredness she felt at the end of each day, she wasn't sure she'd trade any of it. Sure, a crisis with a million-dollar client was much easier to handle than squabbling siblings, but the perks of hugs and kisses were becoming priceless to her.

Ed waded his way to the middle of the creek, then trod water to keep his head above the surface. "I had another couple express interest in your house today, but when I told them where it was located, they said no. Said they'd been talking at a party with one of your neighbors about all the vandalism problems and weren't interested in moving into a questionable neighborhood."

Cassie let her feet touch the gravelly bottom. "Questionable neighborhood? Was that neighbor perhaps Richard Haney?"

"I'm afraid so. And whether or not it's true isn't at issue. Either way, it's getting harder and harder to find somebody for your house."

She regarded him closely, wondering again who it was he reminded her of. "You know, Ed, I was thinking about this the other day. Instead of selling it to you, I could just rent it for a while. It would mean I could return to New York that much quicker and it wouldn't be such a pain for you trying to sell it."

He dipped his head in the water, slicking the hair back off his face. "Well, that might make things easier, that's for sure. And it would also give you time to think and reassess what you really want to do with the house." He tilted to the side and began sidestroking across the creek. "I'm assuming you heard about the town-council meeting. Sam may have won the battle for an ordinance against more teardowns, but he won't win the war. It's just a matter of time. We're having a referendum in January, and I can guarantee the people will vote down the ordinance. The majority of our citizens are pro-progress, and a few sticks-in-the-mud like Sam Parker won't make a bit of difference."

He put his face under the water again, and when he came up, he spewed a mouthful of water out through his teeth. "But you just tell me what to do, darlin'. I know how anxious you are to return to your career and maybe patch things up with that fiancé of yours. I am here to do your bidding."

Cassie stopped treading water and just stood still for a moment, contemplating going back to New York and confronting Andrew again. She hadn't heard from him about the VisEx account, and she assumed he'd either dropped her completely or had managed to buy her more time. Strangely, it didn't seem to matter to her; it was as if that life were one thousand light-years away from the docile creek and splashing children. She flipped over onto her back, letting the water over her ears muffle sound. Why was everybody clamoring for a piece of her flesh? Even the reporter from *Preservation* magazine was relentless with his weekly requests for a feature article and a photography shoot.

She did the backstroke over to the bank and crawled out of the creek, pulling herself over to the large diving rock. Grabbing her towel, she began drying herself off. "Ed, how much monthly rent do you think I should—" Her words were cut off by a scream from Sarah Frances.

Cassie jumped back into the water and swam as quickly as she could to her niece. The girl was clutching at something under the water, making it difficult to hold her head above the surface. She was screaming and choking on water when Cassie reached her and pulled her to the bank.

An ugly gash, about two inches wide, bisected the bottom of her left foot. Blood ran freely from the wound, washing pink down her drenched skin. When she saw the blood, Sarah Frances began to scream louder and continued her wail as Joey held up the rusty can lid out of the water.

On autopilot, Cassie reached for the T-shirt she had worn over her bathing suit. It was a crop top with spaghetti straps and the perfect size for wrapping around a small foot. She tightened it as much as she could, trying to calm the hysterical child at the same time.

Ed threw on his shirt. "Come on—put her in my car. I'll drive y'all to the clinic."

Cassie nodded. "I'll wrap towels around her foot so as not to get blood on the upholstery."

He nodded as Cassie carried the sobbing girl and settled her in the backseat. She quickly gathered the rest of their belongings before she and Joey piled into the car. Ed drove a little faster than she would have liked, but they got to the clinic in record time, even with dropping Joey off at home first.

To Cassie's surprise, Ed carried Sarah Frances inside the empty waiting room himself. Mary Jane stared with shock at Ed in his T-shirt and Speedo carrying the little girl but quickly adjusted her expression. Cassie, wearing just her bikini top and cut-off shorts, explained the situation. With a cool smile, Mary Jane disappeared into the back to call Sam.

Sam appeared and took Sarah Frances from Ed. Her sobbing quieted once in Sam's arms, and Cassie couldn't help but notice how he seemed to have that effect on most women, herself included.

She followed Sam and Sarah Frances into an examining room that resembled an underwater adventure. Blue walls with painted bubbles and pudgy fish swam around the perimeter, with bright rays of sun covering the ceiling. The little girl sat on top of white paper in the middle of an examining table, her skinny legs stuck out in front of her and her tear-stained face a mask of childlike suffering. Cassie put her arms around the girl's shoulders. "She stepped on a rusty can lid in the creek."

He nodded and slid on a pair of latex gloves before bending to examine the little foot. "You did a good job with this tourniquet." His eyes moved from his patient and boldly examined Cassie's chest. He turned back to unwrap the impromptu bandage. "I'm assuming this was your shirt. Then again, it could have been another one of Ed's bathing suits. It's small enough."

Cassie smoothed back the wet hair from Sarah Frances's face and kissed her cheek. "Stop it, Sam. Ed was nice enough to drive us here."

Sam sent a reassuring smile to Sarah Frances as he started his examination of her foot. Pressing a button on the wall, he addressed the little girl. "I don't think we'll need stitches. I'll send Miss Harden in to clean it and bandage it, and then you can pick something out of the goody box, okay?" The little girl nodded, her cheeks pale and stained with drying tears.

Stripping off the gloves, he turned to Cassie. "You wouldn't happen to know if her DPT is current, would you?"

"Actually, I do—and it is. I had Harriet go over all that stuff with me before she left." She shrugged, trying not to look too proud. "You know, just in case."

Sam's eyes widened in surprise. His words were cut short by Mary Jane's entrance. Sam gave her instructions, then asked Sarah Frances for permission to speak with her aunt in private. With a promise to be quick, he ushered Cassie out of the examining room to his office at the end of the hall.

He went to a small refrigerator and pulled out two Cokes, handing one to Cassie. The air-conditioning blew strong from the overhead vent, making Cassie all too aware of her barely dressed state. From the interested look on Sam's face, she could tell he was quite aware, too. She pulled the tab on the can and took a long swallow.

Sam continued to watch her closely without speaking, so she turned her back to him and examined the small but well-furnished office. "So, this is where you work."

"Yep. When I'm not lancing boils or saving houses, that is."

She sent him an arch look before returning to admire the neutral tones splashed with bright colors on throw pillows, the curtains, and a quilt hanging on the wall. Cassie walked over to the quilt and touched it, admiring the tiny handmade stitches. "Did your mother make this for you?"

He took a long swallow from his Coke. "Actually, Mary Jane did."

"Oh." Something in her gut clenched. She turned back around to face him. "So, what did you need to talk to me about?"

He leaned against the wall and took a deep breath, just like a man ready to open a box he knows contains something unpleasant. "I just got off the phone with Joe right before you got here. They're coming home tomorrow."

"Tomorrow? Why didn't they call me to let me know?"

"They did. You haven't been home. Gallivanting with Ed Farrell, I expect."

"I don't gallivant with anybody, especially not Ed. I was just at the creek, and he showed up." She crossed her arms over her chest, hugging herself. "So, that's good news, right? That she's coming home?"

He sat on the edge of the desk nearest her. "Why don't you take a seat."

His voice had turned suddenly serious, and she obeyed without question.

"Harriet wanted me to speak to you first, before they got home. I guess they need you to know so you can help them with the children. Especially Maddie." His blue eyes were gentle as he regarded her, but they did nothing to still the rising tide of fear inside her.

Unbidden, her fingers reached up to the gold charms around her neck and began fingering them one by one. She noticed Sam's gaze following her hand, and he looked at her with such understanding that she wanted to fall into his arms and let him kiss all the hurts away.

She held his gaze and kept her voice strong. "What do they need me to know?"

"They had her charts and test results faxed over to me, and I was on the phone with her oncologist for over an hour this morning, discussing her care." He looked down at his hands for a moment. "So, I can explain this to you in black-and-white terms, in medical terminology, in words that won't make a lot of sense to you. Or I can tell you what you don't want to hear."

Cassie stood, walked over to the window, and jerked up the venetian blinds, sending a small cloud of dust motes into the late-afternoon sunshine. "Tell me . . ." She cleared her throat, her voice stronger now. "Tell me everything— medical and otherwise. I need to know everything." Her voice sounded far away to her, reminding her of the same voice her father had used when he told her that her own mother had gone to heaven. She felt small and scared again, and the need to run away and hide made her foot twitch. But she reached inside herself and found the inner reserve, her particular brand of stubbornness, and clung tightly to it. "Shoot," she said with false bravado.

He took a deep breath. "She has breast cancer with lymphatic invasion—a stage-four cancer. Aggressive, multimodality therapy is warranted, but we can't undertake it because of the pregnancy. Radiation is out of the question because of how widespread the tumors are, and Harriet won't consider the chemotherapy because of the chance of miscarriage or fetal damage, however small the risk at this stage of the pregnancy. Surgery is also not an option at this stage because of how much the cancer has spread." He paused for a moment as if gathering strength. "She, with her doctor's knowledge, will wait until the baby is born before beginning treatment—if any is even warranted at that point."

Cassie made her way back to the chair, sat heavily, her legs no longer able to hold her, and began to shake with small trembles at first, which then erupted into visible limb movements. She realized she still held her Coke can and let Sam take it out of her shaking hand. Then he moved to stand next to her, draping his lab coat over her bare shoulders.

Cassie stared at the wall. "If she's at stage four now but waits four more months for treatment, what's her survival probability?"

He squatted by her chair and looked her in the face. "It's almost nonexistent now, Cassie. Cancer cells have spread everywhere—including her liver. Even without the pregnancy, her chances are very, very low."

Her voice was calm, belying the trembling in her arms. "And the baby?"

"The baby is healthy. There have been no known instances of a maternal-fetal transfer of cancer cells." He touched her arm, a glimmer of light in his voice. "It's another boy."

"A boy." She gripped the coat around her arms, unable to control their shaking. Squaring her shoulders, she sat up straight in the chair and looked directly at him. "So, after the baby is born, what do we do then?"

He stared at her for a moment before speaking. "This isn't an advertising plan, Cassie, where there's a solution to everything. This is the human body, and I'm afraid it just doesn't work like that. We're in a wait-and-see mode right now, but her survival is given now at about six months."

She stood so quickly, her chair flipped on its back. "So what do we do?" she repeated, her voice rising and cracking. "What's the next course of treatment?"

He stood, too, but slowly and deliberately. "We make her comfortable. And we . . . manage the pain."

The overhead air vent shut off, and all was silent inside the office except for the muffled voices down the hall and Sarah Frances's childish laugh. Cassie gripped the edge of the desk, unable to move or form words. Yanking the coat off her shoulders, she threw it to the ground.

"So you're going to give up—just like that?" She slapped her hands on the surface of the dark wood desk, making a piece of paper slide off the top, then slowly drift down to the floor like a fallen spirit.

She tried to move, but he held on to her with both hands on her shoulders. "Cassie, you're not being reasonable. This is Harriet's decision, and she needs your support."

She struggled, not even trying to keep her voice down. "You're all a bunch of quitters. None of you know how to fight." Biting her lip, she struggled to get away from him.

Gently, he said, "No, Cassie. I think we realize when it's time to pick up the pieces and go home—wherever that might be. Harriet has made her choice. Let her do this in peace."

"No!" She jerked away and headed for the door, leaving Sam behind.

She ran to the examining room and found it empty. In a panic she started opening all the doors down the corridor, shouting Sarah Frances's name. When she came to the waiting room, she stopped. The little girl was at a kid-sized table, coloring. She looked at her aunt with a smile and held up the picture she had been working on. It was a picture of a house with seven stick people in front. One of the figures with long blond hair held a small baby in her arms.

"I'm drawing this for Mommy. I'm going to give it to her when she comes home."

Cassie knelt by the child and hugged her tightly.

As if sensing something, the child stiffened and began to cry, "I want my mommy."

Cassie patted the back of the girl's head and whispered softly to her, "I know, I know. Let's go home."

Then she lifted the little girl, the picture clutched tightly in the small fist, and carried her out the door.

Chapter 22

The dog days of summer had arrived with a vengeance, and there was little respite from the heat to be found anywhere. Cassie had already taken the children to the Piggly Wiggly for MoonPies and Cokes, lingering in the well-chilled frozen-food aisle.

Now she sat on the porch swing with Maddie at the old house, the ceiling fan whirring overhead and a metal tub of peas between them. Joe and Harriet were set to arrive any minute, and Cassie had to have something to take her mind off it. Sensing Maddie's agitation, Cassie knew she'd better find something for them both.

Cassie stifled a yawn as she struggled to shell a pea. She'd been up half the night researching cancer on the Internet, hoping to find mention of some new drug, some miracle cure. A lot of what she'd found had been mostly gibberish to her, but she'd printed it all out, anyway, sure it would mean something to somebody. Despite what Sam had told her, she, at least, was not going to give up. She threw peas at the tub on the floor, missing the bucket and sending the small green projectiles scattering across the floorboards.

As she bent to pick up the errant peas, she heard the sound

of tires on gravel and looked up to see Joe's van, followed closely behind by Sam's truck. Walking to the screen door, she opened it and shouted to the younger children to come outside.

The two vehicles parked amid clouds of dust, and the two men got out and went to Harriet's door. Cassie stood on the top step, her breath in her throat, watching as they assisted her sister out of the car.

Harriet seemed smaller, somehow, more frail. They had only been gone three weeks, yet the woman that stepped out of the car was years apart from the woman who had left such a short time ago. Her pregnancy was a little more pronounced, but still barely caused a bump in the A-line cotton dress Harriet wore. She had made it to the porch steps by the time the sound of running feet could be heard in the foyer. As the screen door slammed, she was seated on the bottom step and had her arms spread wide.

Knoxie, Joey, and Sarah Frances vied for their mother's limited lap space but were all given turns before being handed over to Joe for bear hugs and big kisses. Aunt Lucinda appeared with Amanda in her arms. When the baby saw her mother, she squealed and reached for Harriet with chubby arms.

Maddie stayed on the swing, shelling peas and letting them plop into the bucket until her father approached. "Hey, peanut. Aren't you going to give your favorite daddy a big hug and kiss?" His eyes were full of reproach, but he kept the warm smile on his face.

The girl shrugged, causing Cassie to prod her on the arm. Reluctantly, Maddie reached up and gave her father a hug and a quick peck on the cheek before returning to her shelling.

Harriet stood with Amanda in her arms, wobbling slightly. Lucinda took the baby as Harriet approached her eldest child. "Hey, Maddie. Can I have a hug, too?"

Maddie looked up far enough to see the swell of her mother's abdomen, then resumed shelling peas without comment. Cassie, seeing the hurt in her sister's face, gave Harriet a hug. She felt small and brittle in her arms, making Cassie pull away and look carefully at her sister. The skin on Harriet's face seemed thinner, almost translucent, as if stretched too tightly over the fine cheekbones. Her blond hair seemed to have lost much of its luster, but her eyes, glowing with brilliant radiance, had not changed. An odd sense of déjà vu came over Cassie as she held her sister at arm's length and said, "Welcome home, Harriet."

She dropped Harriet's hands and gave Joe a hug. She tried to read his eyes but could only see a deep and abiding weariness in their clear depths. Hugging him again, she wondered how she could have once had more than just brotherly feelings for this man. The past fifteen years without her sister suddenly went spinning through her mind, leaving her with a bitter taste in her mouth at the abject waste of it all. Looking at Harriet again, all she could see was a decade and a half of wasted time and profound loss.

Studiously avoiding Sam, Cassie motioned for everyone to go into the kitchen, where Lucinda had prepared a home-coming lunch. After the children finished fighting over who got to sit next to their mother, Cassie found herself once again seated next to Sam. For the blessing, she reached for his hand without looking at him and waited for him to take it.

Harriet took a single bite of her chicken salad and chewed slowly. Dropping her fork, she stood, leaning heavily on the table. "Excuse me, everybody. But I've got to go lie down on the sofa in the parlor. I'm just so tired from the trip."

Cassie excused herself and followed her. "Are you all right?" She grabbed an afghan off her father's reading chair.

"Besides the cancer, yes, I'm fine. Just tired is all."

Cassie cringed. "I'm sorry, I didn't mean . . . well, I can't believe you can joke about this." She tucked the afghan around Harriet.

Harriet leaned back and closed her eyes. "I'm sorry, Cassie. It's just that if I don't laugh—" She let her voice die.

Cassie straightened and went to the bookcase to take out

a stack of papers. Pulling up the ottoman in front of the sofa, Cassie held them up. "I printed these off the Internet last night. It's a whole list of clinical trials you can sign up for. There's also a few articles on drugs that they expect the FDA to approve in the next year. I think you and Joe need to look at these."

Harriet nodded, her eyes soft, and reached out her hand. Cassie gave her the pages, expecting them to be read and examined right away. Instead, Harriet dropped them on the sofa beside her.

"I'll give you some time to look at those while I go make sure the kids eat their lunches, all right?"

Harriet nodded, and with a small squeeze of the shoulder, Cassie retreated to the kitchen.

She seated herself between Knoxie and the highchair and began mushing bananas to feed to the baby. Maddie hadn't come in yet to eat, and the others were busy wolfing down their sandwiches so they could go outside and have some of Aunt Lucinda's homemade ice cream.

When the older children had deserted the kitchen, leaving the back door open, as was their habit, Cassie addressed Sam and Joe.

"I've printed a bunch of stuff off the Internet that I think you should read. I didn't understand most of it, but there's a lot there that I think might be of help to Harriet, including a list of clinical trials and a few new experimental treatments." She glanced up hopefully, her gaze moving from one man to the next.

She saw them exchange a look as Joe shifted uncomfortably in his chair.

Sam put down his sandwich. "We've already gone over every possibility, Cassie. We've looked down every avenue, and this is the course of action that Harriet has chosen. And you need to remember it's *her* life we're talking about."

With deliberate care, Cassie put down the fork she'd used to mash the bananas and dumped the food on the highchair tray. Amanda immediately dove into it with both hands.

"So what you're telling me is that those five children—soon to be six—don't need their mother. You're giving up."

Sam's jaw began twitching as he slid back his chair, leaning forward on the table as he spoke to her with precise words. "We're not giving up. We're making the best decision we know how with the situation we are given."

She slid back her own chair, bumping the wall behind her. "The hell you are." The baby stared up at her with wide eyes, and Cassie's heart skipped a beat. Lowering her voice, she said, "There's a world's worth of information on the Internet, and you're not even going to look at it, are you?"

Sam spoke with a great deal of control, keeping his voice low. "Damn it, Cassie. Don't you think I already have? Maybe if you saw the X-rays yourself, you'd understand the situation better."

She stood and slapped her hands on the table. "I don't want to see any X-rays. What I do see now is my sister and those children, and I'm the only one around here who seems to care about any of them."

The baby began to whimper, and Joe, with an anguished look on his face, took her out of the highchair and left out the back door, Lucinda following close behind.

Sam came around the table in two steps but kept his clenched hands at his side. Despite bright red patches of color on his face, he did not raise his voice. "You're not the only one upset here, Cassie. Don't you think that Joe is grieving for her, too? Don't you think we're all angry at what has happened? Because I'm angry as hell. I'm angry that she's sick, and I'm angry that this baby is complicating things." He turned to face the wall and pounded a fist on pale blue wallpapered cornflowers. "You should be thanking God that this wasn't a decision you had to make and respect Harriet enough to comply with her wishes and not make this any harder for her." He took a deep breath, facing Cassie again. "Don't fight her on this."

She tried to walk away, but he blocked her path. Looking up at him, she bit her lip, willing the tears not to spill.

"She's going to get better with or without your help. I don't have time to take a wait-and-see approach. And I guess it will be up to me to make sure that she gets the care and treatment she needs as quickly as possible."

She made a move to get by him again, but he held her back with his hands on her arms. His hands trembled as he spoke to her with measured control, his face only inches above her own. "You're acting like a spoiled child who can't get her own way. I'm sorry if things are messing up your plans to return to New York and that you're being forced to get involved with other people's lives more than you want to." He shook her gently. "Now listen to me, because I'm not going to tell you again. Let Harriet die in peace. And if you feel you can't, then go back to New York. It's where you think you belong, anyway."

Yanking away, she ran out of the kitchen, biting back the bitter taste of tears. She stopped for a moment, pressing her forehead against the wall, willing her strength and composure to return. Walking into the parlor, she noticed that all the pages she had painstakingly printed out the night before had slid off the couch in a white waterfall and were now covering the rug under the coffee table.

Her sister's voice called her over to the sofa. Stopping, Cassie knelt and took Harriet's hand. "Do you need something?"

Harriet nodded. "I need your understanding."

Cassie looked down, ashamed that Harriet had heard her arguing with Sam.

Harriet squeezed Cassie's hand lightly. "Even without the pregnancy, my chances of survival are almost nonexistent. I could fight it with chemo and radiation, but it would only prolong my life by a few months—if any. Why risk the life of my unborn child only to give me a little more time?" She swallowed, closing her eyes for a long moment. "I know Maddie is angry about the baby. She thinks I'm choosing it over her and the others. I want you to help her understand something . . . and maybe that will help you, too." Her chest rose and fell in shallow breaths, her skin blanched as if in pain. "I have been blessed by being allowed to give life to Maddie and her sisters and brother. It is all this baby is asking of me and all that I will ever be able to give him. Allow me this, please." She closed her eyes again. "Please," she said again, her voice barely louder than a whisper.

Cassie dipped her head, hot tears spilling on their clasped hands. "I don't want to let you go. Not now . . . now that I've found you again. You're . . . all . . . I've . . . got."

Slowly, Harriet shook her head, her eyes remaining closed. "No, Cassie. You'll never be alone." Her voice faded, and Cassie continued to hold her hand until Harriet fell asleep. Leaning over, she kissed her sister's forehead and left the room.

Crossing the foyer, the phone rang, and Cassie rushed to get it in her father's study before it could disturb Harriet.

"Hello, Cassandra. It's me."

"Andrew." She waited for a rush of emotion—any emotion—but none came. She was completely tapped out. "How are you?" The background noise of pulsating music and laughing people made it hard to hear. She wiped the tears from her face and searched to find a stronger voice.

"Never been better. As a matter of fact, I'm in the midst of celebrating."

She leaned against the desk, feeling so very tired all of a sudden. "Celebrating what?" The sound of a woman's voice came from close by. It sounded a lot like Cynthia Moore.

"We closed the VisEx deal today—it's mine."

Cassie felt a faint tingle reminiscent of the old adrenaline rush course through her veins. "That's wonderful, Andrew—and congratulations."

His voice broke through the background noise. "I couldn't have done it without you, Cassandra. You were the one who made the initial contact and set the groundwork. You deserve as much credit as anyone."

"To be honest, I'm surprised. When you didn't call back after our last conversation, I assumed the deal had fallen through. I guess you got them to agree to it without having my name attached."

There was a long pause and the woman's voice again, faint but insistent. Then Andrew spoke. "Actually, that term of the agreement didn't change. I told them you'd be back in January to manage the account."

She stared at the phone, speechless for a moment. "You told them what? Andrew, you out-and-out lied! I told you I wasn't sure. How could you do this?" She rubbed her temple, feeling the beginnings of a headache. She almost welcomed it. It was so much easier to deal with than heartache.

"Because I knew you'd come back when I offered you a partnership."

The air seemed to leak out of her like a punctured beach ball. "A partnership? As in 'Wallace and Madison'?"

"Yes. That's exactly what I mean. What do you think?"

"What do I think? My gosh, what could I think? I'm . . . flattered. More than flattered, really. I don't know what to say." She tried to force enthusiasm into her voice.

"How about just saying, 'Okay, Andrew, I'm on the next flight out'?"

She brushed the hair off her face, feeling her hand shake. Why couldn't she just say yes? God, that would make her life so much easier. Instead, she heard herself say, "It's just . . . well, things are complicated here. I need time to sort things out." For some reason, she didn't want to tell him about Harriet. Maybe if she kept it to herself, it would go away.

Another pause now, with the distinct sound of clinking glass coming through the receiver. "The Cassandra Madison I knew wouldn't take more than a second to think about it."

Irritated, she said, "Well, maybe I'm not the same Cassandra Madison you remember."

"Yeah, well. The thing is, you don't have to decide right away, although I was hoping you would so I can put all my people in place. But VisEx won't be able to make the move until after the first of the year. How about if I give you until January first to decide? Will that give you enough time to sort through your complications?''

Her gaze rested on the family picture of Harriet and Joe with the kids, then moved to the framed crayon rendering of her with her nieces and nephew catching fireflies. ''Yeah. That should be plenty of time.'' As if Harriet's life was a complication. As if January could even be looked forward to without thinking of the intervening months and the specter of diminishing life that haunted the time between.

''Great. Because there's also the matter of the apartment. Your name's on the lease, remember, and the renewal is coming due in February. We need to sit down and talk about it—among other things. I feel we haven't really settled everything between us.''

She nodded, then remembered she was on the phone. ''Yes, you're right. We've a lot to talk about. I'll let you know.''

''Cassandra?''

''Yes?''

''You don't sound like you anymore. I hardly recognize you.''

Her fingers strummed the charms at her neck, her soul oddly comforted by their presence. ''Yeah, I hardly recognize myself anymore.'' She sniffed, hoping he didn't hear it. ''I've got to go. We'll talk soon.'' She hung up the phone, then stared at it for a long time, her blood pumping heavily in her brain. When she looked up, she spied two familiar hats through the sidelights of the door, and she ran to open it before the Sedgewick twins had a chance to ring the doorbell.

Their orange lipstick matched the plastic flowers on their hats and the antiquated Corningware casserole dishes in their gloved hands. Thelma spoke first. ''We hear that Harriet is back, so we brought some food. We stopped by their house first but figured they were probably still here. It's backbone and dumplings and macaroni mousse ring.''

Selma patted Cassie on the arm before marching past her

with what appeared to be the mousse ring. "We don't want you or Lucinda or Joe having to worry one single minute about anything else but taking care of Harriet. Let us do the rest. The garden club has already set up a list of ladies to bring fresh flowers to her house, and the Daughters of the Confederacy have already got a meal schedule started." She turned an orange smile on Cassie. "We got to go first, since we're president of both associations."

Seeing Harriet asleep on the sofa, the ladies, with their practical navy pumps, tiptoed past her and into the kitchen.

Feeling strangely defeated and utterly useless, Cassie climbed the stairs slowly, ignoring the reproving glare from Great-great-great-grandfather Madison.

Chapter 23

Cassie grabbed the top of the plastic garbage bag and hoisted it on top of the already full trash can outside the back door. She caught sight of her college-freshman picture staring out at her through the thin sheet of plastic, the mousy hair and goofy grin preserved forever. With two fists, she smashed the bag into the can and closed it.

Harriet and Joe had been back for almost two weeks. Even though Cassie played her role as dutiful sister by watching the children or running errands, she had avoided any more serious discussions with her sister. She hadn't seen Sam at all, through a mutual avoidance. She wanted to apologize for insinuating he had failed Harriet somehow as her doctor, but his words about her acting like a spoiled child and being angry with Harriet for complicating her life still stung. Worse, she recognized the truth in them and wasn't yet ready to admit that to anybody.

As she pulled open the screen door to go back inside, the distinct sound of somebody humming nipped past her ears. It was so faint that at first she thought she was imagining it until she heard it again. Lucinda had been staying at

Harriet's, so Cassie knew she was alone. Gently, she closed the door, careful not to make a sound.

She crept to the side of the house and stuck her head out. An old tire swing, strung to a low branch of a towering oak, moved back and forth, the young girl who sat snug inside of it oblivious to her audience.

"Maddie?"

The girl stopped the swing abruptly, making the rope vibrate wildly. "Hey, Aunt Cassie."

Cassie walked toward her niece, her hands behind her back. "Aren't you supposed to be in school?"

Maddie gripped the sides of the tire swing and hung backward, her light brown hair falling behind her and touching the tips of the dried grass. "I didn't feel like it."

"Um-hm." Cassie leaned against the tree trunk and regarded her niece carefully. "Does it have anything to do with that trick you played on Lucy Spafford?"

Maddie sat up, her face flushed red from being upside down. An impish grin lit her face. "Heck, no. It's actually made me pretty popular." She tilted her head as one bare toe propelled the swing in a wobbly fashion. "How do your floors look, by the way?"

"Very nice, thank you. The upstairs needs doing, too, so just be aware that I'm looking for the first opportunity to get that done."

With a little snort, Maddie began twisting the swing, making the rope bunch on the tree branch. "How come you didn't tell my parents?"

Cassie reached up and plucked a leaf from a limb. "Because I didn't want to see you get in trouble. And because I don't think your parents need to be worrying about something like that right now."

Maddie lifted her foot, allowing the swing to twist her around in tight circles. With her head dangling and her hair over her face, she said, "Thanks."

"So, why aren't you in school?"

She answered with a shrug.

Letting the shredded leaf drift from her hand, Cassie said,

"Is it because of your mother? Are you trying to punish her?"

Maddie kept her head down, her hair a confessional curtain. "Maybe."

Cassie slid down the trunk to a sitting position at its base. "I wish you'd talk to me, Maddie. I might be able to help you. I know what it's like to be the oldest child and to have a mother who's dying."

There was a long pause, but Cassie waited patiently for her niece to speak. Maddie kicked a stone with her toe. "Yeah, but at least your mother didn't *choose* to die. My mother doesn't love me enough to want to fight." Her voice broke, but her hair still obscured her face.

Cassie's heart clenched in her chest. "Oh, no, Maddie. I used to think that, too, but that's not it at all. I wish I could tell you how much your mother loves you." She looked up toward the lower branches, fighting the stinging in her eyes. "Your mother has had to make the most difficult decision of a lifetime. Neither you nor I can know what she's going through, and I hope we never do. But she's made this decision without thinking of herself. It's not a matter of her life or the baby's. It's a few stolen months or an entire lifetime. Can you understand that? And that takes more courage than I know I've got in my whole body."

She grabbed a dead leaf nestled among the roots of the ancient tree and let it rest on her open palm. She said a brief prayer of thanks for her newfound wisdom and let its grace settle deep inside her. With renewed fervor, she faced Maddie. "You need to go to your mother. Talk to her." She reached out and touched the young girl's knee. "There will be times, later in your life, when you will wish you had. Do it now so there will be no regrets."

A sob came from the girl on the swing, and Cassie rose, her need to comfort making her heart ache, not just for Maddie but for the lost girl she herself had once been. Maddie reached out for her, and Cassie met her halfway, clutching her tightly and letting Maddie's head fall on her shoulder. Her hand cradled Maddie's head, and she felt as if an unseen hand cradled hers, too. She was a girl of eight again, and through her own hurt and anger, she felt her mother's love.

"You'll never be alone, Maddie. As long as I'm alive, you'll never be alone."

Maddie's body shook with sobs. "But I'm so angry—angry at Mama for dying and angry at the whole world for letting it happen. I know it's not her fault, but I can't help it. I can't help it if I think this lousy life is so unfair." She choked, and Cassie held her tightly, her own tears falling lightly on the brown head that reminded her so much of her own.

"You're damned right it's not fair. But we're not always given choices. Sometimes these awful things get plunked down in the middle of our lives and we're left to just deal with it. Some people handle it better than others, but we all find a way. You're strong, Maddie. You'll find your way. Just like I did."

Maddie looked up, her face red and streaked with tears and sweat. "You ran away."

With the pads of her thumbs, Cassie smoothed away some of the tears. "Yeah—and that wasn't the right thing to do. I think I've almost come full circle now, but it would have been a lot easier if I'd taken a more direct route."

Her niece looked at her with confusion. Cassie smiled. "What I mean to say is that running away is usually the easiest thing to do but rarely the right thing in the end."

"But you've had such a great life in New York. Would you trade that for anything?"

Cassie stilled, the answer that popped into her head too frightening to confront. "If you'd asked me that last year, I would have said no." She lowered her voice in a conspiratorial tone. "Don't tell anybody, but I think I've grown up a bit in the last few months, and my answer would definitely be different now. Sure, I've had a great life in New York, but at a very high price. My decision to run away cost me fifteen years with your mother."

Maddie sniffed loudly, then banged her fist against the side of the tire. "I'm so mad I could just spit."

The rope groaned as it slipped on the tree branch. "Go ahead and spit, Maddie, if it makes you feel better, but you do need to talk to your mother. She loves you and is worried about you. I think she could use your forgiveness—and understanding—right now."

"I don't know . . . how. It's too hard."

Cassie blinked, fighting the strange urge to laugh. Maddie was as stubborn as a rock when it came to asking for or giving forgiveness. The apple certainly didn't fall far from the Madison family tree. Cassie pushed the damp hair out of Maddie's eyes. "All we have to ask ourselves is to give it a try. Sometimes it's all we can do. And it's definitely a step in the right direction."

Maddie sighed. "So what should I do?"

"Go to your mother. You don't even have to say anything, and I doubt she'll notice that you're skipping school, because she'll be too excited to see you." She tugged on her arm. "Just go. Now."

Maddie squeezed herself out of the tire but continued to stand there uncertainly.

"Remember, all you have to do is try. It's a start. Everything else will fall into place."

She shook her head. "I can't. I can't! Not now—but maybe later. I promise. I'll try later." The young girl hugged Cassie, then left with a slow gait, her brown hair swaying softly behind her.

Cassie wrapped her arms around herself, feeling goose bumps bead her skin. Her own words reverberated in her head, and she felt like a hypocrite. Giving advice to others had always been easy; taking it never had been. Grabbing the swing, she threw it in a wide arc, watching it spiral into ever-tightening circles.

Without even realizing where she was headed, she followed her own feet across the lawn and down the drive. Harriet had told her that Sam had bought the old Duffy house and was in the midst of restoring it himself. He'd moved out of the second-floor apartment he'd been renting from Mrs. Cagle and had moved into his new house the same day. Neighbors said he worked like a dog on it during every spare moment.

As Cassie approached, she spotted Sam standing in the front yard, working over a sawhorse. His bare chest glistened with sweat, and she noticed he wore work boots and shorts— the first time she'd ever seen him wear anything except cowboy boots and jeans. She stood at the corner of his property for a moment, glad for the chance to observe him unnoticed. As he sawed through a piece of wood, muscles rippled in his back, and her gut tightened. Her eyes lowered, enjoying the show. When her gaze finally made it up to his head, her eyes met his, and she blushed.

George barked and made a move to run to her, but Sam held him back. He returned to his work, his back turned toward her.

She had to shout above the sawing. "I've come to apologize."

He paused. "Well, gosh, that's certainly news. Did you call the *Walton Sentinel?*" Without waiting for an answer, he picked up the saw and turned it on.

"Sam," she shouted again, moving closer so he could hear her.

He turned off the saw and put it down, then straightened. He lifted his eyebrows expectantly.

"I . . . I had a call from Andrew. He's offering me a partnership in the agency."

His face remained rigid. "Congratulations. When are you leaving?"

"I haven't given him an answer yet. I have until January."

He pulled a handkerchief out of his back pocket and wiped his forehead. She gave him a lopsided grin. "I see you still have one left."

"Yeah, guess so. You can mail the other ones from New York. Just make sure you wash them first." He leaned down and hoisted another two-by-four onto the sawhorse and began marking measurements on it.

''Sam, you're not making this easy for me.''

''That's a first.'' He clamped a pencil in his mouth, as if to effectively shut off all conversation, and flipped on the circular saw again.

She stared at his back, bare and brown from the sun, and she suddenly realized how very much she needed to touch him. The moment her fingertips touched his bare flesh, he stiffened and took a deep breath, flicking the saw off and dropping it onto the table. She splayed both hands wide, marveling at how good he felt.

Stepping closer, she felt the heat from his body, and it made the blood jump in her veins. ''I wanted to say I'm sorry, and you know that's not easy for me. I'm sorry for the way I talked to you about Harriet. You were right; I see that now. I know I need to focus on her needs right now and not what I want or think would be best.'' She rested her cheek on his back, feeling his intake of breath. ''And . . . I need you right now. You're the only one who understands me and puts up with me, anyway. Harriet's dying, and I can't face it alone.'' She closed her eyes, tears teasing her eyelids. ''I can't promise you what's going to happen in January, but . . .'' She stopped, trying to find enough air in her lungs to continue.

His breathing came in long, deep, deliberate breaths, his muscles tense. ''But what?''

She touched his back with her lips, and he sucked in a quick breath. ''I . . . I need you. I need you now. And I can't imagine not always feeling this way.''

She pressed her lips against the smooth skin on his back between his shoulder blades, tasting him with her tongue this time and feeling his skin ripple over his spine. ''You do something to me, Sam Parker, that makes me forget all reason. Maybe I could stand to eat grits every morning for the rest of my life, or maybe I'm destined for a bagel from the corner deli. I don't know. But every time I picture a future without you in it, I feel more lost and alone than I've ever been in my life.''

Her arms reached around his torso, rubbing his ribs, but

still he didn't speak. She could feel the tightness in every single one of his muscles. "Please tell me that's enough— for now."

Finally, he turned around in her arms. His eyes were dark blue and brooding, but she recognized the glint of hope in them. "What about the partnership? Are you telling me you'd consider not returning to New York and your job?"

She nodded, not trusting her voice to speak.

He studied her face for a long moment, as if weighing his words. "It's enough—for now. But I won't wait forever. Even Job had his limits." He stared down at her, his gaze dropping to her lips. He glanced in the direction of the neighbors' houses. "I have a feeling that these trees have eyes. Would you like to go inside for a glass of sweet tea?"

She licked her lips, but not because she needed anything to drink. Nodding, she led the way, trying to ignore the rubbery feeling in her legs. He followed her into the small foyer, closing the door with a booted heel while simultaneously pinning her to the wall.

"You're not doing this because you have an itch, are you?"

She shook her head, her mouth dry. "No, Sam. You're the only one who seems to make things right in my world." She placed the palm of her hand against his cheek. "I can talk to you about Harriet and cry and rage and know you still love me, anyway."

He slid her hand to his lips and kissed the open palm, sending shock waves up her arm.

With a breathless whisper, she said, "And you do give me this terrible itch. . . ."

"Then let me scratch it." Slowly, he slid his hands to the waistband of her shorts and then underneath her panties. Cupping her buttocks in his hands, he pressed her against him. "Where did you say it itched?"

He smothered her moan with a kiss as his right hand worked its way between her legs. She whimpered, and he grinned against her mouth. "Did I find the right spot?"

"Oh, yes," she managed, heat coiling like a spring deep inside her.

Suddenly, his hand stopped but didn't move away.

She opened her eyes, barely inches away from his. She stared at him, breathing heavily. Groaning, she squirmed against him. "You're driving me crazy."

His eyes were serious. "Now you know what it feels like." He kissed her deeply, then pulled away again. "It's not nice to be toyed with, is it?"

She shook her head, moving her hips to make contact with his fingers again. Instead, he opened the waistband farther and slid her shorts and panties down her legs. When they hit the ground, she kicked them out of the way, fighting for her composure. "We don't have to do anything right now if you think I'm toying with you. I might die of frustration, but I'd rather do that than for you to think my feelings for you are anything less than serious."

She read the answer in his eyes and in his mouth as he lowered his lips to hers. "I need you, Cassie Madison. You're stubborn, bullheaded, and mean to boot, but God help me, I need you." He lowered his mouth to her neck and lingered there for a long moment. "I also need to take a shower." His fingers deftly began unbuttoning her blouse.

"Call me anything you like, just please don't stop this time." She reached for his belt buckle and opened it.

"How are you at scrubbing backs?" He shifted backward to allow her better access to his fly.

"Would you like to find out?" Her voice gave out on the last word as he unhooked her bra and his mouth found her breast. Without removing his lips from her, he managed to shuck his boots and socks, sending them flying across the room.

"Sweet Jesus, Cassie, you're killing me." With a swift motion, he removed his shorts and underwear. Then, hoisting her up, her legs around his waist, he headed for the stairs. Nimbly stepping over paint cans and tools, he made it to the top floor and the master bathroom. Still holding her, he switched on the showerhead and stepped in.

He wedged her up against the tile wall, making her gasp from the coldness of it, while his fingers slid between them again, making her gasp for an entirely different reason. He caressed her, heating her skin until she bucked against him.

"Please Sam—now."

He moved between her legs, but paused. "I'm not going to make it easy for you to leave."

Water splashed from the showerhead onto his back, spraying her in the face. She clenched her eyes shut. "You already have." Pressing her forehead against his chest, she murmured again, "You already have."

A low growl came from his throat as he slid into her in one slow thrust. The water beat down on them, sliding between them, easing its way down their bare bodies. Sam began to move more quickly as she felt her core begin to melt. He pressed her harder against the shower wall and she whimpered, sucking on his shoulder as her release struck her, knocking the air out of her lungs, and Sam shouted her name, the sound of it more of a caress than anything he could do with his hands.

They remained locked together for a few long minutes; then she slowly lowered her legs. She had to lean against him for support; his heart beat under her ear. Without speaking, he gently began to dry her off, then carried her to his bed. She fell asleep immediately, her head cradled by his arm.

The phone rang at four-thirty the next morning. Sam came fully awake immediately, reminding her that being awakened in the middle of the night was something he did with regularity. He answered the phone, then gave it to Cassie. She recognized Lucinda's voice immediately.

"How did you know I was here?"

Lucinda sounded groggy with sleep. "Diane Eames, next door to the Duffy place. She called me last night to let me know she had seen you and Sam in the front yard at about three o'clock and then hadn't seen you leave."

Cassie ran her hand over her face. "So are you calling me to tell me to come home?"

"No. I wanted to let you know there's been another incident and the sheriff wants to talk to you again."

Cassie sat up, and Sam flipped on a bedside lamp. "Is Mama's magnolia—"

"It's fine. But the grass in the middle of the yard isn't."

"Oh, Lord. Is anybody hurt? What happened?"

She heard Lucinda yawn into the phone. "No, thankfully—nobody's hurt. Somebody used gasoline or something to spell out an obscene word in the front yard and then set it on fire. I don't know what stopped it from spreading across the lawn and to the house, since nobody was home to notice it. Richard Haney was out walking his dog and saw it, thank goodness. He was the one who called the fire department."

Cassie ignored the tone of reproach in her aunt's voice. "An obscene word? Which one?"

"Really, Cassie. I don't think I can say it."

"Aunt Lu." She rolled her eyes. "Can you at least spell it?"

"It's the one that starts with sh. But you'll see it soon enough once you come home. And Joe's fit to be tied, worrying about your reputation and such and trying to field questions from the fire department and the sheriff."

"For crying out loud, Aunt Lucinda! I'm thirty-five years old. But if it will make everybody happy, I'll come home now, all right? One more thing. When you see the sheriff, make sure he knows it was Mr. Haney who called the fire department. I find it interesting that the man would be walking his dog at this hour."

"He's always walked his dogs in the middle of the night, sugar." She yawned into the phone. "But I know Hank has already questioned him. He's off the hook, but I don't think his sons are. Somebody spotted the oldest one running down the street shortly before the fire was spotted."

"That's great. If you see the sheriff, tell him I'll call him first thing in the morning and we'll talk about it."

Lucinda yawned into the phone again. "Is Sam going to drive you?"

"I imagine he will."

"Just ask him to drop you off at the end of the road so no one—"

"Stop right there. I don't want to hear any more. I'll come home soon, so tell Joe not to worry and to go back home to Harriet. I'll have Sam keep me company."

"Now, Cassie . . ."

Cassie hung up the receiver before she could hear any more.

Sam bent to kiss her neck. "What's wrong?"

"Well, it seems the whole town knows I've slept with you again, and somebody has burned an obscene word across my front lawn."

His lips moved down to her collarbone. "At least I have an alibi. And to think you used to find New York City exciting. . . ."

She knocked him over the head with her pillow, then kissed the spot where it had landed. "Come on. I need you to drive me home." She slid out of bed, taking the covers with her. "And don't be surprised if Joe asks you for a duel at dawn over my honor."

Sam's eyes darkened as he regarded her. "Maybe I'll have to make an honest woman of you instead."

She looked away, reaching for her pile of clothes Sam had brought up in the middle of the night. "Sam . . ."

He stood too close to her, but not touching. "What if I told you I loved you enough to let you go?"

Shaken, she turned to face him, searching his eyes. "Remember how you once told me about angelfish and how they mate for life? And that when one of them dies, the other does, too? I thought you told me that for a reason."

His finger traced the line of her jaw. "Yeah, but there's also the black widow. Maybe loving somebody else would be safer, if not as exciting."

She looked away for a moment, feeling the stillness of the night and the crickets singing to the dark sky outside.

"Would you marry Mary Jane if I left?" She shivered, but she wasn't cold.

"I could," he whispered.

"You'd be willing to settle, then? Be happy with 'good enough'?"

"Sometimes we have to make the most of what we're given and make compromises."

She moved away, slipping into her blouse. "Like your medical career. You settled for Walton when you could have gone anywhere."

He took a deep breath. "Sometimes you have to reach deep down in your heart and decide what road you're going to take. And all choices involve some sort of sacrifice. But in the end, you know whether or not you made the right decision." He bent down to pick up a pair of jeans from a chair. "And, no, I didn't settle by coming here. I used to think that I had, but now I know I made the right decision."

She attempted a light tone. "When did you figure that out?"

He regarded her calmly, his blue eyes searching hers. "When I saw you at my dad's service station the first night you came back. I thanked God that I hadn't stayed in the big city long enough to become like you."

She sucked in a mouthful of air. "I guess that means you wouldn't consider coming to New York with me."

He dropped his hand and said simply, "No." A lone car sped by on the street outside, its radio blasting a heavy beat into the dimly lit room.

"We could be happy there. With your degree, you could pick and choose which medical practice you joined."

He took a pair of underwear from the drawer and slid them on, followed by the jeans. "You don't believe that any more than I do. If I really thought that's where we belonged, I'd start packing now. But I don't. Nor will I stand in your way if that's what you want." He pulled a boot over his foot. "Like I said, maybe I love you enough to let you go." He faced her, a failed attempt at a smile on his face. "Besides, I just don't think I could ever eat sushi or start using words like 'suppose' and 'do lunch.' It's just not me, Cassie. And it's not you, either.'' He slid on the other boot.

She sighed. ''This isn't something we have to decide right now.'' Rubbing her hands over her face, she said, ''Come on. Let's go.'' Without waiting to see if he followed, she left the room and went down the stairs, the old wooden steps creaking under her weight. The sound, familiar and haunting, crept around her heart. Pushing any nostalgic thoughts away, she let herself out the front door.

Chapter 24

The heat of summer gradually gave way to the cooler temperatures of fall, although it stayed warm enough for the children to wear shorts to school. The grass in the yard turned the shade of weathered wood, except for the newly seeded spot in the middle, where the ugly word had been burned. The Bradford pears bordering her property with the Haneys' gave a last breath of life, with brilliant red and orange leaves, before they, too, gave way to the season and settled one by one onto the ground beneath.

But Cassie's magnolia stayed a vibrant green, as if mocking autumn and all the other lowly plant species not strong enough to face the colder months. Cassie looked with pride at her tree, seeing it as a living thing among all the shriveling plants in the front yard, and she hung all her hopes and dreams on its sturdy branches, with their bright, glossy leaves.

Each passing week, Harriet's belly grew larger, while she grew frailer. It was hard for Cassie not to see the child growing within her sister as a cancer itself, drawing the very life from the person whose only desire was to give it freely. Harriet managed the weekly trips into Atlanta for tests and progress reports but refused to stay in the hospital even as her delivery date neared and her condition worsened. She insisted on being home with her family as much as possible, and Cassie and Lucinda helped make that possible by filling in at Harriet's Skirts 'n Such. As Harriet got sicker, Cassie and Lucinda found themselves running the business, much to Harriet's apparent relief.

Despite Harriet's fatigue, Cassie found them both rediscovering the closeness they had once shared, sometimes staying awake late into the night and just talking. At times, Harriet would doze off, and Cassie would just hold her hand and watch her restless sleep. Then Harriet would awaken and remember something about their childhood, and they would talk again, whispering and giggling like the young girls they once were.

Thanksgiving came and went with only a nod to the usual holiday preparations. Even Aunt Lucinda had told Cassie that she didn't feel much in the mood for celebrating, since there wasn't too much to be thankful for. Maddie had skipped coming to the dinner table completely, and it nearly broke Cassie's heart to see Harriet forcing herself to keep up her spirits while blatantly ignoring the empty chair at the dining-room table.

Even with Harriet's illness, there was no reprieve from whoever had been tormenting Cassie for the last six months. The fall annuals she had spent an entire weekend planting with Aunt Lucinda had been dug up with incredible brutality. The flowers hadn't just been uprooted; they had been shredded. Bright fuschia petals littered the flower beds like pink teardrops and scattered over the lawn with every teasing fall breeze.

Sheriff Adams had been by to investigate and had assigned two detectives to work the case full time. But, like the other incidents, few, if any, clues had been left behind, and he and his department had no more answers for her than they had when the vandalism had begun with the stripping of the oak trees. As for the oldest Haney boy seen running down the street, the account had come from Mrs. Ladue, who was legally blind and admitted to not having her glasses on at the time. Footprints had been found, and they matched the first set found, but there seemed to be no connection with the Haney boys.

Now Christmas preparations had begun in earnest, and Cassie tried her best to push all the unpleasantness away, if only temporarily. The streetlights downtown were wrapped in red and white, like candy canes, with big red bows crowning their tops. Every store window blinked colorful lights along with the required faux snow dusting the storefront displays. The weather obliged by sending a cold blast south from Canada, making the Walton residents break out their heavy woolens for the first time in over two decades. The weathermen threatened snow, sending everybody to the grocery store for milk and bread. Snow had been as scarce as shoes in summer ever since Cassie could remember, and she wished on every star in the sky that it would snow just this one winter so Harriet could see it.

Joe surprised Cassie by asking her to go with him and the kids to pick out a Christmas tree on Christmas Eve. She had assumed Christmas would go the way of Thanksgiving, but Joe's words made her reconsider.

"It's her favorite time of year, Cassie, and I want to make it real special."

Cassie smiled. "Sure, I can do Christmas. I, after all, learned at the hand of the masters, my mother and Aunt Lucinda. They used to do everything but tie-dye the toilet paper red and green." She touched his arm and was surprised at the look of gratitude in his eyes.

Gently, she said, "I haven't really stopped to think how hard this must all be for you. How are you doing, Joe? Really?"

He looked away, his eyes reflecting the cool gray sky. "I can't say I've gotten over my anger. No—I'm not mad at Harriet. Not anymore, anyway. I'm mad at fate for doing this to her. To us—and our family. But she's made me strong." He shook his head, looking back at Cassie again. "If I had a quarter of her strength, I could do anything."

Cassie smiled up at him. "I know. I feel the same way." Impulsively, she reached up and kissed him lightly on the cheek.

They piled into the van with all five kids, Maddie included, and drove to the gas station, where several rows of fresh-cut pines from the Georgia mountains waited to be chosen and taken home. They ended up with the largest one they thought they could squeeze under the ten-foot living-room ceiling.

Harriet clapped her hands as they drove up to the house, the tree hanging over the front and end bumpers of the van. From her chair, she hustled the children inside to direct them as to which nook or cranny to find the decorations. Cassie noticed she had a notebook with her and jotted everything down in the form of a list. She dared not even consider what her sister was doing.

With Harriet and the children inside, Joe and Cassie were left to untie the tree and bring it into the living room. As Cassie reached inside the back window to cut the length of twine, Joe put his hand on her arm.

"I need to talk to you about something."

Cassie jerked herself out of the car, hitting her head on the doorframe. "What?" She felt something lodge in her throat. "Is it about Harriet?"

Joe shook his head. "No. It's about you and Sam."

Cassie colored, suddenly finding her boots very intriguing to look at. Sam had been spending every night with her in her house, and the sex had been frequent and satisfying, filling an aching need in her. When they made love, it was as if he held her very soul in his hands, keeping it from shattering in the depths of her grief. He held her and cherished her; and the feeling of coming home was never as strong as it was while in his arms.

"Um, what about us?"

Joe coughed. "Well, I, um, was just wondering if it was going to lead anywhere."

Cassie watched the blood flood his face, and she couldn't

resist teasing him. "You mean, if our relationship means anything more than just great sex."

Joe studied the Christmas tree closely. "Well, um, yes. I guess so."

She punched him gently on the arm. "Joe, I appreciate your brotherly concern. But it's not necessary. We're in a sort-of trial period, and we're just not sure how it's going to work out right now. But you'll be one of the first to know, all right?"

He yanked on the tree, sliding it off the top of the van. "I was just wondering. Lucinda said Sam's been spending just about every night with you and that people keep calling her to let her know about it, in case she didn't already."

Cassie shook her head, hoisting her end of the tree. "This town doesn't need telephone lines, does it? Just hang out at the backyard fence."

Joe groaned, lifting the trunk end. "That's not such a bad idea, if you think about it."

They began walking toward the porch. Under her breath, Cassie said, "Sometimes the anonymity of a big city holds a great deal of appeal."

After cutting two feet from the bottom of the monster tree, they brought it in and settled it in the newly discovered tree stand, following Harriet's meticulous directions on the perfect placement.

The children watched like vultures, ornament boxes held in each hand, until the tree was ready to be decked out in all its holiday finery. Harriet lay back on the sofa in the living room, her skin yellow against the crisp white cotton of her pillow. She watched with eyes that now seemed too large for her face as the children decorated the tree. They'd bring the boxes of ornaments to her; then she'd select one and give it to the proper person to hang.

"Maddie, come here." Harriet's voice sounded weary and hoarse.

Slowly, Maddie came to where her mother lay. Harriet handed her a tissue butterfly, the wings iridescent with multi-

colored glitter. "Do you remember making this in kindergarten?"

A reluctant smile crossed Maddie's face. She shrugged.
"Yeah, I guess."

Harriet handed it to her, and Maddie took it, holding it
up to the light to make it twirl and sparkle. She bent her
head closer to read the inscription on the wings. " 'Butterfly
flutter, near my mother, please tell her, that I love her.' "
Her voice cracked, and she looked back at her mother, her
green eyes pooling with tears.

She knelt by Harriet, the butterfly clutched in her hands,
her voice very quiet. "I still love you, Mama. I never
stopped. I didn't. And I'm so sorry. . . ." Maddie placed her
hands gently around her mother, as if holding a glass doll,
then laid her head on Harriet's shoulder and began to sob.

Harriet held her firstborn, stroking her hair, as she had
for fourteen years. "Shh, Maddie. There's nothing to be
sorry for. I never thought you'd stopped loving me, okay?
Not for one minute." She continued patting Maddie softly.
"I remember when you made that butterfly, and when you
gave it to me, it made me cry. And you didn't understand
when I told you that sometimes beautiful things make people
cry." She pulled Maddie up so she could look her in the
face. "Now, promise me something. Promise me that when
you see this butterfly you'll remember how much I love
you, and if it makes you cry, I want them to be happy tears."

Maddie nodded, sniffing, then wiped her nose with the
back of her hand. She kissed her mother on the forehead
and stood, examining the tree closely. Finding a spot on the
side of the tree, she hung it on a high branch, a butterfly
fluttering over a candy-cane reindeer and a toilet-roll angel.

With a sigh, Harriet leaned back wearily on the pillow,
and Cassie stooped to take the ornament box from her hand
before she dropped it. Harriet pointed at the box. "These
are my favorites. All were made by the children. I keep this
box in the linen closet upstairs. Make sure that's on my list
for Joe."

The doorbell rang, and Harriet tried to sit up. "I'm a

wreck. Quick, Cassie. Hand me my lipstick in my purse over there."

Joey ran to answer the door as Joe turned to his wife. "You're always beautiful in my eyes, Har. Don't change a thing."

Cassie's eyes misted as she watched Joe and knew that he was telling the truth.

Harriet raised a limp hand and rested it on the bulge of her abdomen. "Did I mention I'm having a torrid affair with Gus Anderson over at the hardware store?"

Joe sat down next to her and cradled her in his arms. "If I didn't know how crazy you already were about me, I'd believe it."

Harriet buried her face in his arm, hiding a grin.

Knoxie sidled up to the sofa and squeezed in between her parents, snuggling deeply into their embrace. Amanda, just learning how to toddle, grabbed a glass ornament in the shape of a peach and threw it just as Sam walked into the room, Joey wedged tightly under his other arm. He caught it and held up his prize. Putting the ornament down and out of the baby's reach, he swooped down on the little girl and scooped her up in his other arm, making her squeal with delight.

Cassie eyed Sam, and his ease with the children, and felt her heart tighten. He looked at her, and she felt the tension between them—the tension that had been there ever since she had told him about the partnership offer from Andrew. The only time it went away was when they were making love and he held her heart in his hands.

Cassie stood. "I was about to go get some leaves from Mama's magnolia to spray-paint gold and use to decorate the tables and mantel. I could use some help."

Sam nodded, setting Amanda and Joey on the floor. "Sure, Martha Stewart. I'll go."

Bending to kiss Harriet, she said, "We'll be right back, and then we'll make your house worthy of a spread in *Architectural Digest*."

Harriet grabbed her hand and winked. "Just don't do anything I wouldn't do."

Cassie grinned. "You're nine months pregnant, Har. And I have no intention of wobbling anywhere." She bit her lip, regretting her flippant remark.

Harriet bent her head, sending her sister a serious look. "Don't worry about it, Cassie. The day you don't feel it's okay to make some smart remark is the day I'll be glad not to be here to see it." She waved her hand back and forth. "Now shoo, you two. And make my house glamorous." She leaned back on the pillow with a smile that became a grimace of pain. "Ah, the advantages of being an invalid."

After slipping on her jacket, Sam ushered Cassie out of the house, and they walked the few blocks in silence. Her cheeks stung from the wind, and she bundled more tightly into her coat. Sam put his arm around her, drawing her close, until they reached the old house.

Maneuvering a wheelbarrow under the tree, Cassie and Sam began picking up the fallen leaves, now brittle with frost.

One spiraled down from the tree, and Cassie caught it. Bending her head, she examined it closely, observing how the sinuous veins ran to the edge of the leaf, then disappeared, like a fragile life reaching its end. Sighing softly, she let the leaf drift into the wheelbarrow. She sifted her gloved hands through the pile, searching for the glossiest ones she could find and remembering her mother doing the same thing as she and Harriet stood back, their dresses held out in front, ready to collect their treasures.

"Just think, Sam. This time next year, Harriet's baby will probably be walking. Hard to believe, isn't it?"

He nodded, then reached down for another handful of leaves.

Cassie watched him while her fingers searched in vain for the chain under her jacket. She stopped and stood very still. "You don't think she's going to be here to see it, do you?"

Straightening, he fixed her with a gentle look, his eyes reflecting the scattering clouds. Slowly, he shook his head. "How much longer?"

His hands fell to his sides. "Her doctors are surprised she's lasted this long. I think she's living to bring that baby into the world full term. Either way, it'll be soon. Not more than a month."

She stared at him, feeling her face crumple, and he gathered her in his arms and let her cry.

"I'm sorry. I know that's not what you wanted to hear."

She buried her face in the soft suede of his jacket, inhaling deeply. "No, it's not. But . . . thanks for being honest with me." She bent her head back to stare into his face. "And thank you . . . for being there. For me."

He took her face in his hands, his eyes soft. "I love you, Cassie, and I guess I always will. I'll always be here for you, whatever you decide to do."

Fresh tears filled her eyes, and she took a deep, shuddering breath. She stared into his face, with all its beloved curves and angles, as if seeing it for the first time. "I love you, too, Sam Parker. You're stubborn and irritating, and you make fun of me way too much, but I do love you. Now kiss me before I start crying again."

His eyes bright, he lowered his lips to hers and held her in his arms while the wind whipped at the old magnolia, its leaves shaking in applause.

Long after the last ornament had been hung on the tree, the children tucked into bed, and the final present wrapped and beribboned, the men retired to the back porch for a beer and a cigar, and the two sisters bundled up and headed for the front-porch swing.

The sky had cleared, the wisps of clouds giving birth to brilliant stars and a rising moon. It rose, full and heavy, pregnant with untold stories. Harriet sat close enough for Cassie to feel the bones of her hips, her silk scarf soft against Cassie's skin. Cassie reached her arm around her sister and stilled. She was so fragile, as if so much of her had already gone. How would they ever bear saying good-bye to what remained?

Their breaths came in little puffs, and Harriet shivered. Cassie pulled her closer. "It's too cold out here for you. Let's go inside."

Harriet closed her eyes and shook her head. Cassie noticed how translucent her eyelids had become, almost like those of an infant. "I like the cold." Harriet's voice sounded tired. "It reminds me that I'm alive."

Between them their hands entwined, squeezing tightly. Cassie turned to her sister. "Are you scared?"

With teeth chattering, Harriet shook her head. "No. I'm ready. For whatever happens." She touched her forehead to Cassie's. "But I'm worried about you."

Cassie moved back. "About me? Whatever for?" She gave the swing a shove with her foot, letting it sway gently.

Harriet smiled, her teeth almost bluish in the light. "Because you don't know your own heart. You're almost thirty-six years old, Cassie. It's time you started listening to it."

Cassie shook her head and laughed softly. "I can't believe *you're* giving *me* advice. When did that happen?"

Leaning her head back against the swing, Harriet grinned. "I think I've gained a lifetime of wisdom these last few months. I guess dying does that to a person."

With a jerk, Cassie faced her sister. "Don't say that, Harriet. I can't stand to hear you say that."

Harriet touched her sister's cheek. "Dying is as much a part of life as loving. I've accepted it. And I've had a good life, Cassie. I've had the privilege and the honor of loving and being loved by the most wonderful man and bearing our children. It's been a full and happy life, and I have no regrets—except for those years without you. Promise me . . ." She took a deep breath and clenched her eyes shut, as if in great pain. After a pause, she continued, "Promise me that you will live your life without regrets. Find your heart and listen to it and you can't go wrong."

Cassie laid her head on Harriet's shoulder and let the tears freeze on her cheeks. Finally, she said, "I love you, Har."

Harriet patted her gently on the head. "I love you, too."

They stayed outside for a while longer, watching for shooting stars to wish upon. But the sky lay still and cold, the faceless moon climbing in the interminable sky. Cassie stood, pulling Harriet with her, and they went into the house, shutting the door firmly behind them.

Harriet went into labor in the frigid morning hours of Christmas Day. While the town of Walton slept and the children dreamed, Harrison Madison Warner came into the world, kicking and screaming. Cassie and Sam had to rush back to the house they had just left so Cassie could stay with the children and Sam could drive Harriet and Joe to the hospital in nearby Monroe. Sam called shortly after six A.M. to tell her about her new nephew, who had all ten fingers and toes and, as he put it, was in fighting form.

As the children awoke one by one, Cassie told them about their new baby brother, whom Harriet wanted to call Harry, and then everybody joined her in blowing up light blue balloons and draping blue-and-white streamers over every stationary object in preparation for his homecoming. The blend with the red, green, and gold was controversial, but the two events had to share the limelight.

Sam appeared around nine o'clock, and he, Cassie, and Lucinda celebrated Christmas with the children, videotaping them unwrapping and squealing over their presents. Harriet had to stay in the hospital for a few more days, and Sam wanted her to be able to share this Christmas with her children.

Harry came home first, a small bundle in a blue blanket and a delight to his older siblings—except for Maddie. Reserved at first, she soon succumbed to his charm and began vying for a chance to hold him.

Three days later, Joe brought Harriet home to die. It was never spoken of, but it was plain to the adults that it was time to prepare and to let go. Joe moved a bed into the living room next to the Christmas tree, and that room became the heart and soul of the family. Sam came daily to visit and to minister her morphine drip, and life seemed to hang on a tenuous web for Cassie and the rest of the family as Harriet slowly slipped away from them.

Cassie spent the week between Christmas and New Year's at Harriet's. She was sensitive to Joe's need to be with his wife by staying away at times, but always close enough to be available if Harriet needed anything. Most of the time, she sat by Harriet's bed and held her hand and talked or read to her. The ebb and flow of family life moved the days forward, each single hour interminable in its pain and grief but each close of day gone far too quickly.

On New Year's Eve, the bleak winter sky had darkened to a charcoal gray, sending frigid winds through the town of Walton and urging the people to stay inside. Those lucky enough to have fireplaces stacked on the pine logs and enjoyed the novelty of a roaring fire to warm a cold winter's evening. Harriet kept her face turned toward the flames, a small smile on her lips.

Cassie was reading aloud to Harriet an article on holiday cooking from *Southern Living* magazine when she felt the air shift. It was nothing tangible and nothing that she could describe, but it was there. She glanced at Harriet, whose half-opened eyes were now focused on Joe feeding baby Harry a bottle. Despite being glazed from pain and morphine, the love that shone in her eyes was unmistakable.

Cassie let her gaze move across the room to Sam, who sat cross-legged on the floor, playing go fish with Joey, Sarah Frances, and Knoxie while Maddie sat curled up in a chair by herself, busily scribbling in her diary. Amanda was upstairs, being put to bed by Lucinda, and the peace of a day's end had settled over the house.

Quietly, Cassie closed the magazine, but nobody seemed to notice. It was as if she were an audience in a play and she wanted nothing more at that moment than to close the curtain and prevent the final scene from playing out.

She stood and crossed to the window and looked out into the night sky. The moon lay murky and swollen behind the cover of clouds, laying a silver blanket over the slumbering garden below. She moved to the door and stepped out, sniffing deeply.

Excitedly, she ran back into the room. "It's going to snow. I'd bet old Grandma Knox's red hair that it's going to snow tonight." As soon as she spoke, great white flakes began to fall from the sky.

The children squealed, and even Maddie put down her pen to rush to the window and peer out. In unison, they turned to their father. "Daddy, please can we go out in the snow—please, please?"

Joe, out of years of habit, turned to Harriet. In confusion, he turned back to the children and then to Cassie.

"If it's okay with your dad, I say go get yourselves all bundled up and we'll go out and watch the snow fall."

All four children ran out of the room and headed toward the hall closet. Cassie made to follow them when a small sound came from the bed. Harriet's voice had grown so weak that Cassie had to bend close to hear. "I want . . . to see . . . the snow."

Cassie looked at Joe, then at Sam. "Harriet wants to go out, too."

Joe stood, a wavering smile on his face. "I think she should. She's always talked about going skiing someplace so she could finally see snow. Who would have thought she could do it right in her own front yard." He knelt in front of Harriet and kissed her forehead. Turning to Cassie, he said, "I'll go put the baby down, and if you'll get Harriet bundled up, I can carry her outside."

Cassie nodded, and Joe brought the baby over so Harriet could kiss him. She touched his cheek, then buried her nose in his neck before saying good-bye.

Sam removed the IV drip, then helped Cassie with getting Harriet in enough layers to be able to stand the frigid cold. She had lost so much weight since Harry's birth, and the pain medication made it difficult to hold anything in her stomach. She hardly weighed more than Sarah Frances, and it scared Cassie to her core.

Joe came down the stairs, and after he had put on his coat and hat, he bent to pick up Harriet. He scooped her up with ease, but when he asked her to hold on to his neck, she couldn't find the strength. Instead, Sam tucked her hands between her body and Joe's; then he and Cassie followed them outside.

The snow came down in hard, heavy swirls, like God's fingerprints on the landscape. The withered grass and bushes now glistened with springlike fervor, wearing fresh coats of new-fallen snow. Joey and Sarah Frances crunched their feet on the frozen ground, trying to make tracks, as Maddie stared up in wonderment. Knoxie raced around the yard, her tongue hanging out like a puppy's in an open car window, trying to catch a flake.

Icy snowflakes coated Harriet's hat and coat, sticking to her eyelashes and brows. Cassie touched her arm. "Open your mouth, Harriet. See if you can catch one."

With mouth wide open, Harriet turned her face to the sky, her eyes clear, reflecting the joy that emanated from her. She caught one and grinned. "It tastes cold."

"Yes, it does, doesn't it?" Cassie laughed, and Joe joined her, the sound hollow in the snow-dusted air.

She watched then as Harriet lifted her hand to Joe's face, the exposed wrist thin and fragile. Harriet whispered something to him, and then her hand fell and lay perfectly still.

Sam stuck out his arm, holding Cassie back, and she stepped away without resentment. What passed over Joe's face as he realized his beloved wife was gone cut into her heart at the same moment she realized that she had just lost her sister, her Harriet, her constant. She bent her head and wept until Sam pulled her into his arms, and they cried together.

First Maddie, and then the other children, one by one, stopped and came to stand around their mother still cradled in their father's arms. The weeping started, but nobody thought to go inside yet, as if doing so would make what had just happened to them too real. Joe bent his head to protect Harriet from the snow, his body shaking as his tears fell on her face.

And still the snow continued to fall, covering the houses and trees with a thick white blanket and whispering a gentle hush to the grieving family.

Chapter 25

The snow fell for three days, paralyzing five counties. Without anything to clear the roads, life came to a virtual standstill. Power and phone lines were down and not expected to be repaired for a week. Cassie's deadline came and went, but she found relief from the reprieve of the downed telephone service. She felt as if she were walking in a dream world, with no beginning and no end, and could not even imagine thinking about her future, much less making plans for it.

Harriet lay at Murphy's funeral parlor, her service on hold until the snow cleared and the ground thawed. But every evening during visitation hours, the home was packed with mourners. They brought poinsettias, holly, and evergreen wreaths, since no fresh flowers could be found, and Joe brought a small Christmas tree, decorated with their children's ornaments, to rest at the foot of the coffin. The whole effect was a fitting tribute to a woman who had loved the Christmas season with the bright-eyed glee of a child.

The food began piling up again in Cassie's kitchen as the citizens of Walton rallied around Harriet's family. Cassie had gone several times to Joe's to see him and the children, but the house was always swimming with visitors or the children were at friends' houses. She felt useless and unneeded and the old pull again for the calming distraction of work. She even practiced saying the name Wallace & Madison, and the ghost of the old rush came back to her, beckoning her. She longed to be in charge, in control again; even the cool anonymity of the city pulled at her. She wore her grief on her face here, and everyone knew it. But in New York she could hide beneath her business persona and push the grief far away.

Harriet had told her to find her heart and follow it. Work had been her heart for so many years. It was black and white and easily understood, and she knew how to navigate it. Wallace & Madison. She'd be foolish not to follow this opportunity, especially when it was so obvious that she was unneeded here. The town took care of its own, and Harriet's family was safely tucked into the security of that knowledge.

Sam. Hadn't Harriet once said that love was about sacrifice? He would be her sacrifice, for surely whatever was between them now would be destroyed if he were to come with her to New York or she were to stay in Walton. She'd visit Harriet's children and Lucinda and maybe even see Sam until he married Mary Jane. Then she'd wait until the pain went away, because none of it would matter in New York, where she'd be a partner in a top advertising firm. It was what she had always wanted.

She sat at the edge of her bed in the old house and looked around at her pink rosebud bedroom, listening to the silent house around her. Lucinda had moved into Harriet's house to help Joe with the children, and the house sat creaking, muted by the unfamiliar mantle of snow. Cassie spoke aloud to the quiet around her. "Harriet, you were wrong. Love's not just about sacrifice. It's about making tough decisions, isn't it?" She took a deep breath, then moved to the closet, dragging out her suitcases and a handful of clothes on hangers.

She had to call Ed. She needed to find a renter for her house as well as somebody who could put everything the renters didn't want into storage. But she would definitely hold on to the house. It was her family legacy and all that she had left now of her childhood with her parents and Harriet. She imagined leaving it to Maddie one day and hanging her own portrait in the stairwell to scare future generations of Madison children.

After leaving a message on Ed's machine, telling him she would be there at nine o'clock in the morning, she left the room and wandered through the house, visiting old memories and replaying past conversations. She paused at the threshold of Harriet's old bedroom, seeing the girls she and Harriet had once been sitting on the bed and sharing secrets. Clenching her eyes shut, she listened carefully to hear girlish voices, but only the bereft call of the winter wind bristled through the empty room. Slowly, Cassie closed the door, clutching the brass knob tightly.

She returned to her room, her resolve to leave renewed. Dumping clothes on the bed, she opened the largest suitcase in the middle of the floor, then emptied out a dresser drawer and jewelry box and stacked the contents next to the suitcase. Lifting a pile of underclothes, she placed them into the suitcase. A drop of moisture hit her hand, and she realized she was crying. *How am I going to tell Sam? How will I be able to leave him and not have it tear a chunk out of my heart?*

She sniffed loudly, using her sleeve to wipe her nose. Pushing herself up, she sat on the bed, facing the wall, and allowed her fingers to play with the charms around her neck. Headlights raced around her room, followed by the slamming of a car door. Peering out the window, she recognized Sam's truck and walked slowly down the stairs to meet him. She opened the door before he could knock, then waited for him to stomp the snow off his boots before coming inside.

He reached for her, but she pulled back, causing him to draw himself up. "Are you all right?"

She nodded, her eyes avoiding his. "I'm ... I'm fine. I've been thinking about Harriet ..."

He touched her cheek softly, then let his hand fall. "That's what I came by to tell you. The snow's still on the ground but not falling anymore, so they scheduled the funeral for Saturday. Joe wanted me to tell you.''

She nodded, feeling very much like a third party. ''Thanks. For letting me know.''

He tilted his head, looking at her with narrowed eyes. ''Are you sure you're all right?''

''I'm sure.''

He stood in the foyer in his jacket, as if waiting to be invited in. Finally, he said, ''The referendum on further development is tomorrow night at Town Hall. I was wondering if you could come and maybe offer your support.''

She swallowed, offering him a lopsided grin. ''Are you sure I'm going to support the right side?''

He smiled. ''Well, since you haven't bulldozed this place, I have to assume you're in favor of preservation.''

''Yeah, I'll be there.''

They stood facing each other awkwardly for a long moment. Finally, Sam spoke. ''What's wrong, Cassie? Why won't you let me touch you?''

Something halfway between a laugh and a sob erupted from her throat. ''I . . . I've decided to go back to New York.''

His face went absolutely still, but his eyes glittered in the dim light from the ceiling chandelier. He stared at her for a moment without speaking. ''So, Cassie Madison does yet another great disappearing act. As soon as the going gets rough, she runs away. I guess I should have expected this.''

Being confronted with the truth had always been too large a chunk of meat for her to swallow. She straightened her shoulders and faced him. ''I am not running away. I've just been visiting here, remember? I have a career in New York and a great opportunity. I'd be an idiot to turn it down.''

Sam slammed his fist on the wooden doorframe, making her jump. ''Damn you, Cassie. What about Harriet's children? Don't you think you're needed here?''

Cassie fingered the gold chain around her neck, her fingers popping up and down along the charms in agitation. ''They don't need me; the town's taking care of everything. And they've got Joe and Lucinda. And the rest of the town is lined up at their door to offer aid or food or whatever it is they think the children might need. I'm pretty much superfluous.'' She dropped her hand to her side.

"Superfluous? Your nieces and nephews have come to love you and depend on you. And what about me?'' He kicked at the entryway rug, folding a corner of it over. "I guess I never even crossed your mind.'' Raking his fingers through his hair, he shook his head before leveling his gaze at her. "You want to know what's superfluous? It's your heart. You don't seem to use it, so why's it there?''

Cassie stood, stilling her shaking hand by clutching the banister. "You're not being fair, Sam. You just don't understand.''

He shook his head and stared at her for a moment. "You're like a crop duster. You just dump your stuff in a puff of smoke, and then you're gone into the wild blue yonder. You're right, Cassie. I don't understand you. I used to think you had a heart under all that big-city hardness. I guess I was wrong.'' He leaned in closer, his face flushed red, and spoke very quietly. "Your sister has died, leaving six motherless children, and you're thinking about leaving, and you don't seem to see anything wrong with that. Go, then. We don't need you here.''

He turned on his heel and, with long, angry strides, left the house.

Unmoving, she watched the empty space where he had stood, listening to his heavy footsteps cross the porch. It wasn't until she heard his footsteps crunching in the snow that her breath came back to her with a loud sob.

"Sam!'' she shouted to the empty house. She couldn't let him go. Not like this. Forcing her feet to move, she ran after him, not bothering to put on her shoes.

She burst through the front door, letting the screen slam behind her, and cried his name again. He stopped by his truck and faced her in the dim light.

She shivered as her feet sunk into the cold snow blown

onto the porch. "Please don't go." Tears threatened behind her eyes, but she held them back, fighting for her precious control—the one thing she could always depend on.

He took a step forward, his breath coming out in big puffs in the frosty air. "What else do you want from me? Do you want me to rip out my bleeding heart and lay it in your lap? Because that's the only thing I have left to give that you don't have already. And I won't do it, Cassie. I won't." He turned back to his truck. Speaking over his shoulder, he said, "It'll hurt for a while, but we'll get over it. This town has a wonderful way of coming together and helping each other in bad times. I don't expect your departure to be any different." He opened the door.

"Sam, please!" Her voice held a desperation that she had never heard before, and it frightened her. Why had admitting weakness always been so hard for her?

Sam looked back.

She clambered down to the bottom porch step, her arm clutching the railing and holding her steady. Her teeth chattered. "Don't go. Please. I . . . need you."

Leaving the door open, he walked toward her. "You what?"

She looked at him with narrowed eyes brimming with tears. "You heard me."

He retraced his steps back to the truck and got in. He was about to slam the door when she shouted his name again.

Cassie had stepped off the bottom step and away from the railing's support. Without it, she swayed. "Sam, please! I . . . need . . . you." She fell to her knees in the cold snow, her control gone and her heart hammering in her chest. She felt herself drowning in her own desolation and knew only Sam could pull her out. Her body shook as she screamed at him, "I'm so afraid!"

Sam left the truck and came to stand in front of her, his face in shadow. "What are you so afraid of?"

She dropped her head into her hands. "That . . . that I'm going to die from this grieving. That I'm going to lose control. That I'm making the wrong decision." She shook her head. "God, Sam—I don't know what I want! I thought I had all the answers when I came here, and now I don't. And I'm so afraid I'm not smart enough to make the right decision."

He knelt in front of her and held her shoulders, his hands two welcome spots of warmth. "Bullshit, Cassie. You know exactly what you should do. But if you think that all the promotions in the world are more important than staying here with the people who love you and need you, then go." He shook her shoulders. "And the only thing you've ever been afraid of in your life is admitting you're wrong. Try it, Cassie. The world won't end."

She sat back in the snow, and he let her go. "How can she be gone, Sam? Who's going to tell the children too young to remember what a wonderful mother they had? And about their grandmother and grandfather and about how to care for roses and make sweet potato pie and why it's important to wear a slip?" She sniffed loudly, her tears freezing on her face.

He stood slowly. "If you don't know the answer to that question, then I give up. I've done everything I know to help you. There's nothing more I can do. You've got that suitcase upstairs, and you alone can decide what you're going to do with it." He shook his head. "But nobody's going to bribe you with those kids, Cassie. That would make it too easy for you."

She shuddered, her voice stumbling between words. "It's hard ... I can't ... say ... what I want." Looking at him with a fierce frown, she shouted, "It's too hard for me."

Gazing down at her, his eyes were unforgiving. "I love you, Cassie, and that's why I'm not going to say it for you. You're on your own with that." He turned and headed back toward his truck.

She felt like a small child in the midst of a tantrum, but she couldn't seem to stop herself. She was too miserable. "What if I wanted to say that I'd made a mistake, that I think this is the damned finest place on earth and that I never want to leave? Huh?"

Sam stopped but didn't turn around. "Then you'd better come right on out and say it." He waited for a moment, keeping his back to her, but Cassie kept silent. With a swift kick, he sent a tightly packed drift of snow flying before climbing into the cab of his truck and gunning the engine. With a long look at Cassie, he dipped his head, then took off out of the drive, the crunching snow a terrible, final sound.

Cassie spent the remainder of the night alternating between crying and packing. By four o'clock in the morning, she was nearly done. Pulling the last load from the dryer, she plucked out three handkerchiefs and began ironing. She cried some more as she moved the hot iron over the crisp linen, her tears sizzling into steam under the iron's hiss. Folding them neatly, she tucked them into her purse, next to the letters she'd found under her bed.

The first rays of dawn were streaming through the fan window as she wearily made her way up the steps, a stack of clean and folded laundry in her arms. Dust motes flitted through the air, tracing a path to Great-great-great-grandfather Madison's portrait. She leaned against the banister on the landing, staring at her ancestor in the murky light. Setting down the laundry, she moved closer, and her eyes widened.

Why had she never noticed it before? In the millions of times she'd climbed up and down those steps, not just in the last several months but in all the years she'd spent living in this house, she had never once noticed. The shape of the eyes, the curve of the nose and jaw—it was just so obvious. And if Great-great-great-grandfather Madison didn't have all that hair, she'd bet he had large ears that slightly protruded from his head.

She sat down on the steps for a few moments, letting her newfound knowledge sink in. In the long run, it didn't really matter anymore. It was just one more loose end to tie up before she left. One more person to say good-bye to.

With heavy steps, she climbed up the steps to her room.

She had three hours to sleep until her appointment at nine o'clock. She lay down on her bed and waited for the slow ticking of the hall clock to put her to sleep.

Lou-Lou greeted her warmly, her pink lips curved in a sympathetic smile. "Hey, Cassie. I'm so sorry about Harriet. Ed's closing the office on Saturday in honor of her funeral. We'll both be there."

"Thanks, Lou-Lou. It'll be good to see her friends there."

Lou-Lou's lip trembled a little. "I know the whole town's going to turn up. I mean, she knew just about everybody, and everybody loved her. And those poor kids . . ." Her voice cracked, and Cassie had to turn away, knowing if she didn't, she'd start crying again and wouldn't be able to stop.

"Is Ed here? We have a nine o'clock appointment to talk about the rental agreement for the house."

Lou-Lou pressed a tissue into the corner of each eye. "He sure is. I'll just let him know you're here."

Before she had the chance to press the intercom button, Ed opened the door to his office. Cassie stared at him in surprise. He looked as if he'd slept in his clothes with his tie undone, his shirt hanging out, and his hair standing at attention in short, dark bristles. Dark circles hovered under his eyes, and his jaw was shadowed with whiskers. He helped her take her coat off, then ushered her into his office. She followed him, allowing him to close the door behind her.

He sat down behind his desk, indicating the chair opposite for her. She sat down, regarding him closely.

He cleared his throat. "I've got all the rental agreement papers, and all are in accordance with what we discussed. The rental rate is on there, as well as my commission. I will act as your agent and as your landlord in absentia. You shouldn't have to worry about a thing except for any large repairs and general maintenance. Just check on the last page that your New York address is correct so I can make sure you're getting your monthly rent checks—as soon as I find a renter, of course."

She nodded and began to read through the sheaf of papers, initialing the indicated paragraphs and signing at the bottom of each page. When she was done, she laid the pen down and slid the papers over to him. Then she sat still, facing him.

"You took Daddy's writing box, didn't you?"

A look of shock was quickly replaced by one of relief. "Yes, I did. And I assume you know why."

She was surprised at his candor but realized he had no reason to hide it anymore. "You're my missing sibling. You're the baby Miss Lena gave up for adoption in 1963, aren't you?"

Ed looked down at his desk and toyed with a pen. "I was wondering how long it would take you to figure it out. You almost caught me that once, when I called you outside the Dixie Diner. I wanted to make sure it was you who was trying to find me."

Cassie leaned forward. "Why didn't you just tell me? Why all this deception?"

He slid his chair back and swiveled it to face the large picture window, his profile illuminated by the bright morning sunshine reflecting off the snow. His resemblance to Great-great-great-grandfather Madison was more apparent than ever. He shrugged. "Because I didn't think it would be news you'd be too happy about." He glanced at her briefly. "I still remember how you and Sam and the rest of them treated me back in school. Didn't think you'd take too kindly about finding out I was kin."

Cassie looked down at her hands, still reddened from her long walk in the snow. "I'm not proud of that, Ed. But that has nothing to do with now. We share a father. And I'd be honored to call you my brother."

A dark flush covered his face, and he shifted in his chair. "Yes, well, I thought it best."

Lou-Lou knocked briefly, then brought in coffee and cups on a tray. Cassie welcomed the interruption, using the time to study Ed with fresh eyes. She noticed again his unkempt state and mulled over the reason why.

She emptied a blue packet of sweetener in her cup, noticing that her hands shook. "How long have you known? And did you ever approach either my father or Miss Lena?"

Ed held his cup in front of him, the steam distorting his features for a brief moment. "When I was twenty, my parents died. I found some papers in their things that spelled out who my real parents were." He turned back toward the window and took a long sip of coffee. "You can imagine how shocked I was. My father was rich and lived in a big house with the two kids he wanted, and I was living on some dirt farm with a man who beat me and a woman whose spirit had been crushed too long ago to care."

Cassie winced. "He didn't know. I know he didn't. If he had, he would have taken you in. It wasn't because he didn't care. . . ."

Ed snapped around in his chair, spilling coffee over the brim of his cup. "Don't you stand up for him. He could have taken me away at any time if he had wanted to. But he didn't. I was left there to nearly starve to death."

"That's not how it was, Ed. . . ."

He cut her off again. "Don't try to defend him. You weren't there when I approached him after my parents had died. He wouldn't acknowledge me publicly; he was too embarrassed about me. He gave me money for my education and even set me up in business, but the deal was, I couldn't come out with who I really was."

Cassie leaned forward. "You've read the letters now. Surely you can see why he did that. It wasn't about you. It was Miss Lena's reputation. It would have killed her for people to know she had had an illegitimate child. He did it to protect her. Can't you see that?"

Ed swiveled away from her and rubbed his hands over his face. "Those letters. God. I wish I'd seen them years ago. It would have changed a lot of things."

"Like what?"

He faced her, his eyes wide. "Nothing. It's nothing."

Cassie sat back. "Does Miss Lena know?"

Ed shrugged. "I've tried talking to her about it, and sometimes she even seems to understand, but most times her mind just drifts away, and I don't think she understands anything. It's almost funny, though, because I've had the most lucid discussions about my business with her. And then she'll look at me in the next minute like she's never even seen me before.''

Cassie set her cup gently on the desktop. "I . . . I'd like to acknowledge you as my brother. If you think Miss Lena would still be embarrassed, it could just be between us and a few friends—for now. But I'd like to. Besides Lucinda and Harriet's children, you're the only family I've got now.''

He turned away from her, giving an almost imperceptible shake of his head. "I wouldn't go sharing the news with anyone just yet. You might find it's something better kept inside.''

"What do you mean?" She leaned forward, wondering again at his rumpled clothing and hair. It seemed he'd been in the office all night, wrestling with demons.

He shook his head and stood, a clear sign of dismissal. "It don't matter. It's nothing that can be fixed, anyway.''

She stood, too, a questioning look on her face. "Maybe, since we're family, I can help with whatever problem you're having.''

He strode away from his desk toward the door, pulling it open for her. "I don't think so. Now don't get me wrong. I like you and all. In fact, I like you a lot. But you're still your daddy's daughter, and I'm just not ready to trust you.''

Touching his arm lightly, she said, "Well, you know where to find me if you change your mind." She walked through the door, then turned around, reaching into her purse. "I almost forgot. It's a letter to you from Daddy. It must have fallen out of the writing box when you dropped it on my bed. I found it under the bed with two other letters from your mother.''

He colored again and took the envelopes.

"I don't know why he didn't give it to you when he learned of your existence. It was written so long ago, I'm wondering if he simply forgot about it.''

Ed fingered the envelopes gently but didn't move to open them. "Did you read it?"

"Yes, I did. And I hope that any doubts you have about our father's love and concern for you are answered in there."

He nodded, and she felt him watching her as she turned around and headed for the door. She stopped halfway and faced him again. "I'd like you to sit with me and Joe at the funeral, if you're comfortable with that."

Slowly, he shook his head. "No, I can't do that. But thank you. I do appreciate the thought."

"All right." She said good-bye again and waved to Lou-Lou, then let herself out.

It didn't occur to her until later to ask for the writing box. And then she was glad she hadn't. She had been given many happy years with her father, sharing his life. The least she could do was give his lost son his old writing box and the letters inside that spoke of a child born of love and then given up.

Chapter 26

Christmas lights still glistened in the snow outside the Town Hall as the square and available parking spaces quickly filled. Clouds had been threatening more snow all afternoon, and the smell of it was thick in the air as Cassie pulled into a parking spot in front of the Statue of Liberty.

The weather didn't seem to deter Walton's citizens as they streamed in from all directions. Cassie recognized most of the cars, including Sam's and Ed's, both parked near the Town Hall steps as if they had been the first to arrive. She waved her mittened hand in response to shouted greetings and climbed the steps.

The meeting room was quickly becoming standing room only as Cassie made her way down the center aisle, looking for a place to sit. The radiators spewed out a thick heat as people in sweaters and coats seemed to melt as quickly as the snow on their shoes.

"I didn't expect to see you here."

Cassie spun at the sound of Sam's voice close to her ear. "I told you I would be here."

His face was closed to her, unreadable. "Thank you. Hope it doesn't take you away from your packing."

She pulled off her mittens. "Sam . . ."

"When are you leaving?" His words were clipped and impersonal, and they hit her right in the gut.

"After Harriet's funeral. Lucinda's taking me to the airport at five. I . . . I called Andrew and accepted the partnership."

"Congratulations." He looked over her head, watching as the town councilmembers took their seats up on the podium. "I've got to go."

"Wait." She put her hand on his arm, and he stopped, a small flash of hope in his eyes. "I've been meaning to return these to you. I ironed them myself." She reached into her purse and handed him the small stack of pressed handkerchiefs.

The flash in his eyes flickered, then died. He took the handkerchiefs from her. "Thank you. And good-bye. I hope you'll be happy."

Without waiting for her to respond, he turned and left her. Feeling a hundred pairs of eyes staring at her, she looked around for a vacant seat and was surprised to spy Miss Lena, an empty chair next to her.

Cassie stepped over feet to reach her, then settled herself down, trying not to bump anybody as she slid out of her coat. Miss Lena had on her ubiquitous pink sweater over a flowered dress and navy blue woolen hose covering her legs. She reached over and squeezed Cassie's hand. "I'm so sorry to hear about your sister. How sad you must be." She patted Cassie's frozen fingers. "I'm keeping you and her husband and darling children in my prayers."

Cassie coughed to clear out the lump in her throat. "Thank you, Miss Lena. Thank you very much." She looked into the old lady's eyes and saw that they were clear and bright.

The room gradually quieted as people shuffled into spots, and the meeting started with the usual formalities. And then, one by one, people stood up and began talking about their town and using their words to hopefully sway an opinion one way or the other.

Senator Thompkins stood up and spoke about his great-

great-grandparents who had settled the town almost two hundred years before and were now buried in the cemetery behind the old Methodist chapel—the same chapel that was slated to be destroyed by a new industrial complex constructed by Roust Development.

A half-dozen more people stood to tell similar stories. And then Richard Haney stood to speak about the areas of neglect and decay on the outskirts of town that had been rejuvenated and renewed, courtesy of Roust Development. Several other respected town members approached the podium to state their support of Roust and the terrific job he was doing for the town.

Cassie looked around for a man in a dignified suit, or at least somebody she didn't recognize, to be able to pick out the representative from Roust Development. She couldn't believe that somebody from Roust wouldn't be present at this important town meeting. But she saw no one she didn't know and wondered if Jim Roust could be so conceited that he thought his pillaging of her town a done deal and this meeting inconsequential in the grand scheme of things.

Finally, Ed Farrell stood. His tie was askew, and he looked uncertainly around the room before gathering up an easel and approaching the podium. He set an oversized posterboard town representation up on the easel, then stepped back for everyone to see, an uncomfortable grin on his face.

Ed cleared his throat and began to speak. "Ladies and gentleman, I offer you the great compromise. I suggest that we say no to the grand development scheme of Roust Development and instead let one of your own plan a new and more vibrant Walton. Sure, Walton was a great place for our great-grandparents. But that was back then—before computers and highways and supermarkets." He took a handkerchief out of his back pocket and wiped his brow. "Yes, we know everybody in town, we go to church with our neighbors, and we marry the girl whose pigtails we used to pull back in fourth grade." A small chuckle rumbled through the gathered people. "But that's not what is going to keep Walton from becoming an economic disaster in the new millennium. We need revitalization. We need it to keep our young people here as much as we need it to bring in new people who can inject capital into Walton's economy.'' He stepped aside so people could get a better view of the easel. ''This is what I'm suggesting—a new and improved version of Walton.''

Cassie sat up in her seat, mesmerized. The map on the easel shouted with color and beauty and perfection—the ideal Walton. Nice cars traveled the wide boulevards of the town as people pushing carriages and walking dogs strolled down the pristine sidewalks. There was even a group of children flying a kite in a field—a field that currently housed a block of businesses that included the Dixie Diner.

There was something so wrong about it—so unreal and incomprehensible. The rendering wasn't her Walton. It was some dreamer's idea of the perfect town. Whatever it was, it wasn't the Walton where people knew each other from birth and neighbors helped each other and chipped in to bring food and care to an elderly woman. It wasn't the town where children swam in the old creek behind Senator Thompkins's house or had church picnics in the park where a new Piggly Wiggly was now drawn on the map. Whatever that town was on the map, it bore no relation to the wonderful place she'd grown up in. From the look on Sam's face, she could see that he was thinking the same thing as she.

Slowly, Sam stood. He had no easel or pointer, nor did he wear a suit. Instead, he sauntered to the podium, wearing his jeans and boots and waving to neighbors and friends. He leaned toward the microphone.

Very succinctly, he said, ''Pardon my French, people, but this is all bullshit.'' A murmur passed over the crowd, and Miss Lena giggled. ''Just because Ed here says he's one of us does not mean he's got the town's best interests at heart. Sure, this town could use revitalization in areas, but not mass destruction of old homes and business. We need to focus our efforts on preservation. Because that is the only way we can hold on to the integrity of this town.''

He paused for a long moment, his eyes scanning the

room and meeting the gazes of individuals sitting out in the audience. "And if you decide to vote against preservation, I don't think it's going to matter who does the construction in the town—Ed Farrell or Jim Roust. Either way, they will ruin Walton. They will ruin it just the same as if they burned it and then sowed the ground with salt. People will move out, and strangers will move in. We'll start keeping our doors locked and won't know our neighbors anymore. There won't be any more Dixie Diner or Bitsy's Beauty or Skirts 'n Such. Everybody will be going to the mall for those services, and the empty shops will be boarded up and abandoned."

Cassie sat up even straighter, feeling the passion of his words. Sam continued. "And I ask you all this. Where are Jim Roust and his people? Don't you think somebody who wants to change this town so much would be here tonight? At least to listen to what the town's citizens have to say about proposed changes? Don't you think he'd care?"

Cassie watched in surprise as Miss Lena stood, her gnarled hands gripping the chair in front of her. Her high voice rang out over the quiet crowd. "But he is here. He's standing right there in front by that easel."

Ed's face seemed to drain of all its color as he gazed up at his mother. He took a step forward, forcing a smile. "Now, Miss Lena, I think you're getting confused. Why don't you have Cassie take you outside for some fresh air." A tick began in his jaw, belying his otherwise calm expression.

Miss Lena did indeed look confused as she tilted her head and stared down at the men near the podium. "But Ed, you told me yourself that you'd bought the Roust company and that you're the big boss now. Right, Ed?"

Ed sent an apologetic shrug to the audience. "I'm sorry for the outburst, ladies and gentlemen. Perhaps Miss Lena just isn't used to being out so late."

The old woman began to shake, her expression wiped clean of any confusion. Her voice, though trembling, came out clear and compelling. "No, Ed. I'm not used to being lied to, especially by my own son." She ignored the gasps and whispers coming from the audience around her and continued to stare straight ahead at Ed. "I'm sorry if your childhood was not what it should have been. I only did what I thought was best at the time. Punish me then, Ed, instead of these people—the same people who take care of me now and made sure you had clothes on your back and food on your plate when you were a child. Look at yourself! It doesn't look like your upbringing or this town held you back from becoming a big shot." She paused for a moment, taking a deep, calming breath. "I just wish that you were a little younger and I was a little stronger, because you deserve to have a switch taken to your backside."

Her voice seemed to falter for a moment as she glanced around at her rapt audience before turning back to Ed. "Since I was never able to give you motherly advice, perhaps you'd indulge me just this once." She wagged a gnarled finger at him. "Be nice to people, because all mean acts always come back later to bite you in the butt."

Miss Lena sat down with a thud as a stunned silence permeated the room. Her eyes seemed to cloud over as she regarded the people nearest her, as if trying to figure out where she was and why she was speaking. Cassie put her arm around her shoulders, pulling her close.

Ed stuck out his arms, his hands turned palms up in supplication. "Come on, y'all. She's obviously confused." He stopped for a moment as a steady murmur began in the room, accompanied by accusatory glances. Ed's expression became belligerent. "Hey, even if I did own Roust, so what? I'm still the guy with all the great ideas for this town. I mean, look at the Dixie Diner." He pulled out a large glossy picture from a portfolio by his feet and propped it on the easel. "It's ugly as sin. Yeah, they've got colorful awnings and window boxes, but it's still just an ugly, old building. That whole block is. There are some major national retailers who are just chomping at the bit to get ahold of that real estate. Imagine the business that it will bring in to Walton— and the jobs."

Sam narrowed his eyes at Ed. "Sure—low-paying,

minimum-wage jobs. All the higher-level jobs will be
filled by the companies on a corporate level. The people
now owning and working for those businesses on the block
will be unemployed.'' Sam took a deep breath in an obvious
attempt to control a rising temper. ''What it comes down
to, Ed, is that you want to destroy this town little by little
so we don't notice it right off. You're trying to cut us down
to our knees because of something that happened more than
thirty years ago. I'm sorry, Ed, but I just can't seem to be
able to let you destroy Walton without a fight.''

Sam strode toward Ed, stopping not a foot away.
''Because I will fight you, Ed. I will fight you to my last
penny and my last drop of blood. This town and its people
are my life—and more precious to me than all the money
in the world. I feel real sorry for those who sneer at it and
who feel they've outgrown the need to belong. For all the
education and wealth in the world, they're just too damned
stupid to know what a gold mine they have sitting right here
in this room.''

A tight lump lodged itself in the middle of Cassie's throat,
and she knew Sam's words had been aimed not just at Ed.

Ed looked around, his mouth open, a hostile look on his
face as his gaze scanned the crowd. When his eyes met Miss
Lena's, he stopped. They held each other for a long moment
before she narrowed her lips and turned away, burying her
face in Cassie's shoulder.

Sam spoke softly, but his words carried out over the
mesmerized crowd. ''And don't think that we'll forget that
you've lied to us. Look out at the people of Walton, Ed,
and see if you can look any of them in the eye without
flinching. See if you're man enough now to tell us the truth.''

Ed actually looked chagrined as his shoulders slumped
and he looked back at his mother. She refused to meet his
gaze. With a brief sigh of resignation, he collapsed into a
chair, holding his handkerchief to his upper lip. The crowd
began to murmur as he shook his head as if to clear it.
Finally, he gave Cassie a quick nod and said with a weak
voice, ''It's all true.'' With a prompting look from Sam, he

continued. "I'm behind all the proposed development in Walton by Roust Development."

People stood and began shouting and waving their arms; Miss Lena just shook and buried her face in Cassie's shoulder. A councilman banged a gavel, causing a silence to descend on the room once more.

Sam's voice was calm as he faced Ed, but Cassie could see his jawbone working furiously. "Why, Ed? I think we all need to hear why."

Ed kept his gaze focused on Cassie. "My reasons are personal."

Sam stepped forward, his face screwed up in a menacing cast. "I suggest you get real personal, Ed. We're listening."

Ed glanced up at the doctor for a moment, looking, for all Cassie could determine, as if he'd just emerged from a Come to Jesus revival. Quietly, he said, "I never planned to go forward with my planned town. I wanted to bulldoze Walton and build over it."

A stunned silence captured the audience, and Ed looked as if he wished the ground would open up and swallow him whole. But Sam was relentless in his inquisition. "Keep going, Ed. We're not leaving until you've told us the whole story."

Ed coughed and took a drink of water. A look of what Cassie could have sworn was relief crossed his face. With a deep breath, he began speaking, the easel standing between him and the people of Walton like the screen in a confessional. "For almost twenty years I have lived my life feeling as if I had been done a great wrong. And it has only been recently that I have found out the truth and that I have been the one wrong all these years." His gaze fastened back on Cassie, and she thought back to the letters between his parents and from his father to him. "And the one person I have deceived the most is Cassie Madison. I lied to her about my intentions for her house—abusing her trust—and only because she had the great misfortune to be her father's daughter." He looked around the quiet room. "It was her father I was after—and everything he loved. His house, this

town. I thought I could only feel peace if his beloved house
was buried under a huge shopping mall.''

Glancing at the bowed head of Miss Lena, he said, ''I
also seem to have lost the trust of the dearest, sweetest
woman I have ever had the pleasure to know, and I am
ashamed. For the first time in my entire life, I feel horribly
ashamed.''

Cassie turned, sensing Sam watching her. Their gazes
met, and she knew instinctively that Sam realized who Ed
was. Miss Lena had finally stopped shaking, and Cassie
hugged her tighter.

Ed faced Hank Adams. ''And it was me and men I hired
who've been doing all that vandalism over on Cassie's property, not Mr. Haney or anybody else. Yes, Richard Haney
worked for Roust, but he never knew I was behind it. I take
full responsibility for all damage and will take whatever
punishment is due.'' He rubbed his hands over his face,
hiding his eyes for a long moment. ''I guess I should be
thanking you all. I haven't felt this relieved in years.'' When
he moved his hands away, Cassie could see the bright sheen
of tears.

The poster board slipped off the easel and slid, facedown,
across the wood-plank floor, stopping at Sam's feet. Sam
left it there, not looking down.

Sheriff Adams began walking toward Ed as Ed addressed
the room again. ''I'm sorry. I really am sorry—as pitiful as
those words must sound to you all. I have tried for so long
to ignore the evidence, but Miss Lena, and those of you
who care for her, have done your dangdest to make me see
the stuff this town is made of. Tonight has taught me that
I can't ignore it any longer. Miss Lena has shown me what
a special place this is. Y'all truly care about each other—
and for each other. It's something special and rare, and with
people like me in the world, it will be a dying breed. If
anything I say here tonight is going to have any weight, I
hope it's this.'' He faced the town councilmembers. ''I hope
you vote no to more development and yes to preservation.
I hope you vote no to people like Jim Roust and Ed Farrell,

who want to indiscriminately tear down old buildings. Sure, Walton could use some improvement, but it should be done smartly. I hate to say this, but on this point, I agree with Dr. Parker.''

Before the words had time to sink into Cassie's ears, the double doors at the back of the meeting room flew open, and Joe stood on the threshold. He was bundled in a ski jacket, snow clinging to the hood and his eyelashes. ''I'm sorry to interrupt everybody, but I've got an emergency, and I need your help.''

Her mind reeling from the recent turn of events, Cassie handed Miss Lena over to Mrs. Crandall, who sat on her other side, and got up to go to Joe.

He continued, his face a mask of worry. ''Maddie's run away from home. She left a note.'' He pulled a crumpled up piece of notebook paper from his pocket and handed it to Cassie. ''It's starting to snow real bad out there, and I'm afraid . . . we need to find her fast. Can I have volunteers to do a search party?''

While men and women streamed into the aisle toward Joe, Cassie bent her head to read the note.

I can't live here anymore. Nobody seems to realize that things will never be the same again without Mama. I don't know how Daddy is going to manage with all us kids, so I figured I'd make it easy for him by leaving. I've never felt I belonged here, anyway. I've decided to move to New York. I look old for my age, and I'm sure I can get a job waitressing or something— anything just to get away from this stupid little town where nobody will miss me, anyway.

It wasn't signed, but there was no doubt as to who had written it.

Quietly, Cassie gave the note to Sam, who had come to stand by her, and watched as he read it. He handed it back to Joe, then quickly began organizing search teams and giving out his cell-phone number.

He turned to Joe. "Is Lucinda with the children?"

Joe nodded.

"Good. I want you and Hal Newcomb to go door to door to Maddie's friends' houses. Insist that the parents physically check the girls' bedrooms to see if Maddie is there. She could be hiding."

Ed managed to shoulder his way through the crowd. "Let me help. Please."

To Cassie's surprise, Sam nodded. "You can go with Hank. I don't think he wants you far from him, anyway." He pointed at Hank. "I want you to head out toward the interstate. God forbid she thinks she's going to hitchhike her way up north, but I wouldn't put it past her, either."

Hank and Ed headed toward the door, and Cassie grabbed her coat, running after them and calling to Sam over her shoulder. "I'm going with them."

Without waiting for a response, she followed Hank and Ed out to Hank's truck, the four-wheel drive easier to handle in the snow than his patrol car. They trudged out to the truck, and as Ed held the door open for her, he said, "I am sorry, Cassie. For what I've done to you and your house and for lying to you. If it hadn't been for those letters—"

She held up her hand, cutting him off. "I'd be lying if I said I wasn't angry, because I am. And we've got lots to talk about, and we will talk, later. But right now we have to focus on finding Maddie and bringing her home safely."

Ed nodded, and they both climbed in as Hank started the engine. Cassie forced a smile. "I never thought I'd see the day when I was grateful for a four-wheel-drive truck."

Hank's face was grim. "Yeah. Let's just hope we don't get stuck on any icy patches. Nothing but ice skates can get you off of that."

They pulled forward on what used to be the paved road in front of the Town Hall but was now just a flattened ribbon of white winding its way around town.

Cassie spotted Sam's truck pulling out behind them, his face illuminated briefly by the flash of another set of headlights. People walked quickly out of the building, hurrying to spread the word that young Maddie Warner was lost somewhere out in the snow. If there had been time, Cassie would have hugged each and every one of them for not once considering their own safety. They had come together in a time of need to help one of their own, and it filled Cassie with pride to be among them.

Hank headed out toward the interstate, flipping on his high beams and illuminating snow and more snow and the occasional flakes blown off a tree branch.

Ed spoke from the backseat. "Why would she want to go to New York, do you think?"

Cassie looked out the window. "For some reason, she puts me on a pedestal. I think she wants to be like me."

Ed leaned forward, resting his arms on the back of the seat in front of him. "What better way to do it than to make her way to your big city, huh?"

"It's not *my* big city. I just live there."

He looked at her closely for a moment, then sat back.

Hank flipped on his scanner. "I'm sure with the snow falling like it is there won't be too much traffic on the highway. That might be a good thing for us."

Cassie clutched her knees tightly, not wanting to think about the implication. "Does she expect to walk all the way through the snow?" She leaned her head back against the seat. "My God, she doesn't even have boots." Tears welled in the back of her throat, but she swallowed them down. "What could she have been thinking?"

Ed waited a moment before answering. "When you were fourteen, do you remember ever thinking things through? Heck, I don't think I've had a clear thought for almost twenty years."

Cassie didn't answer, her eyes remaining focused on the empty road in front of them. Hank drove slowly as their gazes scoured the sides of the road. Twice Cassie thought she saw something, but both times what she thought was a leg or a head peeking out of the glaring white had turned out to be either a fallen branch or an icy rock.

When they reached the access ramp to the interstate, Hank

slid to a stop. "I'm afraid to go any further in the truck. It's all icy here, and we might just flip over and end up upside down on the road below."

Cassie strained her eyes to see the six-lane highway, but no car lights or light source of any kind came from the road. Her gaze came to rest in front of the truck in the yellow arc of the headlights. She sat forward. "What's that?"

Hank squinted. "I can't tell from here. Stay in the truck and I'll go look."

Ignoring him, Cassie jumped out, reaching the object at the same time. Picking it out of the snow, she shouted, "It's Maddie's backpack. See? It has her name tag on it." A foot away lay a headband, the glassy beads covering it reflecting the lights from the car.

"Maddie!" Hank and Cassie screamed her name at the same time and were quickly joined by Ed. Hank took a step forward and slipped, his legs flying out from under him, landing awkwardly on his arm. The sound of snapping bone echoed in the snow-dusted air.

Hank grunted, then lay still, his face contorted in pain in the broad beam of the headlight.

Cassie kneeled. "Don't move, Hank. I'll call Sam on Ed's cell phone, okay? Just try not to move."

Ed had crawled his way to the edge, moving slowly. He tossed his cell phone to her, and she caught it. "Be careful. It's all ice under the snow. Maddie must have slipped over the embankment."

A small whimper came from the bottom of the hill. "Help me! My ankle. I can't move it!"

Hank grunted again as he struggled to sit up before collapsing in pain. Cassie put a restraining hand on his good shoulder. "Don't move, Hank. We don't need another casualty. And if that's Maddie down there, Ed and I can bring her up. Just lie still."

She dialed Sam's number while she watched Ed flatten himself on his stomach and peer over the embankment, where no guardrail prevented a potential fall. "Is that you,

Maddie? It's Mr. Farrell and your Aunt Cassie. We've come to get you out of there, okay?''

"Please hurry. I'm so cold." Maddie's voice sounded faint and far away, as if being absorbed by the surrounding snow.

Sam answered on the first ring. "Sam, it's Cassie. We're at the entrance ramp to the interstate. We've found Maddie, and she might be hurt, but she's talking. And I think Hank's broken his arm."

There was no emotion in his voice when he answered back. "I'll be right there." His good-bye was the click of the phone.

Ed looked back at Cassie. "Go inside the truck and look on the floor of the backseat. There's some kind of rope back there. Grab it and bring it to me. I might need it to tie Maddie to me to bring her up."

Cassie nodded and did as she was asked, also bringing a blanket she'd found on the seat to put over Hank.

Ed stood rubbing his arms with his hands, trying to generate heat. "I'm going to go down and see if she's seriously injured. If she's not, I'm going to try and bring her up. I need you to stay here with Hank and wait for me—and let Sam know where I am when he gets here."

Her teeth chattered uncontrollably. "Okay. Be ... be careful."

Wrapping the length of rope over his shoulder, Ed began to move slowly down the embankment, scooting down on his backside and using his heels for traction.

"Maddie, I'm coming down. Don't try to move."

Again, they heard the whimpering, but nothing more.

The short minutes it took for Ed to reach her seemed like hours. When Ed had completed a cursory examination and announced he would be bringing Maddie up, Cassie shouted with relief.

He tied Maddie to his back—piggyback style—while he dug through the layers of snow in search of handholds to grab on to. He slipped several times, once almost back to the bottom where he had begun, but eventually made it to the edge. Cassie grabbed Maddie's arms as Ed untied her and, after two failed attempts, pulled her off of Ed's back before waiting for Ed to roll forward onto level ground again.

As soon as they were both up, glaring headlights and crunching snow announced Sam's arrival. He smiled with relief when he spotted Maddie. After examining her ankle, he directed Ed to bundle her in a blanket he had brought and put her in the backseat of his truck.

He then turned to Hank. The sheriff's face now appeared as white as the snow around him, and he'd begun to shiver. Sam knelt in the snow next to him. "Always have to be the center of attention, don't you, Hank?" Leaning closer, he said softly, "I'm going to have Ed help me put you in the backseat of your truck to keep you warm while I immobilize your arm. Then Ed's going to drive you and your truck to the hospital to have it set properly. The snow's tapering off, and he won't have any trouble with it in your truck."

Hank nodded weakly, then allowed himself to be lifted and carried back to his truck. Cassie climbed into Sam's truck next to Maddie and wrapped her arms around her, waiting for her own teeth to stop chattering. And when they did, she wasn't sure what she'd do first—yell at Maddie for scaring her or tell her how much she loved her.

She watched as Ed drove away with Hank and then waited as Sam climbed in behind the wheel and turned his own truck toward town.

Cassie was amazed at the calmness in her voice. "Maddie, why did you run away? Don't you know that your family loves you and that we were worried half out of our minds?" She remembered the anguish on Joe's face when he announced the news about Maddie running away, and Cassie wasn't sure whether she should kiss or strangle her niece.

Maddie started to cry. "Don't be angry, Aunt Cassie. I didn't think anybody would miss me."

"Oh, I'm not angry, Maddie. I was just so worried about you." She squeezed her tighter. "And nobody miss you? Did you know that half the town is out there in the snow, searching for you, or that your father is going crazy with concern over you?''

Maddie just sobbed louder. ''No, I didn't. And I'm only crying now because my . . . ankle . . . hurts.''

''Yeah, yeah, yeah.'' Cassie patted her shoulder, smothering a grin, relieved that she could still smile.

Sam turned around in his seat, eyebrow raised. ''Gosh, she sounds like somebody I know.''

Cassie sent him a hard stare.

''I'm sorry, '' Maddie sobbed, burying her face in Cassie's shoulder.

Cassie's eyes misted, her heart swelling for this girl who reminded her so much of herself. She touched Maddie's cheek and spoke softly. ''Sweetheart, all the love and belonging you could ever want in your life is right here. If you'd only stop for a minute to look around, you'd know. They will love and accept you even if you decide to grow spots and join the circus. They're your people, Maddie. And most people spend their whole lives searching for what you've already got in this little town. Don't you ever forget that.''

Sam's eyes met Cassie's in the rearview mirror, and in that moment her mind cleared. As if watching a movie in vivid color and exaggerated detail, she saw Joe, the children, Lucinda, Sam, her beautiful house with the magnolia in the front yard and creaking wood floors, and the longing in her heart that she had carried around like a suitcase all these years disappeared. She had what she wanted; she'd had it all her life. And finally she knew what it was.

Chapter 27

Harriet's wake was held at Cassie's house to accommodate the large number of mourners. As if by divine intervention, the skies had cleared, and the temperature rose to the low sixties. Gutters overflowed with melting snow as cleverly made snowmen became nothing more than disfigured lumps of carrots and hats in the middle of yards.

She was pleased to see Ed and kissed him on his cheek. He fidgeted awkwardly in his new suit, the result of a shopping trip to Atlanta with Cassie. "I'll be at your hearing next Thursday, and so will Joe and a bunch of other people, to support you."

He flushed, the white skin of his forehead, exposed by a recent haircut, turning a deep red. "I appreciate it, Cassie. Sheriff Adams says that I'll probably just get probation and community service. Plus I'll have to pay restitution to you for the property damage." He blushed deeper and shifted his feet. "I know I'll never really be able to apologize for everything I've put you through, but, well, I thought that as part of my community service I'd like to build a park. I was thinking of putting it over there off of Sycamore Street where the Olsen house used to be. And I'd like to name it the

Harriet Madison Warner Memorial Park, if that would be okay with you."

Impulsively, she hugged him and blinked back tears. "I think it's a wonderful idea. Especially a park for children—it would be such a fitting tribute to her. Thank you, Ed. Thank you." She looked around the room for a moment before her gaze rested on her brother-in-law. "I'll let you tell Joe. I know he'll be as thrilled as I am."

Ed nodded and headed toward Joe.

Sam came to stand next to her. "How are you holding up?"

She smiled, feeling shy with him. They hadn't spoken since the night Maddie had run away. It had been as if Sam were giving her time for the words that she had spewed out in the backseat to her niece to sink in. "I'm doing fine. I can almost feel Harriet here with us, celebrating her life with us. When I think that, it's not as hard to . . . to face that she's gone."

He nodded and looked down, a quirky smile on his lips. "Lucinda told me that you'd unpacked your things and put the suitcases in the attic. Like you were planning on staying awhile."

Cassie busied herself by picking up a few paper plates and stacking them. "Well, gosh, I guess I can tell Joe to disconnect his phone service. He won't be needing it anymore, since Lucinda's moving in with him. She's better than a town crier."

He lifted her chin to face him. "Were you ever going to tell me?"

She felt lost for a moment in the blue intensity of his eyes. "Yes. Of course. I just wanted to get the details worked out first."

"Details?" He dropped his hand.

"Yes. It appears that I'm going to be the southern partner of Wallace and Madison. I'll be establishing new accounts in Atlanta and handling them from my home office."

"Home office? As in this house?"

Cassie concentrated on lining up the silverware on top of the dirty plates. "Yep. The one and only."

"Cassie?"

She looked up at him. "Yes?"

"I'm glad."

"Glad?"

His eyes twinkled. "I'm pleased as a pig in mud."

She tried to hide her smile. "Don't be so cocky. I'm not doing this for you."

He raised an eyebrow. "No?"

"I'm doing it for me. And my family."

He took the plates from her and dumped them in the kitchen. When he returned, he joined her, his arm around her shoulders, and they faced the mourners as a unit, accepting condolences and sharing their grief. Maddie, having suffered a sprained ankle during her fall down the embankment, hobbled around on crutches, bending over now and then to take a kiss on the cheek from one of her mother's friends or to hug someone's neck.

Joe still seemed to be in a daze but was surrounded by his and Harriet's friends. They talked about her as if she were still alive, telling stories of her thoughtfulness, her kindness, and her love for her family. Joe smiled, and the aura of unbridled grief that surrounded him lifted slightly. Cassie walked over to where he sat with Harry in his arms and gave him a squeeze. They would get through this. With the help of all those who loved them, they would get through it.

After the last mourner had left, Joe led her outside to the porch. "I have something for you. Harriet asked me to give this to you after she . . . left us." He reached into his coat pocket and pulled out a square black jewelry box.

With a trembling hand, she took it and slowly opened the lid. Six gold heart charms lay nestled against black velvet, each one winking at her with the sun's reflection. Her other hand went to her mouth. She looked up at him, afraid to speak.

"These are for her children. She wanted you to be the

keeper of their hearts." His voice cracked, and neither one could speak. He hugged her while they wept, and when they were done, she drew back and looked at the hearts again.

"I'm going to need a larger chain to hold all these." A small laugh bubbled at her lips as she clutched the small box to her chest.

They sat down on the swing and stayed there until the sun set, its long golden rays waving its last good-bye.

Epilogue

Time marched slowly in Walton, and Cassie sometimes wondered if it marched at all. She watched the winter of her sister's death pass into the brightness of spring and the heat of summer. And then it was the autumn of the year again, with old leaves falling, shedding their brilliant plumage, her magnolia still staying resplendent, with its glossy green leaves.

The children grew, lost teeth, and shed tears, and Cassie was there at school plays, cheerleading tryouts, and late-night algebra sessions. Joey lost his first tooth, Harry learned how to crawl, and Knoxie decided she didn't want red hair anymore. Cassie treasured each milestone, each one made more poignant by the memory of the mother who couldn't be there to share them.

Maddie struggled the hardest with the loss of her mother, but Cassie made it clear that her niece would always have a warm shoulder to lean on when she needed it. Cassie looked back on that first year with a mixture of grief and joy, realizing life would always be a mixture of both but also knowing that her little town would give her whatever she would need to cope.

And then it was December again, filled with bittersweet memories. It had been Maddie's idea to hold the wedding at Christmastime, and Cassie had agreed. Harriet had always loved Christmas, and it was now Cassie's duty to bring back happy memories of the season her sister had dearly treasured.

In the confusion and hustle and bustle of Christmas and wedding preparations, Harry's first birthday was almost overlooked. But Cassie remembered and baked the cake herself, following the advice of Mrs. Crandall, who was more than happy to lend a hand.

As if to thank Cassie for her trouble, Harry decided it was time to walk; he took his first steps, landing in the outstretched arms of his beaming aunt. She held him tightly for a moment, silently thanking the woman who had given birth to him.

The ceremony itself was small, with Reverend Beasley officiating. Cassie grinned at his sign in front as she was driven into the parking lot of First United Methodist: Feeling Tired? Rise with the Son. And, below that: Congratulations Sam and Cassie.

Joe and Lucinda left the limousine first, and then Mr. Murphy helped her out, making sure she didn't step on the antique lace train of her gown. She hadn't been crazy about riding in the funeral director's limousine, but it had either been that or the sheriff's car if she wanted to arrive at her own wedding in style. Joe grinned, offering his arm, and she took it, trying to ignore the frigid winter weather that had once again descended on their little town and blew up her billowing skirts. Around her neck lay a longer gold chain, now filled with shining gold hearts and one golden key.

Joey, his shirttail hanging out of the back of his tuxedo jacket, proudly bore the rings down the aisle. Following him to the bright thumping of the church's organ, played by Brunelle Thompkins, came Knoxie and Sarah Frances in forest green velvet, dropping white rose petals as they walked. Finally, the wedding march began, and a brightly beaming Maddie, as maid of honor, preceded her aunt, glow-

ing in the ivory wedding gown that had been worn by her
mother, then packed away with love and hope in the attic
of the old house.

As Cassie marched down the aisle on Joe's arm, she
wondered if her mother had felt even half the joy that was
now coursing through her veins as she approached Sam and
contemplated the life that lay before them. An escaped ray
of sun peered through the stained-glass window over the
altar, and it seemed as if her parents and sister were announcing their presence. Joe kissed her cheek, then handed her
over to her groom.

Following the reception, held at the house, Cassie stood
on the front porch, her new going-away outfit tucked under
a heavy wool coat, and tossed her bouquet into the waiting
crowd of women. It landed in Lucinda's outstretched hand,
who sniffed it with a coquettish smile. Cassie wondered if
anybody else noticed the bright red blush suffusing the sheriff's face.

In a hail of rice, they ran to Sam's waiting truck, brightly
decorated with red and green streamers and with beer cans
tied to the bumper. They pulled out of the drive, then headed
for the cemetery.

Harriet's marker had been placed next to their parents',
and both had been decorated with potted poinsettias draped
with homemade ornaments from Harriet's children. From
her pocket, Cassie took a gold tree ornament in the shape
of a heart and tied it securely to a poinsettia. She stood as
a chill wind blew down from the north, making her shiver,
and Sam put his arms around her.

"I miss her, too," he said.

Cassie nodded and looked up at the graying sky above
them, the cloud edges heavy and thick. "If I didn't know
any better, I'd say it's going to snow."

Sam followed her gaze and nodded. "I guess you did
learn a thing or two while up north."

She elbowed him gently, then rested her head on his wool
jacket.

"Do you think Harriet and my parents are watching over us?"

He squeezed her tightly. "Hopefully not all the time." Then, his eyes serious, he kissed her lightly on the lips. "Yes, I do."

As she looked up at him, three snowflakes drifted down from the sky toward them, twirled and buffeted by the whim of the wind before settling on the barren winter grass. Cassie watched them melt, then turned her face to the sky in search of more.

"Snow in Walton for the second year in a row. What's the world coming to?"

Sam laughed, then took her hand and began walking toward his truck.

They drove through town on the way to the interstate, hoping to make it to the airport before everything shut down. Bermuda in December held enormous appeal to Cassie as she flipped the heater in the truck to the max position.

The old oaks on the tree-lined streets bowed over them in greeting, their leaves winking and swaying, as if celebrating a homecoming. Cassie sighed, turning her head to watch a group of bundled children playing tag on the front lawn of the Harden property, her warm breath fogging the window. She touched the gold necklace around her neck, reveling in the abundance of gold hearts, and she smiled. Home no longer seemed like a place where one is born and then outgrows, along with skinned knees and childhood dreams. Instead, it seemed to her, it was a place that lived in one's heart, waiting with open arms to be rediscovered.

They drove through the town slowly, the cans and streamers tittering gently behind them. They passed Madison Lane and the old high school and Principal Purdy's house, the front porch long ago painted a bright pink. They drove past Miss Lena's and found her with Ed, helping her up the porch steps. They'd been at the wedding and reception, with Miss Lena's pink sweater over her Sunday dress, loving the opportunity to talk to so many people about her beloved books. The Dixie Diner and Lucinda's Lingerie, formerly Skirts 'n

Such, slid by their window, and two blocks later, the Harriet Madison Warner Memorial Park, its playground equipment hibernating under a kiss of snow.

As Sam and Cassie turned into the town square the flakes fell heavier, dusting the grass and leaves like little blessings from above.

"Stop, Sam."

He pulled the truck over to the curb. "What's wrong?"

"Just a minute." She climbed out of the truck and crunched through the frozen grass to the statue of liberty, her driftwood head now a pale green beneath the smattering of snow. Hoisting herself up onto the base, Cassie stared into the face of Miss Liberty, with her perpetual come-hither look aimed at the Confederate soldier on horseback at the other end of the green.

Taking off her red knit cap, Cassie slipped it onto the crown, then jumped down and returned to the truck.

Sam pulled away with a laugh as she turned around to see the effect of Miss Liberty's new look and grinned broadly. Yes, Cassie Madison had returned. It had taken her fifteen long years, but she had finally found her way home.

ABOUT THE AUTHOR

After playing hooky one day in the seventh grade to read *Gone With the Wind*, Karen knew she wanted to be a writer— or become Scarlett O'Hara. In spite of these aspirations, Karen pursued a degree in business and graduated with a BS in Management from Tulane University. Ten years later, after leaving the business world to stay home with her children, she fulfilled her dream of becoming a writer and wrote her first book. It was published in August 2001.

When not writing, Karen spends her time reading, singing, playing the piano, carpooling children and avoiding cooking.

A graduate of the American School in London, where she lived for seven years, Karen now lives outside Atlanta with her husband, son and daughter. This is her third book.

You can contact her on her website at http://www.karen-white.com or at P.O. Box 450181, Atlanta, GA 31145-9998.

DO YOU HAVE THE
HOHL COLLECTION?